Desert Wind

Desert Wind

Mac McClelland

Library of Congress Control Number:		2021903713
ISBN:	Hardcover	978-1-6641-5956-3
	Softcover	978-1-6641-5957-0
	eBook	978-1-6641-5958-7

This is a work of fiction. Names, characters, places and incidents either are the product of the author's imagination or are used fictitiously, and any resemblance to any actual persons, living or dead, events, or locales is entirely coincidental.

Cover illustration by Rasha M. McClelland

Print information available on the last page.

Rev. date: 03/01/2021

To order additional copies of this book, contact:
Xlibris
844-714-8691
www.Xlibris.com
Orders@Xlibris.com
825447

Dedication

To my children: Jonathan for his wisdom, Caroline for her grace, and Emily for her energy. Curious, smart, and inquisitive, they inspire, motivate, and humor me. All parents believe their children are the best but I know mine are.

To Rasha, who sits on the couch next to me each evening listening to another thousand words, some for the nth time, offering opinions, suggestions, and an emphatic *no* to some of my ideas. Thank you: this couldn't have happened without you.

To Rasha's parents, Aroub and Fawaz, who raised such a remarkable woman.

Thank you also to the *Desert Winders* who proofread and critiqued the manuscript as it went through various iterations. If there are still mistakes after all your effort, they are mine alone.

And, finally, to those individual Marines, hard-charging, low-crawling, straight-shooting, highly motivated, roguishly handsome global soldiers of the sea, members of the finest fighting force the world has ever seen, dedicated to defending our great country and protecting our way of life. *Long live the United States and success to the Marines!*

Endorsements

"McClelland educates and then rewards you, taking you on a ride through Middle East history and then skillfully tying your newly earned knowledge to present-day international politics, issues, challenges, and heroism. *Desert Wind* leaves you wanting more. Bravo Zulu, Marine!"
– Lieutenant Colonel Paul W. LeBlanc, U.S. Marine Corps (Retired)

"An absolutely great read. History meets adventure and suspense, from the oldest continuously inhabited city in the world to the Libyan desert. Don't start it if you don't have time to read—it's a page turner, to say the least."
– Dina Storey

"Fasten your seatbelts! Mac brings to life millennia of Middle East history, setting the stage for an exciting tale that blends fact and fiction into a fast-paced, contemporary military thriller. Dr. McClelland weaves his lifelong passion for the region with his career experience as a Marine officer and diplomat to *Desert Wind*...bring it on!"
– Colonel Frank Duggan, U.S. Marine Corps (Retired)

"*Desert Wind* is aptly named, blowing the reader through the Middle East and North Africa on an adventure with Captain Katy Morgan. You'll find yourself sitting next to her as she races to accomplish the mission as only she can. Thanks for allowing me to ride shotgun!"
– Nagham Al Zahlawi

"Densely packed with the human experience from early man's discovery of habitable geographies to post-modern humanity and global politics, *Desert Wind* moves across Arabia with a tale of intrigue and achievement. Mac joins a solid cadre of top tier writers who will entertain and educate readers for years to come. I, for one, am looking forward to his next installment."
– Captain Scott Massey, U.S. Army, The Citadel Class of 1992

Chapter 1

10,426 BC
Aleppo, Syria

The small group moved westward across the tundra, looking for warmer weather in which to settle, hunt, and grow the tribe, now numbering four men, eleven women, and fourteen children. Survival meant finding food and water. It also meant procreating to have enough girls of childbearing age and virile young men to impregnate them, thereby keeping the tribe alive through the millennia.

Olaq was the tribe's leader by virtue of his age and experience. At twenty-eight, he was the oldest man in the group and within six or seven years of the end of his life. He had thus far successfully led them through five cold winters from Ulan Bator in Mongolia, north into Russia, turning south through Kazakhstan over the mountains in Kyrgyzstan and Tajikistan, before turning west through Uzbekistan and Turkmenistan, the area between the Amu Darya and the Syr Darya, which the Romans would refer to ten millennia into the future as Transoxiana. They landed on the eastern bank of the Caspian Sea in Northern Iran. Olaq thought it offered hope, but the winter proved too harsh, so he decided once again to move on after the snows melted.

Two of the men hunted ahead of the women and children while the others stayed behind for security. Two donkeys and a two-humped Bactrian camel—Bactrians and their one-humped dromedary cousins would not be fully domesticated for another hundred centuries—were packed with all of their worldly possessions, mainly rough pots and bowls for cooking, stone tools and spare weapons, water bags, and some skins and pelts to protect them from the winter cold and rain. The men carried spears and sharp stone knives, and all carried the scars of battle against other groups attempting to steal their women and against wild animals reluctant to be the tribe's next meal. Other than one very lean winter in the high mountains when they lost eight members of the group to hunger and a donkey to the elements, the men had provided well; everyone was healthy with enough body fat to last a few weeks without food if necessary.

Some members of the small group found the air at such low altitudes heavy and moist. Descended from archaic primordial human Denisovan tribes high in the Tibetan mountains, their ancestors survived at eleven thousand feet and were conditioned to the lack of air so high above sea level. Survival in an environment with 40 percent less oxygen was facilitated by a mutated blood-cell gene known as ESPA-1, one of the strongest instances of natural selection; the gene is still carried by descendants some 160,000 years later.

The gene atrophied with disuse and through interbreeding with anatomically modern ancestors of *Homo sapiens* originating in Africa, but some still retained the disposition that made dense air more difficult to breathe. Although they never considered or understood why, Olaq and another man and two of the women in his small tribe were among a handful of modern humans who still carried the gene and fit that category.

Pushing on from the Caspian, Olaq led the tribe through Mosul in northern Iraq and continued westward, eventually crossing the Euphrates. They kept moving, as there was too much human activity along the big river; the four men could not hold off large groups of marauders intent on stealing women and food.

Almost by accident, they stumbled on an encampment of several hundred foragers in southeastern Anatolia in modern-day Turkey near Göbekli Tepe, the largest number of people the tribe had ever witnessed at one time. Laboring to erect round monoliths some twenty feet high and weighing up to ten tons, the group had already laid out twelve circles of ten pillars each—to what purpose the tribe could not fathom, the onsite semiotics pointing perhaps to evidence of the earliest evolution of a proto-religion. Encouraged to join the working party, Olaq declined but accepted the group's hospitality, staying for a few days to rest and repair equipment for the continuing journey.

Dozens of workers left the temenos each morning, returning later in the day with baskets of grain previously unknown to the tribe. They watched with fascination as women and children ground the grain, later classified *einkorn wheat*, for use in making flour for bread and a thick, viscous gravy. Although they found the bread tasty and filling, they also found it difficult to digest; their stomachs ached if they ate too much of the wheat.

Olaq enjoyed a drink he was offered made from the fermented grain called *boza* by the foragers. The low alcohol content meant they could drink throughout the day with nothing more than a slight buzz, but it made conversations lighter and full of laughter while making the drinkers warmer and stronger, at least in their own minds.

One afternoon after a heavy meal and a half dozen cups of *boza*, Olaq watched the construction crews tip up the columns on one end using three wooly mammoths—known to the workers as *mammut*—and drop them into prepared holes twice his height in depth. The work was made light by the beasts' strength and the guides' adept handling of the animals using the handmade hemp ropes and leather reins. Ten of the monoliths were installed that afternoon, completing the thirteenth circle. The workers then began digging holes to support the next set of columns.

But the mammoths interested Olaq most; never had he seen such large and strong animals, capable of doing difficult and heavy manual labor for their minders. He noticed that when not working, the mammoths would graze passively on the wild grasses surrounding the mound, oblivious to the men scurrying around them, content to eat and drink until they were next called on to lift the columns into place. Although afraid of them, he nonetheless approached one to touch the fur, noticing a longer layer of hair on top of a shorter layer.

Olaq correctly surmised the layering helped keep the animals warm in cold weather, particularly during the ice age now in its final throes after a hundred years that at one point had forced sapiens into the lower latitudes. He tucked that fact away for later when they were designing clothes to protect them during the cold mountain transits. He didn't know they would be extinct in only a few hundred years as humans encroached on their grazing and breeding grounds, save a few animals trapped on islands far to the east of where he sat; they too would die out over the next forty centuries.

Other animals that caught Olaq's attention were the dogs. Domestication of Pleistocene wolves had begun twenty-five generations previously, yet man's influence over them already yielded loyal and obedient dogs capable of being scouts, retrievers of game and birds killed by hunters, and guards for people or animals. Olaq hesitantly fed scraps to one of the dogs, and by the time they were ready to leave, he and the dog were inseparable. Naming him Canis seemed natural; it was the tribal word for *tooth*, and Canis certainly had long and sharp teeth. The dog followed him everywhere and challenged any person or animal appearing to threaten Olaq and his family.

The tribe pushed on after farewells and exchanges of gifts, rudimentary as they were—Khalpe was delighted with the two bracelets the group said were made from the tusk of a *mammut*—never understanding the purpose of the monoliths or the group's need to build the temple almost seven thousand years before its more famous cousin at Stonehenge in Britain. Within a few weeks, the tribe came to the banks of a smaller river with fast-running clear water, arriving in late spring just as the frost was receding and the earth was coming to life. Olaq decided to halt the journey and enjoy the bountiful game and abundance of edible plants surrounding the river, and he grunted his approval to the tribe.

He didn't know, or even consider, whether this was a one-season halt or where the group might eventually settle; his simple thoughts were on surviving this day and hoping to wake up in the next. The river seemed to offer hope, and the game and edible plants around it boded well for food in the next several seasons at a minimum should they decide to stay that long.

Three of the women belonged to Olaq, two of them again pregnant. No special consideration was given to their condition, and they were expected to work alongside the others. Olaq's favorite woman, Khalpe, would deliver within the month. Given the upcoming summer, the child faced the advantage of being stronger when winter closed in on the tribe. The other woman, Sitt, was due in mid-winter, and Olaq privately held out little hope for the baby's survival. With six other children to feed and having lost two more in previous winters, he knew the necessity but also the danger of bringing children into the world.

Right now, though, Olaq and his small tribe were delighted at their good fortune of finding a small flat meadow on the banks of the little river. They fished and hunted close to their adopted home and began the process of gathering rocks with which to build shelter. Although they had six months to construct a dwelling—one they might only use one season—they were unsure how the winter would announce itself: a rainy season straight into snow, a mild autumn and winter, or something else. Because they had already witnessed several scenarios over the years, Olaq decided prudence was best and set about erecting four houses, one for each man with his respective family and share of the animals. The women gathered thick branches to serve as a support frame for the roof, and the children were tasked with picking berries for food and roots with which to make tea. Everyone worked together; they knew innately that if they were unprepared for an uncertain winter, it could mean death to the entire tribe.

What Olaq would never know and could not comprehend was the dwellings his tribe built and expanded over time would survive and be discovered as some of the earliest remnants of human civilization. The area near the river, known even in modern day as Tell as Sitt—he named the small hill after his second wife—would be excavated almost twelve thousand years later and the stone houses moved to a safe location to preserve them so the river's course could be rerouted by the Syrian government. Olaq knew only that their survival was based in large part on security, food, and shelter. Since they had plenty of food, their main concern now was shelter. The crude huts offered them protection from the weather and wild animals.

They worked for weeks, stacking the rocks row on row and fixing them with a mixture of mud from a hole they dug and clay from the river's bottom. The children kept the hole filled with water and used another in which to mix the mud and clay with straw that formed a cement-like substance. The tribe finished the dwellings in two months, with plenty of time before winter to hunt, fish, and gather and dry fruit. They made rope from long vines and improved their tools for hunting and cooking. They were prepared for the winter and took the opportunity to explore the surrounding area while movement was still easy.

One rock near the riverbank was distinctively different than the rest. Shiny, black, twenty inches across, and an irregular oval shape, it had a center recessed about four inches below a distinct rim. It caught Olaq's attention, and he carried it to his dwelling, noticing how heavy it was compared to other stones of similar size. He neither understood that meteors hit the earth's surface from time to time, nor that he was holding one; he knew only that as leader of the tribe, he could claim it for himself. Generations of his offspring would ultimately use it as a sign of fertility, likening the recessed center to a woman's genitals.

On one of the excursions, Olaq watched a bird floating on the river—he had never seen ducks until they arrived to this area—calling to an unseen mate. The bird made a noise that to him sounded like *kwaik*; Olaq took that as an indication of the river's name, and in his primitive language, it was pronounced *queiq*. The tribe had already added two dozen new words to their primitive language of four hundred words since arriving on the Queiq only four months previously because of the many new sights and sounds in the area. Olaq was satisfied that they were ready for the coming season with enough food stored and a sturdy roof overhead; and naming the river seemed appropriate since their lives were now inextricably tied to it. Also unknown to Olaq was that the Queiq would support life for half a thousand generations and would be a major source of trade and transportation throughout history.

The winter was mild and relatively dry, and equally surprising was that both newborns survived and were thriving. Unlike their previous habitats in Asia Minor and the Himalayas, there was little snow and many days were relatively warm. The children were able to play outside most of the winter, and the men continued fishing and hunting throughout the season. Spearing three of the fat birds on the river before the flock inexplicably flew off as winter closed in, Olaq had Khalpe cook them, and the small tribe ate duck for the first time, finding it tasty and filling. A year to the day after they arrived at the Queiq, the group decided to remain another winter along the river as their needs seemed to be fulfilled better than in previous locations.

Two weeks later, the group was forced to remain inside their huts for almost a week when three of the strangest creatures they had ever seen decided to camp along the river, much to Canis's displeasure. With a furry reddish-brown coat and standing taller than any of the men in the group by more than half, this strange beast had one large horn on the end of a long snout and a shorter second horn between the eyes. The animal—fossils identified it eleven thousand years later as one of the few remaining wooly rhinoceroses left over from the recently ended Ice Age—weighed more than all of Olaq's tribe combined. On the third day, the cow birthed a calf half as tall as Sitt; and a few days later, the three adult rhinos moved west, with the newborn trailing along behind them, and never returned.

In honor of his favorite wife, Olaq named the area where they lived Khalpe—she was still jealous of Sitt's hill—a name that would survive for thousands of years. He would never know that his tribe was the foundation of what would become the oldest continuously inhabited city in the world—although it would not become a formal city for almost seven millennia—with conquerors and potentates changing its name to eventually become known as Aleppo seventy-five hundred years after Olaq ate his first duck. Khalpe's son Halam would be the first child born in Aleppo. For now, in Olaq's perfect world, the area was Khalpe, the hill was Sitt, the river was Queiq, Canis was by his side, and life, however primitive, was good. Ten thousand years before Abraham would milk his ashen Zebu cows in exactly the same location, human needs were basic in the extreme.

Olaq was also unaware that the foraging lifestyle he witnessed at Göbekli Tepe was quickly coming to an end. Whereas previously humans found food where it grew, grazed, or roamed, now they started to grow crops from their favorite grains and herded cattle, sheep, and other animals into pens to hold for milk or slaughter. The hunting-and-gathering society of man's entire existence was just starting to evolve into an agricultural revolution, necessitating static dwellings and villages, tracts of arable land and pastures, larger families to mind the flocks and tend the fields, and continuous sources of water for the crops and animals.

The transition from foragers to agriculturalists happened so slowly that people were unaware of the changes in lifestyle, work, and planning. No longer could they hunt until they found food and then relax with family and tribe until they were again hungry; the work tending crops and animals never ceased, and they now lived in fear of famine, starvation, and deprivation. Scottish anatomist and anthropologist Arthur Keith would declare twelve thousand years into the future, "The discovery of agriculture was the first big step toward a civilized life," but Olaq could hardly have understood that as he camped on the banks of the Queiq.

The tribe cleared land adjacent to the river and began the process of planting wheat, barley, and corn. They solved the problem of irrigation by constructing elevated troughs—later called aqueducts by the Romans and *aflaj* by the Arabs—to carry water from the river directly to the crops, a technique they observed during their brief stop in Turkey. Simple sliding panels regulated the flow and direction of the water, obviating the need to carry water by hand for irrigation and for the livestock. The favorable climate meant an ample harvest and a second winter living comfortably along the riverbank.

Olaq and his tribe encountered other groups moving through the area, but for the most part, they were left alone. One small group traveling north from Jordan—offspring of the original Natufian culture from the Judaean Hills near the Sea of Galilee—stopped for a few days before continuing northeast to Göbekli Tepe. Although the two groups spoke no common language, crude drawings and hand signals by the

Natufians convinced Olaq they were traveling to the monoliths—for what reason, he could not discern. The visitors also taught Olaq's tribe secrets of agriculture and harvesting, tillage in hoe farming, how to use a mattock to prepare the earth for planting, cleaning fish and fowl, and the use of concave stones as mortars for grinding grains, nuts, and seeds. The Natufians had moved to a sedentary lifestyle a thousand years earlier and had tamed crops and animals long before the Asian tribes had.

Khalpe experimented with the grains they were domesticating, cooking them with wildflowers, berries, and meats to create new dishes. She and the other women learned how to tenderize the newly slaughtered game by cooking it slowly, often having to push the children away from the open flame as they tried to steal small bits of the roasting meat. They devised a technique of pushing meat onto a tree-branch spit and roasting it upright, carving the cooked meat onto rudimentary bread the Natufians taught them how to bake and allowing the newly exposed raw meat underneath to continue cooking. It would be another six thousand years before domesticated chickens arrived to the Middle East from Burma, offering a choice of lamb or chicken, much later claimed by the Ottoman Turks as an original dish of their empire called *shawarmas*.

Olaq and the other men, meanwhile, experimented with making boza, and even placed some in a homemade palm-frond container in the cold river to make an ice cream–style slush favored by the children. They soaked meat in boza for a sweeter taste, and the Natufians helped them crush berries into the concoction to create flavored drinks. When the harvest came, they made boza from corn and barley, each with its own taste and intoxicating characteristics.

Although never consciously deciding to stay, Olaq and his offspring remained along the river for hundreds of generations and thousands of years, the group waxing and waning over the millennia through wars, famine, disease, and abundance.

Chapter 2

5121 BC
Timbuktu, Mali

Humans went through different developmental stages depending on where they lived, what they ate, what animals preyed on them, and how the climate affected their existence. A skull was found by a miner digging for baryte in 1960 at the archeological site in Jebel Irhoud southeast of Safi, Morocco, one of a number of hominin fossils originally believed Neanderthal but since reclassified *Homo sapiens* from just over three hundred thousand years ago in the Middle Paleolithic era.

French and Moroccan researchers reacted to the discovery, unearthing over thirty species of mammals across twenty-two layers of rock; the biostratigraphy of the dig included a child's mandible and a woman's humerus and hip bone with evidence of trauma. Microcomputed tomographic scans provided a composite reconstruction of the many *Homo sapiens* fossils found at the site, reinforcing the notion that modern humans were present across Africa at least a hundred thousand years earlier than previously believed.

Of particular interest, the lower thirteen layers included evidence of human habitation linked to an industry classified as Levallois Mousterian—a technique of shaping flints and rocks into stone tools called knapping, normally associated with the earliest anatomically modern humans in North Africa and West Asia. From the strata, it became obvious that humanlike mammals had lived in the same location over hundreds of thousands of years, probably because of the dry, open steppe-like environment full of game animals and predators; and the theory is further supported by the discovery of lumps of coal used for cooking, extraction of marrow from charred bones of slaughtered animals, and butchery marks caused by sharpened tools.

What the discovery could not show was the migration of a young man with his wife and child away from Jebel Irhoud. Banished from the tribe because of a dispute with one of the elders who coveted the man's wife, Tog and Buctou decided it best to leave their village and head east, away from the Berber tribes occupying the Maghreb coast in the north.

Berbers—the word *berber* was originally Greek, meaning "barbarian"—were agriculturalists who populated Northwest Africa since at least 10,000 BC, illustrated in cave drawings in Tassili n'Ajjer in southeastern Algeria with prehistoric Tifinagh scripts (the *abjad* Berber language) in the eastern region of Oran close to the border with modern-day Tunisia. Arab influence reached even Berber writing as *abjad* is based on the first four letters of the original Arabic alphabet corresponding to *a, b, j,* and *d* to describe a language with only consonants, leaving it up to the reader to fill in the invisible vowels. The transition to Neolithic societies was the final step of the Stone Age as farming and subsistence agriculture spread across the region.

Various Berber kingdoms claimed land in Morocco, Algeria, Tunisia, Libya, Mauritania, and northern Mali and Niger, changing in strength and influence over the millennia. They consisted primarily of the Mauri tribes of Mauritania, the Numidians of Carthage, and the Gaetuli from the Atlas Mountains. Although the Berbers tended to keep mostly to themselves, due to the financial success of Carthage, they increased the scope and sophistication of their politics to control the markets.

The Holocene geologic epoch—the Greek words *holos* means "whole" whereas *cene* means "new"—began only eight hundred years after Halam's birth and signaled the end of the previous glacial period, not because of anything humans did but, instead, because of a sudden increase in global temperatures brought on by seismic shifts deep inside the earth and changes in its orientation to the sun, alternating equally between the warmer hypsithermal and the colder neoglacial periods. Continental motion caused by plate tectonics accounted for only a thousand yards' difference over the course of ten thousand years, but ice melt resulting from the warmer temperatures caused ocean levels to rise over a hundred feet, inundating coastal settlements and creating new bodies of water where they didn't previously exist.

Tog and his wife headed first to Fez, centrally located in the northeast of the Atlas Mountains, with Rabat and Casablanca to the west, Tangier to the northwest, and Marrakesh to the southwest leading to the Trans-Saharan trade route. While they were barely classified as villages at the time with different names that evolved over the millennia, they nonetheless represented the largest trading posts in northwest Africa.

The small family then joined a caravan heading east through Algeria before turning south to very sparsely inhabited Mali, stopping when they reached the river later call the Niger, possibly derived from the Berber word *gher* meaning "river." They found the weather temperate, the land arable, and the river capable of providing food, transportation, and fresh water from its source in the Guinea Highlands. It also helped that their new homestead was two thousand miles from the village elder, significantly reducing the chance of him dropping by to lure Buctou away from her husband.

The last five thousand years witnessed birth, life, and death, not only of humans but of other species as well. Global warming and glacial retreat spelled the end of many animals that had adapted to the colder weather of the receding Ice Age but were unprepared when it ended so abruptly, further supporting Charles Darwin's maxim: "It is not the strongest of the species that survives, it is the one most adaptable to change."

A stone tower twenty-eight feet on each side constructed over nine thousand years ago confirmed the emergence of Jericho, among the oldest continuously inhabited cities in the world. Cattle were domesticated about the same time. The megatherium, Irish elk, cave bear, and saber-toothed cats all disappeared. Byblos was settled, cultivation of barley and wheat began in Mesopotamia, and an African culture developed across the current Sahel region.

The identical ancestors point was reached; all people at that point are common ancestors to everyone living today, or they are ancestors of no one living today because all lines of descent are extinct in every branch of their lineage. Jiahu culture began near the Yellow River of China, known locally as Huang He; and copper smelting was practiced in Pločnik in modern-day Serbia.

The oldest known gold hoard was deposited in the Varna Necropolis burial site in Romania, and the Minoan culture in Crete was born and died in the blink of the geological eye. Evidence of a wheeled vehicle emerged about fifty-five hundred years ago, enshrined on ceramic pottery near the Nida river in Poland. The prehistoric passage tomb monument at Newgrange in Ireland predated the pyramids of Egypt by almost six hundred years.

Tog was ignorant of the many changes happening around him, focused only on shelter for his family and food to eat. Their hospitality extended to welcoming travelers coming overland on foot or by riverboat; and as a result, the settlement grew quickly to over fifteen hundred inhabitants in their lifetimes, becoming one of the largest and most important autonomous desert ports.

Buctou assumed responsibility for bringing fresh water from the river for their little family. Tiring quickly of the tedious process that never ended, through good weather or bad, whether she was healthy or sick or pregnant, she decided instead to dig a well large enough for everyone in the growing village to use. She became the foreman and site manager, operating from crudely sketched diagrams and labor shifts so as not to burden one person or family over the others. The well—synonymous with life—was completed in just ten weeks to a depth of two hundred feet; and it would serve the people into modernity. The villagers combined their word *tin* meaning "place" with her name and Timbuktu was born.

Descendants of Tog and Buctou would populate the village that would eventually grow into a major Malian city, with tribes of Africans arriving from less hospitable areas and claiming land to settle and animals to breed and eat. Among them, the Mandinkas quickly established themselves as the dominant ethnic group in the region. A caste of griots in their social organization—historians, poets, storytellers, praise singers, and musicians, known locally as *jelis*—recounted tales of conquests and heroes, about strong and powerful women celebrated by the culture, and countless other stories of their oral society. Successive generations would produce strong offspring favored by East African slave traders, plucking them out of the villages along the Niger River, anxious to sell them to the Arabs and, eventually, to ship captains heading west to the New World over sixty-five hundred years into the future, victims of their own success.

Chapter 3

2227 BC
Aleppo, Syria

Spring came slowly this year, the winter snows finally melting in early April, fully four weeks later than in previous years. Although the sun rose just before five o'clock, the air was still cool an hour later as villagers made their way to the blacksmith's shops, the animal stables, and the bakery. Fields were being prepared for planting, and skins were tanning in the bright sunshine. Traders loaded their wagons for the journey overland to the Euphrates River, with the ultimate destination for their goods at towns and villages along both coasts of the Persian Gulf, the body of water known simply as "the sea above Akkad."

Naram-Sin rose at dawn before his wife awoke and stepped out onto the balcony from the bedroom. As always in the early morning, he nodded toward Thuban, the polar star to the north, acknowledging the constant around which the other stars rotated. He had a restless night, preoccupied with the affairs of state, of defense budgets, and of his pregnant wife. His army was camped in the area surrounding Khalpe—it was increasingly referred to as Halam, although history didn't remember it as the name of the first child born in Aleppo—taking defensive positions on the eight hills surrounding the inhabited areas close to the Queiq River with its clear drinking water and delicious perch, trout, and other freshwater fish. Their victory against a ragtag militia was swift and brutal; many men surrendered immediately so they could go back to their farms, their families, and their livelihoods. Most were never enthralled by the local governor's desire to fight the invading force, realizing quickly that they stood no chance against the Akkadian army.

The Akkad dynasty under Naram-Sin was the largest it would ever be, stretching from the Zagros Mountains in modern-day Iran to the Mediterranean Sea. This included the Land of the Amurru—named for its Amorite inhabitants—in what is today called Syria, stretching from Mount Lebanon across the Euphrates to the Khabur River valley in Mesopotamia, with Aleppo at its heart. He was so enamored with his conquests that he became the first Mesopotamian king to proclaim himself a god, angering many of his subjects and fomenting dissent among some of his soldiers. Naram-Sin promptly quashed the rebellion, adding to his reputation and enhancing his divinity and the folklore surrounding his reign.

None of that was on his mind as he stood on the balcony, the house taken as a spoil of war. It was a grand structure, built for and belonging to the governor of the region, who was now being used as live target practice by the archers, live at least until the arrows moved up from his legs into the torso and the head. The house was replete with beautiful pottery and cutlery finer than any Naram-Sin had seen previously. The furniture had been carved by skilled carpenters, and the beautiful curtains and linens woven tightly and adroitly. He appreciated the refinements the governor had enjoyed and felt for an instant that he could get used to such luxuries—but that was what worried him most this morning.

He saw the same look in his men's eyes, the same appreciation, the same longing for peace and stability rather than war, conquest, fatigue, and privation. He was certain a handful soldiers would desert, a normal event as they moved across the kingdom; but he feared the beautiful women, the amazing local food, and the mild climate might corrupt more men than he could afford to lose. He decided it was the priority issue for today.

Khalpe had evolved over the last eight thousand years since Olaq and his ragtag tribe arrived—centered around the river with cell-like quarters throughout the village segregated initially into tribal areas and much later into religious and ethnic cantonments. A walled city was in its earliest days of taking shape, and the central marketplace was becoming more defined, albeit seemingly disorganized.

The governor's mansion would over time be assimilated into the iconic citadel dominating the high ground in the middle of Aleppo, eventually becoming one of the oldest and largest castles in the world. Farms sprung up on the fertile land outside the village while shepherds grazed their livestock on the grass and clover blanketed the eight hills surrounding the small but growing town.

Naram-Sin felt rather than heard his wife come up behind him, pushing her warm body close to his in the morning chill. She pulled her robe around both of them and reached around his stomach to pull him to her. He could feel the bump swelling in her belly and smiled inwardly at the thought of the arrival of their first child. He was twenty-seven years old, king of the Akkadians, a god in his own right, with subjects across thousands of miles of his dominion.

"Come back to bed," Mozan-Al implored in her ancient native Tamil language, quickly repeating it in broken Akkadian for his sake. From her look, he knew better than to resist. She summoned the best-looking of her handmaidens—a tall girl named Jos-El with dark hair, large breasts, and almond-colored eyes, taken several battles ago from the arms of her dying father—and ordered her to strip and excite Naram-Sin, forcing her down onto her knees in front of him. The young girl obeyed without question or hesitation.

Although Mozan-Al wanted to please him herself, she found the pressure of him lying on top of her during the pregnancy was too painful to endure for more than a few moments; she used the girl to stimulate him so he would mount her and finish quickly. In another month, when she was even bigger and more uncomfortable, Jos-El would actually finish him on her knees, never lying down; Mozan-Al guarded her husband's seed jealously, not allowing him the chance to impregnate another woman whose children might challenge hers for the throne.

Mozan-Al would issue a daughter named Tar'am-Agade two months later, after the victory at Urkesh. This morning, though, she sought only to please Naram-Sin, and the slave girl served the purpose of getting him ready. He seemed to enjoy having the young girl start things off, and Mozan-Al found herself aroused by the girl watching them as she waited to clean the couple after they finished. Her arousal served to heighten the experience, and Mozan-Al shuddered in delight like never before. Her husband pulled her closer, believing she was shivering from the cold morning air.

Over the next few months, and even after delivery, the girl would continue to satisfy her husband, and she would from time to time push the girl's head into her own groin to experience the arousal again. Mozan-Al considered all of this training for the young girl; she was already thirteen years old and ready to be married off to one of the soldiers. Even though still a virgin, she had already learned many skills that would make the lucky soldier happy he was a man.

Still feeling the effects of the early-morning session with his wife and the maid, Naram-Sin crossed the road and entered the villa his army was using as its headquarters. Two of his corps commanders were late arriving, reinforcing his belief that this place was making his men soft and complacent. During the daily briefing by his staff, one detail caught his attention: twenty-three soldiers were absent at morning roll call and presumed deserters. Although he was already considering launching a new campaign, he was now convinced more than ever that the army needed a new purpose and mission away from here. He ordered the generals to get them on the move before sundown.

The Hurrians of Urkesh in the foothills of the Taurus Mountains were again resisting his rule. Although only a few hundred miles from Khalpe, the area around Urkesh was undeveloped and held very few attributes to attract his men and divert their attention away from pillaging and plundering as they moved across the land. It gave them something meaningful to do, and they were away from Khalpe with its vices and vamps—necessary distractions from time to time but not as an ongoing lifestyle.

His generals counseled conquering Iobaritae across the Kebrit Peninsula—later called the Arabian Peninsula—because of the reported wealth they could plunder, but Naram-Sin felt disposing of a recurring irritant was more acute. Urkesh was two hundred miles away, whereas Iobaritae was two thousand miles south and across the desert; the choice was obvious. They could discuss conquests through the peninsula later.

The Hurrians were an easy target, the real attraction being the beautiful women in their camp, bred from Persian stock mixed with eastern Europeans with long legs, dark hair, and penetrating eyes. Spirited was the best description of their personalities: often mercurial, they were nonetheless passionate. One had to take the good passion with the bad, well worth the experience, and Naram-Sin knew his soldiers would be motivated just thinking about it. Khalpe, and even Iobaritae, was quickly forgotten with expectations of something even better.

The cooks set off immediately with wagons loaded, looking for a campsite and cooking area several hours' march from Aleppo. They were already roasting the large game animals on the mobile barbecue grills because the last thing they wanted to do was be unprepared for the arrival of a hungry army marching to battle—never a good idea.

Naram-Sin chose to walk alongside his horse on the road heading east to Urkesh. He didn't like backtracking his army and knew they should be moving west toward the Middle White Sea, but failure to subdue the Hurrians might lead some to believe he was afraid of their reputation as warriors. He wasn't. Rather than allow their raids on his supply wagons and possibly lose men and equipment—and some of the women as well—to guerilla attacks, he thought it prudent to solve the problem once and for all as he had done in Khalpe.

His thoughts drifted back a few days before they left Khalpe, when his wife wanted to visit the river. After being bathed by three of her handmaidens and washing her hair in the crisp, clear waters of the

Queiq, they sat together in the noonday sun, enjoying the fresh air and watching the bees begin their work of pollenating the flowers and plants. They ate the snacks prepared by the servants, and Naram-Sin ordered some of his aides off into the surrounding forest to hunt deer, wild boar, rabbits, and game birds. The remainder of his entourage moved away to give the couple some privacy, but still stayed close enough to respond immediately should they need something.

The only one who stayed was Jos-El; she rarely left Mozan-Al's side. She had even taken to sleeping with the couple—his wife slept in the middle of the bed between the slave girl and him—with his wife justifying it by suggesting the warmth of Jos-El helped her sleep better. He didn't mind it, and often woke to see the two women satisfying each other late in the night. He would watch them and then pull the girl to him while his wife watched.

The melting snow had taken some of the topsoil with it as it ran off the small hill, leaving behind bare earth and rocks. The servants dug several holes, always hitting rocks just a few inches below the surface, until finally they were able to scratch away enough dirt to build a firepit. What caught Naram-Sin's eye was the straight line of the holes: random rocks were never organized like that, and it piqued his interest to discover what was hidden beneath the soil.

He ordered the servants to excavate the area surrounding the rocks, quickly discovering the four walls of what was obviously a dwelling of sort, slowly covered by the earth over the millennia since it was built. While ducks were being roasted over the fire, Naram-Sin watched curiously as the workers uncovered the structure and finally found a way in.

Although some mud had seeped into the building, the roof had held remarkably well, and they were able to go inside standing upright. Using torches made of cloth wrapped around a tree branch lit at the campfire, they could see it had at one time housed several people, with sleeping areas spread around a central firepit. Rough pots, knives, and other tools were scattered around the pit, as well as what served as cups full of a brown beverage long ago dried and hardened.

Naram-Sin pried the top off one of the pots and poured out the contents; the container would be rediscovered along with two *mammut*-bone bracelets twelve thousand years later and displayed at the Louvre Abu Dhabi as one of the earliest artifacts found in Arabia. He emptied some grain resembling wheat onto the dirt floor.

As he did, he caught sight of a black rock prominently displayed in one corner on an earthen mound with smaller polished stones surrounding it. He picked it up, noticing its heavy weight and trying to guess its purpose. The artifact was valued by the original inhabitants of the dwelling, Naram-Sin surmised, given the obvious prominence of the shrine where it rested. He ran his hands over the smooth edges and recessed center of the rock, trying to discern its significance and wondering about the men who placed it there. He passed it to his senior aide with orders to have it delivered to his quarters, rightly assuming its previous owners wouldn't miss it.

Naram-Sin slowed so his wife's wagon could catch up. He looked inside and saw her resting, her cheeks pink from the warm sunshine. Although she knew he considered her his equal, he could not express that certainty in front of his officers and men. He valued her company and her counsel, often seeking her ideas and opinions regarding military strategy, disciplining the troops, and how best to spend the treasury's money. The Akkad dynasty was flush with wealth that grew with each conquest. Mozan-Al implored him to help the widows of the fallen soldiers, friend or foe, and provide for orphans and the elderly. Naram-Sin felt it unnecessary but enjoyed watching his wife's face light up when he announced another charity. Even with such largesse, the donations didn't make a dent in the treasury.

When they arrived at the first camp on their short journey, the men were already enjoying themselves with *deynek*, a sport similar to jousting. Organized into two six-man teams on horseback, the players alternated throwing the blunt javelin at and chasing an opponent, expertly maneuvering the horses to their tactical advantage. Players hit by the javelins were sent off the field; the first team to have all its players hit by the opposing team lost.

Horses had been domesticated in Kazakhstan some fifteen hundred years earlier and spread quickly across Europe and Asia. The Akkadians preferred smaller horses for battle and sport because they were able to turn and accelerate faster than larger horses, with progeny of Przewalski's horses from Mongolia their first choice for *deynek* and combat. The game remained popular for almost a hundred years until the end of the Akkadian Empire, then forgotten for two thousand years until it was resurrected by the Turks, renamed *jereed* by the Ottomans in the 1600s, and today remains a sport of skilled horsemen in the Central Anatolian province of Konya. The breed didn't fare so well; by the 1960s, Przewalski's horses would be extinct in the wild.

Naram-Sin maintained the camp at that location for two full weeks, allowing his soldiers time to rest and relax, bathe and wash clothes in the nearby stream, repair weapons and shields, sharpen swords and knives, and send reconnaissance forces ahead to scout the Hurrians. Wounds and injuries were tended to, new sandals fitted, and garments mended. The Akkadians wove plants into crude horseshoes, protecting the horses' hooves and enabling them to run faster than horses not similarly equipped. One of the wagons in the long procession carried the required vegetation and a group of women whose sole purpose was to weave the shoes. It would be another fifteen hundred years before cast iron horseshoes were nailed to the hooves; they could be removed quickly, melted, and repurposed into weapons if the need arose.

The Hurrians had originally been allied with the Akkadians under Naram-Sin's father and grandfather, but recent pronouncements by the Indo-Iranian–speaking Mitanni kingdom of dominion over Urkesh emboldened the Hurrians to resist Akkadian rule again and renege on trade agreements. Mitanni king Kirta had grand ambitions of uniting all of Asia from the Pacific Ocean as far west as Constantinople. Atalshen, king of Urkesh and Nawar, subordinated his forces under the protection of Kirta, believing he was capable of resisting any force that might come his way.

Naram-Sin moved his forces slowly toward Urkesh so they would arrive fresh and ready to fight. He was concerned when the scouts were unable to locate Kirta's army that might reinforce the Hurrians; he doubled the scouting parties and pushed them beyond Urkesh into the Taurus Mountains so they didn't overlook possible encampments.

Reconnaissance over thousands of square miles surrounding Urkesh yielded nothing of value, although one of the scouts was missing and assumed captured, adding to the uncertainty. Naram-Sin didn't simply want to win the engagement; he wanted instead to crush any ambitions of Kirta, Atalshen, or others who might cause him problems later. History must record the victory as decisive, profound, and absolute.

On the thirty-third day after leaving Aleppo with his forces surrounding Urkesh, Naram-Sin attacked from every direction and prevented anyone from leaving the city or reinforcing the Hurrian army from outside the cordon. Atalshen was captured alive; rather than kill him, Naram-Sin allowed him to watch the battle from a strategic vantage point in the foothills of the nearby mountain range as Akkadian forces swept through the town. The army was defeated but not destroyed; Naram-Sin wanted to ensure the Hurrians could defend themselves from other invaders, fresh with the memory that they were no match for the Akkadians. Atalshen was left on his throne after pledging fealty to the Akkadian man-god, removing a threat to Naram-Sin and his army.

The Hurrians and Urkesh would suffer defeat by the Amorites, the Assyrians, the Hittites, and other armies over the coming centuries, never again reaching their full glory. Despite its military weakness, Hurrian cultural spread westward and influenced civilizations throughout Western Asia, North Africa, and modern-day Europe. The work of masterful ceramists would make Hurrian pottery renowned for its craftsmanship and beauty, with wheel-made Khabur and Nuzi ware adorning palaces and dining tables west of the Euphrates as far away as Egypt. Hurrian metallurgy would survive the decline of its empire and be used in crafting tools and fashioning weapons for almost two thousand years; they would be introduced into Europe after the First

Crusade when skilled blacksmith slaves from Urkesh were brought with the retreating Christian armies around 1100 AD.

Naram-Sin eventually turned his army west again, defeating Manium of Magan, several tribes in the Taurus foothills, and Turkish cities lining the Amanus Mountains. The Sumerians submitted to his rule rather than be exterminated, with the seal of the governor of Lagash proclaiming, "Naram-Sin, the mighty God of Agade, king of the four corners of the world, Lugalushmgal, the scribe, *ensi* of Lagash, is thy servant." He signed a peace treaty with the Elamite king, Khita, who declared "the enemy of Naram-Sin is my enemy, the friend of Naram-Sin is my friend."

Conquests of Anatolia in Turkey and Armanum and Elba on the Mediterranean coast cemented his rule across thousands of miles and made him the undisputed ruler of the known world. Naram-Sin's grandfather Sargon, the first ruler of an empire, reigned for fifty-six years before relinquishing the throne to Naram-Sin's father, and ultimately to his grandson. The Akkadian empire had now reached its maximum strength; it would take another hundred years before it would collapse. But for now, the God of Akkad, King of Akkad, King of Sumer, King of the Four Corners of the World, and King of the Universe, husband of Mozan-Al, and father of Tar'am-Agade contented himself with surveying his dominion.

Chapter 4

526 BC
Iobaritae, Arabian Peninsula

Amr bin Jafna loaded his wagon with the day's frankincense crop for the short trip to the village, where it would be prepared for northbound shipments. There was urgency in his activities; the weather was cooling, making his long journey through the vast desert easier for both the animals carrying it and the man who would sell the aromatic resin in Dimashq, Rabbath Ammon, and the Sumerian city of Urim, the birthplace of the patriarch Abraham. Derived from the Old French expression *franc encens* meaning "high-quality incense," the Bedouins of the Arabian Peninsula referred to it as *al bukhur*, but in any language, it was more valuable than gold.

Dating from 3800 BC, Urim—Ur in today's Iraq—would become an important Akkadian city named for the Assyrian-Babylonian moon god, Nanna. Once a coastal city in the pivotal point where the Euphrates River and her sister the Tigris emptied into the Persian Gulf, Ur became a strategic trading center and, as a result, wealthy. Over time the coastline shifted, the tundra grew, and the city was no longer on the river or the Gulf; and owing to a sustained drought, it would be abandoned in another hundred years.

For now, though, Urim was Amr's best customer for his desert gold. Wealth brought many conveniences and luxuries to the city and the region, among them the rectangular-shaped ziggurat, the massive pedestal supporting the White Temple, constructed to connect heaven and earth. Wealthy businessmen raised money to build and operate the temple that would ultimately consume two tons of frankincense every year; in years when significant festivals or remembrances were planned, that amount could easily double.

Amr struggled to keep up with demand, a good problem to have for a commodity supplied exclusively from his properties where the *Boswellia sacra* trees grew in valleys south of the Empty Quarter in modern-day Oman and Yemen. He guarded the trees jealously and kept them healthy, never cutting them more than once a month for the valuable resin that seeped from the wound.

Iobaritae—the Land of the Ubarites—encompassed the region along the southern end of the desert, centered on a market town just north of the escarpment of *Thurifero regio*, or "incense land," an apt if not simplistic description of the area. Over the centuries, its fortunes would rise and fall with the demand for and price of frankincense.

A massive earthquake that originated in the Cherangany Hills in the western highlands of the Great Rift Valley in Kenya and traveled under the Red Sea into the Arabian Peninsula would strike around 300 AD. Tremors and aftershocks were felt throughout Arabia, the Levant, Mesopotamia, and even across the Gulf into Persia, where coastal cities were decimated by a forty-three-foot-high tsunami. Iobaritae, the Atlantis of Arabia, would sink into the desert sands and not be rediscovered for almost sixteen hundred years when images from the Space Shuttle's low earth orbital spacecraft missions photographed ancient tracks converging on a central area in southern Oman bordering *al Rub al Khali*, Arabic for "the Empty Quarter."

Amr was a Sabaean Arab typical of South Arabia, part of the Saba Kingdom of which the Queen of Sheba would become famous and where the prophet Job was buried. Although pre-Islamic pagans, their religious beliefs were similar, requiring a pilgrimage to Mecca. Men were forbidden to marry both a mother and her daughter or two sisters or his stepmother; and they performed circumcision among other rituals. He was a member of the Azd tribe, branches of which would leave indelible marks in the region throughout history.

Imran bin Omar took his extended family to Oman—this would lead to the creation of the al Said dynasty a thousand years later—along with Jabir ibn Zayd who founded the Ibadi sect of Islam dominant in that part of the peninsula. Imran's descendants would also form the Bani Yas tribe along the coast of what is now the United Arab Emirates, of which the al Nahyan branch in Abu Dhabi and the al Maktoum branch in Dubai would rule their respective emirates for centuries continuing into modernity. Amr's father, Jafna, relocated his clan to Syria and founded the Ghassanid dynasty. His descendants included the Roman emperor Philip the Arab and the Byzantine emperor Leo III the Isaurian centuries later.

Amr made it a point to visit other cities and temples before traveling to Urim. As the last stop, the priests who offered prayers and gifts to the gods housed in the White Palace never wanted to be without and would buy not only their consignment but whatever he had remaining from his earlier stops. Besides, selling smaller quantities along the way yielded more income per mina (an ancient unit of weight divided into sixty shekels) than he would get from the priests who would push for lower rates with the higher volume.

Frankincense traders from Somalia and Ethiopia were sailing across the Red Sea and Gulf of Aden to Arabia; although their resin was not as good as his, they nevertheless presented a challenge to his market monopoly. At this point he was the wealthiest man in all of Iobaritae with vast groves of fruit trees and ownership of many of the remarkable buildings in the village, so losing some business wouldn't hurt much. As long as he kept the priests content and protected his trees, though, his frankincense trade would continue unabated.

On this trip, he headed northwest to Dimashq, traveling as best he could along established trade routes through oases at Umm al Melh, Wadi al Dawasir, Al Khurma, and to the coast at Yanbu. He followed the Red Sea until forced to go inland northeast to Irbid, Dara'a, and, finally, to his first destination.

Artisans in Dimashq would melt the resin into perfumes, make scented soaps and shampoos, and fashion candles for temples, funerals, and weddings. Amr would use the time while they worked to recover from the trip across the Empty Quarter and seek new customers for his frankincense in the vast trading area in the city center. Long before the Souq al Hamidiyah would be built as the central marketplace, the area next to the citadel inside the walled city would serve as an informal farmers' market and trading area for centuries in what had already become the world's oldest continuously inhabited capital city.

Amr moved throughout the market, seeing exotic birds, monkeys, and snakes in one area; slaves of every size, shape, and description in another; and gold, silver, and precious stones being crafted into jewelry in a third. What he didn't see was frankincense, which made trading his monopolistic product so much easier because everyone wanted it and few had it to offer.

His habit was to return home with something from each trip for his wife and children, and this time was no exception. For each daughter, he bought a gold bracelet; for his wife a necklace adorned with amethyst from Hellas and Panjshir emeralds and rubies from the Khorasan province in Kapisa (now Afghanistan); and for his boys, two ancient Egyptian board games called *senet*, the rules of which evolved over a thousand years, and Game of Twenty Squares played with sixty pawns and two dice.

These small gifts traveled well and allowed plenty of space for virgin olive oil from Syria, bulgur from the parboiled groats of durum wheat from Byblos in the eastern Mediterranean region of Phoenicia, and sorghum brought by sailing ships from North Africa. He ordered what he needed and arranged for it to be ready after his trip to Urim on his return through Dimashq to Iobaritae.

What really caught his eye, though, was a black rock unlike any he had seen before. Smooth to the touch, it was unusually heavy for its size. The vendor regaled Amr with stories of kings and cavemen alike coveting the stone in an obvious attempt to drive up the price, a tactic with which Amr was already well familiar. He feigned indifference, left the store, but returned a while later. Then he left again after haggling about the price, slept on it for two nights, and went back on the third day to buy it, paying less than one-fourth of the original asking price. Concerned about leaving it with the vendor during his trip to Ur—Amr had never done business with this man before and was unsure the stone would be waiting for him on his return—he decided instead to take it with him. Because of the amount of resin he had already sold in Dimashq, the load was lighter on the trip to Ur, even with the black rock.

Amr departed for Urim a few days later with his black rock safely cradled in one of the bags in the wagon. The four-hundred-mile trip was usually uneventful even with so many travelers on the same road heading north or south. He stopped every so often to rest the animals, have a good meal, and sell some of the resin, an early example of the traveling salesman, predating similar merchants on the Silk Road by some three hundred years. Sometimes travelers would keep him company, usually seeking work.

Lulled into complacency both by unseasonably warm weather and having completed the same biannual trip for the last thirty years, Amr did not notice or suspect the four men traveling toward him in a forested area with few other passersby. He was already thinking about the return trip to his wife and family, and that his wife asked him to bring honey and juniper from the ten-thousand-foot Al Souda mountains at the far southeast corner of the Empty Quarter. The finest wild honey was found at six thousand feet elevation, and the women in Iobaritae mixed the juniper from the higher elevations with the frankincense to create their own bespoke scents. Because his load would be considerably lighter after selling the remainder of his . . .

They set upon him quickly, disarming him of the curved *janbiya* knife (*janb* is the Arabic word meaning "side") he carried on his right hip before he could unsheathe it. Two of the men bound and guarded him while the other two went through the wagon to determine what they could pilfer. Recognizing the frankincense resin's value, the men decided to take the entire wagon and its contents.

Amr's body would be seen beside the road by several people as they headed to or from Dimashq, speeding up their own walk and looking over their shoulder so the same fate would not befall them. They could not have known the bandits were already in Dimashq selling what they could of Amr's belongings. One of the four men was tasked with selling the black stone; the man who bought it did not let on that it left his store only five days before, nor did he inquire about Amr's whereabouts.

    It would be two full seasons before Amr's family reluctantly accepted that he wasn't returning, correctly surmising he was attacked and killed by bandits. His eldest son began the monumental task of rebuilding his father's trading network with Ur and the cities along the way. Within ten years, he had tripled Amr's revenue and acquired half again as many clients for the resin. The family business not only survived Amr's death but thrived under his son's dedication and perseverance.

Chapter 5

202 BC
Zama, Tunisia

As queen of the Phoenician city-state Tyre located on the coast in modern-day Lebanon, she enjoyed all the trappings befitting her throne. Born in 839 BC, she grew up accustomed to wealth, not only of the palace but also as a result of being raised in the largest and wealthiest trading hub of the Eastern Mediterranean. Daughter of the Tyrian king Mattan I and his wife, Sychaeus, Dido was loved both inside and outside the palace. Her name, from the same root as *David*, confirmed it. Translated from the Semitic language, it meant "beloved," although the Greeks would later call her Elissa, meaning "fire," referring to the intensity of her commitment to her people, to commerce, and to fair play.

Dido was eight years old when her father died, succeeded by her brother Pygmalion, who elevated her to the throne in Tyre, where she was out of his way. Tyrannical and ruthless, he was the antithesis of his sister and did not want to be reminded by her of their parents' benevolence. Even as she got older and began pushing back against some of his excesses, she was far enough away that most of their conversations were in letters carried by riders on horseback; he could choose to ignore them and saw her in person only once or twice a year, something he usually could tolerate. He also knew Dido was their father's favorite child, and had Mattan lived longer, he likely would've put her on the throne instead of his son.

Rome had been a minor city-state for much of the past five hundred years after it was first settled, with little appetite for war or expansion. Roman citizens preferred their bathhouses and debates, perfecting the wines that would make them eternally famous, and relaxing in the soft Mediterranean sun eating the locally grown fruits, vegetables, and livestock.

Traders arriving from outside the Italian peninsula brought fabrics, jewelry, and trinkets from foreign lands, selling or trading their wares in *il mercato* in central Rome, the marketplace for everything from animals to food to garments and slaves. The silver denarius had become the coin of the realm, its influence lasting to modernity as the currency in Tunisia, Bahrain, and other nations where the dinar is still used.

But the situation had changed. By 200 BC, the Roman army had conquered Italy, and within the next two centuries Greece, Spain, France, and Britain. The Roman Empire expanded over time but became unwieldy and ultimately split in half. Germanic tribes defeated Emperor Romulus and occupied Rome in 476 under the leadership of Odoacer, the first Barbarian to rule in Rome. The eastern half based in Constantinople survived for several centuries as the Byzantine Empire, becoming the launch pad for conquests of Asia Minor, or today's Turkey, as well as Palestine and Syria in the Levant and Libya and Carthage in North Africa.

Rome effectively controlled the entire Mediterranean coast and beyond for over a thousand years, with forts connecting the empire across Europe east to the Krak des Chevaliers in Syria and south in Libya, establishing a foederati system of peoples and cities bound with Rome by treaties. North Africa served as a winter haven for Romans with the major cities along the Libyan coast at Leptis Magna—the largest of the ancient cities on the south shore of the Mediterranean Sea—with Sabratha and Oea in the Limes Tripolitanus frontier zone of defense, and in Tunisia at Carthage, the mausoleum in honor of a Numidian prince at Thugga, Theveste, and the terra cotta industry and second largest coliseum outside Rome around Thysdrus, or modern-day

El Djem. So much trade developed between North Africa and Rome that ports were built at Diarrhytus, Curubis, Gightis, Sabratha near Tripoli, and Carthage to handle and redistribute the cargo.

Five hundred years earlier, Pygmalion had Dido's Tyrian priest husband, Acerbas, assassinated believing she would transfer her husband's wealth to the king; she met with her advisors in the tiny village of Dbayeh to decide whether to stay and fight or leave, ultimately deciding to flee her murderous brother to Carthage where she established a trading post.

Because of her royal lineage, Dido at age twenty-five became the first queen of the North African city-state in what is modern-day Tunisia, where she would rule for almost fifty years. By the third century BC, it was the most advanced city in the region, wealthier than Rome, and possessing a significant naval force that could not only defend Carthage but also project power abroad.

The Year of the Consulship of Canina and Lepidus in 285 BC and the decades before and after were significant for several reasons. Egypt's Ptolemy I Soter abdicated and was succeeded by his son Ptolemy II Philadelphus, a few short months before the lighthouse in Alexandria's harbor was completed; the 360-foot tower became one of the seven wonders of the ancient world, a model of lighthouses of the future, and a prominent landmark for ships transiting the eastern waters of the Mediterranean. Halley's Comet appeared in the skies in 240 BC, portending a disaster according to the priests; an earthquake destroyed the Colossus of Rhodes a dozen years later, validating their supposedly prescient claim.

Seleucus accepted the surrender of and imprisoned his predecessor Demetrius I when the latter's troops mutinied and deserted him in Macedonia in 288 BC, setting up dozens of wars over the next two centuries as Seleucus and his successors attempted to replicate the empire of Alexander the Great of Macedon. Ptolomies re-excavated the Red Sea canal originally dug by Persian king Darius I, opening a significant maritime trade route between the Mediterranean and the Indian Ocean.

Realizing the economic potential of this development, Rome began exerting control over the littoral states of the Middle White Sea, completed by defeating Cleopatra of the Ptolemaic dynasty in Egypt in 31 BC. Farther east, work began on the first stretch of the thirteen-thousand-mile Great Wall of China as a barrier to prevent invasion by the Mongols from the north. Within a few years, the Greek astronomer and polymath Eratothenes in the Libyan city of Cyrene would accurately measure the circumference of the earth using maps and charts from the Library of Alexandria, built one hundred years earlier, where he served as chief librarian.

Hamilcar was born in Carthage in 275 BC and rose to command the city-state's forces in Sicily toward the end of the first Punic War—Punic representing the Roman word for Phoenicia—and returned home after the surrender of Carthage in 241 BC. He was recalled to duty over the years and fought campaigns in Spain and Italy, frustrating the Romans with his tactical prowess and military strategy. Hamilcar was so successful the Romans were forced to raise a fleet and learn maritime power projection that would facilitate the ultimate defeat of Carthage and expansion of the empire.

One of Hamilcar's sons accompanied him on campaigns from the age of nine, learning the art of war by his father's side. *Hanno*—a typical Carthaginian boy's name—was joined to the Canaanite name *Ba'al*, meaning "Lord," rendering Hannibal, son of Hamilcar, with a prominent name that would be remembered through the ages. Hamilcar made his son promise to never be a friend to Rome, going so far as to suspend the boy over a sacrificial funeral pyre until Hannibal swore he would use fire and steel to stop Rome's ambitions.

As Hannibal matured and eventually commanded Carthaginian forces, first under his father and later under his older brother, he studied fighting, how best to deploy his soldiers and equipment, and how to use terrain to his advantage. He practiced masking his forces from view until the last moment to surprise the Romans, and he perfected the use of small reconnaissance units that gave him intelligence of the enemy's disposition and movements. By the time he rose to commander in chief of the army at age twenty-six, Hannibal was ready for the job.

The island of Bint al Riyah—the name is Arabic for "Daughter of the Winds" because of the strong gales emanating from the North African coast—fifty miles east of Carthage was a useful vantage point from which Hannibal could surveil maritime traffic moving through the central Mediterranean. The ten-mile-long, five-mile-wide island oriented northwest to southeast was formed by volcanic activity forty-five thousand years ago, resulting in two calderas in the center crowned with a twenty-seven-hundred-foot peak. For the two hundred soldiers stationed on the island to provide early warning of Roman, Greek, and other foreign troop movements, the Carthaginians built dozens of small structures from the volcanic rock called *dammuso*, topped with domes painted white to reflect the heat. They built the local acropolis just outside the enclave and buried their dead in Punic-style tombs at a small sanctuary used for worship.

Duty on the island was easy, bolstered by sweet wines made from local Zibbibo grapes and olives from trees transplanted from the Tunisian interior and the natural hot baths from the geothermal springs remaining from prehistoric volcanoes. On a clear day, they could sight the Tunisian coastline thirty-seven miles to the west, a blunt reminder of why they were in uniform and what they were fighting for.

Carthaginians referred to it as Yarmar, from the Punic language of the Canaanites, Greek cartographers named it Kossyrus, the Romans called it Cossura, and in the Arabic language, it became Qawsirah. Over the years, dominion over the island changed, eventually becoming part of the Sicilian province of Trapani; the city council there labeled it on local maps as Pantelleria, named for the silica-rich volcanic rocks called pantellerites found strewn across the island.

Hannibal was able to take advantage of the outpost during most of the second Punic War. His scouts' visibility was over forty miles, and they were able to report a sizable Roman flotilla crossing the Strait of Sicily aiming for the North African coast. He moved his forces to the inland village of Zama, allowing him access to roads leading northeast and northwest, depending on where the Romans came ashore.

The Roman general Scipio insisted on meeting the Carthaginian before the battle. Whereas Hannibal guaranteed they would relinquish control of any overseas territories if Scipio were to leave Tunisia immediately, the Roman said the only acceptable solution was Hannibal's unconditional surrender. Believing his eighty war elephants offered a significant tactical advantage because of their intimidating size, Hannibal was unaware of Scipio's plan to open gaps between his units and allow the beasts simply to run past the legionnaires, rightly figuring they could attack in a straight line but not adjust quickly to a changing situation. The Romans slaughtered the elephants at the rear of the formation before they could turn for another assault.

Despite the advance warning, home field advantage, a brigade of war elephants, and a numerically superior force, Hannibal suffered a profound defeated at Zama. The Carthaginian Senate sued for peace and accepted the humiliating terms imposed by Rome, ending the seventeen-year war and preventing Carthage ever again from challenging Rome in the Mediterranean. The treaty also bankrupted the city-state, obviating the Senate's ability to raise an army even for self-defense, although the seeds of trade planted by Dido five centuries earlier allowed a quick and prosperous economic recovery. Successive leaders kept a detachment on Pantelleria to watch the Romans to the north and, eventually, new invaders from the east.

For now, though, inhabitants on the tiny island harvested olives; the prized oil of the Chemlali olive was sought after throughout the region and would be named in 2019 by the New York Olive Oil Competition as the best in the world. The rare but extraordinarily adaptable Zibibbo grape—the scientific name is Muscat of Alexandria, suggesting a possible connection to Egypt, translated as "dried grape"—flourished under Arab domination that cherished the sweet raisins for cooking and snacks. It was also fermented into an aromatic white wine with intense honey, date, and nut aromas, drunk mostly with fish, white meat, cheese, and dessert. Such was life on Pantelleria for centuries to come.

Chapter 6

January 21, 605
Mecca, Arabian Peninsula

In the eight hundred years since Hannibal's defeat, the Roman Empire had undergone tremendous upheaval and change. Its rule spread throughout Europe, North Africa, and the Middle East, conquering thousands of square miles with dozens of ethnic groups. At one point in the early fourth century, when the empire got too big, Emperor Diocletian attempted to rule more effectively by dividing it in half with capitals in Rome and Byzantium.

He appointed Maximian as Augustus, effectively co-emperor, with Diocletian ascending the throne in the Eastern Empire. He also appointed Caesars Galerius (reporting to him) and Constantius (to Maximian). The arrangement enabled each to rule one-quarter of the empire and secure the borders against foreign invaders. The tetrarchy proved effective while Diocletian was alive but collapsed after his death when the sons of Maximian and Constantius held competing dynastic claims to the empire.

Constantius's son Constantine ultimately defeated Maxentius's army to become the sole ruler of both halves of the empire, building a new imperial residence at Byzantium and renaming the city in his honor. Constantinople, later Istanbul, would be the capital of the Roman Empire for more than a thousand years. He was the first Roman emperor to convert to Christianity, probably influenced by his Greek mother,

Helena, who had converted previously; he even ordered construction of the Church of the Holy Sepulchre in Jerusalem at the purported site of Jesus's tomb. He designated the day devoted to the sun god Sol Invictus a day of rest for Christians; Sunday would also become a holy day through the ages. By the time of his death in 337, more than half his subjects voluntarily had become Christians.

Within sixty years, successive emperors had hardened in their interpretation of Christianity: whereas Constantine tolerated other faiths and beliefs, Emperor Theodosius in 393 proclaimed Christianity the religion of the empire. He ordered the destruction of pagan symbols, such as the temple at Serapeum at Alexandria, and abolished the Olympics. The games would not reemerge for almost fifteen centuries. Jews were given the choice of converting or facing death, and conquered subjects found themselves designated Christians without redress or remedy.

Meanwhile, the western part of the Arabian Peninsula had developed over the centuries under the Thamud civilization, with maritime trading perfected by the Phoenicians using Alpha Ursae Minoris as the North Star to navigate away from sight of land. (It would later be known as Polaris, succeeding the "Guardians of the Pole" Thuban, Kochab, and Pherkad—described by the ancient Egyptians as the Indestructibles lighting the north, used when orienting the pyramids of Giza—in the twenty-six-thousand-year precession of the earth on its axis.)

It had been five hundred years since the Banu Judham tribes of Yemen ruled the city and controlled much of the Eastern Province along the Red Sea coast. At over a million square miles and as the largest peninsula in the world, it would eventually consist of seven independent countries sitting atop huge fields of petroleum and natural gas deposits. For now, though, it was a collection of coastal villages and nomadic desert tribes with loyalties of convenience and fungible alliances.

Abraham and his son Ismail had been commanded by God to leave Aleppo some twenty-six hundred years earlier and build a house in His honor on a holy site in Mecca. Over the centuries, the house was destroyed, rebuilt, reshaped, and repurposed; but it always remained a physical manifestation of God's commandment toward men to remain obedient and pious, at times housing almost four hundred idols of the various tribal gods.

When floods destroyed the structure in 605, the Quraish tribe inhabiting Mecca and the self-appointed guardians of God's house rebuilt it. Abu al Qasim Mohammed ibn Abdullah ibn Abdul Muttalib ibn Hashim of the Banu Hashim clan of the Quraish tribe, then about thirty-five years old and the religious, social, and political leader who would found Islam half a decade later, participated in the construction project and insisted on installing the black stone—named al Hajar al Aswad by the Arab traders and brought to the area by caravans originating two thousand miles north in Aleppo—into the structure.

An orphan since age six, the young man felt it appropriate to place the rock in the eastern corner of the building, by then referred to as the Kaaba because of its cubic shape, to face the west winds responsible for bringing rain to the parched region. Eight years after placing the black rock in the Kaaba, Mohammed was publicly preaching in Mecca, his hometown, although he was largely ignored and considered crazy. Within seventy years of his death in 632, there were more non-Arab than Arab Muslims, growing eventually to over one billion of the faithful.

The enigmatic black rock discovered by Olaq ten thousand years ago along the Queiq River near Aleppo, coveted by Naram-Sin and Amr bin Jafna among others, finally found a home and sacred significance that would endure throughout history.

Chapter 7

June 12, 1325
Tangier, Morocco

At twenty-one years old and already trained and recognized as an Islamic scholar, Shams al Din Abu Abdullah Mohammed ibn Abdullah ibn Mohammed ibn Ibrahim ibn Mohammed ibn Ibrahim ibn Yusuf al Lawati al Ṭanji in the patronymic system, including the forefathers' names after his given name—known locally as ibn Battuta, likely a nickname since it means "son of a duckling"—was finalizing his personal affairs and packing the few items he intended to take on his journey.

He had announced to his parents and friends a desire to explore the world after completing the hajj, or pilgrimage to Mecca, required of Muslims, waiting until he finished formal education in Islamic jurisprudence as had his father and grandfather and great-grandfather before him, before setting out on his epic journey.

He was born into the Lawata Berber nation during the Marinid dynasty, and his forefathers served as legal scholars and judges for centuries after Islam came to North Africa. The tribe originated in Cyrenaica, eastern Libya, under Roman rule, and started a westward migration through Tripolitania in the third century, first to Tunisia and Algeria before reaching the Atlantic Ocean where ibn Battuta was born.

Under Roman rule the city was known as Colonia Julie Tingi—the Julian Colony of Tingis—retaining the Berber word *tingis*, meaning "marsh." Early Arabs referred to it as Boughaz, and it carried nicknames such as "Bride of the North" and "Door of Africa" because of its strategic location on both the Atlantic Ocean and the Mediterranean Sea. The name developed in Portuguese, *Tânger*; Spanish, *Tánger*; and French, *Tanger*, before entering English as Tangier, with modern Arabs and Berbers now calling it Tanja. By adding *al Tanji* to his name, ibn Battuta announced his hometown to the world.

In sheer distance, ibn Battuta would travel more than seventy thousand miles, twice as far as Zheng He, five times farther than Marco Polo, and the equivalent of circumnavigating the globe three times. As with any journey, his first step set the tone: he slipped on the stairway outside his parents' home and almost broke his ankle, potentially obviating one of the greatest journeys in history. The Son of a Duckling stood, dusted himself off, and headed east out of the city for what was normally a sixteen-month journey to Mecca by foot, with no horse or companion to accompany him. He would not see Tangier again for twenty-four years.

After leaving Morocco, he crossed the sultanates of Abd al Wadid and Hafsid before arriving in Tunis—from the Berber word *tns*, meaning "encampment"—enjoying the city so much he remained for two months, discovering Carthage and the ruins of several Roman cities, Sidi Bou Said, and the beaches of Hammamet and Djerba. He took a side pilgrimage to Kairouan in northern Tunisia's inland desert, the fourth holiest city in Islam after Mecca, Medina, and Jerusalem. He spent the night in the small farming village of Siliana at the invitation of a family he met on the road and stayed in the underground Berber-speaking town of Matmata in southern Tunisia. It would be made famous as Luke Skywalker's home in the fourth episode of the Star Wars movie series 650 years in the future.

As he prepared to continue his pilgrimage, he met a group of sailors who encouraged him to accompany them to the small island east of the Tunisian mainland. Ibn Battuta took them up on the offer and traveled to Pantelleria, spending a few days exploring the extinct volcano, feasting on the local foods that were a mix of Tunisian and Sicilian cuisines, and learning of the many cultures that had occupied the island over the centuries. When he was ready to depart, the boat deposited him on the Libyan coast near Sabratha; he found it an outstanding example of Roman architecture and lifestyle. From there he continued east, arriving in the Egyptian coastal city of Alexandria almost a year after leaving home, having covered twenty-two hundred miles on foot.

Ibn Battuta eventually reached Mecca and completed his pilgrimage, earning the honorific title El Hajji. Rather than return to Tangier, he kept moving east, with side trips to Persia and Mesopotamia, into Hebron, Jerusalem, and Bethlehem, and back to Mecca for a second pilgrimage. On a return trip to Baghdad, he met Abu Sa'id, the last Mongol ruler of the domain including modern-day Iraq, Armenia, Georgia, Afghanistan, Turkmenistan, Pakistan, and parts of Dagestan and Tajikistan, collectively known as the Ilkhanate area. Ibn Battuta joined the royal caravan for a while, then left them and turned north on the Silk Road toward Tabriz, the first major city to open its gates to the Mongols only a hundred years earlier, with the Arabian al Azd tribe of Marib residing in the city after the Muslim conquest of Iran.

He would eventually travel from Yemen to the east coast of Africa, visiting Somalia and the Swahili coast of Kenya and Tanzania; through Turkey and Central Asia; cross the Khyber Pass to India, Sri Lanka, and Bangladesh; south by ship to the Maldive islands; and then east to Sumatra, China, Malaysia, and Vietnam. He found cowrie shells were used as cash in many of the countries he visited, considerably easier than converting from one currency to another, and making it the first attempt of money unification similar to the euro almost seven hundred years later.

On his return, he was forced to stop in Syria, alternating his time between Safita and Homs to avoid the Black Death plague that ultimately would kill 200 million people in Eurasia and North Africa from 1347 to 1351. He arrived home three years later and dictated *A Masterpiece to Those Who Contemplate the Wonders of Cities and the Marvels of Travelling*, the only original source of information on Ibn Battuta's travels, before crossing the Sahel to visit Taghaza, Gao, and Timbuktu in Mali; Oualata in Mauritania; and Takedda in Niger, among other sites. He continued exploring until his death in 1369, although his cultural agility would be admired and emulated throughout history.

Chapter 8

March 3, 1672
Port Royal, Jamaica

Robert Morgan was not particularly excited about the birth of his tenth child and sixth son, although at that point, there wasn't much he could do about it. He was a farmer in Llanrumney, a largely rural agricultural community in the mild, wet climate in Monmouthshire, incorporated into Cardiff three hundred years later, bordering the Bristol Channel in the far south of Wales. Morgan's small family farm was located on a relatively flat plain adjacent to the mountains dominating the area, making his land not only valuable but an absolute necessity for the communities that relied on his wheat, barley, and rapeseed oil crops.

Henry was born six weeks prematurely in the middle of winter; the infant struggled to survive, suffering early from croup, four times before he was six years old, leaving him with a deep, raspy voice that served him well later in life as a sea captain. As soon as the boy was able to walk, Robert put him to work in the fields with the other children, offering no solace for Henry's breathing difficulties made worse by the crop dust.

Henry learned quickly and used his natural leadership abilities to organize his siblings and the other workers, all older than him, to produce a higher yield and profit from the existing crops. With the additional revenue, Robert was able to buy some adjacent land and expand into cattle farming by breeding and milking Welsh Black dairy cows, suitable for grazing on the poor-quality pasture and moorland. He even raised chickens for eggs, at one point selling a hundred dozen eggs a day to the surrounding villagers. Henry's initiatives had another effect on the region; at its height of its success, two hundred men, women, and children worked at the Morgan farm, making it one of the largest employers in Monmouthshire and the southern third of Wales.

As the youngest boy, Henry understood full well he was not entitled to a share of the property upon his father's death; that would go to the eldest son, Daniel. Welsh property law could be superseded only by a properly attested will, something Robert failed to sign before he died suddenly. Against their mother's wishes, Daniel gave the other children thirty days to find another place to live.

Henry was only twelve years old when the nine siblings left the Morgan farm to find work and accommodations elsewhere. None of them ever returned to the farm and openly celebrated when Daniel went into debt and lost the farm to a prominent businessman who acquired it through the courts when he paid the taxes on the property, already five years in arrears. Daniel died penniless.

The Port of Cardiff sits on the north side of the Severn Estuary and serves as a major port to move Welsh coal from the Rhondda Valley to England, Ireland, and Scotland; it was also a stopping-off point for coal-fired ships before crossing the Atlantic Ocean to the Caribbean and the Gulf of Mexico. Adventurers and traders from Europe and Africa were now making the transit regularly, providing passage for anyone with money to buy a ticket; those who couldn't pay were indentured, forced to work on the ship to pay for the trip.

Henry understood he was unlikely to find work in southeastern Wales at his age. He heard stories in the bars and shops lining the docks in Cardiff about the New World, a land of opportunity for any man or woman willing to work hard and take a risk. Because he had no other obvious choice, Henry found the correct quay for the next ship sailing west, signed an indenture contract as a ship's hand, and went to work.

Having never been aboard a ship, and not understanding the ferocity of the North Atlantic Ocean in winter, he was seasick for the first three days, working as best he could but often creating more of a mess than he was able to clean. By the fourth day, he found his sea legs and never looked back, returning only once to Llanrumney in his late forties, the captain of his own ship. He wanted brother Daniel to see what became of the boy he banished three decades earlier.

Henry Morgan cast about Jamaica looking for work into his late twenties, finally joining Vice Admiral Sir Christopher Myngs's raiding parties during the Anglo-Spanish War. Morgan realized he would be unable to sustain the standard of living he wanted by working on the docks or aboard the normal shipping that traded between the Caribbean, Europe, and Africa. Instead, he found that working for Admiral Myngs entitled him to part of the spoils in the Spanish Main, the coastal cities along the Caribbean littoral, and American towns on the Gulf of Mexico.

After proving himself, Morgan convinced the admiral to let him command one of the ships and give him autonomy on the ports and towns he could raid and the foreign ships he could plunder. With experience, Morgan understood where the money was in the form of gold, silver, and Spanish doubloons, and how frequently and when the ports were resupplied.

As Morgan's wealth grew, he chose to spend some of it buying property in Jamaica, where he originally landed after his indentureship. The land proved fertile for growing crops, particularly sugarcane, and the revenue soon equaled what he was making in the raiding parties. He sailed periodically to the West African coast to buy slaves for his plantation and found the Mandinkas, Muslim descendants of the former Mali Empire, the strongest and most able to endure the weather and working conditions in Jamaica. Although most of the slaves were uneducated and spoke nothing beyond their native Mandingo, a rare few stood out. Twelve-year-old Jedediah was exceptional.

From a village in the southern part of Mali, Jedediah descended from corn farmers dating back hundreds of years and probably earlier if accurate records had been kept and preserved. He was the only person in his tribe who could not only read and write Mandingo but could also read, write, and speak English, the result of European missionaries working throughout West Africa. Jedediah and his brother and his family all secretly had converted to Christianity, something they kept hidden from the neighbors who respected and admired his work ethic.

At night when he could steal away from the village, Jedidiah—his name meant "friend of God"—met secretly with Helmet Krause, a Lutheran lay minister, who taught him about Jesus, which Jedediah in turn taught his family. Krause attempted several times to proselytize in the village but was beaten and threatened each time.

Krause's grandson's grandson Jerry would return to Mali in the 1990s, flying his Beechcraft 1900C throughout West Africa, bringing supplies to other missionaries. In April 2013, Krause and his plane disappeared on a flight from South Africa to Mali via a refueling stop in São Tomé. Although reports of him being held by rebel groups in the Sahel surfaced from time to time, several years went by without proof of life and with no group claiming responsibility, ending a multigenerational pilgrimage of missionaries on the African continent.

Every task Morgan gave Jedidiah was completed to perfection, and faster than Henry estimated and expected. Within a couple of years, Jedidiah was running the farm, improving crop yield, reinvesting profits, and expanding Morgan's land holdings. Because Morgan was still traveling the oceans, Jedidiah often was the senior man present, prompting Henry to sign a power of attorney for the Malian slave to act in his stead, although the magistrate and other landowners and prominent businessmen warned him not to do so, particularly at Jedidiah's youth. He was only sixteen. Henry ignored them, promoted the slave to his assistant, and included him in all decisions and activities.

Jedidiah never let him down, accounting for every penny of revenue and expenses without ever being asked.

On one occasion, Morgan sent for Jedidiah, who appeared with a drink in hand: fermented and slightly alcoholic, it was made from sugarcane using the same process as a drink Malians called *boza* made from corn. Although Jedidiah's fermentation process was crude and unscientific, Henry found the drink tasty and refreshing. Morgan forgot why he called for Jedidiah in the first place and instead asked the slave to show him the still. Jedidiah took Henry through the entire process, and even made suggestions on how to improve the makeshift moonshine with a little money and better equipment.

By the time Morgan returned from his next two-month trip, Jedidiah had built an entirely new contraption and was distilling five gallons a day of *boza*. He ran the mash through the process twice to increase the alcohol content and sweetness and filter out more of the impurities before storing the liquid in used and discarded oak wine barrels—he found them abandoned in the barn—until it was bottled and sold to the neighbors. Morgan served the drink to one of his French-speaking visitors from nearby Haiti, who exclaimed, "It is *arôme*!" Although the Haitian meant it had a good aroma, Henry and Jedidiah heard him say the liquid was *rum*, and the name stuck.

Within twelve months, Morgan's distillery was producing fifty barrels of rum a month, four times as much a year later, fermenting increasing amounts of sugarcane from the farm and forcing them to buy all the used wine barrels they could find. It was much easier to ship the rum in barrels than in glass bottles, and they found that the longer it stayed in the barrels, the better it tasted, wicking the residual wine taste from the oak. Jedidiah stored two of every four barrels in an old warehouse on the estate, letting the rum age for a few years. He learned from French vintners visiting Jamaica the techniques of winemaking, which he also used to improve the rum.

French and Spanish colonists and fur traders were pushing into the New World, first referred to in 1507 by cartographer Martin Waldseemüller as North America, with some settling near the terminus of the Great River translated from the Algonquin Indian words *Misi-ziibi*, anglicized to Mississippi. Although it was still another forty years before the city of La Nouvelle-Orléans would be incorporated by the French, it was already popular among pirates and priests alike—a den of iniquity begging for redemption and salvation. Word reached Jamaica of the bars and brothels springing up near the port, with riverboats coming from settlements north along the river and steamships arriving from Europe, South America, and even Africa. *The City That Care Forgot* accurately described the outwardly easygoing bohemian nature of the city's immigrants, now numbering almost five thousand.

Jedidiah raised the idea of Morgan relocating to New Orleans to take advantage of the huge trading potential along the Mississippi, leaving the slave to run the plantation and distill the liquid gold; and while Henry was certainly interested in the revenue, he had no interest in living in America.

"Why don't you go and represent Morgan rum there?"

As intelligent as Jedidiah was, he still thought like a slave. He worked for Morgan, and it was therefore necessary to be by his side to serve him. He had never considered leaving Jamaica unless Morgan did too and they would go together. But Henry was insistent.

"I'll sign a Certificate of Freedom, have it attested by the magistrate, and pay for you and your family to live in New Orleans. Once you're there, I'll ship you full barrels and money to purchase a warehouse where you can bottle the rum and sell it throughout North America."

When Jedidiah realized Captain Morgan—he would promote himself to admiral two years later—was serious, he spent a few days trying to talk Henry out of the idea. Morgan wouldn't listen. Henry made the appointment to sign the affidavit, and the two men rode horses five miles into Kingston.

"First name?"

"Jedidiah, sir." He spelled it out when the magistrate hesitated. "Like in the Bible, sir."

"Family name?"

"No family name, sir."

Henry spoke up, "Morgan, Your Honor. Jedidiah Morgan." He looked at Jedidiah, who seemed to agree.

And just like that, Jedidiah Morgan was a free man, along with the members of his immediate family, although he had never really felt like a slave working for Captain Morgan, it being a legal rather than emotional distinction. Still, it felt good. And *Jedidiah Morgan* sounded good too.

Chapter 9

April 4, 1718
New Orleans, Louisiana

The directive to establish New Orleans in the name of ten-year-old King Louis the XV of France was debated by many aristocrats and politicians regarding the form it should take; there was a sense of urgency to the directive in an effort to deny the riches of what would ultimately be Louisiana's largest city to the English and Spanish who were encroaching on other territories in the New World. Scottish investor and economist John Law even suggested forced migration of six thousand settlers and three thousand slaves into Louisiana, managed by a for-profit corporation that would enrich individual shareholders if the European monarchies didn't support his plan.

Addressed to Jean-Baptiste Le Moyne de Bienville, stationed in Mobile, the directive arrived in the winter of 1717 and provided instructions on incorporating the city, the form of government, the courts system, taxation, and other governance issues. Bienville began loading six ships with supplies and equipment he needed for the voyage to the site he preferred for New Orleans, arriving mid-March and anchoring off what is today the French Quarter. Three hundred years ago, it was little more than swamp with some high ground—no more than ten feet above sea level—next to the river. Clearing the area began immediately, somewhere near the 500 block of present-day Decatur

Street, with the work performed by thirty convicts he brought from Mobile for that purpose.

Although Bienville would've preferred more time for preparation of the site to draw crowds of observers and members of the nascent press corps from the surrounding cities, he also wanted to complete the incorporation before Easter on April 6. Deeply religious, he wanted a conjoined celebration for a risen Christ and a new French colony rising from the banks of the Mississippi River.

Easter fell on Wednesday on the Julian calendar in use by European countries at the time, so Monday was designated for the ceremony. Heavy rainfall common to Louisiana in the spring began early morning and continued until the evening, although it didn't dampen Bienville's spirit even if it reduced the number of observers on hand for the proclamation. Because the media didn't show, Bienville drafted a press release and dispatched riders with strict instructions to get it published and return with a copy of the newspaper; of the twenty-three riders who departed the new city, only two returned.

Newly appointed Governor Bienville's every decision was second-guessed by the authorities in France as well as by settlers in the city. With Louisiana prone to floods and mosquito-borne malaria emanating from the surrounding swamps, those closest to the king implored him to order Bienville to relocate the entire city with its name to Bayou Manchac near present-day Baton Rouge. Others felt Natchez, or even Dauphin Island, near Mobile was more suitable. In the end, Bienville prevailed, and the city stayed on the banks of the river near its terminus in the Gulf of Mexico.

By this time, Jedidiah had been in New Orleans for almost thirty years, building a rum and trading empire on behalf of his benefactor in Jamaica. Even after Henry Morgan's death, the former slave continued sending monthly dividends to the widow with annual audits of the books for her review. He tried to get Morgan's son to work with him in Louisiana. The boy declined—probably a good decision, considering his natural sloth and the string of fatherless children he left strewn throughout the Caribbean.

Jedidiah thrived in this setting; naturally affable and polite, businessmen first believed they could cow him into agreeing to a bad deal but soon found he was a skilled negotiator with impeccable business conduct and ethics. When Jedidiah promised something, he delivered it, often citing Matthew 5:37 commanding him to let his "yes" be yes and his "no" be no. As they got to know him, traders realized they could rely on his word regardless of the circumstances.

In one instance, Jedidiah replaced twenty-six barrels of rum ordered by a bottler in St. Louis, even though he had no obligation to do so after the riverboat carrying the goods sunk just outside Vicksburg. Explaining to his customer that the delivery was not made as agreed, and to keep his word, replacements were immediately dispatched on the next boat heading north up the river. As word spread of his actions, three dozen new customers and four new bottlers signed up, knowing he would honor agreements and contracts without fail.

Jedidiah took the opportunity to have his Certificate of Freedom and the power of attorney from Jamaica attested in New Orleans and registered with the sheriff when the new government was installed and judges and magistrates appointed. As a former slave, he knew how fragile his freedom was, particularly if bounty hunters could convince the authorities he was an imposter. It certainly didn't hurt that cases of rum arrived to the judge and sheriff a few days later—a small price to pay to ensure he and his family remained freemen entitled to citizenship, franchise, and other privileges. A case even found its way to the governor's office; Jedidiah never knew when he might need Bienville's help in the future.

The business and profits grew, and Jedidiah improved the warehouse and offices, relocating them to higher ground and storing the rum on the upper floors of a six-story building to prevent flood damage recurring on the ground floor. His prescience paid off when a hurricane destroyed most of the buildings in New Orleans in 1722. Most of the damage was caused by the tidal surge that undermined the integrity and foundations of many structures hastily built over the last fifty years.

Seizing on the opportunity created by Mother Nature, city engineer Adrien de Pauger commenced laying out a grid system of streets and drainage. Jedidiah's warehouse became a key survey point with geodetic markers around which the city would be built.

On a sales and marketing trip north through Memphis, St. Louis, and Minneapolis all the way to the headwaters at Lake Itasca, a small glacial lake in northern Minnesota, Jedidiah found that the rum tasted better the longer it stayed on the paddle steamer. After returning home and running several tests, he discovered the gentle rocking motion of the boat and the fluctuating temperatures in the cargo hold gave the rum a deeper and richer flavor.

Jedidiah immediately bought and anchored a wooden barge near his warehouse, storing barrels of rum for at least three years on the vessel; he posted twenty-four-hour security around the boat when news of his unusual aging technique became known. When the barge was sufficiently full, he would charter a tug to push it up the river, stopping along the way to sell the rum. Jedidiah described the process as *barrelized*; although the word did not survive his death, his concept that the rum left longest in the barrel fetched the highest price did. Henry Morgan followed his example and also stored barrels of rum on a barge near Kingston, Jamaica.

They discussed distilling sugarcane already being grown in Louisiana, but the tax policies and labor laws at the time favored importing the bulk finished product from Jamaica, with the justification being that it provided local bottlers more business. By the time of Jedidiah's death in 1858, two years shy of his centennial, the operation was the largest rum distiller and distributor in the world, making both men rich—one the boisterous captain of a raiding ship with a raspy voice who lent his name to the endeavor, the other a former slave who kept a low profile even as his decisions grew the company into one of the wealthiest in the Americas. Jedidiah's offspring would operate the business and continue sending dividends and royalties to Henry's family through the years; in return, they shipped rum to New Orleans for the insatiable American market.

Chapter 10

April 30, 1867
Yerevan, Armenia

Gregor Mazloumian finished preparations for the journey and bid farewell to his family. Riding his favorite horse and leading three packhorses carrying supplies and clothing, Gregor—most everyone called him Baron, the Armenian word for "master" because of his immense land holdings and considerable wealth—was realizing his lifelong desire to see the beauty of Jerusalem, Bethlehem, and the surrounding Christian sites. Deeply religious and financially secure such that his absence would not cause his family distress, he set off on a personal pilgrimage from Yerevan, Western Armenia, across the Anatolian Plain in Turkey, en route to the Holy Land. The year was 1867.

Armenia is a mountainous region bordered by modern-day Turkey, Georgia, Nagorno-Karabakh, and Azerbaijan to the east as well as Iran to the south, at the crossroads between Western Europe and the Eastern Hemisphere. Originally known as Hayk, landlocked and formerly a kingdom, it was the first nation-state to adopt Christianity as the country's religion, with prominent religious sites dotting the landscape, such as the Greco-Roman Temple of Garni, the fourth-century Etchmiadzin Cathedral—home of the Armenian Church— and Khor Virap Monastery pilgrimage site near the dormant volcano Mount Ararat just across the border in Turkey, all of which Gregor already visited. He was ready to open the aperture of his Christian experience and expand his knowledge through pilgrimage.

After celebrating Easter with his family, Gregor bade them farewell and set off southwest, dividing his journey into equidistant thirds. His first objective was to cross the mountains in eastern Turkey and reach Diyarbakir; there he could rest, take on provisions, cross the Tigris river barely sixty miles from its source, and take advantage of the relatively flat plains all the way through Syria to the eastern Mediterranean. Crossing the mountains was a challenge for any group, much more for a man traveling alone.

Although relatively warm during the day, Gregor huddled against the bitterly cold nights next to a campfire that also kept wild animals at bay. He had worked hard all his life—Gregor was a self-made man—but he never experienced such harsh weather and inhospitable conditions. In a fever one night, he imagined a warm hotel with hot water, a tasty meal, and a clean bed; he awoke cold, wet, and hungry to a storm that was more rain than snow.

Gregor walked and rode almost four months to cover roughly five hundred miles through the fifteen-thousand-foot Anti-Taurus Mountains from Yerevan to Diyarbakir, sometimes covering less than a mile a day, losing one horse and thirty-five pounds in the process. Unbeknownst to Gregor, at one point he was camped directly above the ark Noah built on God's command, slowly consumed by the earth and snow after settling in the mountain when the flood receded. The Baron's pilgrimage was well under way but, he was unaware of it. The ark was barely twenty feet underground where it would remain forever, a story in the Bible and a quest for explorers and archeologists throughout time.

Although he planned to stay in Diyarbakir three days before moving on, he checked into what passed for a hotel, where he spent three weeks regaining his strength and preparing for the next leg of the journey, hoping to make Aleppo in northern Syria within a month or so. Situated on the banks of the Tigris river, Diyarbakir is one of the largest cities in southeastern Turkey's Anatolia region, over the years a flashpoint between the Turks and various Kurdish groups.

Roman rule toward the end of the third century included building a defensive wall around the city they renamed Amida, only to be overrun by the Arabs under tribal leader Bekr bin Vail, who again renamed it Diyar Bekr, or Bekr's country. Crude stone tools would be discovered in caves in the nearby village of Hilal where Olaq's tribe sought shelter from the weather as they traveled to Aleppo twelve thousand years before Gregor's pilgrimage.

Gregor resumed his trip refreshed and resupplied, unknowingly following a path similar to that Olaq had traveled six hundred generations before. The two-hundred-mile trip took thirty-five days, as he expected, across a gentle downhill southwest slope most of the way. He arrived in Aleppo to find a bustling commercial site dominated by a citadel perched on a hill in the city's center.

Western expatriates filled the ancient city with one recurring complaint: there was no hotel comparable to those of Europe in the late 1800s, forcing visitors to rent rooms in private homes or brave the traditional eastern caravanserais, roadside inns left over from the Silk Road, with shared accommodations, outdoor toilets, bedbugs, and few discernible amenities. Returning home to Armenia after the pilgrimage to Jerusalem and other biblical cities, and recognizing the growing importance of this crossroad between Europe and Asia, he resolved to find a solution to the problem.

Gregor returned to Aleppo and in 1872 opened the Ararat Hotel with clean but basic rooms. It attracted few Europeans who were by then used to the grand hotels in the great cities of Europe. Gregor formulated another plan and in 1911 opened the Baron Hotel with two floors of rooms and suites, the first of its kind in Syria.

The hotel was an instant success; Aleppo was the last stop on the newly constructed Berlin-to-Baghdad Railway before reaching the Iraqi capital, and many tourists wanted to stop for a few days before continuing their journeys east or west. The hotel bar was stocked with all the wines and whiskeys preferred by the Europeans—including original bottles of the first blended Johnny Walker Red and Black label whiskeys in 1909—and served as a welcome respite on the long trip.

The Baron hosted numerous guests and momentous events over the years. King Faisal in 1920 declared Syrian independence standing on the balcony of room 215. Agatha Christie spent the second half of the 1930s in room 203 while writing *Murder on the Orient Express*, bidding the staff good morning as she descended the staircase to the restaurant to take her English breakfast and tea. American aviator Charles Lindbergh, the late Egyptian president Gamal Abdel Nasser, English army officer and writer T. E. Lawrence (room 202), and others stayed at the Baron over the years. Even Yuri Gagarin, the first man in space, as well as Valentina Tereshkova, first woman in space, both Russian cosmonauts and heroes, resided in the Baron in the 1960s.

It would serve as a refugee center during Aleppo's occupation by the Islamic State militants a hundred years after the hotel's grand opening, still owned by the Mazloumian family and managed by Gregor's great-grandson Armen and his wife, Rubina.

Chapter 11

April 17, 1906
San Francisco, California

When Henry Wells and William G. Fargo—two of the original founders of American Express Company—formed Wells Fargo & Company in San Francisco in 1852, they wanted to focus exclusively on western markets underserved by East Coast banks, hoping to provide express and banking services to California that had gained statehood only two years before. A series of mergers and acquisitions over the years saw their startup grow to become the seventh largest public company in the United States, at one point worth 2 trillion dollars and for a brief period the most valuable bank in the world.

Caleb Morgan dispatched the latest quarterly report by mail to Antoinette Davidson, the great-great-great-granddaughter of Henry Morgan sitting atop the Morgan rum empire, and then entered the original Wells Fargo building in San Francisco. As his forefathers had done before him, he dispatched dividends to the Jamaican "wing" of the Morgan family within three working days after the end of the financial quarter.

Today he would sign the paperwork directing the bank to transfer over 18 million dollars to Antoinette, although none of the Morgan family heirs, including Antoinette, had any interest in running the company, waiting only for their share of the profits from New Orleans, where Caleb still maintained the U.S. headquarters of the company.

Caleb's brother Barnabas was dispatched to run the Jamaica operation, appointed by the board of directors and shareholders who saw the Caribbean headquarters falling farther behind competitors simply because of sloth. Antoinette's family made a half-hearted attempt to appear upset when told about Barnabas's appointment, although they privately cheered the decision so they didn't have to work for their keep. Old man Henry's industry and perseverance did not pass from one Morgan to another as they hoped it would, leaving twenty lazy and corrupt relatives to split the Jamaica pie any way they chose. Jedidiah's descendants, on the other hand, were hardworking and reliable in honor of their good fortune and God's blessings.

Just after five o'clock the following morning, a 7.9 magnitude earthquake leveled 80 percent of San Francisco. The shaking and tremors were felt throughout the state, becoming one of the worst and deadliest earthquakes in America's 130-year history.

The bank building was still standing but would be razed within a month; its architectural integrity was compromised, and officials were concerned about the burgeoning lawsuits arising from the natural disaster. They set up banking facilities and teller windows on the sidewalk to ensure their customers had access to their own money in a time of need. This certainly qualified as an act of God for insurance purposes but solidified customer loyalty toward the bank that went above and beyond to help its members.

The Palace Hotel where Caleb was staying was fairly untouched by the tremors, although one couple fled the hotel when the shaking began, wrongly believing it would collapse on their heads; they tripped and fell into one of the sinkholes that opened up around the city, this one almost forty feet deep, and were pronounced dead twelve hours later when rescue crews finally reached them.

Caleb—his name meant "wholehearted"—set up a temporary command center in the hotel to coordinate the company's response to the disaster. He bought and distributed tents, cooking oil, food, and washing powder to help average citizens get back on their feet; he arranged fresh water from the Klamath, Colorado, Truckee, and

Applegate rivers supplied to the city by horse-drawn bowsers; and he helped local distributors of Morgan rum reestablish their businesses.

A fire destroyed the hotel a few days later and forced him to relocate; unbeknownst to the management, the fire started during the earthquake smoldered for almost a week and then began burning in earnest in the subbasement and spread throughout the building in a matter of hours. Because of the large cracks in the roads leading to the hotel, the fire department was unable to get close enough to extinguish the fire.

Caleb returned to New Orleans a few weeks later exhausted but satisfied he did everything in his power to help the residents of San Francisco in their time of need. He felt blessed to be alive—over three thousand deaths were recorded on the day of the earthquake—and redoubled his efforts to help people who were less fortunate in the image of Jedidiah so many years before.

Caleb's daughter Ariel—the literal meaning of her name is "lion of God," but in the Bible the name is given to the city of Jerusalem meaning "victorious under God"—would eventually take over the business from him some twenty years later, teaching her children and grandchildren (Dan was among them and would become the first Mali Morgan to graduate from college) to not hate, to not hide, and to not be a victim, lessons that would continue serving the family well for centuries to come.

Chapter 12

April 2, 1979
Aleppo, Syria

Sixty-eight years after Gregor Mazloumian opened the doors of the Baron Hotel and five hundred generations since Olaq first settled his small tribe along the banks of the Queiq River, Ahmed was celebrating the birth of his first child. The new father left his wife, Soumaya, at the hospital with her sister and their mother and joined his friends at the Baron for drinks, cigars, and small cups of strong Turkish coffee as they discussed the issues of the day.

Soon forgotten was the newborn girl since it was more than a little embarrassing to Ahmed that his firstborn was not a boy. Rasha—Arabic for "female deer"—through no fault of her own would be less worthy and less important in Ahmed's eyes than the sons Soumaya would bear him over the next decade. He wanted a buck but got a doe.

Although all his friends knew Ahmed had a daughter—word spread quickly in his circle of friends and acquaintances who gathered in the hotel bar for the promise of free Johnny Walker Black Label—none raised the issue, and each silently thanked God their first was a son; those still without children prayed to not suffer the same ignominy as Ahmed. Each knew he would lose face by admitting Rasha's birth, and they spared him the embarrassment.

A quirk of fate gave Ahmed a girl instead of a boy, an expense rather than a productive human being, someone to marry off quickly and restore honor to the family. Rasha knew none of that this evening as her father celebrated her short existence and she slept peacefully by her mother's side. She would eventually feel his shame and resentment, but right now she felt only the warmth of her crib and a stomach full of her mother's milk.

Mohammed Ahmed Al-Shibli—in Arab culture only the second half of the double first name Mohammed Ahmed is used—was a typical proud and confident Aleppian man. The youngest of three boys, he never quite measured up to his older brothers; Ahmed cast around Aleppo for work, for something that gave him enough money to marry Soumaya. Finding employment in the late 1970s in Aleppo was hard, and he eventually agreed to work in his father's bakery and confectionary shop to make ends meet. He and Soumaya married, and she was immediately pregnant.

A few months after Rasha's birth, Ahmed followed a friend's advice and moved his small family to Abu Dhabi in the former Trucial States of the Arabian Peninsula. When Great Britain decided to pull its forces out of the region, the Foreign Office agreed with the sheikhs of Abu Dhabi and Dubai to allow them to unite under one flag and form a government, ultimately becoming the United Arab Emirates.

With oil discovered a decade earlier, jobs were plenty in Abu Dhabi, and Ahmed brought the tools of his father's trade to open a shop. From meager beginnings, the bakery grew in popularity and reputation and made Ahmed comfortable, if not wealthy. Soumaya worked with him in the early years, but he made her quit as soon as his income allowed it. Wives of successful men did not work outside the house, and even there, they had maids to do the cleaning, cooking, washing, and ironing, and other manual jobs.

Rasha grew into a girl full of curiosity and intensity, preferring her own company over playdates and parties with others. Possessing innate intelligence and good judgment, she should've excelled; instead, she watched passively as one opportunity after another went to her brothers, as was the custom in the region. Her schooling was mediocre; piano lessons were given by her mother while her brothers enjoyed professional teachers, and she was expected to come home immediately after school to help her mother prepare dinner instead of participating in the many social and sports activities the community offered. The boys took horseback riding lessons, they went boating with friends late into the night, and Ahmed ensured they were licensed to drive as soon as their age permitted. Rasha got a bicycle and a sketchpad.

Rasha celebrated her first birthday in Abu Dhabi with a small cake her father made of dough and icing left over from a wedding cake he had prepared for a member of the ruling family. Shorter than her brothers would be, Rasha had dark-brown eyes that penetrated the soul of those who looked into them. With dark hair, soft features, and olive skin, she would grow into a beautiful woman who constantly sought but never quite received her father's acceptance or blessings.

Her education was unimportant to Ahmed; he sent her back to Aleppo to live with his family while she attended the local university that satisfied the requirement even if it did not educate her. When she returned to Abu Dhabi, he employed her in his shop so he could watch his daughter and look out for a suitable husband. As with everything else in her life, Ahmed did the absolute minimum necessary but acted as though he moved heaven and earth to please his eldest child. His sons would all attend Ivy League schools in the United States with all of his attention and adoration while Rasha had to settle for much less.

A few days later and a world away in Nashville, Tennessee, Mark Masterson was celebrating his seventh birthday with his older brother and sister and younger twin brothers. As with most American boys his age, life revolved around baseball and football in their respective seasons, riding his bicycle with friends, and playing board games, cards, and checkers with his brothers. Because both of his parents were teachers, Mark would understand and appreciate the importance of education and did well throughout his schooling.

When his mother, June, asked Mark what present he wanted for his birthday, he answered immediately: to see a show at the Grand Ol' Opry. The family ate an early dinner and drove downtown, parking behind the Baptist Church on Broadway where June volunteered at the soup kitchen, walking two blocks to the Ryman Auditorium to enjoy the two-hour show. As they were leaving the performance, two Marine Corps noncommissioned officers in dress blue uniforms were standing in the lobby; both decorated veterans, the Marines impressed Mark so much he confidently approached them and introduced himself.

The Marines told Mark of their visits to exotic ports and battlefields in faraway places, of drill instructors at recruit training at Parris Island, South Carolina, and of riding in helicopters to training exercises in Korea and Japan. Mark asked questions about weapons and marching and uniforms and physical exercise; he soaked in what they had to say and made them explain what each medal on their chests represented.

From that day forth, Mark's singular purpose was to be a Marine; he never succumbed to boyhood fantasies of being a policeman or pilot or a firefighter. Second Lieutenant Mark Masterson was still fifteen years into the future, but he began his Marine Corps journey on his seventh birthday.

Chapter 13

April 14, 1986
Near Tripoli, Libya

Al Aziziyah lies approximately twenty miles south of the capital. A major trading center on the al Jifara Plain with a road that runs almost due north to Tripoli, it is the site of the hottest location ever in Libya when, on September 13, 1922, the official recorded temperature in the shade was a 136 degrees Fahrenheit, although the locals there claim it was actually five degrees warmer.

Eighty years later, the International Atomic Energy Agency would claim the military facility there, codenamed Site K by the IAEA, was a storage facility for equipment related to the rogue state's nascent nuclear weapons program. On this spring evening, though, it was a pleasant seventy-eight degrees, with a southerly wind blowing gently through the tent erected for the Leader.

Mu'ammar Mohammed Abu Minyar Gaddafi was approaching his seventeenth anniversary as Leader of the Socialist People's Libyan Arab Jamahiriya, relaxing in the shade of the date palm trees surrounding the Bedouin tent, equipped with telephones and televisions and, in the cold desert winters, heaters to take away the chill. The tent and its location in the desert away from traffic and noise reminded Gaddafi of his childhood days as a son and the youngest child of a nomadic Berber shepherd in the desert region of Sirte. Born in 1942 at Qasr Abu Hadi in western Libya, he had a traditional religious education in primary school and attended Sebha Preparatory School in the southern Fezzan province. Of note, his mother, Aisha, was Jewish, a fact Gaddafi went to great lengths to protect from disclosure.

Gaddafi entered Benghazi Military Academy after studying law at the University of Libya, and entered the army as a cadet in 1965. He was sent to the Royal Military Academy Sandhurst in the United Kingdom, returning to Libya a year later a second lieutenant in the Signal Corps, responsible to the commander for radio and other forms of communication.

Three years later, he and close friends from his Sebha school days overthrew Idris al Sanussi, the first king of Libya and the man who united the three provinces of Cyrenaica, Tripolitania, and Fezzan into the modern country of Libya when it gained independence from England in 1951. King Idris, already seventy-nine, was in Turkey for medical treatment when Gaddafi seized power. The old monarch would never return to his homeland before dying in Cairo fourteen years later.

Al Aziziyah was the one place on earth where Gaddafi felt safe from the world, and the one place he felt comfortable bringing his whole family together at the same time. His second wife, Safiya, would not allow Gaddafi to gather her children with him in any other location other than here. They both felt they had enough warning should something happen that could affect their safety. Gaddafi even had a red phone installed in the tent modeled after the hotline linking John F. Kennedy and subsequent American presidents directly with the leadership in the Soviet Union; this phone was connected to the Command Center in the military headquarters in Tripoli and was designed to keep him informed of anything out of the ordinary, particularly should radio signals be intercepted or interrupted.

The Americans won't be back so soon, Gaddafi said to himself. Barely two weeks previously, the Libyan army fired Russian-made SA-5 surface-to-air missiles at planes from the U.S. Sixth Fleet ships as they conducted Freedom of Navigation operations and crossed Gaddafi's self-declared *line of death* in the Gulf of Sidra. Not only did the missiles not hit any American targets, but the Sixth Fleet aircraft returned to the Libyan coast after dark that night, sinking several Libyan military attack boats and killing fifty-six Libyan sailors.

They're gloating over the attack on our ships and don't want to appear overzealous, Gaddafi thought. *It's why they're weak—they won't go for the kill.*

A scorching wind from the desert, called a *ghibli* in the Libyan dialect of Arabic, blew itself out the night before, and Gaddafi was grateful for the beautiful weather this evening. It would soon be hot in the Libyan summer and wouldn't cool off again until October. The family ate dinner on the ground in the traditional way and drank Moroccan mint tea.

Seven hours earlier at 1736, twenty-four U.S. Air Force F-111F Aardvark fighter aircraft took off from airfields in the United Kingdom along with twenty-eight refueling tankers and five EF-111 Ravens equipped with jamming equipment to accompany the fighters, kicking off Operation Eldorado Canyon. When French, German, Italian, and Spanish leaders refused to cooperate in a strike with the Americans, or even to grant overflight clearance for U.S. aircraft, flight time to Libya was extended an extra six hours and required a half dozen in-flight refueling operations, making it the longest fighter combat mission in the history of military aviation, with most of the aircraft flying for thirteen continuous hours.

"This is Remit 23, feet wet," air force captain Don James called to military air traffic controllers as he crossed the southern English coastline over the North Atlantic Ocean. He was leading a strike force of nine Aardvarks around the Iberian Peninsula. James's copilot was his college classmate, Captain Bruce Sherburne of New Roads, Louisiana, a Cajun who escaped the Bayou State with an appointment to the Air Force Academy.

Five hours after the Aardvarks took off from the United Kingdom, fourteen U.S. Navy A-6E Intruder all-weather attack aircraft launched from the aircraft carriers USS *Coral Sea* and USS *America* in the

Mediterranean Sea. Able to cruise at over 400 knots and sprint to almost 600 when required, the Intruder could fly 3,000 miles before refueling and could also do so in-flight. The A-6 in all of its variants would be the navy's workhorse for fifty years and prove itself worthy time after time. On this evening, though, the Grumman-built A-6E hosted laser-guided bombs and a variety of other munitions.

Commander William C. Morris, United States Navy, commanded the VFA131 Wildcats, the squadron of F/A-18s, or Hornets as they were called, an all-weather fighter jet designed to attack both ground and aerial targets, capable of flying off aircraft carriers. In this case, six Hornets were catapulted into the night sky from *Coral Sea*, heading toward the Libyan coastline near Benghazi. Entering service two years before, the Hornet was designed to be the multirole fighter of the future.

Commander Morris, call sign "Catboy," organized his squadron and its ingress routes to achieve maximum surprise and reduce the ability of Libyan air defense systems to engage the planes as they flew their assigned missions. Now just after 0100 on a moonless night in the central Mediterranean, air force and navy aircraft joined forces to attack five different objectives simultaneously across the Libyan landscape.

Gaddafi turned as the phone rang in the tent. Although not the first time the Command Center had called him on the hotline, he had convinced himself that tonight would be quiet and was irritated at the intrusion. As he rose to take the phone from his aide, he heard the jets flying in from the north and east, his instincts telling him they were not Libyan Air Force MiG-23 or IL-76 aircraft.

"Get into the bunker—now!" he yelled to his wife and children. He scooped up their only daughter, Aisha, and ran toward the reinforced steel-and-concrete bunker built near the tent for just such a purpose. He dropped the girl near the entrance to the bunker and then moved toward the Military Command Center fifty meters from the tent where he could better speak with his commanders to get information and coordinate a counterattack. He saw members of his personal security detail moving toward him and watched as a half dozen vanished in one of the many explosions in the camp.

Captains James and Sherburne in Remit 23 piloted the first plane over the target, dropping two Mark 84 2,000-pound Paveway II Plus laser-guided gravity bombs on the barracks. The first bomb struck the northwest corner of the building, blasting metal and concrete shrapnel in every direction. Of the four subordinates with Gaddafi, one was immediately decapitated, the body taking five more steps before it realized there was no brain controlling it, finally falling in a heap in the sand. Another junior officer raced to his right into a building he thought would afford him protection, but that collapsed on top of him, crushing him to a death two hours in the making.

Gaddafi and the remaining two aides continued running through the line of buildings toward the Command Center. One aircraft after another flew over the camp for eleven long minutes, dropping the thirty-six bombs they carried with uncanny accuracy and turning back north toward the sea and to safety.

"Remit 23, Tranquil Tiger," Captain James reported, indicating his bombing run hit the intended target. He and Sherburne listened to the radio traffic and heard twelve more "Tranquil Tiger" success stories and only three "Frostee Freezer" reports indicating that those targets were not hit.

"Don, we've got an engine overheating," Bruce reported as they went feet wet over the Mediterranean. They would ultimately have to divert to the airfield in Rota, Spain, well before the engine seized and the airplane fell from the sky. They reported the problem to the airborne air traffic controllers and vectored toward the Spanish coastline, declaring an emergency before landing safely. The two officers were ferried back to the UK within an hour after landing in Spain for debriefings and recuperation after the long flight and the physical and mental stresses of live combat.

Catboy Morris was first to go feet dry over the Libyan landmass en route to his intended target at the Benghazi Air Base. Air defense radars lit up Morris's instruments, indicating he was being targeted by an SA6 Gainful surface-to-air missile system just as he crossed the beach, and he fired a missile to destroy it. Naval records would record this as the first HARM ever fired in combat from the new Hornets.

The AGM high-speed anti-radiation missile is an air-to-surface missile fired at radar-equipped air defense systems. When the enemy's radar is turned on, the seeker in the nose of the missile finds the emission and locks in on the signal and follows it back to the source. In the case of the HARM, the missile's proportional guidance system homes in on the radar and the missile streaks along at Mach-2, roughly 1,500 miles per hour, to destroy the transmitter. Originally developed by Texas Instruments and later by Raytheon Corporation, it is one of the most effective weapons against the radar systems that control enemy air defense weapons.

"Wildcat 31, Magnum on SA6 along the coast," Morris reported, indicating that he fired the HARM at the surface-to-air missile site.

Why do they light up their radars since they know all we're gonna do is take 'em out? Morris asked himself. At the correct time after launching the missile, Morris noted that the radar stopped transmitting, a good indication of a catastrophic hit. At twenty miles in the distance, exactly where the radar should be, Morris actually saw an explosion, further confirming the kill. *All they're doing is committing suicide*, he thought.

The six F/A-18s continued their runs to the air base accompanied by the A-6 Intruders, destroying several targets along the way. Morris sent another HARM toward a Gainful site at the air base, recording a direct hit that killed six air defense soldiers at that location.

"Let's go home," Morris instructed the Wildcats and led them back to the carrier steaming in the central Mediterranean. Without so much as a scratch, the squadron completed its mission and destroyed fully one-third of Libya's air defense system in a little over twenty minutes. Customers of Russian-made air defense systems were not pleased with what they were told was the best product in the world; the evening's activities would significantly slow sales of these systems for the next several years and force Moscow to make significant technology improvements to one of its biggest defense export money-makers.

As the last American plane dropped its payload, the two aides saw the Leader hit by shrapnel in the shoulder and blood rushing from a head wound where the scalp and skull were blown away. They would later tell officials that they saw Gaddafi go down to his knees and collapse into the doorway of a building. As they moved to check on him, another bomb exploded nearby, sending them both cartwheeling away from the Leader and into unconsciousness.

Fourteen hours later, Gaddafi walked into the Command Center— the only building still standing after the attack—with a wound on his right shoulder and a bandage around his head, wounds just as the junior officers had reported but seemingly less severe and life threatening. He immediately demanded that the senior officers in the Command Center accompany him to inspect the damage.

As they walked through the camp, Gaddafi let out a cry of anguish and called out Aisha's name. All eyes focused on the body of a young girl as the Leader scooped her up in his arms.

"Great One, that's not your daughter, Aisha," an army major said.

"Then who is she?" Gaddafi looked confused, trying to focus on the little girl as he looked at those around him.

A woman sitting ten feet away staring at the ground answered, "She is Hana. She lived most of today with her wounds. She was brave and didn't cry. She was ten years old. Her father was also killed by the bombs."

Gaddafi seemed distant, off guard, confused, saying only, "I take this girl Hana as my own daughter, then, in accordance with the Holy Koran."

The little girl was buried before sunset the next day, forever and always remembered as the adopted daughter of the Leader of the

Revolution, Mu'ammar Gaddafi, who miraculously survived the day's attacks to lead his country against the aggressors.

Gaddafi's aides were dumbfounded when they saw him walking through the camp. Unable to reconcile what they saw the night before with what they were now witnessing, they agreed quietly among themselves to say nothing.

"It is God's will," one of them professed. That seemed to satisfy both of them, and they returned to the Leader's side as though nothing was amiss.

The western media would report that Gaddafi was missing over twelve hours, leading some to believe he died in the attack. Instead, television reports of his walk through the camp, holding the limp body of the dead girl Hana in his arms, confirmed he was very much alive.

Within the Arab world, television reports convinced many viewers of the Leader's failure to lead his country. If he couldn't protect even his own family, the reasoning went, how could he protect the people?

"I must be confident," Gaddafi confessed to his aides. "I must stay in power and direct this country. Our security is at stake, and I cannot fail."

But everyone close to Gaddafi noticed the differences. Whereas before he was flamboyant, boisterous, and confrontational, particularly toward the United States, he became reticent to attack the West directly. The man that U.S. president Ronald Reagan described as the "mad dog of the Middle East" was restrained and subdued after the raid. More and more, he retreated into the Sahara before emerging several years later to inflict more terror on the West.

One of the first people to see differences in his attitude and personality was the commander of the Amazonian Guard, his personal security detail, an African woman named Aisha, just like his daughter, with whom Gaddafi had developed a close relationship. The Leader had recruited, screened, trained, and equipped a private personal security detail of African women bodyguards—tall women who were referred to as Amazons—who swore allegiance only to him.

A special course was developed to educate the women in surveillance detection, evasive driving techniques, specialized shooting, interrogation, and other skills needed to protect Gaddafi. At the end of the rigorous training, held twice a year for eight to ten recruits, he personally chose the one or two graduates who would be added to the unit guarding him; the remaining women immediately were scooped up by African despots and dictators for their own personal security details. By his side at all times except inside the tent at al Aziziyah—his wife, Safiya, did not like them close to her and directed that only family be allowed in the tent— Gaddafi insisted they remain virgins throughout their service to him.

Captain Aisha, as she preferred to be called, had been commander of the Amazonian Guard for ten years and was Gaddafi's favorite among the forty women in the security detail. Despite the requirement to remain chaste while part of the guard force, Aisha performed special "additional duties" for the Leader that violated her covenant with him but with his full consent and encouragement. Always by his side, she traveled abroad with him, and even saved his life a dozen years earlier when she threw herself over the Leader as would-be assassins riddled his car with bullets.

For now, though, she watched him closely and could not fail to notice remarkable changes in his personality, priorities, and patterns. In the months following the raid, he no longer expressed an interest in her joining him at night and appeared more aloof than previously. He conducted more closed-door sessions with his two senior aides, to which she was no longer invited, and he seemed more removed from his family and close friends than before.

The death of that little girl he thought was his daughter really affected him, Captain Aisha said to herself. *He's what the Americans refer to as a basket case. He's strong, though, and he'll come out of it over time.* Captain Aisha pushed her thoughts and feelings to the back of her conscious thinking and moved up to protect Gaddafi, coordinating the activities of the other women of the security detail.

"The Roman Empire conquered and occupied the entire Mediterranean coastline, the only nation to do so, at least until now. Libya will rise to its former glory"—no definition what glory he was referring to—"and conquer not only the coastal countries but also all of Europe without firing a single shot. We will unite Africa and the

Middle East and erase references to the colonial and Zionist nations from all of history."

It would take Israeli agent Avraham Abelman almost a year to completely embed in his new role and really *become* the Leader. A member of Israel's elite Sayeret Matkal secretive special operations brigade, Avraham had participated in Operation Thunderbolt, the raid on Entebbe, Uganda, in 1976, to rescue Israeli hostages from a hijacked Air France flight from Tel Aviv to Paris that was diverted to Africa by two members of the Popular Front for the Liberation of Palestine – External Operations and two members of the German Revolutionary Cells. Formed in 1957, Unit 269, as it was also known, had gained an impressive reputation for deep reconnaissance, counterterrorism, hostage recovery, and direct action missions, training at the Camp Mitkan Adam facility along the Jordan Valley on the road from Tel Aviv to Jerusalem.

Avraham bore a striking resemblance to Gaddafi, already spoke Arabic, and had trained in the Libyan dialect for almost four years, studying every film clip, photograph, and speech of the Libyan, becoming his double in the chaos created during the American strike. The real Gaddafi didn't survive the attack, leaving an opening for Avraham to be inserted in his place at Al Aziziyah. The body was checked for birthmarks and other features that were quickly replicated on Avraham before Gaddafi's miraculous return from the dead. Not since Eli Cohen infiltrated the Syrian Ministry of Defense twenty years before had Israeli intelligence been able to penetrate another Arab government at the highest levels; now Avraham was the Leader.

U.S. secretary of state George Shultz was quoted as saying Gaddafi "retreated into the desert" after the bombing. Americans felt the strike on his bases was necessary and justified to atone for the recent West Berlin discotheque bombing and other attacks against the West. Gaddafi retreated for a while, but as former National Security Advisor Zbigniew Brzezinski said, "We haven't really dealt a blow to terrorism; we've just made ourselves feel good." The good feeling would not last long. The Leader would emerge from the desert revitalized, with a grander vision for a united Arab federation that would stand up to the West and directly challenge the United States of America.

Chapter 14

May 2, 1988
The Libyan Desert

The four-wheel-drive bounced over the potholes of the makeshift road after turning off the highway at Ra's Lanuf. Once a month, more often during the season with the most sandstorms, a truck swept and packed the road—really more a tarmac track than a road—to help drivers see it in the vast desert. The cars and trucks passing through this part of the Sahara usually helped keep the road intact, but the desert sands could erase it if a strong wind blew for any length of time.

The car headed south-southeast along this seemingly endless track. Every half mile or so was a fifty-five-gallon drum, filled and weighted with sand with a twelve-foot iron pipe welded to its side, to help demarcate the road, so that when it was covered by the desert, provided the dune was no more than twelve feet high and one could find the pipes, one could dig out the track. It would be ten years before commercial global positioning technology made this procedure obsolete. In the 1980s, though, it was still the only way to preserve the overland route from the coast to the oilfields deep in the Sahara.

He shook his head, marveling at the simplicity of life, yet questioning how silly some things really were. *Sahara* is the Arabic word for "desert," yet Westerners insisted on calling this piece of arid soil the Sahara Desert. It brought to mind a movie he and Laverne had seen a few years before when they took the girls to the United States for summer vacation, *Bridge on the River Kwai*. *Kwai* was the Thai word for "river." *Why do they do that?* Daniel Jedidiah Morgan wondered to himself.

At least driving through the desert gave him long moments of undisturbed thought, which he usually didn't squander thinking about Arabic or Thai words and their meanings. Both girls were asleep, as best they could, particularly given the heat of the desert and the noise and movement of the car. He studied their faces in the rearview mirror, marveled at how similar they were to their mother, marveled at how different they were from each other—Katy who was in constant awe of each new experience, Caroline expressing what appeared to be detached boredom to almost anything that confronted her, a seriousness older than her years—and he realized he knew little about them, of the things on the inside that mattered most.

He was home more than many of the oilmen who worked in Libya, with most of his trips being three or four nights at a time to the rigs many miles south of the family's rented home in Tripoli, actually more south of Benghazi, and it wasn't because they were girls—he simply didn't know how they felt about many things, save wanting to be with him. They would miss school, which both of them loved, just to drive with him four hundred miles into the desert, spend a night or two among the roughnecks and tool pushers and foremen, of the rough talk softened only slightly when the girls were around, the heat of the summers or the cold of the winters, the huge portions of food and soft serve ice cream in the mess hall, and then drive the same route home.

Something attracted his attention, broke his train of thought, forcing him to look to his right, west of the car—something that wasn't the sameness of the desert surrounding them. He slowed, pushed the clutch, turned off the engine, and just let the car coast along the track until it came to rest, well, nowhere, but in the middle of the road. Both girls looked up from the back seat to see if they were at the rig but quickly realized that they were still in the high desert, watching their father leave the vehicle and walk toward the sun still ninety minutes from setting.

They got out of the car and followed Dan, seeing what he saw, a collection of stumps, like dark trees casting shadows toward them, thick at the base but at most five or six feet tall, most of them under three feet. One tree was over two hundred feet tall when it was still standing, but now a dozen pieces eight to ten feet long all in a row where the tree had fallen thousands of years before. Their father looked back and saw them following, waving and calling to them, encouraging them to catch up to him. He waited just in front of the forest, alternating looking at the girls and the stumps.

"What is it, Daddy?" they asked, almost simultaneously.

"It's a petrified forest, and we're seventy-five miles into the desert. Look at that tree—it must've been two hundred feet tall, and over fifteen feet across!" he answered the question, not quite believing what he was saying, but saying it anyway as it was rather obvious what they were looking at. They moved through the forest, now no more than a hundred stumps still visible, as hard as rock but trees nonetheless, some broken with pieces on the ground. He picked up one log three feet long and started back toward the car with it, carrying it in front of him with both hands and then slinging it on one or the other shoulder when it got too heavy.

"Your mother will never believe us unless we bring back proof of our forest," he said, more wanting to show it to friends at the office than to his wife. He looked toward the car and saw somewhat incredulously an old Bedouin man coming from the other direction, walking through the desert as casually as they would be walking through the streets of Tripoli where they lived. Again the girls followed his gaze and started after him back toward the car, interested in where the man came from and what he was doing this far from anything, at least as far as they could see.

He loaded the ancient log into the back of the vehicle and even had enough time to retrieve two more pieces before the Bedouin reached the car. The girls watched as the old man arrived, with seemingly nothing to support him, no water, no map, nothing save the clothes he was wearing with his unusual blue headscarf and a stick that, if not petrified, was certainly as old as the man appeared to be, which was ancient. They would've been shocked to know he wasn't yet forty-five.

"Assalamu allekum," the old man issued the greeting as he got within earshot even though he recognized they were not Arabs.

"Wa allekum asalaam," Katy answered in Arabic she knew from constant use over the last five years in Tripoli. She was as fluent in the language as a non-native child could be, and when her father asked her to place long-distance calls for him through the local operators, they never suspected she was not native, not even Arab; her command of the language was that good.

Her parents had enrolled her in a Libyan school at age four with the idea that she could learn the language and catch up with English later; with Caroline, they thought she was too young and wasn't mature enough to do the same, and started her at the Oil Companies School, a nine-hundred-student kindergarten-through-ninth-grade American curriculum school in Tripoli set up by the various oil and oil services companies.

After a few years when they were ready for Katy to join Caroline, she refused, preferring instead to remain in the Libyan school, so they arranged tutoring in the afternoons to make sure she stayed up with the other American students. She excelled in both languages; she had just a few months earlier begun studying French with a second tutor and even more recently began expressing an interest in learning Italian and German. They did not discourage her and just made arrangements for more tutors; Libya was full of European expatriates seeking employment opportunities in the emerging economy.

Katy and the man carried on a conversation for the next few minutes while Caroline and her dad listened and watched, neither of them understanding much of what was being discussed. Katy stopped to tell them that the old man, whose name was Mohammed and was proudly Tuareg and Berber—rather than Arab and Bedouin—of the Kel Ferwan tribe, had a son working in the Barrut North oilfield another 250 miles to the south and was looking for a ride.

The old man knew that when he got to the makeshift road, someone would eventually come along; this wasn't the place where you left anyone behind, local or expatriate, clean or dirty, smelling or not, heading north or south. Katy said he had been walking for two nights, how far he didn't know—not that it was important to know the distance from the tribal camp. His son, Omar, had been hurt at the rig, although the old man didn't say how he knew this, and he was traveling to see what condition Omar was in, perhaps to bring the boy home to the collection of tents in order to recuperate, perhaps to bury him in the desert, he wasn't sure which.

The Sahel encompasses the area in the middle of the Sahara comprised of Mauritania, Mali, Niger, Chad, and Sudan. A vast no-man's land of desert and scrub, hundreds of ethnic groups like the Hausa and Tuareg used the Sahel as a superhighway to move across the continent, largely without interference from or observation by the region's governments. The Kel Ferwan was one of hundreds of tribes within the Tuareg nation, a loose ethnic federation of nomads, whose native language is Tamashek although many speak Arabic, enabling them to conduct business with the northern coastal nations.

Mohammed told Katy of Omar's requirement to pay the *taggalt*, or "bride-wealth," which according to his tribal traditions would, under normal circumstances, be up to three camels for a young woman's hand in marriage, more if she were a virgin—Katy shook her head although she didn't actually understand what that meant—considerably more if she were from a wealthy family. Omar wanted to marry the tribal chief's daughter Hinan, so he was facing a *taggalt* of twenty camels, some cash, and the *tisrar*. The *tisrar*, he explained, was given by the groom to the bride and her parents, consisting of food to help with the wedding feast, pieces of cloth for various skirts and headscarves, and two pairs of *takalmi*-type sandals like the ones Mohammed wore on his feet.

He went on to explain that just the food for the wedding feast—two hundred kilos of millet, fifteen liters of butter, five liters of Sudanese honey, and an ox—were more than his little family could afford. And although that completed the statutory obligations of the groom to his new bride, he was really expected to provide her jewelry shortly after the wedding.

Mohammed seemed relieved that the bride's family was responsible in their custom for providing an *eben*—the mat tent the couple would live in—and the materials for a bed, or *tedabut*, as well as sundry cooking utensils, and even a number of domestic animals to round out the bride's dowry. He told Katy that Omar went to work in the oilfields to help finance his impending marriage to the chief's daughter. Now that all seemed in jeopardy.

Katy's skin was almost as dark as Mohammed's, and Caroline's certainly was, yet the girls were neither Arab nor Tuareg. He respected Katy's command of Arabic—he nicknamed her Amira, the Arabic word for "princess"—but she was still a foreigner and, while not yet ten years old and soon old enough for marriage, she was nonetheless female. He spoke with her but didn't get too familiar, as much because she was a girl as a foreigner. Women were for bearing children, cooking, and caring for the animals, not for conversations of consequence, even if she was your wife.

Another hour down the road, Dan Morgan pulled the car over and announced that they would be stopping for the night. The girls moved with the confidence of having performed this routine several times before and soon had the small camp set up. Meanwhile, Mohammed moved away from the Americans to settle in for the evening. Although Katy wanted to learn more about the Tuareg tribes that spanned the area roughly from Sudan and Libya in the east and north to Niger in the south, Mohammed instead rested after his considerable walk. More than once, Dan had to stop his elder daughter from disturbing the old man's sleep.

The next day, they made it to the rig after another five hours of driving, passing several other oilfields and rig camps along the way. Mohammed went to find Omar, with Katy following at a respectful distance. Dan and Caroline went to the site office to get an update on the drilling operation.

Mohammed found his son in the infirmary with casts on both legs up to his waist, awake and in good spirits. He had put on some weight— the Westerners brought food from abroad, and Omar had developed a fondness for chocolate ice cream. Katy translated from the Irish nurse that some drill pipe fell on Omar's legs while the boy slept under the pipe stand. That was strictly forbidden, she told Mohammed; but under the circumstances, it was irrelevant.

Omar would be bedridden for six weeks, followed by three months of physical therapy, and would then be released to his parents and home in the desert to convalesce. He could probably come back to work in twelve months, she told Mohammed, provided he followed the safety rules he was taught. Given that the rigs were the only good employment outside the coastal cities of Tripoli and Benghazi, Omar would most certainly be back and would, hopefully, find another place to sleep. The wedding could wait.

Mohammed stayed with Omar over the next few days while Dan Morgan went about his business at the rig site, and Katy/Amira used this time to talk with the old man and his son. By the time the family and their hitchhiker were heading north again, the conversation between the two was more relaxed, and Mohammed was almost amused by this young girl who could discuss so many different things about which he knew little to nothing. Katy learned more about the Tuareg and their general antipathy toward organized government rule. The tribes were generally left undisturbed so far out in the desert, but the new government in Libya was not as conciliatory.

Installed in a bloodless coup that ousted King Idris al Sanussi, Captain Mu'ammar al-Gaddafi rose from the ranks of the army to lead the nation for the last two decades. While the king was in Turkey for medical treatment, Gaddafi at age twenty-seven, organized officers to seize power and changed the very fabric of Libyan culture and way of life. The Libyan Army had recently begun insisting that the Tuareg move into the villages built for them by the state and register with the various ministries responsible for keeping track of citizens and expatriates, a move the Tuareg resisted.

Dan slowed the car and again let it roll to a stop with the petrified forest now to their left as they headed north. Mohammed eased out of the car, thanked his hosts for their hospitality over the last few days, and set off in an easterly direction toward his camp far in the desert. The Morgans watched him for a few minutes, honked the horn, and waved as he disappeared over a dune, and then continued their journey home.

Chapter 15

December 21, 1988
Stockholm, Sweden

The young man moved unobtrusively through Stockholm's Arlanda Airport with obvious familiarity. Khalid had walked this route three dozen times over the last three months, careful never to wear the same disguise or clothes twice. He wanted to be sure he knew exactly how long it would take to cross the departure hall, which counter to go to, and who would be on duty, leaving nothing to chance.

A young blonde woman, not at all uncommon in Sweden, was behind the counter as he expected. Her nametag read *Anna*, and he knew it was her shift. She had never seen him in this disguise, so she didn't know he had even spoken with her on several occasions. She would never have known it from his demeanor. Unlike previous encounters, he was businesslike in his bearing and almost curt in his manner. He stepped up to the counter and said, "London. Last name is Jalili. You should have an aisle seat reserved for me."

Anna checked the computer for his reservation and seat information. He gave the same instructions to the ticket agent who originally booked his flight and had already been assigned seat 1B in first class to London Heathrow. He pulled his wallet out of an inside coat pocket while Anna calculated the price of the ticket in U.S. dollars. Khalid paid it, knowing he would get change in Swedish kroner. It was important that everything appear normal to the woman, even though it was anything but normal to Khalid. Today was the day.

"How many bags do you have, sir?" The young girl feigned sincerity in the question she had asked a hundred times already today and several thousand more times over the last few years.

"Just one. I think I'll carry it on with me since it's so small." He hesitated momentarily. "On second thought, go ahead and check it." Khalid laughed to himself as he knew all along he would check the bag.

The girl started to caution him to put his name on the bag in case it got lost, but he held up the luggage tag already attached to the small suitcase. She completed the process and handed him his passport, his ticket with the luggage claim check attached, and the boarding pass.

"Sir, you are on SAS flight 66 to London, seat 1B, leaving from gate 7 at 1130. You need to clear immigration and be at the boarding gate in about forty-five minutes. You have one bag checked—here's your claim check—all the way to London Heathrow. Here's the pass for the SAS first class lounge. Have a nice flight."

Khalid listened intently for the slightest hint of suspicion in Anna's voice or demeanor but found none. She pointed vaguely to her right as she asked the next person in line to step forward and produce his ticket and passport. The man behind Khalid seemed eager to move closer, hovering over the woman and staring intensely at her tight V-neck sweater. She seemed not to notice or to care.

Khalid cleared immigration immediately and moved to the gate for the SAS flight without going to the lounge. He was not fond of Sweden in the winter, but it was not his decision to use this airport. Abdelbaset Ali Mohamed al Megrahi, a Libyan intelligence officer and head of security for Libyan Arab Airlines and Khalid's boss, had made that decision for him; and he only belatedly found out the reason why. Swedish law prohibits checks into the backgrounds of airport personnel, including those who handle the baggage.

Khalid knew his luggage would make it onto this flight to London and from there be placed on a flight to New York. A fellow Libyan who had worked here for eighteen months would switch the luggage tag on Khalid's bag with one bound for JFK. The authorities would initially focus on an American woman who visited Stockholm on business and was returning to New York City for Christmas to determine her role in what would be the deadliest act of terror in the twentieth century, wasting three months of the investigation on a misdirection instigated by Jalili.

Khalid would retrieve her real bag in London and pass it to a Libyan embassy operative, who would quickly destroy it. When his shift ended this evening, the baggage handler would walk away from his Swedish wife, his newborn daughter, and their nice apartment in a comfortable neighborhood in Stockholm and return to his "real" family and home in Tripoli. His work here would be completed.

Khalid had every reason to hate the current regime in Libya, but longevity did not accompany his hate. Before the revolution, his father, Salim, worked at the sprawling Wheelus Air Base outside Tripoli, having helped the Americans as a young man during World War II against the German tanks led by Field Marshal Erwin Johannes Eugen Rommel. The Desert Fox commanded the Deutsches Afrika Korps, later taking part in an assassination attempt on Hitler before committing suicide to escape the Führer's wrath when it failed.

Salim supplied the Americans with information on Rommel's movements and was later rewarded with a key position at Wheelus, the largest U.S. military facility outside North America. He was particularly fond of the last base commander and one of the Tuskegee Airmen, air force brigadier general Daniel "Chappie" James, who would go on to become the nation's first black air force four-star general. Salim would often tell Khalid stories of how General James would walk into barracks, hangars, and offices unannounced and unaccompanied and, after motivating his people, would leave the same way. The airmen loved him, as Salim did, because he was a real human being first and then an officer and a general.

Khalid remembered vividly how his father was dragged off the base after it was turned over to the Libyans in June of 1970. Gaddafi's security forces took Salim away and returned his body to the family for burial ten days later, saying only that he died of a heart attack. The gruesome marks indicating torture suggested otherwise, and Khalid as a young man remembered his mother saying that God's mercy had taken away the pain by allowing Salim to die. Khalid told himself at the time that he would fight the dictator at all costs.

I couldn't resist the regime forever, Khalid reminded himself. *They hold the strings to everything in our lives, including whether we live or die. I couldn't subject my family to more suffering at the hands of these people.* Although Khalid tried justifying his actions, he was left feeling empty and tired. He found the rich rewards of actually helping the regime were more than he would see in a lifetime of resistance, and he was thus able to send his three younger brothers and a sister abroad for education and, hopefully, to better lives outside the country.

Besides, he suggested to himself, *the Americans are arrogant and don't care about us.* He couldn't reconcile that with his father's impression of General James, but Khalid merely closed his eyes and continued on his flight to Great Britain, shutting out once again the struggle he faced during all his waking moments and in many of his dreams.

The trip to London was uneventful. After arriving, he moved quickly to the Pan Am gate and watched the luggage being loaded onto the Boeing 747-121 named Clipper Maid of the Seas with hull number N739PA. He caught a brief glimpse of the small bag going up the ramp into the underside of the giant plane.

After waiting a few minutes to make sure the bag wouldn't inexplicably be unloaded, he made his way to a public phone. He inserted several coins and dialed a number in downtown London that was automatically routed to Tripoli. The call was answered, but no one on either end of the line said a word. Khalid held the phone up while an announcement was being made over the public address system about a flight leaving from London Heathrow to Prague. When he was certain the person on the other end of the line—his boss al Megrahi—heard the announcement, he hung up.

Khalid did not wait for the big plane to finish loading and taxi away from the terminal. He retrieved the woman's bag, now with his name on it, checked its contents in the men's room before he cleared customs, walked out of the arrival lounge, and headed for the London Underground. In a few minutes, he was rushing toward downtown

London and into anonymity. No one noticed him switch bags with another commuter who got off at the station closest to the Libyan embassy. The other man would dump the suitcase into the incinerator at the embassy, effectively eliminating any proof the bag and its contents ever existed.

Later that afternoon, Khalid heard of Lockerbie, Scotland, for the first time and saw the carnage his actions had caused. Pan Am 103 was scattered over much of the Scottish countryside around the villages of Lockerbie, Dumfries, and Galloway; and an investigation was initiated to determine why the plane crashed.

They will never know for sure, Khalid said to himself as he sipped a Courvoisier while a very young redheaded English girl began undressing in front of him. He tossed two hundred dollars on the bed and commanded her to slow down. She did.

Chapter 16

May 25, 1999
Charleston, South Carolina

Kathryn Emily Morgan moved down the aisle following the long gray line of cadets toward the stage. She looked up to see her parents and younger sister, Caroline, and her father gave her a "thumbs up." Her mother smiled the tight smile she always did indicating she wouldn't relax until the act was done. She had that same smile four years earlier when Katy got the envelope telling her that she was accepted to The Citadel, the Military College of South Carolina, one of the very first women to enter the Corps of Cadets and notably the first black woman. And when she was nominated to the National Honor Society. And when she was competing to be the university's sole Chief of Naval Operations Distinguished Naval Midshipman Graduate of that year.

Before she realized it, the diploma was in her hand, hats were thrown into the air, and she was walking arm in arm with her family toward the car, the rental condominium on Isle of Palms, and her future as an officer of the Marines. Having been commissioned a few hours before the commencement ceremony—she was only nineteen and needed a waiver from the U.S. Congress to be commissioned so young—Second Lieutenant Morgan was bound for Alpha Company, 1-00, at the Basic School, a.k.a. TBS, at the sprawling base at Quantico, Virginia, where every new commissioned or warrant officer was indoctrinated as a leader of Marines.

The drive to the island was almost surreal. Everyone spoke at the same time, her father making pronouncements about Katy's career and professional exploits, her mother warning her not to volunteer for hazardous duty—"That's what the men do, dear"—and Caroline telling their mother that Katy would be as much an officer of Marines and warfighter as any man was. The girls, really young women, laughed hysterically as they replayed stories from their childhood of Katy climbing to the roof of a barn to rescue a cat, standing on the peak, beating her chest, and declaring that the Marines had landed and the situation was indeed well in hand.

Katy had ten days of leave before reporting to Quantico, and she wanted to spend them with her family before heading off to who knew where and God knew what. Family was important to her, and this family had been around the world together. Now one of the tribe was going out on her own, and regardless of how hard they tried, the relationship would forever be different than the way it had always been. Katy's parents had even retired to Charleston so they could be close to her while she went through The Citadel, and they saw her most weekends when she was competing in one sport or another and several times during the week since her grades allowed her local leave.

Before she went to TBS, though, she had leave with her family on the beaches of the Atlantic Ocean, swimming, playing, eating, and laughing—a time of fellowship, family, and reflection. She could not have known at that time on that beach the course her life would take, the highs and lows, the unimaginable joy and the inconsolable sorrow. For now, though, she was with her family, warmed by their love and secure in their protection.

The days went quickly. Dan and his wife, Laverne, brought the old 8mm movies and an ancient projector to the beach condo, and each evening the family laughed over the antics of the girls as they were growing up. There were pictures of them visiting the ancient Roman cities Sabratha and Leptis Magna and the Greek city of Cyrene in Libya. They rode camels, watched the Apollo missions fly overhead in the unpolluted night sky devoid of artificial light, and swam in the Mediterranean Sea, all captured on Kodak film Laverne was already having converted to videotape, anxious to protect the memories before deteriorating to the point they were lost to this family.

Katy and Caroline were out every evening dancing and partying with friends and sleeping until noon. Laverne made it her mission to make things as easy for Katy as possible before she left to start her life in the Marine Corps. Brunch was ready for the girls when they awoke, clothes were already cleaned and ready, and the car always had a full tank of gas. The girls were invited to The Citadel beach club one evening for a classmate's bachelor party, and there was always time to stroll the beaches before the huge crush of summer vacationers descended on the tiny island.

Dan and Laverne were immensely proud of both daughters and felt they had taught them well. Being black in America even at the start of the new millennium could still be challenging, but they encouraged their children to not hate, but also to not hide. Fully enfranchised in an America of hope and belonging, the Morgans would not permit themselves to be victims, instead seeking every opportunity to achieve, excel, and succeed.

Katy would find a new home in the Marine Corps that evaluated her on performance and the content of her character, not on an abundance of melanin pigment in her skin, a trait that began a million years ago over which she had no control. She would learn that hard work, brains, and good judgment would carry her forward as well as any other Marine.

Chapter 17

June 12, 1999
Quantico, Virginia

Two weeks later, Katy found herself driving into Camp Barrett, the secluded area around the Basic School at Quantico. She spent the previous summer at Officer Candidate School in the same part of the base, proving to one and all that she had the mettle to be a Marine officer. Now the screening took a different turn, whereby her peers were judging her; each would express their opinion of whether the other measured up to the challenges and ideals of what an officer should be.

The Basic School. *I'm finally here*, she said to herself. Every second lieutenant of Marines in modern times learned to be an officer at TBS. Five platoons of about fifty officers each formed for the twenty-six-week training period. Hundreds of hours of leadership, history, weapons handling, tactics and strategy, and warfighting skills are taught with almost half the courses conducted in the field.

She entered O'Bannon Hall in her Summer Service "C" uniform, quickly found the check-in desk, and reported for duty to Company A, Class 1-00, or one double naught as some called it. She and her classmates referred to themselves as the "Naughties."

"Katy O.," a husky voice called out from behind her. "You still mad about that flare I shot at you last summer?" Katy had been so dedicated and meticulous in her training at OCS that members of her platoon had nicknamed her Katy O'Bannon, reminiscent of the famous Marine lieutenant Presley O'Bannon after whom the large training hall at TBS was named. Katy made the mistake of telling her classmates she grew up in Libya and the link was made to Lieutenant O'Bannon who led the Marines to Derna in 1806 in a battle memorialized in the Marine's Hymn opening line "From the halls of Montezuma to the shores of Tripoli."

Katy knew without turning around who was behind her. "Lieutenant Stephens, you made it out of OCS?"

Second Lieutenant Paul Stephens was one of her best friends at Officer Candidate School, and they had stayed in touch over the last year with periodic phone calls in the era just before electronic mail would make communicating easier and cheaper. "How are you, Paul? Are you still seeing Judy?" She knew he wasn't.

"Nah, she left me for a mere mortal. How y'doin'?"

"I'm great. I'm anxious to finish TBS and get to the Fleet. Have you decided on your MOS?" Katy was referring to the Military Occupational Specialty, the primary job each Marine is assigned, officer or enlisted, in addition to being a rifleman.

"O-3 Infantry, of course. What else would a Marine want to be? What are you trying for?" Paul knew she was ineligible for infantry since that field was not yet open to women.

"Haven't decided yet," Katy lied a little bit. She knew she was perfectly suited for intelligence work, but most of the women in the class would try for logistics, intelligence, or administration; she didn't want to get shoved into admin. "But if my esteemed peers would allow me to serve in intelligence I would be eternally grateful."

The banter continued as the two caught up on the year's events since they last served together. Other classmates drifted in and out of their conversation before they moved into the Bachelor Officers Quarters—the BOQ—to unpack and get settled. They were down the hall from each other: Katy with another woman named Cheryl Atkinson and Paul with college classmate Steve Marliss. They moved together to the mess hall for the evening meal, where they met dozens of other friends from college, OCS, and their summer training cruises.

The schedule began at 0800 the next morning with a welcome by the Commanding Officer of TBS, Colonel Charles Duncan, followed by Major Ray Hannifen from Sterling in the Commonwealth of Virginia, the commanding officer of Company A. Hannifen discussed the sacred bond they shared as officers and Marines and gave them a rundown of his career in the artillery. He then introduced the staff platoon commanders—SPC—who would lead and mentor the second lieutenants through their six-month training syllabus at TBS and who would, to a large extent, determine the first step in the course of their professional lives.

Katy watched with anticipation as Captain Robert Robichaux of New Orleans, Louisiana, was introduced. Robichaux had been assigned to third platoon, Katy's group of fifty-one second lieutenants. While she found him physically attractive, she reserved judgment on his ability not only to lead these officers but also to coax each of them to excel in their own way.

The next twenty-six weeks were spent training 251 lieutenants in the science and skills of being a Marine and the art of being an officer.

Chapter 18

September 18, 1999
The Rifle Range, Quantico

Don't wimp out, Katy reminded herself a dozen times this morning already and two hundred times over the last three months since TBS started. Although they fired weapons the previous summer at Officer Candidate School, the lieutenants were now expected not only to shoot but also *to qualify* with the M16A2 service rifle. Katy had never fired a weapon before OCS and was now faced with her biggest challenge since entering the Marine Corps.

Staff Sergeant David J. Mersino could see the look on her face. *Not another one,* he said to himself. *Why do I always get the ones who can't shoot?*

"All right, Lieutenant," he began, trying not to let the sarcasm drip to the point of being disrespectful, "this weapon will keep you alive if you know how to handle it properly. How much shooting have you done before the Marine Corps, ma'am?"

"To be honest, Sergeant, none." Katy decided not to bluff.

"Ma'am," Mersino began slowly, "I am a staff sergeant, not sergeant, and your Marines will always assume that everything that comes out of your mouth will be honest, so never start your sentences that way." He paused long enough for that to sink in. "I'm here to teach you, so it's good you won't have to unlearn bad habits." Mersino wasn't sure why he liked this lieutenant, but there was something about her he did.

"Thank you, Staff Sergeant." Katy laughed at her mistakes. "I appreciate your experience, and I'm ready to learn."

The two Marines—one with eight years' service and three wars, the other with eight weeks' training and lipstick—spent the next two weeks learning sight alignment, sight picture, breathing techniques, and rapid fire. Toward the end of the first week, Staff Sergeant Mersino admitted to himself that this woman had that special something when shooting that comes along only so often, and she was a better shot even than him. Three of the five qualifying days of the second week she actually shot "possible," meaning that as far as the scorers could tell, she scored 250 out of 250 possible points, a perfect score. He saw real genius in her shooting and brought it to Major—he had been promoted the previous week—Robichaux's attention. The SPC moved down the firing line where he could watch her shoot without making Katy self-conscious, and he agreed wholeheartedly with Mersino's assessment.

The following week was Mess and Maintenance, the period when the lieutenants got a feel for what the enlisted Marines did when not training with their units. The lieutenants were split into two groups: one to work at the dining facilities on base and the other in various supervised maintenance jobs. Robichaux assigned Lieutenant Morgan to Weapons Training Battalion, specifically to work with Mersino. He trusted the staff sergeant; they had served together when Mersino was a corporal, squad leader, and sniper in a reconnaissance platoon Robichaux commanded as a first lieutenant. Mersino was promoted to sergeant meritoriously on Robichaux's recommendation.

Mersino "invited" Lieutenant Morgan to the rifle range Monday morning and began a series of shooting exercises meant to reinforce what she learned the previous two weeks and to test her ability to proactively engage an enemy through fire and maneuver with a proper gun-target line. Katy excelled under Mersino's disciplined approach to weapons training, successfully hitting targets at a thousand meters downrange. She learned how to compensate for wind, humidity, gravity, and other atmospheric conditions when engaging targets at longer ranges.

On the last two days—the final days of her third consecutive week on the rifle range—Mersino moved her a full mile from the target and introduced her to the .50 caliber sniper rifle. He taught her how to select the correct ammunition with the best ballistic coefficient for the weather conditions. By changing her shooting position, Katy learned how to measure the cosine angle, adjusting for targets physically above or below the line of her weapon.

She believed he was pulling her leg when he described the effect caused by rotation of the earth as bullets travel to targets over a thousand meters away; Mersino demonstrated how the Eötvös effect would cause rounds to hit lower when shooting to the west and higher when shooting to the east. The Coriolis effect, he explained, would cause rounds to hit to the right of the intended target in the northern hemisphere, with the opposite effect below the equator.

Katy finished the week with appreciation for shooting surpassed only by respect and admiration for her teacher.

"Staff Sergeant Mersino, I hope all the NCOs in my Marine Corps are as professional and disciplined as you are. I would be honored to serve with you anywhere, anytime."

After Mersino sent the lieutenant back to O'Bannon Hall, he called Major Robichaux to update him on what could only be described as an extraordinary three weeks, made more so since she had never picked up a weapon in her life before OCS and TBS. Whatever it was, Mersino told the major, "She just has it," and it was something Mersino had never before witnessed.

Chapter 19

November 10, 1999
The Basic School, Quantico

One of the most celebrated of military traditions and soldierly virtue is observance of the anniversary of the original founding of the United States Marine Corps. Although formal commemoration of the birthday only began in 1921, November 10 was chosen because on that day in 1775 the Second Continental Congress decreed,

> *That two battalions of Marines be raised consisting of one colonel, two lieutenant-colonels, two majors, and other officers, as usual in other regiments; that they consist of an equal number of privates with other battalions; that particular care be taken that no persons be appointed to offices, or enlisted into said battalions but such as are good seamen, or so acquainted with maritime affairs as to be able to serve with advantage by sea when required; that they be enlisted and commissioned to serve for and during the present War with Great Britain and the colonies, unless dismissed by order of Congress; that they be distinguished by names of First and Second Battalions of American Marines, and that they be considered as part of the number which the Continental Army before Boston is ordered to consist of.*

One hundred forty-six years later, General John A. Lejeune, thirteenth commandant of the Marine Corps, issued Marine Corps Order no. 47, Series 1921, in which he summarized the history, mission, and tradition of the Corps. In the order, General Lejeune directed that it be read to every command on November 10 each subsequent year in honor of the birthday of the Marine Corps. Seventy-eight years later, the Naughties of Company A were repeating the same celebration as all Marines would be around the globe.

Predating the birth of the United States, Marines served aboard ships of the Continental Navy to board foreign vessels and seize them for the colonies, and to repel boarders from enemy ships. Marines perched in the riggings of American ships acted as sharpshooters to target enemy commanders, naval gunners, and helmsmen.

One of the earliest symbols associated with the Marines came about as a result of the difficulty the shooters had in identifying friendly forces on the enemy's ships. Once the Marines boarded the other vessel, it was virtually impossible for the sharpshooters high above in the riggings to distinguish them from enemy combatants. To solve the problem, Marines sewed a quatrefoil of rope on top of their hats; Marines in the riggings shot at anyone lacking that insignia. Marine officers continued the tradition with a quatrefoil on their barracks covers.

Lieutenants were seated at tables of ten, with eight seats for the junior officers and the remaining two for senior Marine and Allied officers or for guests. A captain who worked at the Presidential Helicopter Squadron, HMX-1, headquartered at the air facility at Quantico, occupied one of the seats, and an elderly woman sat in the other. The lieutenants had been instructed by Major Robichaux to entertain the guests at their table, and three of the lieutenants who were bound for flight school after TBS sat around the captain, picking his brain on what to expect when they reached the training program at Naval Air Station Pensacola, Florida.

Katy and her roommate, Cheryl, sat on one side of the woman, with Lieutenants Steve Marliss and Paul Stephens on the other. Although she was introduced to them as Mrs. White, they had not yet found her connection to the Marine Corps.

"Is your husband a Marine, ma'am?" Cheryl was curious why the woman was at the celebration without obvious ties to the Basic School or any of the senior officers present.

"No, my dear, he retired as a sergeant major in the army." Her voice was so quiet the four lieutenants were forced to lean in to hear her. "He passed away ten years ago."

"I'm sorry to hear that, ma'am," Katy offered. "I noticed you have an accent. Where are you from originally, if you don't mind me asking?"

"Not at all, dear. I was born in Portugal, but my family moved to China when I was two years old. That's where I grew up and went to school, so my accent is very confusing to most people. I eventually left China before moving to Germany and then to the United States after I married my husband." The old lady had obviously answered that question many times in her long life but offered it as though it were the first time. She smiled inwardly, knowing the lieutenants were curious why she was there but didn't want to ask her directly, nor did she want to volunteer the answers until asked.

"My grandfather served in China as a Marine during World War II," Steve told the group. "He was in Peking and Tientsin."

Mrs. White smiled gently with a certain twinkle in her eyes as she remembered a past that was seventy years old. She shocked the lieutenants as she spoke. "Yes, I met Lieutenant Colonel Jack Marliss in Tientsin in 1949, and that's why I wanted to meet his grandson this evening. It's late, though, and I must go now." Lieutenant Marliss stood and helped the old woman out of her chair and out of the ballroom. "May I visit with you again?"

"Yes, ma'am, of course," Steve offered, handing her one of the new visiting cards he purchased through the Marine Corps Exchange. "Let me write my parents' phone number on the back just in case I've graduated from TBS before you call."

Mrs. White thanked him and accepted his help to get into the back of her car. The chauffeur returned to the front seat and drove off into the night.

"Can you believe she knew my grandfather?" Steve asked the group when he returned to the table, incredulous at the thought of it.

"Did you hear her say she wanted to meet you again?" Paul was weighing her words, trying to understand what she said and why.

"She wants to tell me more about him. He died before I was born, and my folks never gave me the details of his service, if they even know." Steve knew little about the man save that he served his country as a Marine before and during the Second World War.

The four lieutenants continued their discussion and talked about the upcoming final weeks of their training. Most important was MOS selection, when the officers would know to which specialty they would be assigned. The night ended with the entire gathering singing "The Marines' Hymn" and drinking a toast to their beloved Corps, a ceremony they would repeat annually on November 10 for the rest of their lives wherever two or more Marines were gathered.

Chapter 20

January 5, 2000
Dam Neck, Virginia

Katy was anxious to start the training that would define her military occupational specialty for the remainder of her Marine Corps career, whether four years or forty. She got the MOS she requested; as the honor graduate of her TBS class—the first woman to do so in the mixed gender training cohorts—she was entitled to her first choice. She was ordered to the Navy-Marine Corps Intelligence Training Center, or NMITC, at Dam Neck just south of Virginia Beach and adjacent to the Oceana Naval Air Station, learning how to be an intelligence officer supporting Navy and Marine Corps units. When Major Robichaux informed her she would attend NMITC, Katy sought out intelligence officers stationed at Quantico to understand the job and what was expected of her, and she even drove 180 miles to Virginia Beach one weekend to get the lay of the land.

Not surprisingly, Katy excelled at NMITC, graduating first in her class of fifty-seven naval officers, one FBI special agent, a foreign service officer, and two army officers on an exchange program. Four of her TBS classmates were also assigned to the school, giving her an advantage early in the program to work with officers she already knew until she could make new acquaintances. Katy was pleasantly surprised by how professional and motivated her classmates were; for most of them, this was their first choice of specialty after officer basic training, and they all wanted to do well.

The class section leader wasn't a fan; Major Jason Pellish was a prior enlisted intelligence specialist, promoted to warrant officer in the intelligence field, and finally commissioned a limited duty officer captain as a ground intelligence officer. LDOs were specialists and couldn't serve in unrestricted specialties outside their area of expertise; they were ineligible from being promoted above lieutenant colonel, and they could not command units except in unusual circumstances. They were limited not in their authority but, rather, in their career progression because of the considerable prior training and expertise. Coming *sursum ab ordine*—up from the ranks—Pellish, like some LDOs, had little time or patience for officers entering directly from America's colleges and universities, believing they should instead spend time in the enlisted and warrant officer ranks before commissioning.

And his belief that women shouldn't be Marines, although unspoken in public, was legend.

Katy ignored what she couldn't change and focused instead on being the best at every training exercise, personal fitness test, and academic examination, reminding herself of her father's words: *Don't hate, don't hide, don't be a victim.* Even with the headwinds of Pellish's prejudices, Katy knew he couldn't ignore her superior performance and unwavering commitment to be the finest intelligence officer in her class, if not in the Marine Corps. He begrudgingly acknowledged her competence despite just learning the trade and the perseverance that motivated her every action. She simply refused to be mediocre.

The capstone project of the course was an intelligence assessment and preparation of the battlefield for an amphibious assault on the island of Cuba. The exercise scenario posited an attack by the Cuban Revolutionary Armed Forces on the Guantanamo Bay Naval Base—also called Gitmo as shorthand because of the common pronunciation of the location—at the southeastern end on the island nation, threatening U.S. and allied forces ashore and the military prison housing unlawful combatants from the ongoing Global War on Terror after the terrorist attacks on September 11, 2001. The oldest U.S. naval base overseas, the yearly lease on the facility rose to $4085 in 1974 where it has remained ever since.

Katy organized the team's S-2, the designation for the command's intelligence section, into a research and analysis cell, a collections cell, and a liaison cell responsible for coordinating activities with higher headquarters represented by Pellish and his staff trainers. The team reviewed archival material on the utter failure of the Bay of Pigs operation in 1961; they studied maps to determine the best beaches for an opposed amphibious landing; and they collected data on the Cuban civilian and military leadership as well as the weapons and tactics of the armed forces. Their mission was to provide the landing force commander the best intelligence assessment of the enemy while assisting in preparation of the battle plan according to available information, but also offering reasoned opinions based on experience, and even gut feelings.

When it came time for Katy to brief the team's analysis, Pellish challenged every statement and assessment; she parried, respectfully, with facts and figures, referring to historical and current data, examples of similar Cuban operations and responses, and focused arguments to support the findings. By the time her turn was over, Pellish's staff acknowledged the professional job she and the team had done and how complete the presentation was. After all the teams presented their analyses, they awarded Team Katy an unprecedented 100 percent on the assignment despite Pellish's protestations, the first time in anyone's memory that occurred.

Katy graduated first in her class at NMITC and received a plaque and certificate from the Naval Intelligence Professionals Foundation recognizing her achievement and leadership in the class as rated by her peers. She was ordered to Marine Corps Air Station New River, North Carolina, adjacent to the base at Camp Lejeune where the East Coast infantry, artillery, and tank units were stationed, to serve as the Assistant Intelligence Officer of the Marine Aircraft Group 26. The MV-22 Osprey vertical/short takeoff and landing tiltrotor turboprop aircraft had entered the fleet the previous year, allowing Katy the chance to be on the cutting edge of Marine Corps aviation technology.

Katy's career had now begun in earnest, doing her job to support Marines "in the air, on land, and sea" as advertised in the Marines' Hymn. She was determined to get it right.

Chapter 21

Wednesday, August 1, 2001
Naples, Italy

A warm rain fell as the trawler moved slowly through the harbor. The man at the helm, Abu Yusuf—known by his *kunya* name "father of eldest son Yusuf" instead of his birth name Abdulaziz—was confident he could steer the ship into position before too much longer, and definitely before the lookouts on the American military ships could identify his flag. He had considered switching flags—more for convenience's sake and not because he was afraid—but Abu Yusuf was a proud man and could not let anyone think otherwise. His flag would remain flying.

And besides, he asked himself, what could the Americans do? This is an international port with dozens of ships from all over the world, and I have been granted permission to enter from Harbor Control. One more ship was of no concern to the sailors, even if she was flying the flag of the Socialist People's Libyan Arab Jamahariya.

The lights of Naples bounced on the dark water in the harbor. Traffic still moved along the waterfront even though it was after midnight, and it seemed as though the nightlife in the city itself was just starting. He noticed the dock for the hovercraft that took scores of tourists daily to the Isle of Capri and the tattletale sound of the ropes and shackles of private boats bobbing in the wake created by his and other passing boats. The U.S. warships were now in full view, although he was sure his actions were still covered by the darkness.

Most of the American sailors were asleep aboard the ships after a night of chasing whores and drinking beer. Abu Yusuf found himself staring, amazed at the size of the guns on the battleship USS *Missouri*; he heard stories of how one shot fired from these behemoths could level 1,000 square meters. In Lebanon, they had done just that during the time before the bombing of the Marine barracks in 1983. Now almost eighteen years later, Abu Yusuf saw for himself the enormity of the guns sitting idle and pointed out to sea. He turned the wheel slightly to starboard.

Just out of visual range from the American ships, he shut off the engine and let the ship slow of its own accord. A group of men who had been huddling in the pilothouse with him moved to their assigned positions on deck and began their work. Abu Yusuf remained at the wheel with the ship's surface search radar on scanning for any approaching vessels that might cause him to turn out of the way or disrupt their plans.

Why exactly he had been chosen to skipper this important task, he didn't know. He was approached less than a month ago by an army captain, who asked if he would be interested in moving some cargo for the Jamahariya and thereby making a nice profit in the process. His immediate response was yes as he recognized the drudgery he would face for opposing the government. The captain promised him that he was not obligated to this task and would suffer no ill effects if he chose not to undertake it. He chose to undertake the mission, and he chose not to believe the captain's promises.

Abu Yusuf knew little of the men who now moved quietly across the deck of his boat. He saw them uncover small motorboats, none of them longer than three meters. They quickly connected battery cables, fueled gas tanks, and made adjustments to some instruments the old captain was sure he wanted to know nothing about. They lowered the nine boats into the water on the starboard side, unseen by the American warships now to port.

One of the men jumped into the closest boat, pulled the rope on the motor, and when it roared to life, he adjusted the throttle. Another man still on deck turned the switch on a small black box whose antenna he had already extended and started adjusting dials. The small boat with the first man began maneuvering toward a second boat, seemingly without control from its only occupant.

Thus the man in the small boat went from one to the other until all nine boats were puttering quietly next to the mother ship. The last boat glided through the water up to the ladder of Abu Yusuf's boat, and the man climbed back on deck with the rest of the group. Nine of them stood with identical black boxes, identical antennas extended, each moving the dials in varying fashion. The apparent leader of the group spoke softly.

"Allahu akbar! Let them know the *jihad* began at"—he glanced at his watch—"3:17 on this day!" Then his eyes became cold and he said, "Send them on their way."

At his command, the nine men moved along the deck as each steered his remotely controlled motorboat toward the ships moored in the harbor. The captain fired up the engines on his own boat and brought her about. The nine motorboats trailed him for a distance and then each on separate command turned toward the ships as their crews lay sleeping in the early morning.

Petty Officer Second Class Carl Zemanski was the stern midwatch of the ship's self-defense force aboard USS *Saginaw*, an amphibious landing ship tank, or LST, homeported at Little Creek Amphibious Base in Norfolk, Virginia. Zemanski had seen the Libyan vessel move through the port although he couldn't see her flag. He thought it strange she was departing only minutes after arriving, but that was someone else's problem. His was to protect *Saginaw* from boarding by swimmers and to watch for his shipmates returning from liberty drunk and possibly falling overboard. He had only moments before checked in with his chief petty officer by radio and was settling in for his last half hour of tonight's watch. He would be relieved at 0400, be in the rack ten minutes later, and not have duty again for another two days.

He heard some sailors at Fleet Landing swearing loudly at a taxi driver they claimed was ripping them off. Zemanski had spent the last seventeen months on *Saginaw*, thirteen of them at sea. He failed to understand how his shipmates, particularly those without families, could have spent as much time on *Saginaw* as him and not have a dime to their names. He saved most of his meager salary and was planning on adding that to the education fund he got with his navy enlistment. He would, if his estimates were correct, have enough money saved to pay for a bachelor of science in computer engineering, room and board, and a little bit for the hours when he wouldn't be studying. He had a Ford F-150 pickup truck already paid off during a previous deployment waiting for him in Norfolk and . . .

What's going on? he asked himself. The noise of the motorboats caught his attention. He stood up from the rail where he had been daydreaming and came to full alert. Even in the noisy harbor, he was able to pick out what was not supposed to be there. He scanned the surface of the water looking for clues where the noise was coming from. Although motorboats were common in the harbor, they weren't at 0330, and certainly not several of them at the same time. He was able to pick out noises from at least three different motors.

He was not yet concerned about the boats, but he was nonetheless curious. He kept scanning the dark horizon until he was able to pick up the movement of one boat. Within two seconds, he found the second, and then the third. All three seemed to be heading in the general direction of the navy ships moored along the various piers in the harbor. One of the boats was coming directly at Zemanski, who unconsciously slipped the shotgun off his shoulder. The boat was still 250 yards from *Saginaw*, and Zemanski was trying to make out the pilot of the boat.

Movement to his right front drew his attention in that direction, and he saw two more identical boats, all moving slowly toward different ships in the fleet. The five were spreading out in a fan from where the Libyan vessel was previously. When he thought of the ship, he sensed she was still there, someone was looking at him from the boat, and then realized that she cut her engines again and was slowly drifting toward the harbor entrance, but still within visual range of the piers. His attention went again to the motorboat aimed at him, and he strained hard to see the person inside. He saw no one.

As he scanned left and right, he saw boats to each side. *That makes seven,* he said to himself, and he directed his spotlight toward a boat 150 yards from him and to his right. There was no one aboard. As he turned, the light reflected off something metallic in the boat, and he turned it back in the direction of the boat. It was headed directly for USS *Nassau*, LHA-4, to his right rear, and was only a hundred yards from her stern.

Zemanski reached up with his Motorola radio, and as he did so, his arm hit the railing. The radio dropped from his hand, bounced once on the deck, and fell into the water forty feet below. He swore as he illuminated the boat coming toward *Saginaw* and found it was now seventy-five yards away. He couldn't contact the chief and thought about yelling at the pilot of the boat, if there indeed was one, but knew he would not be heard above the boat's motor. He looked toward *Nassau* and saw that boat only fifty yards away from the LHA.

He chambered a round in the shotgun and aimed at the boat bearing down on *Nassau*. He pulled the trigger and immediately realized he was picking himself up off the deck. He fired many shotguns before and had never felt recoil like that. When he finally looked up, he saw the motorboat had exploded into a huge fireball sending shards of fiberglass and metal in every direction. It took a few seconds for him to realize the explosion knocked him off his feet, not the shotgun's recoil.

Shocked, he felt he was moving in slow motion and the world was speeding around him. He turned to see where his boat was, the one coming toward *Saginaw*. Barely thirty yards away, he chambered another round, aimed at the crew compartment of the small boat, and fired. He was driven straight back into the superstructure of the LST by the blast of the explosion. Within seconds, Zemanski heard several deafening explosions all around the harbor. Bright flashes tore at the night sky, and what he mistook for fireworks was really ammunition being ignited by the small boats exploding as they were steered remotely into the sleeping ships.

Lieutenant Colonel Bob Robichaux, commanding officer of First Battalion, Eighth Marine Regiment, felt *Nassau* rock violently below him, followed by the deafening explosion that penetrated the hull of the ship. Immediately out of his stateroom, he pushed open the door to Major Jake Noonan, his executive officer, and called to his staff. "Out of the rack, we've got incoming!" Jake rose too quickly, banging his head on the metal bedframe, blinking quickly to get rid of the stars in his eyes.

The officers stumbled out of a sound sleep and moved to the berthing areas where their Marines slept. Robichaux climbed the stairs to the Landing Force Operation Center,—the LFOC—running into the duty officer as he entered the space. "What's going on, Striker?" Captain John James was one of the two forward air controllers in the battalion. Marine aviators by training, Captain James and the other officer were temporarily assigned from active helicopter squadrons to help run air-ground operations for the infantry.

"I don't know yet, Colonel. Radio chatter says we were attacked by small boats. No confirmation, sir." Striker flew the CH-53E helicopters when he was with his squadron, the massive transport helicopters that could move thirty fully armed Marines or a jeep and trailer with other equipment.

"Give me a SITREP"—situation report—"on *Saginaw*, *Sumter County*, and *Trenton*," Robichaux ordered. USS *Saginaw* (LST1188), USS *Sumter County* (LST1181) and USS *Trenton* (LPD14) were the three other ships of the Amphibious Ready Group, or ARG, that carried components of Battalion Landing Team 1/8, Robichaux's reinforced battalion deployed from Camp Geiger, North Carolina. Staff Sergeant Mersino was also in the LFOC, having just returned from Shore Patrol, where he tried to keep the sailors and Marines on liberty from hurting themselves.

"Get down to the pier and organize the medical personnel where they're needed most, Staff Sergeant." Mersino was gone before the colonel finished the sentence.

The captain of the Libyan vessel stared in amazement at the spectacle. Explosions continued as the ships ignited each other and the fuel and ammunition within their own hulls. One of the larger ships, struck broadside by one of the motorboats, had a gaping hole that seemed to be swallowing all the water in the harbor. The ship was already listing, and it was obvious to the captain that unless something was done quickly, she would sink. Abu Yusuf watched for one more moment and then opened the throttle on the trawler and moved the boat out toward the harbor entrance to the open sea. The old man felt the heat from the burning ships and heard the cries of the dying as he steered toward home with his mission completed.

Zemanski also looked on in amazement. The entire harbor and most of the surrounding area was lit up from the fires of the explosions. It had not yet dawned on him that two rounds from his shotgun had saved the lives of hundreds of sailors and Marines, some so drunk they were sleeping through the slaughter. He stayed at his post, watching now more diligently for any further attacks from a silent and invisible enemy. His mind raced through the events of the last hour—in reality it had only been six minutes since the incident at Fleet Landing—and it seemed the harder he fought to recall the details, the less he could actually remember. Now he focused only on what was around him, of the fires and screams and bodies in the water.

Suddenly Chief McCann was there on deck with him. Zemanski heard McCann swear loudly, making the scene that much more unbelievable. Chief Petty Officer Mike McCann, father of three beautiful daughters and an equally beautiful wife, never swore, didn't chase the whores like his shipmates, and only had a beer when his wife was there to drive him home, not that he ever drank enough to require a driver.

"Stay at your post! Keep scoping out the water for swimmers, check for boats, planes—anything out of the ordinary! Self-defense ROE!" Chief shouted the last sentence as though Zemanski had not already defended himself—and his ship—as provided for in the rules of engagement. In any situation, when protecting U.S. government property or preserving lives, self-defense was sanctioned. In this case, deadly force, or the authority to kill in order to preserve life and property, was authorized only if no other action would eliminate the threat.

Zemanski wasn't sure if anyone was in the two boats he shot at, but looking around him, he knew he was right, even had there been a pilot. When things calmed down, he would tell the chief what he saw and what happened. For now, though, he watched for swimmers, boats, planes, and anything out of the ordinary, just as McCann ordered him to do. Without realizing it, he pumped the shotgun and loaded another round into the chamber, just in case.

USS *Sumter County* was taking on water faster than the bilge pumps could force it out. Sailors were working frantically to patch one particularly large hole in the hull of the ship, but they would be unable to do so before she sank. Many of the Marines who had been asleep in the compartment just aft of this one would spend another four days aboard the ship until U.S. Navy divers could remove their bodies and send them home for funerals all over the United States. Twenty-two minutes after she was struck, *Sumter County* came to rest at the bottom of Naples harbor with thirty-two Marines and fifty-six sailors resting peacefully on board.

Abu Yusuf looked north toward Naples. He saw the fantastic fires leaping out of the harbor, and he shuddered at the carnage. He knew to obey his orders would mean countless deaths. To disobey would mean his own death. He was too small a man in the disarray of the Jamahariya to make a difference by dying for his country. He might as well live for himself. He headed home and back to anonymity.

Halfway across the Mediterranean, the old captain's weighted body was dropped to the seabed below in a maritime funeral. There was a single bullet wound in his left temple; he would not live to tell about this evening's exciting activities.

Chapter 22

Wednesday, August 1, 2001
Quantico, Virginia

Mark was now a widower at age twenty-nine, losing his high school sweetheart and wife of six years to breast cancer. He moved through the church service and funeral on autopilot, thanking family and friends for coming and for paying their respects to the only woman he had loved in his short life. He heard their words of advice—time heals all wounds, better to have loved and lost than never to have loved at all, it'll make you stronger, you'll recover and get better soon—but for some reason, their words didn't console him. Mark and Anisa did not have children; after they were married, tests showed that she couldn't conceive; and after three attempts of in vitro fertilization, they agreed to live happily with each other and be thankful for what they had. They didn't realize at the time that included cancer.

When the last guests left his home just after noon, Mark went to the bedroom and changed into his uniform. Now a captain of Marines already confirmed for major, he was waiting to see if he was selected to attend Amphibious Warfare School at Quantico, Virginia, that would, hopefully, set him up for promotion to lieutenant colonel and prepare him to command an infantry battalion. Right now, though, he went through the paces of dressing, climbing into his car, and heading to the office. He had buried Anisa that morning, and the last thing he wanted to do was hang around the house all afternoon; he knew he had plenty of dark, lonely days and nights ahead.

"What are you doing here, Mark?" Jonathan McDaniel asked incredulously. J-Mac attended the funeral that morning and thought Mark was still with his and Anisa's family.

"My job," Mark replied matter-of-factly.

"Come on, man, you need to get your head screwed on straight." A fellow captain, J-Mac was Mark's best friend, having served together at the Basic School in First Battalion, Ninth Marine Regiment in Okinawa, Japan, and now at the training command at Quantico.

"I can't sit around the house day and night. I need something to do." Mark knew he lacked enthusiasm right at this moment, but just getting a complete sentence out was a major accomplishment.

Anisa discovered the lump in January just after they returned from spending the holidays with her family in southern Pennsylvania; barely seven months later, Mark laid her to rest. The doctors at Bethesda Naval Hospital did what they could, consulting with experts from around the country, even referring her to world-renowned MD Anderson Cancer Center in Houston for a second opinion, but finally admitted there was nothing left to do other than to make her comfortable. Mark watched Anisa's condition deteriorate, and then Sunday afternoon, the light in her eyes went out. A navy psychologist would work with Mark to help him understand how he would react; as low as he felt right now, he knew it would get much worse before he could start climbing out of the dark hole he was in.

The two officers were following the events in Naples earlier that day, trying to discern who among their friends and colleagues were injured or dead, looking for clues to who might have been behind the attacks. News reports from Italy played the video footage of the half-destroyed ships over and over again, while the Pentagon began identifying the casualties and notifying the next of kin, a process that would go on for over a week. The navy brass promised to raise the sunken vessels while the president and Congress vowed to bring the perpetrators to justice.

Pundits on all networks and in think tanks around the world speculated on who committed the attacks and the reasons why; the

Russians, the Chinese, the North Koreans, and even the Palestinians were suspects. One surveillance camera caught sight of a Libyan-flagged trawler entering the harbor just before the attack and leaving immediately after, but there was only one person visible on the ship who appeared to be the captain.

Because the Libyan government denied involvement, even suggesting the man had acted on his own, there was little the U.S. or its European allies could do. If they struck inside Libya without justification, the condemnation would be deafening. For now, just like the Lockerbie bombing, they collected data, interviewed witnesses and informants, and bided their time, waiting to act until the preponderance of evidence was in their favor. The right time would come.

Chapter 23

December 28, 2003
Dubai International Airport

The young woman moved purposefully through Terminal 1 toward the Emirates Airlines business class lounge. She checked in with the concierge, turned on her laptop, and plugged it into a landline jack to download any last-minute e-mails she could answer during the seven-hour nonstop flight to Heathrow Airport. She already had several dozen messages in her inbox, but she also knew she would have ample time to do a full day's work en route to the U.K. even if she watched a movie, had two meals, and read several chapters of her textbook.

Rachel Becker was a political officer and second secretary at the Embassy of the United States of America in Abu Dhabi, the capital of the United Arab Emirates, halfway through a three-year tour and heading home to New Orleans for the holidays. Raised in a foreign service family, she lived in seven countries before finishing high school, spoke five languages, and knew her way around four dozen major cities on five continents. Born to American parents, she spoke with a distinctive English clip due to the schools she had attended; American men always commented on her accent and were surprised when she told them that she too was American born and bred, despite all evidence to the contrary.

Her thoughts focused on Christmas gifts, parties she already knew were scheduled and some not yet announced, and on spending time with her family. Three sisters and a brother were flying in from various points of the globe, the first time in several years the whole family would be together.

Rachel got her carry-on luggage and moved to the gate. With over twenty years of flying, she had hundreds of thousands of frequent flier miles on five different airlines, and she chose this time to upgrade since she was too junior in the State Department hierarchy to fly anything other than economy class at the government's expense.

She boarded as soon as she could and took time settling in, finding an extra blanket, collecting her reading material, and getting a bottle of water from the flight attendant. She barely noticed the other passengers and withdrew into her own little world of reading, music, and thoughts of her life after this flight.

The Boeing 747 taxied from the jetway at the scheduled time, rolled to takeoff speed, and rotated off the active runway at 0145. Just as the plane was airborne, two men rose from their seats in the main cabin, reached over, and took the metal hair pins—they looked more like chopsticks—from the women sitting ahead of them, and raced to the front of the plane. Three other men also moved forward, quickly overpowering the flight attendants and taking control of the rear of the airplane. The cockpit crew was so busy with the takeoff, and none of the flight attendants were able to notify them, that they knew nothing of what was happening in the cabin.

A dozen years after the horrific events of 9/11, flight deck doors of airplanes were reinforced and alarms were installed so the crew could alert the pilot of disturbances in the cabin. The pilots right now were focused on getting the jumbo jet to its initial cruising altitude, heading the airplane in the right direction, and preparing the plane for the transcontinental flight.

The door splintered into the cockpit as the two men forced their way forward, quickly overpowering—and stabbing to death with the hair pins—the pilot and copilot. One of the men slid into the pilot's seat and took control of the airplane, speaking with air traffic controllers at Dubai as though nothing was wrong. The whole process had taken less than ninety seconds.

"Emirates 001, passing through 14,000 feet on 348 degrees, switching to frequency 145.3 contact Dubai departure. Roger." The man repeated instructions given him by the tower. The air traffic controller, Milton Goddard, would not have noticed the difference in accent, but the plane had moved off vector and ascended slower than it had been for almost a minute just before the voice changed. "Something's not right," he muttered to no one in particular. Curious, he challenged the pilot before the cockpit crew changed the frequency.

"Emirates 001, Dubai tower, confirm souls on board, sir." The real pilot had only five minutes previously told the tower that there were 217 people on the aircraft, including the cabin and cockpit crews.

Goddard waited for the answer. When he got none, he repeated the question. Still no answer. With almost thirty years' air traffic control experience, Goddard suspected something was wrong and notified his supervisor. The supervisor accepted the veteran's assessment and retrieved the checklist for in-flight emergencies. He began from the top and started working his way through the procedures.

The duty officer at Emirates Airlines took the call and retrieved her instructions for emergencies, initiating calls to the company officials responsible for dealing with these types of situations. On the back channel radio, she hailed Emirates 001. No answer. She tried again. While waiting for a response, she searched Emirates' intranet for information on the flight deck crew, including challenges and passwords to verify their identities. Emirates adopted an industry-wide system of authenticating a challenge by providing a discrete password known only to the two parties.

"Emirates 001, Emirates Corporate. Authenticate November Tango Alpha. I say again, authenticate November Tango Alpha."

"Emirates Corporate, Emirates 001. Unable to authenticate at this time due to in-flight emergency. Hydraulic failure port side."

Charlene "Charlie" Davenport had sixteen years of experience in the United States and ten with Emirates, with fifteen of those working in and eventually in charge of the command center. An American woman working in an Arab country for a local company was unusual, but her reputation and experience couldn't be ignored. She was close to the senior leadership at Emirates and immediately contacted the managing director at his home number.

"Hi, Beverly, this is Charlie Davenport, is Duncan home, please?" Duncan Norman was recruited eight years previously at the request of the ruler of Dubai to set up the airline. A veteran of British Airways, the new airline was bankrolled only long enough to get the company operational and was then expected to make its own profit.

"Good evening, Charlene. I hope all is well?" Norman knew Charlie was not calling for social reasons.

"Duncan, we've got something going on with 001, and I can't get the cockpit crew to authenticate. Milt Goddard is in control. He said the plane slowed its ascent and veered off course for more than forty-five seconds, enough that he also feels something's up. They called in a hydraulic problem on the port side, which could explain the retarded ascent, but it doesn't feel right. They've made no attempt to return to Dubai with the problem." Charlie gave him the facts without embellishment.

"Who's PIC?" Norman asked.

"Pilot-in-command is Allan Stewart, with Mohammed Al Bawardi riding shotgun. Tania Shihab is senior flight stewardess." Charlie still used American slang and had never attempted to conform to the vernacular of the large British community in Dubai. She still felt odd referring to flight attendants as stewardesses, but that was a real rank in the company, and she had to use it to be understood.

"Well, give them a few minutes to get themselves sorted out and then try again. Please call me if anything else happens." *I'm sure it's nothing,* Norman said to himself, *and I doubt we'll have an incident tonight.*

Rachel was oblivious to the trouble in the front of the airplane. She was listening to music and studying her textbook to prepare for her next exam coming up right after the holidays. Someone reached across her and pulled the headphones off her head.

"I said get up! Now!" The man half dragged her out of the seat and stopped only when he realized she was still belted in. "Get to the back of the plane!" Everything he said seemed to be a shout.

Rachel grabbed her purse as she reacted to the threat. The man was herding everyone from the first and business class cabins to the rear and forcibly pushing people into seats. She tripped on her way to the economy cabin but caught herself and kept moving.

Rachel underwent the State Department's hostage training classes administered by the Bureau of Diplomatic Security when she entered the foreign service a few years earlier. The instructor reminded the class to blend in, not to stand out from the crowd, and to remain anonymous. She kept her eyes down, moved quickly without being too obvious, and did what she was told.

Rachel moved to the rear of the cabin and slid quickly in the center seat in the middle row of the cabin. While watching the four men who continued herding passengers to the back of the plane, she removed a credit card from her wallet and swiped it through the telephone provided at her seat. She dialed the State Department and waited for the call to be answered.

"Department of State Operations Center, Rich Carter."

"Rich, this is Rachel Becker from Post in Abu Dhabi. I'm on Emirates flight 001 from Dubai to London, and we've been hijacked."

Carter snapped his fingers and pointed to his ear. Several desk officers punched into his line to listen to the conversation.

"Rachel, we're checking status now." He handed one officer a note with her name and location. He got an immediate thumbs-up that a woman named Rachel Becker was indeed a political officer stationed in Abu Dhabi.

"Rachel, please tell us your mother's maiden name." Carter was running through his checklist to verify the authenticity of the call and identification of the caller.

"Blankenship. They're coming. I'll call back when I can." Rachel placed the phone in the holder in the seatback in front of her and looked down.

With four men moving about the cabin and all of the passengers in the economy section of the airplane, Rachel knew she was taking a huge risk by contacting the Operations Center on the phone. She dialed again, and Rich answered immediately.

"Carter."

"Rich, this is Rachel. There are four men in the rear of the cabin armed with handguns. They moved us all into coach. I don't know where they got the weapons."

"Rachel, be very careful they don't see you. What nationality do they look to be? What language are they speaking?" Carter was concerned with her safety but realized she was the only firsthand information they had available.

"Their dialect sounds North African, but not Maghrebi," she replied. Rich understood she believed they were Egyptian or Libyan, not the Francophone countries of Morocco, Algeria, and Tunisia.

"John, get DoD on the line and let them know what's going on. See if they can get Fifth Fleet and Sixth Fleet HRTs spun up. We don't know where they're headed, so let's be prepared for both regions." Carter directed that the Department of Defense be contacted and to mobilize the hostage rescue teams in the Persian Gulf and the Mediterranean.

"I'm on with them now." The desk officer continued his discussion with an army lieutenant colonel at the Pentagon.

"Rachel, we're moving an HRT to you. Let us know if you hear where they're going and what they want."

"Rich, he's coming again." The line went dead.

Rachel put the handset back, sat back in her seat, and forced herself to not look at the man coming down the aisle.

As the duty officer, Rich Carter was responsible for the tactical response to the situation, leaving the strategic—read *political*—response to the secretary of state, the vice president, and ultimately the president herself. Carter had eleven years of service at State and was three months short of finishing his tour in the operations center.

His immediate task was to inform the community, the elements of the U.S. government responsible for the military or police responses to incidents such as this one. Paul Smith was already coordinating with

DoD, and he knew Roberta Conley was talking with the Situation Room in the White House.

His phone rang again. "Carter."

"Mr. Carter, this is Ned Walker at the Federal Aviation Administration. I understand you are talking to one of your folks aboard a hijacked Emirates flight. Can you fill me in?"

"Mr. Walker, we'll call you back at the approved number. Stand by for our call." Carter wanted to make sure Ned Walker worked for the FAA and that no one outside the core group got information on this operation. He was keeping this on a strict need-to-know basis as required by the procedures in effect.

"Stephen, please call Ned Walker at FAA and fill him in. Thanks."

Carter returned to Paul for an update on DoD. "What assets do they have, Paul?"

"Rich, there's no HRT in the Med right now, so they're going to run this op with Fifth Fleet assets from the Gulf. They'll launch a Gulfstream from Minhad Air Base near Dubai as soon as the team flies in from the Gulf of Oman. The ship is transiting the Strait of Hormuz south to north. They're getting their gear together and will be on the helicopter in fifteen minutes." Paul was talking as he was being briefed by the duty officer at the Pentagon.

"Please get me the names and ranks of the team. The secretary will want to know."

Carter knew the secretary of state was a retired army lieutenant general, a close friend of the president's, and she always wanted to know who was going in harm's way. Carter didn't advertise that the secretary also was his mother. With four dozen Carters in the department, no one suspected any affiliation beyond the name. "Also, get the duty officer in Dubai on the hook. I need to speak with him."

"Her. It's Robyn Ridley. I've got her holding on line 2."

"Kaire, please find someone who can tell us where the plane is in real time. Also see who can give us likely locations where it's going and when it might land."

"I'm on it, Rich." The woman returned to her desk and flipped through her Rolodex.

"Robyn, this is Rich Carter, duty officer at State. Sorry to get you up so late."

"Hi, Rich. What's up?" Robyn was at home after attending a diplomatic reception and had already been asleep for three hours. *This is why we get the big bucks, isn't it?* she asked herself.

Carter filled her in on the situation and asked her to contact Ambassador Dunford in Abu Dhabi and Consul General Lukeman in Dubai. "We're going to need landing rights and overflight clearance from the authorities in Dubai for the G-4 out of Minhad as well as permission from the Emirates team to conduct the hostage rescue. Can you get that quickly?"

"I don't think that will be a problem, Rich. I know the guys at Civil Aviation, and they can help me get to the right people at the Ministry of Defense. I'll talk to Emirates and see what they have too."

"Thanks, Robyn. I'll pass you back to Paul. Please make sure you stay close to him." Carter hung up.

Stephen returned to Carter. "They don't have anyone by the name of Ned Walker at FAA, or Edward Walker or Ted Walker. They have two Walkers, and they're both women." Rich was curious and made himself a note to check it out later.

Where's Rachel? he asked himself. Although he didn't know her, he had read some of the traffic from Abu Dhabi she wrote, mostly political/ economic stuff and well done, particularly for such a junior officer. She had great access to good information.

Rachel was waiting for another chance to check in with State. One of the men stood near her row for ten minutes, scanning the cabin for anyone he might consider a threat.

Charlie Davenport at the Emirates headquarters took the call from Robyn Ridley, whom she had met at the annual U.S. Independence Day party a few months before. She knew immediately that this wasn't a social call, as much because it was the first time Robyn ever called her and because it was well after midnight. The plane had been airborne just under thirty minutes and was still over Iran heading north before turning west over Turkey.

"Hi Robyn, this is Charlie. This can't be good."

"Charlie, we have a friendly aboard EK 001 reporting that the plane has been taken over by at least five armed men of unknown origin and intent. Anything to report on your end?"

"Who's the friendly?" Charlie was already asking one of her subordinates for the flight manifest.

"I can't confirm that to you on an open line—OPSEC." Robyn hesitated for just a second while referring to operational security. "But you know her," Charlie added just as she recognized Rachel's name on the manifest.

Davenport relayed the events of the last thirty minutes to Robyn, and they agreed to keep each other updated throughout the ordeal.

"OK. Let me give you a discrete number where you can reach me immediately. You won't have to go through the switchboard. What do you need from me?" Charlie checked the roster again to see if they had an air marshal on board 001. Anticipating Robyn's question, she said, "No LEO on board, unfortunately." Law enforcement officers were routinely assigned to flights on a random basis; they certainly needed one tonight, but there was none on this flight.

Rachel managed to make another call to the operations center. As soon as Rich answered, she started talking.

"I need your cellphone number so I can send text messages to you. I can't keep calling like this—it's too dangerous, and I'll get caught."

Rich gave her his cell phone number, and she immediately hung up. Within seconds, his phone vibrated indicating a text message had arrived.

`Passenger 57 checking in from seat 46E. R u there?`

Rich laughed to himself because she was using the eponymous Wesley Snipes movie to communicate with him. He answered her immediately.

```
I'm here. Any change?

None. Don't txt me unless I text you so my fon doesn't
vibrat when theyr near me.
```

The man next to Rachel asked her who she was speaking with.

"I'm just letting my family know I'm here," she said, still careful not to divulge too much to the stranger even though he appeared genuine.

"Next time would you ask them to call my wife and tell her I'm here too. My name is Don Stinson. I'm just returning from a mission trip in Pakistan for the church I pastor in Houston." He gave her his home phone number and his wife's name.

"Sure, Pastor. I'm Rachel."

First Lieutenant Paul Stephens was preparing his assault team for the helicopter lift into the United Arab Emirates to link up with the Gulfstream. As part of the Maritime Special Purpose Force, or MSPF, they trained for hostage rescue missions as well as deep reconnaissance, clandestine recovery of personnel and equipment, close-quarter battle, and special demolitions. Drawn from the direct action platoon of the deployed Marine Force Reconnaissance unit, Stephens' team was normally paired with a Navy SEAL platoon, but that unit was currently in Afghanistan conducting operations against Al Qaeda. Paul's HRT was executing this mission alone.

Stephens was selected for captain but had not yet pinned on the new rank. After serving successfully as weapons platoon commander and company executive officer in First Battalion Eighth Marines, or 1/8, he was assigned to Second Force Reconnaissance Battalion and saw action in Iraq and Afghanistan. Well decorated for a junior officer, Paul was in his element leading Marines in combat.

"Make sure we have breaching kits. The target is a Boeing 747. We have fourteen seats on the G-4, so we're limited on who we can take and how much gear we can carry. The assault team will take what it needs—no palletized gear." Paul was briefing Gunnery Sergeant Roger Pippins, his platoon sergeant.

"Lieutenant, I recommend a two-man sniper team. The assault team gets the rest of the seats with you and me. I'll have Sixth Fleet standing by with parachutes in case we need them, as well as any other equipment we can't get on the plane. We'll take the corpsman as part of the assault team, sir." He wanted to make sure they had medical expertise for the types of trauma they were likely to face on missions such as these. Gunny Pippins had twelve years' experience in this business and knew how to get things done quickly. As soon as he got the nod from the lieutenant, he was off to make it happen. He was, after all, in his "office."

Under normal circumstances Paul would have a covering element from the reinforced battalion embarked on the amphibious shipping. Part of the Marine Expeditionary Unit, the battalion trained with the MSPF in the months leading up to the deployment to provide seamless support to the strike unit. Time and distance worked against him since the jumbo jet was moving away from them and the airlift was limited in the time he had to execute this mission. He would be taking thirteen Marines and one sailor, no more.

As his team was preparing for the mission, Paul took the opportunity to brief the MEU commander, Colonel Charles Starling, along with the Amphibious Squadron commander, navy captain Andy Franklin on their progress. "We packed light because of the ride on the G-4, but we've asked Sixth Fleet for support. I doubt we'll need much more, but it'll be there if we do. The Emirates flight is still over northwestern Iran. There's been no radio contact, and air traffic control has just been trying to keep everyone out of its path. There's a State Department officer on board feeding info to their ops center on the bad guys. Anything else, sir?"

Starling spoke first. "Paul, we have already agreed with Sixth Fleet that we'll retain operational control, so you'll talk to us throughout the mission. If the situation changes and we have to relinquish OPCON, we'll let you know. If so, we have a list of the senior officers on the Sixth Fleet staff you'll deal with. We're still waiting on landing clearance for the G-4. Emirates approved our direct action on their airplane, so it's a matter of waiting to see where they land and see if we have permission from that country to act."

"Aye aye, sir. I'll be on the net, gentlemen." Paul returned to the flight deck to finish preparing for the mission.

Rachel contacted Rich Carter to let him know she could communicate for a few minutes. Rich asked her by text message if she could call.

"What's new?" she asked when he answered the phone.

"We have a Marine Corps assault team preparing to trail your plane until you land somewhere. What are you wearing?"

Rachel thought that was an odd question but answered Rich. He gave her what details he had and finished the call.

"Save your phone battery and contact me in half an hour."

Rachel hung up.

Lieutenant Stephens and Gunny Pippins finished preparations for the deployment and moved with the unit to stage their gear on the flight deck. The assault team spent the time loading ammunition into magazines for their automatic weapons, Doc Pete Currall checked his medical kit for the items he would need to treat trauma injuries, and the scout-sniper team marked off a makeshift known distance course with which to zero the scope of the caliber .50 sniper rifle, or CFSR.

Sergeant Matthew Hamel was completing his sixth year in the Marine Corps and had spent five years in the Scout-Sniper Platoon after completing boot camp and Advanced Infantry Training. He was experienced from Operation Enduring Freedom and had twenty-two confirmed kills, all of them fired at distances over 800 meters from the targets. He was the best at his job and already had orders to Scout-Sniper School as an instructor to train the Corps' future sharpshooters.

Corporal Steven Yuravich was the second man of the scout-sniper team, the spotter who would find and identify targets for Sergeant Hamel. The two had been working together for three years and were inseparable on the battlefield.

Gunnery Sergeant Pippins moved through the detachment, letting them know it was time to load the helicopter and depart for Dubai. "Saddle up!"

The Marines moved instinctively to the helicopter, having rehearsed this scenario countless times. Each man knew the mission and his job, and each knew the jobs of at least two others in the HRT in the event of casualties. They were equally proficient with the radio, every type of assault weapon, first aid, and lifesaving techniques, tactics, and even foreign languages. They could multitask in the vernacular of the day.

Thirty minutes later, Rachel sent Rich Carter a text message.

`Herd them taking abt Italy. Cn u confirm?`

Rachel wasn't yet sure where in Italy they were heading but wanted to give Rich as much notice as possible.

`Nothing yet. We r talkin w/Italy now. Hw r u?`

The man in the left seat of the cockpit dialed in radio frequency 118.45, which he knew to be the tower's main approach frequency and was manned twenty-four hours a day.

"Pantelleria Approach, this is Emirates flight 001 declaring an emergency. We do not have approach plates for your airport. Please give me orientation of your runways, sir."

Valentina La Noce was completely unaware of an Emirates flight heading her direction. "Emirates 001, Pantelleria Approach, we have two runways, 03/21 and 08/26. Please state your intentions, sir."

"Pantelleria, Emirates 001, which runway is longer?"

"Emirates 001, Pantelleria, 08/26 is eighteen hundred meters. What equipment are you?"

"Pantelleria, Emirates 001, we are a Boeing 747. I need seventeen hundred meters to land, so there should be no problem."

Valentina stared into her radio, incredulous that a pilot would suggest an additional hundred meters would mean there was no problem. "Emirates 001, Pantelleria Approach, you are not cleared to land due to limited runway length. Divert to Tunis-Carthage Airport, contact Approach Control on 118.1, good day, sir." She turned to contact Tunis Airport.

"Pantelleria Approach, Emirates 001. Madam, thank you for the recommendation, but I have dinner reservations at Albergo Ristorante La Tavernetta that I don't want to miss. Please make preparations for us to land there in about ninety minutes. Emirates 001 out."

He's risking the lives of everyone on board so he won't miss dinner? Valentina asked herself. She turned to report this unusual conversation just as her supervisor handed her the notice from the civil aviation authorities about a hijacked Emirates flight.

```
I herd them say pantelleria. Do we have pepl ther?
```

Rachel messaged Rich as soon as she heard the hijackers talking about it.

```
Wait.
```

Rich got his people focused on the island of Pantelleria, the southernmost spot in Europe and thirty miles east of the North African country of Tunisia. Less than ten miles long and only five miles wide, the volcanic island had not witnessed an eruption in over three thousand years. One of the analysts in the Bureau of Intelligence and Research, or INR, retrieved what information he had on the island and its history. Rich already sent the information Rachel provided to the Department of Defense, and they were scrambling the Gulfstream to land at Pantelleria before the Emirates flight arrived.

"We have a problem," the analyst began with a sense of urgency, "because the longer of the two runways at Pantelleria is only fifty-nine hundred feet, and the landing distance for the 747 at six feet above sea level—the elevation of the runway—is about fifty-five hundred feet. They'll be way down on fuel so that could shave five hundred feet off the landing distance. We're still critical even assuming he hits the runway right at the threshold. Bottom line: Pantelleria can't handle a 747 landing."

"What's the best they can do on a short field landing?" Rich asked the analyst.

"I'll get on the hook with Boeing and see what they say." The analyst moved back to his desk and was immediately on the phone.

Paul Smith had an open line to the DoD command center, and Rich asked that they be put on speaker phone.

"General, this is Rich Carter. I'm the duty officer at State. What do you have on your end?"

"Rich, Frank Duggan here. We had the G-4 move ahead, and the assault team will be on the island twenty minutes ahead of the Emirates plane. I understand one of your officers is on board and reporting back."

"Yes, General, we have a political officer on board from the embassy in Abu Dhabi who's coming home on leave. She's the only link we have with the plane right now. I understand from the FAA that there has been no communication with the pilot after the first exchange. We don't know who they are, what they want, or what their intentions are."

"Same on this end, Rich. Our assault team can enter the airplane through one of the doors or through a breach they create. Our only motivation is to get everyone out alive, including the bad guys if we can. If we can't, well, they chose this course of action, we didn't."

They traded information on the expected destination of the Emirates flight and the requirements from State and Defense once the plane was on the ground.

"OK, General. I suggest we leave this line open so there's no delay in communication. Paul Smith is here as your point of contact. Please let him know what you need and he'll get it."

"Rich, I'm out of pages in my passport. Can someone help me out with that?" The general laughed as he said it.

"No problem, sir. When this is all over, come on down and I'll personally hook you up." Rich laughed and passed the phone to Paul.

Sounds like a good guy, Rich thought with the smile still on his face. He made a mental note to call the general after this crisis to get him over to the department with his passport. *You never know when you need a friend at Defense,* Rich opined to himself, *even if, or perhaps especially because, your mother is the secretary of state.*

The Gulfstream opened the throttles and cut as many corners as it could to reach Pantelleria and landed thirty-five minutes earlier than the Boeing. The plane taxied to a hangar, and the doors were immediately closed behind it so the team could prepare for the assault unobserved.

Paul Stephens watched his Marines going through their mental checklists and gear one more time for the operation. He saw Sergeant Hamel and Corporal Yuravich gather their equipment and prepare to move to positions from which they could provide surveillance and firepower if called on. They quickly scouted and chose the best positions depending on where the plane stopped moving. Although Gunny Pippins had assurance from airport authorities that the plane would be parked on the southeast end of the runway, there was no guarantee the hijackers would play by the rules.

Rachel felt a change in the plane's attitude and realized they had turned farther south toward North Africa. She made note of that in a text message to the State Department, and then as a precaution, she purged all the messages she and Rich had traded back and forth. At about the same time, one of the hijackers caught another passenger attempting to make a telephone call from his seat and shot him in his right eye as everyone screamed. He and another hijacker then moved through the cabin, ripping the remaining telephones from the back of each seat, making further calls impossible.

Rachel sent a text to Rich letting him know why she would not be calling again. Since she still had about half of her battery power left on the mobile phone, she decided to restrict usage to text messages and not use the phone for calls unless absolutely necessary. She did not want to lose contact with Rich, but calling was an unnecessary risk when a text message would suffice.

Hamel and Yuravich moved quickly as they scouted firing positions around the airport. They had commandeered a small pickup truck, and Hamel drove while Yuravich made a rough map indicating the locations of recognizable landmarks. They had four hasty positions identified in fifteen minutes.

"Terminator 3, this is Terminator 6. Over."

Hamel answered Lieutenant Stephens' radio call. "Roger 6, this is 3. Go."

"Three, we have Emirates inbound for landing in one five mikes. They're dumping fuel now. How copy? Over."

"Six, solid copy. Will confirm our position after 001 stops rolling but likely to be position Alpha 4. Over."

"Three, roger. Out."

Paul knew Hamel and Yuravich would be there when he needed them and had no doubt about their ability to get the job done. They knew what his intent was and understood his guidance; they were used to mission orders wherein they were told *what* to do and left to figure out *how* on their own. They worked much better that way and actually produced better results if given plenty of maneuver room.

The assault team took hide positions so they could approach the plane undetected regardless of which way the nose of the aircraft pointed when it stopped rolling. They had run a hundred simulated takedown operations in 747s this year alone, and they knew the plane inside and out. The breach techniques they used were designed to get into the airplane without igniting the fuel cells or injuring the passengers, and they could also enter from a window or door, forward or aft, from under the airplane or from above.

Gunnery Sergeant Pippins was the first to see the landing lights in the distance. "Stand by. Aircraft approaching from the northeast." He spoke rapidly into the radio so the Marines could get oriented and ready for the assault.

Yuravich looked north and saw the plane on final approach. "Will you take out the landing gear when they're facing us?" he asked Sergeant Hamel.

"Yep." Hamel was already concentrating on his shot and imprinted the landmarks in his peripheral vision that he would need once the plane landed. So much of his upcoming work was instinctive although he went through his mental checklist another time to ensure he could deliver when and where required.

"Pantelleria Approach, Emirates 001 on short final to runway 26. Please have the fuel truck standing by and keep all security and police away from the plane. No one approaches the plane, do you understand?"

Valentina knew only that U.S. military forces were at the airport, and she had been instructed to promise the hijackers whatever they needed to keep them calm and talking. There were three people in civilian clothes standing near her, presumably Americans, perhaps officials from their government, and they had been given complete access to the control tower. They would occasionally say something to her supervisor, who would then tell Valentina what to do or say.

"Emirates 001, Pantelleria Approach, we strongly urge you to abort landing and divert to Tunis Carthage. They have longer runways and can handle a 747. Contact Tunis Approach Control on 118.1. Over."

"My dear, I appreciate your concern, but we're coming to visit you. No one approaches the airplane. Do you understand?"

"Emirates 001, roger. How will we get fuel to you?" Valentina asked the question relayed from the Americans to her boss.

"We'll let you know. Now clear everyone away from the runway and stay out of our way. Emirates 001 out."

Rachel could see the ground coming up quickly as the plane settled toward the runway. She sent a text to Carter asking if there was anything else she should do, and his immediate reply was to stay calm and stay down.

The plane's landing gear hit the ground hard just before the threshold, and the passengers fully understood the pilot was standing on the brakes trying to stop it in a hurry. Rachel could smell something burning, presumably the tires and the brake pads made of nickel, aluminum oxide, and lead tungstate with beryllium lining.

As the Jumbo Jet stopped, Rachel thought she felt the plane tilt forward as though stumbling off a low stair step. She glanced down as the text message came in from Rich Carter that snipers had shot the front tires out so the plane couldn't be moved any further, and he warned her again to stay down.

"We have go for takedown," Lieutenant Stephens ordered into his radio. The fact that the hijackers already killed one passenger meant the situation changed to in extremis, and they were not required, expected, or even encouraged to negotiate with the hostiles. Paul readied his weapon and moved with the assault force toward the rear of the plane.

Sergeant Hamel could see the pilot in the left seat of the flight deck and another hijacker moving in and out of the open cockpit door. Corporal Yuravich reported one body in a large pool of blood lying on the floor near the open door on the left side of the fuselage, and he could see the pilot talking excitedly on the radio.

"Terminator 6, this is Terminator 3. Mentor Cabot times three." Corporal Yuravich gave the call sign indicating that they had a clear shot to the pilot plus two others reasonably assumed to be bad guys.

"Three, this is 6, stand by." Paul wanted to time the breach, using the sniper shots to maximize surprise and minimize casualties.

Sergeant Hamel saw smoke from the exhaust of the fuel truck in his peripheral vision to his right front. The pilot was obviously ordering the airport authorities to provide him more fuel, still unaware that he had no front tires on which to taxi back to the runway. The fuel truck was actually empty, so a stray round wouldn't accidentally set off an explosion.

He also saw the assault force moving in from the rear of the aircraft, the only real blind spot for anyone inside the plane. The hijackers were busy getting the stairs situated by the open door, and one of them actually started climbing down the stairs.

Hamel counted three targets in his field of view. He had a clear shot at three of the five hijackers they were aware of, and he mentally checked off how he would engage the targets when given permission to shoot. The pilot was of little threat to the passengers as long as he stayed on the flight deck, so he would be last on Hamel's list. The man on the stairs would also be less of a threat, but he clearly had a weapon, so he would be second. The third man, the one going in and out of the cockpit with an obvious weapon in his right hand, would be the primary target since he was the one Hamel could see who could get to the passengers quickest. He was constantly validating those assumptions so he would be ready when he got the order to shoot.

Paul already had permission for the assault and was waiting until his Marines were in place. When the door opened on the left side of the airplane, he fought the urge to begin the attack. Even hanging out of the door, the hijacker couldn't see behind the airplane on the right side where the assault team had already moved into position.

"We have a confirmed friendly in 46 Echo, no air marshals on board. We have at least five hostiles, maybe more. Hit what you shoot at and keep the bad shots to a minimum. Gunny Pippins, we're good to go!" Paul kept his voice steady and the pitch normal in spite of the adrenaline coursing through his bloodstream right then.

"Three, this is 6. Weapons free after entry." Paul told Sergeant Hamel that he could shoot once the assault team breached the fuselage of the airplane and started into the cabin.

After Sergeant Hamel acknowledged the instructions, he ran another sweep of the bad guys and found he actually had a visual on a fourth man standing in the front cabin with what appeared to be a weapon in his hand. He saw the flash of the small explosive used to open a hatch in the rear of the airplane, and he saw the assault team head into the fuselage.

The sniper rifle he was using, the CFSR, is a line of sight direct fire system capable of engaging targets out to 2,000 meters or about 6,500 feet. When they arrived at their current position, Corporal Yuravich surveyed it at a thousand meters from the target, about thirty-three hundred feet, or roughly six-tenths of a mile. Sergeant Hamel already had the data dialed into his scope and had adjusted for night shooting, the slight left-to-right breeze from the south, and the humidity, all of which had an effect on the trajectory of his shots.

"I see four targets. Number 1 is white shirt behind pilot, number 2 is on the ladder, number 3 is the pilot, and number 4 is in dark shirt in business class if he moves forward. If he doesn't, I'll hit him with one of the Norwegian rounds." He didn't need to tell Yuravich the high explosive rounds were capable of penetrating two inches of steel.

"Confirm four targets, free to engage." Corporal Yuravich would be feeding Sergeant Hamel constant updates as the noncommissioned officer focused on the targets in order.

Sergeant Hamel previously had loaded the ten-round magazine with four standard ball rounds, followed by two high-explosive rounds manufactured in Norway, and four more standard ball rounds. In a second magazine, he had ten ball rounds, and in a third magazine, he had ten more high explosive rounds. He reached down to check their location next to him again, something he did constantly and unconsciously, like a man reaches for his cigarettes twenty years after he stops smoking.

"Breach, breach, breach!" Hamel heard over the radio.

He took up the slack of the adjustable trigger pull and felt the weapon cough the first round downrange to the plane. Before it settled back into firing position, Corporal Yuravich confirmed kill number 1, and Sergeant Hamel was already aiming at the man on the stairs. He squeezed the trigger and saw the man's upper torso explode as the round hit him in the sternum.

With practiced routine, Hamel brought the weapon to bear on the pilot as Corporal Yuravich adjusted his M16 for a shot. The stretched acrylic and high-impact glass window of the cockpit would deflect the first round that hit it even as it shattered, so the two scout-snipers developed a technique wherein Yuravich would fire a round to break the glass and Hamel would follow with the kill shot. They had used this procedure before with great success and had practiced it whenever the mission called for shooting through a window.

"Four . . . three . . . two . . ." Yuravich shot as the countdown reached two. "One" Hamel squeezed the trigger, saw the pilot explode in his seat, and immediately swung the rifle to reacquire the fourth target.

Lieutenant Stephens was first into the rear cabin and was followed closely by the remainder of the assault team. Since they were confident all red forces were inside the airplane, there was no need to put a covering force outside. Besides, Hamel and Yuravich could warn him of a threat outside and dispense with most of them without even informing Paul.

Coming in from behind the hostages, he was required to assess the situation on the run. The intent was to put himself and the assault team between the bad guys and the passengers in the rear cabin, to be a human shield and protect them from harm. That said, there was a real threat from sleepers, hijackers who pretended to be passengers unless needed. It was a common tactic, and one that Stephens and his team had planned for.

Paul knew the Italian police and security forces were now surrounding the plane and would not allow anyone outside a defined area. They would take the passengers off, and law enforcement would go through the tedious process of checking bona fides. They were unwilling to let one of the hijackers follow the real passengers out and walk away from the scene.

As he passed from the rear cabin toward the front of the airplane, he found seat 46E and reached out to touch Rachel's shoulder.

"I'm Paul. I'll be back in a minute." The woman nodded at him and put her head back down.

He was momentarily stunned by the woman's physical beauty, and it took a full second to clear his head before refocusing on the mission at hand. *She's incredible*, he said to himself. *Why don't I ever have a good-looking woman like that sitting next to me on an airplane?* He privately chastised himself for getting distracted in the middle of an op, just as he fired at and hit a man wielding a Glock at the front of the passenger cabin.

The assault team continued forward. Sergeant Richard Meeks from Buckhannon, West Virginia, moved past Paul and raised his weapon to fire at the only remaining hijacker who was standing next to the open door in the business class cabin.

Sergeant Hamel knew his field of fire extended only as far to the right as the back of the business class cabin. Any shot he fired to the right of that point might hit friendlies, so he was limited to the cockpit and business class. He confirmed the fourth target he and Corporal

Yuravich identified was just inside the open door. He fired the one remaining ball round in a safe direction, knowing that the next two rounds were high explosives that could easily punch through the hull of the Boeing. He saw the shadow of the fourth target, gauged center mass of the man's upper torso, and squeezed off the shot.

Before he could get a shot off, Meeks watched as the man disintegrated in front of him. He knew the explosive round belonged to Sergeant Hamel and reminded himself at that moment he was glad they were on the same team. He signaled Lieutenant Stephens, who called cease-fire to the scout-sniper team, letting them know that they were danger close, or extremely close to hitting friendly forces.

It also told Hamel and Yuravich that their mission shifted from shooting to surveillance, and they were additionally required to notify their higher headquarters of the progress of the mission. Hamel's four kill shots had taken ten seconds in total, with four confirmed dead at over half a mile, bringing his career total to twenty-six.

As each Marine in the assault team moved into position and gave a thumbs-up, Gunnery Sergeant Pippins checked to make sure all the identified hijackers were down. He counted five bodies, four clearly the work of Sergeant Hamel.

"All clear, Lieutenant." He stood next to Paul and gave the Marines the signal to start moving the passengers out the back door that was now open. "And that, gentlemen, is the way it's done," Pippins said.

Stephens and Pippins moved together toward seat 46E to find Rachel. As she stood to thank him, a woman in the rear of the cabin stood and fired one round from a small .22 caliber handgun at the three Americans before she and the woman next to her—the two women originally wearing the chopsticks the hijackers used to stab the pilots—were knocked down, disarmed, and bound by the Marines nearest them.

"Gunny, get Doc Currall ASAP." Paul looked down at Rachel, now slumped down in her seat. The woman's shot hit Rachel on the right side of her head and likely penetrated the skull.

Paul moved Rachel into the aisle with the help of Pastor Stinson. "I was talking with her earlier," the preacher said, "and I was amazed at how calm she was considering everything that was going on around us." He introduced himself to Paul, who asked him to stay and comfort Rachel.

"Sorry, Padre," Paul said as he did a quick pat-down to make sure Stinson wasn't carrying a weapon.

"Do your job, Lieutenant. I understand. I was a navy chaplain for twenty-four years." From experience, Stinson knew he was considered a hostile until positively identified as friendly.

"Can you hear me, Rachel? Stay with me. Stay with me." Paul talked to her as the corpsman arrived with his medical kit. One look at the wound, and Doc Currall knew it was so far beyond his capability to help her that he simply shook his head at the lieutenant. Paul heard Gunny Pippins direct one of the Marines to get an ambulance to their location.

Paul could see terror on Rachel's face and in her eyes. There was little blood, enough that it made location of the entry wound obvious, not so much that they couldn't control it.

"All I wanted before I died was to get married, that's all." Rachel mumbled to no one in particular. "I wanted to have a husband, a house with a small garden, three children, and a dog. I just wanted to be married." Paul wasn't sure if she was serious or if it was the effect of being shot in the head.

Doc Currall was checking her pupils and vital signs but knew he was helpless to do anything. He told the lieutenant he was going to coordinate with the doctors when they arrived; Paul saw that the corpsman knew he couldn't help and needed to be somewhere else, somewhere other than here with Rachel, knowing what was obvious and inevitable.

"Rachel," Paul said with the softest voice he could muster, still on a huge adrenaline high after the take down, "I need you to stay with me. Pastor Stinson is here too, and we're going to take good care of you. There's an ambulance coming, and we'll get you to the hospital in a few minutes."

Rachel's eyes opened and cleared for a minute. "Pastor, all I wanted was to be married. Will you marry me?"

Stinson's immediate reaction was confusion. *Who does she want to marry?* he asked himself. *She won't live long enough to get married.*

Rachel insisted. "Please marry me. What's your name, Captain?"

"It's Paul, and I'm a first lieutenant." He immediately felt foolish for offering that last piece of information.

"Will you marry me, First Lieutenant Paul?" Rachel was grasping the sleeve of his camouflage uniform with a sense of urgency he knew was real. "Will you marry me? I just wanted to be married, that's all. I just wanted to be married." Tears ran straight down into her ears, and she broke down sobbing as she repeated her desire to be married.

Doc Currall returned, surprised to find Rachel still alive. Paul pulled Pastor Stinson away from where she was lying in the aisle.

"Can you like, you know, can you do the marriage thing for her?" Paul couldn't believe he was even suggesting this, but the intensity with which she stared at him as she pleaded to be married drilled right into his heart.

"Well, yes, but who is she going to marry?" Dan was still confused at her request and equally confused at Paul's questions.

"I'll marry her right here. It will give her peace of mind before she . . ." He didn't finish the sentence to describe what was obvious and inevitable. "She doesn't know what she's saying with the headshot and all, so if it'll help her go peacefully, then let's do it. What'll it hurt?"

The pastor moved back to where Rachel was on the floor. "Will you stay as a witness?" he asked the corpsman.

"Yes, sir, for what?" Currall was also confused.

Pastor Stinson ignored the question and reached into his bag. Both Marines reacted to what they thought might be a threat and relaxed when he produced a well-worn Bible. He began the ritual but hurried through some parts and deleted others altogether. He got to the end quickly and asked Rachel, "Do you take Paul to be your husband?" He abbreviated the question, asking what at this point in time was the only important question.

"I do, I do, I do." Rachel's voice now was so soft that they all strained to hear her. She was obviously getting weaker, and her eyes were closed more than they were open, tears streaming down her face.

"Paul, do you take Rachel as your wife?"

"I do." Paul's voice was not much louder, the lump in his throat choking off most of the sound.

"I now pronounce you husband and wife. You may now kiss the bride." Paul leaned down and lightly kissed Rachel's lips as he heard her repeating, "I'm married, I'm married."

The paramedics from the ambulance came down the aisle as Rachel whispered to them, "I'm married to First Lieutenant Paul," closed her eyes one last time, a serene smile on her face, and lapsed into a coma toward the inevitable.

Paul would be haunted by her words for months to come. He felt like he failed this woman who had been so strong in reporting the events of the hijacking without concern or fear for her own life. Looking down into her eyes as he moved forward in the plane, and then ten minutes later looking into the eyes that seemed bottomless, he fought his own mind as it drifted back to those few moments when she came into his life and then departed just as quickly.

What a beautiful woman, he often reminded himself. She reached into his soul time and again as no woman ever had, yet he knew nothing about her, save incredible grace in the worst of circumstances and piercing eyes accentuating beauty that took his breath away whenever she frequently entered his thoughts.

Chapter 24

March 7, 2004
Dubai, United Arab Emirates

Newly promoted Captain Paul Stephens waited in Terminal 2—T2 in the vernacular of frequent travelers to London's Heathrow Airport—for Jennifer to arrive from Washington, rechecking the photograph to ensure he recognized her after she cleared customs and entered the arrival hall. Dressed casually and sporting longer hair than he normally wore as a Marine, he looked like a young executive meeting his wife for a holiday. His appearance was intentional; during this trip, he was a businessman, and she was playing the role as his wife.

Jennifer Stephens—they were unrelated but having the same surname actually served them well in this operation—was a Middle East specialist in the Directorate of Analysis at the Central Intelligence Agency, previously serving as an officer in the U.S. Army, most recently at the service's Intelligence and Security Command at Fort Belvoir, Virginia, before joining the Company. She rose quickly up the ranks, and now at thirty-two years old, she was a seasoned officer with several "wins" to her name.

Among them was locating Khalid Jalili, the Libyan identified as being on one of the flights connected to Pan Am 103 sixteen years earlier. Jen, as she preferred to be called, scanned passenger manifests from thousands of flights into and out of London the last two weeks of December 1988, looking for clues to the perpetrators. Her attention focused on a man who arrived from Stockholm the same day as the Lockerbie terrorist bombing, checked into the InterContinental London Park Lane Hotel, checked out the next morning, and flew through Malta to Tripoli.

Jen traced his arrival at Heathrow back to Arlanda Airport in Stockholm and flew there to actually interview ground and terminal staff who worked there at the time of the bombing. One of the baggage handlers mentioned in passing the disappearance of a colleague who he believed was Libyan but was unsure because of the strict labor laws prohibiting asking certain questions of employees. She worked with the human resources department to find the man's file, she tracked down and interviewed the Swedish wife he abandoned on the day of the bombing, and she found the passenger data on him—identified as Mohammed Shalgham—leaving the country later that day. To her knowledge, no one in law enforcement or the intelligence community made the link or had knowledge of Shalgham's apparent complicity in the operation.

By piecing together the puzzle, Jen was able to confirm Jalili's direct involvement in taking down the plane, supported by Shalgham and others still unidentified, at the direction of Jalili's boss and head of security for Libyan Arab Airlines, Abdelbaset Al Megrahi, and sanctioned by the Leader, Colonel Gaddafi. Representing an intelligence coup on par with finding Osama bin Laden in Pakistan seven years later, Jen set about hunting down Jalili so he could be brought to justice. Patience, persistence, and determination paid off. She found him vacationing in Dubai.

Jen had spent several months preparing for an operation that might never happen; they hadn't seen Jalili in several years with repeated assurances that "he just left," stymieing their efforts to locate and apprehend the terrorist. At the Blue Goose, a nondescript CIA training facility at the corner of North Glebe Road and North Fairfax Drive in Ballston, Virginia, she learned some of the black ops techniques she might need if the opportunity arose. Even though she was an analyst, she was the most knowledgeable person in the U.S. government regarding Libyan complicity in the Pan Am 103 bombing, so the training was proactive. She would definitely accompany any operation to bring Jalili to justice, identify him, confiscate any papers or hardware of intelligence value, and to provide other support as needed.

Surveillance cameras at Dubai International Airport photographed him entering the country; it wasn't difficult to learn where he was staying, but the suddenness of his appearance left little time for planning and executing a search-and-capture mission, particularly because many of the Tier 1 assets were already committed to the expanding wars in Afghanistan and Iraq. Jen thought it best to move forward to Dubai while scenarios were being worked out at the highest levels of the National Command Authority. Just before taking off from Dulles International Airport in the nation's capital, she was informed her "husband," Paul, would meet her on arrival at Heathrow.

He recognized her immediately as she entered the Arrivals Hall. "You made it, sweetheart. How was your trip?" Paul greeted her as instructed, with a quick kiss on the lips to make the fictive kinship look real.

"It was so bumpy I spilled my mojito," her programmed reply.

Paul indicated where they needed to go to catch the Emirates nonstop flight to Dubai, departing in just over two hours. They carried identical luggage as married couples would normally do. Jen handed him two first class tickets—he had only ever flown economy—to perpetuate the illusion they were young, wealthy professionals on a vacation to Dubai.

"Go do your husband thing, sweetheart," teasing him as she nodded toward the check-in desk, to which he simply responded, "Yes, dear," and got their boarding passes.

They retreated to a quiet corner in the lounge to await the flight, where Paul took the opportunity to update Jen on details decided while she was still crossing the Atlantic. They boarded with the other first class passengers, were assigned adjacent suites, and took the champagne when it was offered, all in the line of duty.

One stewardess introduced herself as Aneesa and informed them she was from Al Hoceima, a small village on the north coast of Morocco, asking if they had ever visited the kingdom. They assured her it was next on their bucket list, made more attractive when she informed them of the Club Med resort near her hometown. She demonstrated the features of the suite, showed them how to close the door, and pointed out the showers and fully stocked bar at their disposal.

"It's too bad the flight is only seven hours to Dubai," Jen lamented.

Paul wasn't sure if she meant it or whether it was said to support their cover story, and neither was she.

They arrived in Dubai to windy, balmy eighty-degree weather and more sunshine in one day than Washington had seen in the last month. An Emirates staff member escorted the couple through immigration and customs and out to a waiting Rolls-Royce limousine that whisked them to the Burj Al Arab, the iconic self-proclaimed seven-star hotel that opened in 1999 shaped like the sail of a boat and built on an artificial island connected to the mainland by a private causeway, all for a cool billion dollars. Like many things in Dubai, the Burj was over the top, one of the tallest hotels in world with a helipad and a restaurant jutting from the roof almost seven hundred feet above the ground.

"Mr. and Mrs. Stephens, I'm sorry the helicopter was unable to bring you from the airport, but the strong winds today made it dangerous to land on top of the hotel. As compensation, we're offering you a complimentary helicopter tour of the city tomorrow when the weather should be nicer." Boushra was sincere in her apology but thankful she could offer a solution.

Jen spoke up. "Thank you, Boushra. We can be ready around ten tomorrow morning, if that works. I want to spend some time at the pool afterward."

"Yes, ma'am, and you'll return to the hotel not later than noon. I'll make the arrangements and send the booking and instructions to your butler. And I reconfirmed dinner reservations for you at Al Muntaha restaurant at 7:00 p.m." Al Muntaha—"the Ultimate"—is a cantilevered restaurant extending ninety feet from the hotel 660 feet above sea level just below the helipad.

"I also confirmed a couple's session in Talise Spa today at 3:00 p.m. as instructed. It includes a Moroccan bath and the chakra-balancing hot stone massage."

This should be interesting, Paul told himself. Jen was thinking the same as both nodded in approval.

"Finally, your butler, Susanna, has the tickets, guest list, and seating arrangements for tomorrow's reception and dinner party. It begins at 7:00 p.m., it's formal, as you know, and it's in Al Falak Ballroom opposite Al Muntaha. We are so pleased to host the Châine des Rôtisseurs event for this month," she said, referring to the international gastronomic society founded in Paris in 1950. In addition to the outstanding food and wine for which Châine dinners are famous, they knew Khalid also was attending.

"And now let me escort you to the suite. You might know the hotel is 1,053 feet tall with 202 suites, all of them two stories with the living and dining areas downstairs and the sleeping accommodations upstairs. You're in room 2404, as requested, but should you desire to upgrade, we have the Royal Suite available throughout your three-night stay for only twenty-four thousand dollars a night." Boushra smiled and winked as she said that.

Jen replied in the same playful tone, "If it were available all week, we'd take it, but it's not worth it for just three nights, right, Paul?" The U.S. government was already paying thirty-five hundred a night for their room.

"Absolutely, dear, whatever you want."

They settled in quickly, met Susanna, and returned to the lobby under the pretense of going shopping.

"Boushra, do you recommend Dubai Mall or Mall of the Emirates for today?" Jen knew where they were going but asked anyway.

"Mrs. Stephens, should you want to go skiing, Ski Dubai in Mall of the Emirates has a 400-meter-long black diamond run and four easier slopes. Should you want to see Dubai from the observation deck on the hundred twenty-fifth floor of Burj Khalifa, the tallest building in the world, then I suggest Dubai Mall."

The limousine dropped them at Dubai Mall, where they went in and out of the high-end stores pretending to shop; every few minutes, one of Paul's HRT teammates would discreetly hand them a bag. They stopped to have coffee; by the time they paid the bill and stood up to leave, the final two bags were by their table, now totaling seven: Christian Dior, Chanel, and Graff for her, Tom Ford and Canali for him. When they finished shopping, they returned to the limo, still parked immediately outside the door, ignored by the police who were forcing other cars to move along. Wealth—in this case the illusion of wealth—had its privileges.

After returning to the room, they called the butler and ordered a light lunch. When she delivered it, they asked to be alone for a few hours to rest. Paul opened the bags while Jen arranged the equipment for the operation on the dining table. Once they confirmed everything was in order, they packed it away, ate the club sandwiches, drank a beer, and for the first time in the day, relaxed. Paul even fell asleep on the couch.

Paul was relieved that the spa provided disposable shorts for him and a bikini-type ensemble for Jen. Although they advertised their fourth anniversary, hence the holiday, both were apprehensive to take it too far even in the interest of their cover story. They made it through the spa without a wardrobe malfunction, returned to the suite, changed, and prepared for dinner.

The elevator door opened on the twenty-seventh floor; because each floor was actually two stories, they stepped out onto what in reality was fifty-four levels above the lobby, turning left to the reception desk for dinner at Al Muntaha. Because the couple was a little early, they seated Paul and Jen in the Skyview Bar for predinner drinks. Jen ordered a spicy Bloody Mary with celery, while Paul ordered a vodka martini on the rocks with olives, not a twist, in a rocks glass, never feeling comfortable holding a delicate, and in his opinion feminine, conical martini glass, regardless that James Bond drank from one. They were served roasted almonds, dried apricots, and popcorn with black and green olives on the side. They had a spectacular view of the city, Palm Jumeirah in the distance, a pod of dolphins just off the coast, some kids on jet skis getting in one last run, and the setting sun.

Paul scanned the room for security cameras and other sensors, estimating how the same systems on the floor above them would be similarly positioned. He related it all to Jen, who made notations on a notepad she pulled out of her purse, seemingly writing reminders to herself of upcoming girls-night-out dinners, an art exhibition, and other important events. When he excused himself and went to the men's room, he intentionally took a wrong turn and ended up in a service area, eyeing the small elevator used to bring snacks and drinks to the helipad above and offering several excuses as he was escorted back to the common areas.

As they ate, Paul noticed eight of his teammates also having dinner; they would remain clandestine, responding only if the security situation deteriorated. Like Paul and Jen, they came to Dubai from different locations in Europe with seemingly no ties to each other. As Corporal Yuravich passed their table, he surreptitiously dropped a piece of paper with the numbers 2412 on it. Now they had Jalili's room number in case they needed it.

All in all, a good day, they told themselves as they turned in for the evening, Jen in the bedroom, Paul on the couch, staging the bedroom in the morning so the housekeeping staff was none the wiser to their deception.

The city tour the following morning gave them a bird's-eye view from the helicopter, allowing them to confirm facilities and obstacles around the resort that could impact the mission. They took photographs departing from and arriving back to the hotel, measured the distance from the elevator to the helipad, and surveyed the security posture of the contract guards on that floor. They arrived back at the room with more information than they could've hoped for.

Jen went to the pool as she informed Boushra the day before, both to keep the storyline intact and for her desire to get some vitamin D currently in short supply in Washington. She ordered a gin and tonic to document her presence at the pool and chatted with a nearby guest about the hotel and its many features, talking like tourists would; no one guessed the other woman was Lance Corporal Samar Hamwi, part of the team whom Jen was updating on what they learned that morning.

Paul sat in the coffee shop reading *The Wall Street Journal* and drinking coffee, occasionally chatting with a table of men nearby who were playing cards and having an early beer. At their invitation, he pulled his chair closer to them so he wasn't disturbing other guests; the waitress even helped him slide the chair next to one of the men. They continued talking, now much quieter, and he updated them on the helipad and the guards surrounding it. They occasionally laughed or cheered as one or the other won a hand, and remained in place for another hour after Paul excused himself and met Jen at the pool.

"What's this for, Paul?" Jen spoke loudly enough that several of the guests could hear the conversation.

"I feel bad, but I have to leave this evening after dinner to catch a flight to Singapore. We had a major problem with the manufacturer, and the client wants me there to sort it out. Will you forgive me?"

Jen opened the package and held up a tennis bracelet encircled with one-karat diamonds; the approving audience had no idea they were simulants.

"Well, I hope you don't make this a habit, but there are some earrings in the Harry Winston store downstairs I like," she said, her words accompanied with a coquettish smile.

"I know, and that's why I got this," Paul said, reaching into his pocket and retrieving another small box.

Jen opened it to find the earrings inside; they were real but actually given to Jen by her parents a few years earlier when she graduated from college. "Then I forgive you, sweetheart!"

Jen was wearing a royal blue full-length gown with gold-and-silver heels, accentuating her height and beauty—and of course, the earrings and tennis bracelet Paul gave her earlier at the pool—turning the heads of both men and women as she and Paul walked into the reception area above and surrounding the ballroom. He was wearing a black tuxedo with white shirt, dark-gray bowtie and cummerbund, and suede shoes. They blended in perfectly with the decorative ribbons and medals indicating their time and rank in the organization they were provided as part of their cover story.

The Châine des Rôtisseurs originated in 1248 with the founding of a professional guild of goose roasters, expanding later to include all game, poultry, and meat. The brotherhood grew over the four-hundred-year beginning of its history until it was disbanded in 1793, along with other guilds, during the French Revolution, possibly lost to history had four Frenchmen not resurrected it, still based on the traditions and practices of the ancient French organization but now in an international and contemporary context. Paul and Jen had enough information to present a credible story if asked about their participation in the gourmet club.

They spotted Khalid chatting with three men who appeared interested in what he was saying. Jen made her way to the bar and ordered drinks, intentionally stepping in front of Khalid, although he had already noticed. She ignored him, rightly assuming it would motivate him to try harder. He excused himself from the discussion, following her across the room to her table.

"I'm Khalid," he announced as though she should already know that.

"Good evening, Khalid."

"May I join you?"

"I believe the seats are already assigned. Aren't you on the table with the redheaded woman in the green gown who's glaring at me?" Jen put him on notice that she was aware of her surroundings.

He ignored her question. "I'm sure I can get reassigned to this table and this seat," he said with both hands on the chair next to hers.

"If you sit there, where would you suggest my husband sit?"

"I'm sure he would enjoy meeting my date for the evening"—most likely a prostitute, as was his penchant—"although I'm not even sure what language she speaks." He seemed amused with his response.

Paul waited until the hook was set and then moved to the table.

"Here he is now. Paul, please meet—what did you say your name was?—Khalid, who was gentlemanly enough to escort me to my seat."

"I'm pleased to meet you, Khalid, and thank you for taking care of my girl," Paul said, slapping the Libyan on the back in appreciation.

Khalid acknowledged Paul's greeting; because guests were asked to be seated, he bid them both a nice evening and returned to his date.

Paul and Jen conversed with their tablemates and chatted about their vacation, their new home in Dayton—neither had ever visited Ohio—and other superficial items as they went about the exquisite dinner. One of the ladies, who was sitting a few chairs over from Jen at the pool, asked to see the bracelet and earrings, confirming to others at the table they were gifts from Paul because he had to leave their Dubai holiday early.

Promptly at 2200, he stood, wished everyone a pleasant evening, kissed Jen on the lips and confirmed he'd see her by the weekend, and then departed the dinner party, speaking loudly enough for the surrounding tables to hear. Because he knew Khalid was watching the scene, Paul made no effort to look in his direction.

The dinner went on for another ninety minutes, followed by coffee and pousse-café, digestifs normally taken neat. Jen had an Armagnac brandy from the southwest of France; the entire table followed suit, assuming she was well versed in the ways of the Châine and knew the best drink to follow the meal. She completed the illusion by describing how Armagnac is distilled in column stills rather than pot stills, using a blend of Baco 22A, Colombard, Folle blanche, and Ugni blanc grapes. They listened in rapt attention, clapping when she finished the soliloquy.

As the party broke up and guests drifted back to the reception area, Khalid made his way to her side.

"You never told me your name." It was half question and half statement.

"Does it matter?"

He didn't answer, but took it as a signal of her interest to move their budding relationship to the next level, confirmed as she gave the slightest nod toward the exit and handed him the small envelope from her room key.

"Give me twenty minutes." And with that, she was gone, saying good night to those she had met throughout the evening on her way out of the ballroom.

Khalid knocked on the door at the appointed time and was surprised when she opened it immediately, having already changed into a deep-red diaphanous peignoir that accentuated her toned and tanned body and left little to the imagination. An open bottle of champagne sat in a bucket full of ice, strawberries in a dish to the side.

She poured each a flute of Krug Grande Cuvée Brut and motioned to the sofa, where he sat with his back to the window. It was too dark to see the water anyway despite the waning moon overhead; besides, he wasn't interested in the water below in the least.

As Jen approached with the champagne, he felt a sting in his neck followed immediately by strong arms reaching over the couch, pinning him down.

Neuromuscular-blocking drugs work first to paralyze the vocal cords before causing skeletal muscles to relax, shutting off transmission at the neuromuscular junction through action on the post-synaptic acetylcholine receptors. In Khalid's case, it was the drug succinylcholine, a synthetic compound popular in emergency medicine. He tried calling out, but his voice box simply wouldn't respond. He could see but not feel a tube being inserted into his trachea, making it immediately easier to breathe but terrifying him in the process. His outer clothes were replaced with a black jumpsuit and boots, his hands bound with flexicuffs, and another injection caused his muscles to become rigid. They propped him up like a scarecrow.

Two men quickly moved him to the corridor outside the suite and down the hallway to a service entrance; he was aware the lights were off in the hall, but his senses were overloaded to the point that he was unsure where he was or what was happening. He was placed in the dumbwaiter with one of the men and felt they were rising. Upon reaching the top, the door opened, and two other men pulled him from the elevator and moved him to the helipad; neither his fight nor flight reflexes were working, but his fright instincts were operating on overtime, believing they were going to throw him off the building to his death six hundred feet below, bolstered by them moving him to the edge of the helipad. His next emotion was weightlessness . . . falling . . . silence.

With chemicals coursing through his brain, Khalid didn't realize the men had snapped him into a harness for a tandem jump with Paul. The MC1-1C parabolic parachute opened immediately after leaving the platform, with Paul steering it out to sea in the almost-black night sky. They floated silently westward, confident that no one on the shore or at the hotel could see them in the dark. A single strobe blinked, bobbing slightly in the sea, pacing the pair's speed and direction.

At the last second, Paul pulled the steering lines to slow the chute and direct it to the aft section of a small boat, landing gently with Khalid still immobile from the drugs. The Libyan was unhooked from the harness and taken below, after which the pilot opened the throttles. A few miles out into international waters, Khalid was hoisted onto USS *Reuben James,* where he was locked in the brig until being transferred by helicopter to Sigonella. Paul lost track of him after that.

Jen checked out the next morning, bid Boushra farewell while lamenting Paul's early departure for business, boarded a flight for London, and was back at her desk at Langley the following day. Her determination helped close another episode in the global war on terror. She used Khalid's room key while the hotel's security systems were still disabled to collect his laptop, mobile phones, and a briefcase from his suite, in and out in a minute without being detected. Now they were being analyzed in the basement of the CIA headquarters.

All the guards on the helipad deck were mysteriously incapacitated for thirty minutes in the early-morning hours, unsure of what happened or why, although the video surveillance system showed nothing nefarious occurred while they were unconscious; many assumed it was caused by a gas leak, but they were unable to determine the source. Paul returned to his team aboard USS *Nassau* to prepare for the next mission, not realizing he was now a marked man.

It would be less than twenty-four hours before those present at the pool were asked to recall the episode confirming why Paul was not with her when Jen checked out the next morning. A quick review of the Emirates flight manifest indicated that Paul Stephens checked in at 2300 and flew to Singapore on the 0200 flight to solve a manufacturing problem on behalf of his client, even if it wasn't the same Paul who was offering gifts to his wife who wasn't his wife. The investigation didn't satisfy the Libyan embassy concerned about the disappearance of Jalili, not knowing the ruler of Dubai had given the U.S. government tacit approval to conduct the operation.

Chapter 25

July 4, 2004
Algiers, Louisiana

The quiet noise of electrical equipment coupled with the hum of small motors was the first thing she noticed. Next, she felt the blanket, warmed by the sunshine on her stomach and legs, and the smell of, well, *clean*. She had the greatest sense of peace she'd ever felt, like slowly dozing off into a restful nap on a hammock on the porch with a warm rain falling in the background. Not wanting to open her eyes, she was curious why she felt so nice, so much so that she could no longer feign sleep.

Rachel opened her eyes to a hospital room she didn't recognize, for a reason she couldn't remember, at a time she couldn't place. At once frightened, she wiggled toes on both feet and fingers on both hands, confirming she had all her limbs. She simply wasn't sure why she was in a hospital bed.

Rachel looked around until she found the call button and pushed it. When no one responded, she pushed it again and held the button down. The door opened slowly as two nurses peered into the room. They approached the bed, both with tears in their eyes as they stared at the young woman.

"May I have some water?" Rachel tentatively spoke her first words.

"You certainly may, sugar. Bless your little heart!" the older nurse said and nudged the younger one to get some water. "You sure scared us for a long while."

"Why am I here? What happened to me?" Rachel was trying to find her way out of the fog.

"We'll get the doctor. He'll answer all your questions." The older woman hurried off to the nurses' station.

The doctor came in a few minutes later with a huge smile on his face. "We are certainly glad to have you back with us. Your parents are in the cafeteria and will be here shortly." Dr. Dillon did what doctors do—checked her pulse and blood pressure, dilated her pupils with a small flashlight, and looked at her throat. "How do you feel?"

"Very confused but otherwise OK. Why am I here?" Rachel knew she had asked the question at least twice already, but no one had yet answered her.

"Well, you were in a terrible accident that almost took your life," the doctor began, "but the worst is over. You've been asleep for about seven months, so you're going to feel weak and uncoordinated for a while."

"Seven months?" Rachel heard herself ask incredulously. "Where's Paul?"

"Who's he?" Dr. Dillon asked, ignoring the question about how long she had been in the hospital.

"I don't know, really, but I know he's someone close to me." Rachel thought hard but knew she couldn't answer the question. "Seven months? What kind of accident was I in?"

The doctor moved to check the charts and otherwise avoided answering her questions. He finally excused himself and left. In a few minutes, Rachel's parents burst into the room.

"Sweetheart, you're awake!" Her mother broke into tears as she saw Rachel sitting up in bed. Over the next several hours, more of her family and friends came by to welcome her back, as though she'd been on a long journey of which she was unaware.

It was only the next morning when her parents shared with her the events leading up to her hospitalization. At lunchtime, two foreign service officers arrived with whom she had worked before going to Abu Dhabi carrying messages from the secretary, the undersecretary, and several others in the State Department who sent well wishes. They handed her a letter from the U.S. ambassador in Abu Dhabi and a handwritten note from Pastor Don Stinson.

"My dearest Rachel," the pastor's note began, "you cannot know the presence of God I felt in you when we sat next to each other on the flight from Dubai to Pantelleria. Your steadfastness of belief, your unshakable faith, and your absolute reliance on the Lord were as evident as your beauty and courage. Please call on me if you need anything and go in the protection and grace of the Lord. Blessings, Don."

Stinson's reference to Pantelleria stirred something in Rachel's memory. She remembered getting on the Emirates flight, and then the hijackers, and talking to someone about going to Pantelleria.

The next few days were a blur as she remembered bits of what happened, talking at length with her mother and her father. Although she tired easily, she knew she must get up and start rebuilding her strength and stamina.

"Mother, I remember so much, but there's one question I can't answer for myself. Who is Paul?"

Rachel's mother looked at her as she thought about it, but she had no answer for Rachel. "Sweetheart, I don't ever remember you mentioning anyone named Paul. Was he in Abu Dhabi with you?"

Rachel let it go for now, celebrating the love of her family and friends and preparing herself to go out in the real world and get on with her short life.

Paul is someone special to me, she would tell herself over the coming weeks and months, *but none of my family or friends knows anything about him. How can he be so important to me and so anonymous?*

Chapter 26

November 20, 2004
Quantico, Virginia

Paul Stephens heard the doorbell ring and saw someone standing outside the condo. It being a typical Saturday, he rose early, ran a few miles around Dumfries in the crisp November morning, showered and put on jeans, and was pouring himself a cup of coffee when the visitor arrived.

The sight of the young woman at his door made his breath catch again as it had almost a year before.

"Rachel." He heard himself say her name without inflection or surprise.

She stood at the door, not knowing exactly what to do, to come in or leave, to answer him or not, to laugh or cry.

He too stood transfixed by her. How many nights he awoke in the middle of his thoughts about this woman he had known for what— twenty minutes? The woman who had penetrated his heart with only a look, who caused him to look twice at other women whose appearance reminded him of her, who haunted him day and night.

"Would you like to come in?" Paul noticed that she still had not said a word. "Can I get you a cup of coffee?" He moved to the kitchen as she sat on the couch in his comfortable living room. "How do you take it?" he asked as he added one teaspoon of sugar and a little milk just like he drank his coffee.

Paul had faced hostile fire with more composure than he now displayed in front of a woman who, until two minutes ago, he was supremely but sadly confident was dead. After the ambulance arrived at the Emirates plane in Pantelleria, Paul assisted the paramedics in getting her situated on the gurney, out the door and down the stairs to the car. He stood and watched the ambulance drive away, sure beyond any doubt that she was dying.

He had not seen her since the rescue, and no one called to tell him she survived. He simply believed she was sent home to her family to be buried and lost to him and all who had known her. He was not attached to her life in any way that made sense, he was unknown to her family and close friends, and, like so many people, he met her only once for a few minutes, never to see each other again.

"You found me," Paul finally broke the silence. "They told me you wouldn't survive the gunshot."

Rachel put her hand in his and sat there drinking coffee fixed just the way she liked it.

"Tell me what happened last December," Rachel finally asked after sitting quietly by his side for nearly fifteen minutes.

Paul respected her silence, correctly surmising she was trying to sort it out in her mind. It had taken all of her emotional energy to finally ring his doorbell, having come to the condo several times that morning and returning to her car, trying to build up the courage to confront this man who in her sleep gave her the will to live. "Please, Paul."

As gently as he could, Paul related the story to her, of the call from his commanding officer to prepare for a possible mission, to the Gulfstream, to the breach and shooting the hijackers. Without scaring her, he told her how two of the bad guys were hidden among the passengers and fired the shot that hit her on the right side of her head.

"What happened after that?" Rachel was trying to piece it all together. "What did you do?"

"Rachel, you were shot in the head. You were saying things, confused things, and we were trying to keep you conscious. There's no reason you should be alive today."

Rachel sat quietly trying to reconstruct her life on that day last December.

"What confused things?" Rachel knew in her heart that there was something there, but she couldn't quite reach it. She knew it connected her to Paul, yet there was no obvious bond she could imagine. She had not even recognized him when he opened the door and, had he not said her name, she would've made an excuse of going to the wrong condo and walked away.

"How did you find me?" Paul was trying to move the conversation to something less intense.

"After I woke up last July, I contacted the State Department to find out who was the duty officer that day. Rich Carter is his name, and he just moved to Muscat for a two-year tour as the political/economic officer. He was as surprised to hear from me as you were to see me just now. Most people just assumed I died after they brought me home. Rich filled me in on what role the State Department played in stopping the hijacking.

"Rich contacted General Frank Duggan, who runs the National Military Command Center at the Pentagon. Frank and I met at the Ritz-Carlton at Pentagon City a few days ago, and he went through the rest of the events, at least as far as DoD was concerned. He reviewed the log and found your name as leading the assault team. As soon as he said your name, I knew you were the Paul I kept seeing in my mind's eye while I was asleep. It wasn't too hard to find you after that. After all, there aren't too many heroes in the Marine Corps named First Lieutenant Paul Stephens."

"I was just doing my job, Rachel." Paul felt himself blush at her comment.

"Well, my hero, anyway. The State Department has me on medical leave until I'm strong enough to go back to work. They want me to think about staying at the headquarters in Foggy Bottom, but I'm not sure that's what I want right now."

Paul stared at the woman seated next to him, marveling at the peace he felt in her presence. There was an excitement at seeing her, at her incredible beauty, her warmth and passion. He knew he must tell her the rest of the story but wasn't sure how it might affect her. And she was still holding his hand.

"Rachel, you were talking about getting married. After you got shot, I mean. You told Pastor Stinson you wanted to be married."

"What did he say?" Rachel knew this was leading to something but couldn't understand what.

"He married you right there on the floor of the airplane. Remember, though, that no one thought you would survive and we were trying anything we could to calm you as you were slipping away."

"What do you mean he married me? To whom? Paul, who was there to . . . ?" Rachel suddenly understood what happened. "It was you, wasn't it?" Her voice was as quiet as when she said "I do" eleven months previously, and with the same tears in her eyes.

"Yes, Rachel, I married you. It wasn't legal, of course, but you wanted it so badly I couldn't walk away from you. I just couldn't. I was genuinely concerned that if we didn't perform the ceremony right there, you would've given up and died on the spot." Paul found himself saying a lot more than he intended to, and he was fumbling for words in his nervousness.

"That's why I was calling out for you while I was . . . while I was sleeping. I couldn't wait to say your name when I woke up, but I didn't even know who you were."

Both sat quietly on the sofa, collecting their thoughts, processing the information they just received, trying to make sense of it all.

Paul took the initiative of suggesting he prepare breakfast, really, brunch given the time, and moved into the kitchen to get started. Rachel took a seat at the bar separating the kitchen from the dining room, talking, asking questions, and watching Paul move about preparing the meal with Marine precision. Their conversation continued into the afternoon; they found themselves at a small Italian restaurant for dinner just up Highway 1 in Woodbridge, still talking, and after 2300 back at Paul's apartment, when Rachel's cell phone rang.

"My parents were concerned when I didn't call them today. They just wanted to be sure I was OK," Rachel told Paul when she returned to the living room. "I should be going—it's late."

"Where are you staying?" Paul asked, realizing that their daylong discussion was coming to an end and he still knew very little about her.

"I'm staying with a college friend who works up here. Can I come back to see you tomorrow?" Rachel was tired and knew she needed rest.

"What's best for you?" Paul heard himself asking her. "I'm home all day tomorrow. We can go into the District and have breakfast at the Mayflower Hotel."

"That sounds perfect. What about nine o'clock? I can be here by then." Rachel felt excitement despite her fatigue, anxious at the thought of joining Paul again tomorrow. She watched his features closely, looking for any signs of pity that she had witnessed countless times over the last several months when people heard her story. There was none on Paul's face.

"Nine sounds great. Let me walk you to the car." Paul stood and helped Rachel to her feet, then opened the front door to his condo and gestured her out in front of him. They walked down the sidewalk to her rental car parked on the curb, and he opened her door.

Rachel placed her left hand on his right cheek, gently pulled him close to her, and kissed him on the lips. He responded by leaning into the kiss, not tentatively, but softly, one kiss, and then they both recovered.

"Thank you, Paul. I had a great day. That's the first good day I've had in a really long time." Rachel could feel a tear forming, and she reached up to brush it away.

"Me too, Rachel. I've thought about you a lot since we met, but I never could have imagined this happening. Drive safely and I'll see you in the morning." He closed her car door and stood on the street watching until her taillights disappeared.

What am I doing here? Rachel asked herself on the way back to her friend's house in Springfield just north of the Marine base. *Paul has a job and a life, and I have mine. We weren't supposed to meet, but we did. Now what?*

If Rachel only knew, Paul was asking the same questions and having the same feelings of uncertainty. *She's trying to put her life back together,* he observed, *and I'm a speed bump that she can't quite figure out. I'm twenty minutes of her past life, twenty minutes that she can't quite remember, but she knows it's there.*

Rachel nonetheless returned promptly at 0900 the next morning, waiting in the car for a minute to be exactly on time. *He's a Marine,* she reminded herself, *and I'm sure he's always on time.* She smiled at her stereotyping, got out of the car, and walked up the driveway. As she reached up to knock on the front door, it opened.

"Hi, Rachel," Paul said as he reached around to lock the door on the inside. "If we leave now, we can catch the 0930 service at the base chapel and make the 1115 reservations we have for brunch. Let's take the Corvette and open the T-top." Paul took Rachel by the arm and steered her toward the garage door, which was already opening by the remote he pushed.

"Good morning, Paul. That sounds perfect." Rachel chided herself for repeating that phrase from the evening before, but she admitted to herself it was perfect. The weather was sunny and cold, the air crisp and clean, and the day was starting out, well, perfect.

Paul got into the car and reversed onto the driveway. He removed the roof panels, stowed them in their separate covers behind the seats, and opened her door. "Your chariot awaits, madam!" He made a grand gesture, and she laughed as she slipped into the tan leather seats while he pulled a Marine Corps camouflaged poncho liner over her to stave off the morning chill.

"This is beautiful, Paul. What year is it?" Rachel saw it was well maintained, flawless in appearance, and ran smoothly.

"It's a 1980 Corvette, the only true American sports car, bought new and has only been driven by one little old lady—me! I got it as a birthday present from my grandmother before I even had a driver's license. It sat in the garage behind my parents' home for thirteen very long years before I could drive it."

"Why did she buy you a car you couldn't drive?" Rachel was amused and pleased he was sharing this story and some of his life with her.

"I always wanted a Corvette," Paul confessed, "and she wanted to get it for me. My grandmother knew she was dying of leukemia, and it was her farewell present to me."

Paul steered out of the driveway and down the street. Seeing that Rachel was cold despite the poncho liner, he turned on the car's heater and rolled up the windows. The sun was bright and warm, but not enough to keep the chill at bay.

"The weather is so beautiful this morning," Rachel commented, "and if I forget to tell you later, thank you for today."

"You're most welcome." Paul smiled as he approached the back gate at Quantico.

The Marine sentry at the gate—Corporal Roach by the insignia on the collar of his camouflaged utility uniform and the nametape above his right breast pocket—put out his hand to stop the car. "Good morning, sir. One hundred percent ID check," Corporal Roach said as he saluted. Paul dug his military identification card from his wallet and presented it to the sentry.

"Should I get my driver's license?" Rachel asked, realizing she'd never been aboard a U.S. military installation and wasn't quite sure what she should do.

"No need, ma'am. Captain Stephens's ID card does the job," Roach told her.

Boy, a great car and a babe like that, Roach thought to himself, not even considering the fact that the car was older than him. Even with her winter coat and the poncho liner, he could see that she was an amazingly attractive woman, and he wanted to hold the car there for just a moment longer.

"Thank you, Captain, ma'am. Have a nice day." Roach saluted Paul again and waved the car through the gate. Not being covered—he was not wearing a uniform and hat—Paul simply nodded his head, returned the greeting, and drove on.

Paul pulled into a parking spot outside the chapel and went around the front of the car and opened Rachel's door. She took the hand he offered, and they walked up the sidewalk to the chapel.

After the service, Paul introduced Rachel to a few friends, including Katy Morgan; the two women chatted off to the side as Paul spoke with some officers in their Amphibious Warfare School class.

"I'm so glad we got a chance to meet in person," Katy began. "Paul came off that mission a different man. All he talked about was you. He called me last night after you left and told me every detail about your day."

"Really?" Rachel asked since Paul had not shared that part of the story.

"Rachel, he thought you were dead, and he grieved just like I'm sure your family did when they thought they lost you. I've known Paul for over six years, and I've never seen him react this way to a girl he met. You're special to him, and I hope you realize that." Katy felt better that Rachel knew what she meant to Paul. "And he didn't even know your last name!"

"Katy, I don't know why, but he kept me alive. I felt like it was one long dream of Paul that disappeared as soon as I woke up. The dream came back yesterday, I guess stirred up by meeting him again and reliving some of the things that happened." Katy watched as tears fell from the corners of Rachel's eyes.

"Just after he returned from that op, he told me all about you. It was so funny because I asked him how he met you, how long he'd known you, you know, the normal questions. He told me you and he were 'married'—it sounded like you two ran off to Las Vegas! When I asked him why, he told me if your personality was half as good as your looks, you were the perfect woman for him!" Both women were laughing and crying at the same time, attracting Paul's attention.

"All right, ladies, what's going on here? Rachel, don't believe anything Katy tells you about me—she knows too much to tell the truth and will therefore tell you only what benefits her most." They laughed as he joined their conversation.

The trio stood talking for a few minutes until Paul looked at his watch. "We have to get going, Rachel, to make our brunch reservations. Want to join us, Katy?"

"Thanks, Paul, but I've got an exam coming up, and I have to get ready for it. One more course and I finish my MBA. You two have fun!" Katy wanted to go since she really enjoyed Rachel's company but knew better than to intrude. She felt confident they would see more of each other and decided to leave it like that for now.

Paul and Rachel returned to the car arm in arm and talked along the way. "What did you think when we met?" Rachel decided to probe further after getting the information Katy shared with her.

"What did Katy say to you at the chapel?" Paul asked, knowing that he had relied heavily on Katy for the informal counseling he needed after "losing" Rachel on the plane.

"She said you were upset I died," Rachel began, "and that you thought you and I would get along if given the chance. Still feel that way after the last twenty-four hours?"

Paul's feelings for Rachel had only intensified since she walked back into his life the day before, and he knew he was in uncharted waters in the relationship. On the one hand, she was an incredibly beautiful woman with a warm smile and a good heart, and she was good-looking too. On the other hand, he was a Marine prone to short-notice deployments to do what he could not discuss, to places he could not reveal, and sometimes for more than just a few days at a time. He often wondered how he would feel leaving loved ones behind.

"Rachel, I'm having a great time, and I'm really glad you're doing better than the last time we met." He winked and smiled as he said that. "Opening the door to my condo yesterday was like waking up from a dream, and I feel like the dream has continued." He stopped talking and hoped she wouldn't notice how confused he was.

"Thank you, Paul. I'm having fun too, and I know I'm awake and with you." Rachel reached over and took his hand, holding it warmly in her lap. They drove on quietly to the Mayflower.

"Good morning, sir, reservations for two?" The maître d'hôtel looked expectantly at the couple as they approached him.

"Good morning. Yes, the table is for Stephens." Paul held Rachel's hand as they moved through the restaurant to the table on the window. He noticed how well her hand fit in his, how warm it was and how easily they moved in unison. *She's an incredible woman*, he told himself as they sat down and took the menus offered by the waiter, also noticing several heads turning to look at them—or maybe just Rachel—approvingly.

The couple talked throughout the meal, laughing at Paul's stories of his Marine Corps career and Rachel's work as a diplomat. When they noticed the staff cleaning up, a quick survey of the restaurant told them they were the only remaining guests, so engaged in conversation they lost track of time. Paul settled the bill, and they left the hotel.

Paul and Rachel walked through the streets in downtown Washington and passed in front of the National Theater. On a whim, Paul asked if tickets were available for the evening performance of *Les Misérables*; the woman looked through the Will Call tickets and pulled out an envelope.

"These people just called and said they won't make it. They already paid for these two tickets and can't get a refund." She looked around to see if her boss was close by—he wasn't—and she slid the envelope through the slot at the bottom of the window. "They're yours. They're in the balcony to the right side of the stage."

Paul told the woman he wanted to pay for the tickets. "Is there a military rate?" he asked as he slid his military identification card across to the woman.

She looked at it briefly and passed it back. "The tickets are already paid for, Captain Stephens, and the computer will tell me that if you try to pay for them, so it's easier if you just take them." The woman seemed determined to give them the tickets.

"Thank you, ma'am," Paul said, pocketed the envelope, and started toward the door.

"Semper fi, Marine," the woman said with a smile on her face.

"What was that all about?" Rachel asked as they entered the lobby.

"Marines use the Corps' motto—Semper Fidelis means "Always faithful"—to greet each other. She must be a Marine or is close to one." Paul saw the woman talking to another member of the theater staff and gesturing toward him.

"You said she must be a Marine, but she has to be too old. You mean she *was* a Marine," Rachel chided Paul gently as they stood in line for some coffee.

"Actually, we believe that once you earn the title, you're a Marine for life. So, no, Ms. Becker, I meant she must *be* a Marine." They both laughed as he paid for two lattes and turned toward the theater entrance.

An usher took their tickets at the door and gestured them down the aisle toward the stage.

"We're in the balcony, sir," Paul said, pointing to the sign near the stairway.

"Sir, there was slight problem with your tickets. It seems someone else is already sitting in those seats. Would you please follow me?" The usher walked down the aisle, Rachel following, Paul looking confused. The usher stopped five rows from the stage at row E and pointed to seats 15 and 16 center stage.

The usher saw the confusion on Paul's face. "Captain, I'm a retired gunnery sergeant, and I always do what my wife tells me. She's a retired master sergeant, and she'll pull rank on me if I don't! She said to give you the best seats in the house, and these are. Enjoy the show, sir, ma'am."

"Thanks, Gunny, and thank the master sergeant for us too." Paul looked away so Rachel wouldn't see him blushing.

"Anytime, skipper!" He bowed slightly at the waist and moved off to help some others who were obviously tourists.

"Wow!" Rachel exclaimed. "I'm hanging around you more if I get treated like this, skipper!"

"It doesn't happen often," Paul said, nonetheless amazed at the way Marines take care of their own, "but we do help each other whenever we can. And we sometimes refer to a captain as skipper, like the captain of a ship."

They chatted before the show began, watched the performance virtually in their laps, and walked back to the car in the cold evening air. The drive back to Paul's house was quiet as each processed the day's events.

"I had a fantastic time, Rachel. Thank you for coming." Paul decided to start first so there was no awkward silence.

"Me too, Paul. It was a perfect day and a perfect weekend. I hope we can see each other some more." Rachel felt warm and comfortable despite the winter cold and wind.

"I have class tomorrow, but maybe we can have dinner after that. Do you like seafood? I'm cooking." Paul was certain Rachel felt the same as he did and was comfortable talking with her.

"Dinner would be great. What can I bring?" Rachel found herself opening up to him.

"Nothing. I'll take care of everything. I'll see if Katy wants to join us, if that's OK."

"I hope she can make it. I really enjoyed talking with her."

"You mean you want to get more scuttlebutt on me, don't you?"

Rachel hesitated, fearing she had done something wrong.

Paul, sensing she was confused, laughed and explained. "Scuttlebutt is another one of those Marine Corps things we do. It means news or rumors. You want Katy to give you more information on me, right?"

Rachel laughed. "Yeah, I guess you're right. I want to get more scuttlebutt on you," she said, pronouncing the unfamiliar word delicately.

When they pulled up to the house, Paul noticed that Rachel's car had a flat tire. "Drive the Corvette home tonight, and I'll fix the flat tomorrow. It's too late tonight to worry about it."

Katy was between boyfriends, so she came alone; she knew Paul well enough that she wouldn't be a third wheel at dinner. She and Rachel did most of the talking while he cooked, with Katy telling stories about Paul over the years and Rachel relating what she could remember of the events leading up to the hostage rescue operation. In a way, it was cathartic, providing Rachel with the psychological relief of telling the story to Katy's sympathetic ear. By the end of the evening, they were fast friends and vowed to meet again whenever the chance arose.

Paul watched from the kitchen, well aware these were the two most important women in his life outside his immediate family, knowing their lives would be inextricably linked, a reality perfectly acceptable to him.

Chapter 27

May 3, 2004
Monterey, California

Mark Masterson reported to the commanding officer of the Marine Detachment, Defense Language Institute, Presidio of Monterey in California, for duty as a foreign area officer (FAO) student in the Arabic language program. His previous year at Amphibious Warfare School was the break he needed, but he was now facing another two years of school, first at DLI and then in Tunis, before returning to the Fleet Marine Force.

His language aptitude scores were off the chart, though, and the Marine Corps desperately needed officers with Arabic, Russian, and Chinese skills. Mark was assigned to Arabic language training and began the forty-seven-week program in August. Because the June and July classes were already at capacity, he had no other responsibilities beyond checking in with the detachment a couple of times a week, with plenty of time to explore the Monterey Peninsula and nearby towns.

Mark took to Arabic well. Although he never studied the language previously, he worked hard, learned the basics, and progressed through the program with almost-perfect scores. By November, he was bored and looking for another challenge. A friend suggested he check out the Monterey Navy Flying Club and train for a private pilot's license. He found the facility at the far end of the Monterey Airport and filled out the required paperwork to become a student pilot.

Flying became a passion; once he soloed, Mark was able to take short trips to airfields around the San Francisco Bay area. Given the size of the state of California, flying gave him the chance to explore the region on weekends and during the school breaks; he eventually saw everything within a few hours' flying distance, and even to Santa Catalina, one of California's Channel Islands southwest of Los Angeles, for a weekend to complete one of the cross-country flights required for the license. He found a restaurant in the Salinas Valley near Castroville that would send a car to pick him up from the local airport when he landed and return him to the plane after lunch.

His nine-year-old nephew Ryan came to visit for a month at the beginning of the summer just after Mark got his license, allowing him to carry passengers without an instructor in the cockpit. The two Mastersons flew the length of California, spending weekends in Seattle, Sonoma, and San Diego, and went as far as Las Vegas for Ryan to see the illusionist David Copperfield perform at the MGM Grand Hotel.

Mark finished the Arabic program and did the second year of his FAO program at the Foreign Service Institute in Tunis, the Arabic finishing school for American diplomats and military officers. The course was more difficult, requiring him to work harder and spend more time studying; neither Mark nor the Marine Corps would tolerate mediocre performance.

Part of the program in the second year involved regional orientation in countries where the language was spoken, traveling as a tourist to understand the culture, religion, art, and literature, and other aspects of the Arabic-speaking countries in North Africa, the Levant, and the Arabian Peninsula. As he discovered, the language was often the only common aspect, with each country's economic priorities, defense strategies, and regional and global alliances varying broadly.

When he wasn't traveling or studying, Mark retained his flying proficiency by renting a plane at Tunis-Carthage International Airport and flying around the country; crossing borders was difficult and presented security problems he was unwilling to address early in his one-year tour at FSI.

On a whim, he went to the Italian embassy and asked to meet the defense attaché, introduced to him as Colonel Fabrizio di Francesco, an air force pilot on his last assignment before retiring. Mark explained that he wanted to fly to Italy on the weekends and needed assistance with aircraft clearances and immigration procedures. The colonel was more than happy to help and suggested the two of them take the first small step of flying to Pantelleria, the southernmost part of both Italy and Europe and only thirty miles east of the capital, Tunis.

Mark filed the flight plan twenty-four hours in advance as required by the Italian civil aviation authority, met di Francesco at the airport, and prepared for takeoff. After receiving instructions from the tower, Mark taxied to the holding area on runway 28, squawked 2545 on the transponder, and opened the throttle for a smooth takeoff.

Mark did as instructed by the air traffic controller, and they were soon on their way to the island, arriving forty-five minutes later to a bright, sunny day with only a few wispy clouds to the east. The officers made their way to Dammuso Ristorante for Sicilian barbecue and seafood, passing on the offer of wine or beer with their meal to avoid liability should something happen to the plane on their way home.

The fresh olives were unlike anything Mark had ever tasted, and the fruit plate included sweet grapes described by Fabrizio as unique to Tunisia and the island. After lunch they accepted the restaurant owner's invitation to show them the volcano's caldera and the old Carthaginian ruins over a thousand years old. He drove them back to the airport, eliciting a promise to return soon for more pasta and grilled shrimp. It wasn't a hard sell.

Mark and Fabrizio took several trips over the coming months, visiting di Francesco's home in Sicily, Sardinia, and even Calabria on the mainland, and would remain friends over the years.

Chapter 28

July 7, 2006
Abu Dhabi, United Arab Emirates

At twenty-five, Rasha was pushing the envelope to get married. Even in this era, Arab women were expected to wed early and have children immediately, and she was above the middle of the age range with no prospects in sight. Her parents suggested some candidates; finally, in one circle of friends, she was introduced to a Lebanese man who seemed reasonable. Typical of Arab men of his age, Homaid hung out with the same young men, made the same circuit of nightclubs, and lacked a real personal identity outside the group. Rasha found him nominally acceptable and announced to her parents she had a prospective husband for them to check out.

The vetting process was brief. Rasha brought Homaid home to meet her parents. Ahmed also found him good enough and gave his consent for them to be married. But Homaid's lack of wealth concerned him; he expected his daughter to marry into money and get off his bank account. The wedding was not the event many weddings are in the region; it was low-key, about a hundred people, and only family and close friends, attended. They made love on their wedding night and only once more in the marriage when Homaid came home drunk one night; sex that evening was not consensual.

The union lasted barely eighteen months; Rasha sought more from a husband than Homaid was willing to give. He coveted his independence and his girlfriends and was often out late smoking *shisha*, the traditional Arabian water pipe, and roaming the nightclubs at the five-star hotels with his friends. Rasha was not so empowered; as a married woman, she was expected to be with him when he so chose or at home waiting for him if not. She could not go clubbing the way Homaid did, and the many lonely nights got to be too heavy a burden for her to bear. She filed for divorce and returned home to live with her parents.

Her father's culture and generation disapproved of divorce, and he felt ashamed Rasha was no longer married. Although he had not selected Homaid for her, given the fact she was almost twenty-five, Ahmed immediately agreed. Now two years older, again single and living at home, friends were curious what was wrong with Rasha that she would do this to her parents. Nothing was asked or said about Homaid; of singular importance was that Ahmed had a marriageable daughter now divorced from a man with whom she could live an adequate if not passionate life. Ahmed complained to his wife that Rasha was being unreasonable; if her husband wanted to go out with friends at night, that was his prerogative, and she should be happy he even wanted to marry her in the first place.

Rasha retreated into her world of working and painting, going to the gym daily, and spending weekends in Dubai hotels, where she could be alone with her thoughts by the pool or on the beach. One Friday afternoon, she joined a group of friends who rode jet skis to a nearby island for a sunset beach party, only to feel lonelier when she returned home. She politely declined her friends' introductions to single men. A potential suitor referred by her father proposed within a few minutes of meeting, confirming he wasn't concerned she was divorced. Rasha recoiled when he assured her she would be treated fairly as his second wife, and even though traditional Islamic marital jurisprudence allows Muslim men to practice polygyny, she would have nothing to do with it—or with him.

She felt humiliated by Homaid, who more often than not came home smelling of another woman's perfume, sometimes with her lipstick on his shirt collar. When she said something, he would often hit her, fortunately not in the face, but leaving large bruises on her arms and back. She learned to suffer in silence. She did his laundry, cooked meals he rarely ate, and waited at home watching Bollywood and Egyptian movies to pass the time, often waking up alone to find he slept elsewhere for the night.

After moving back into her parents' home and with no support from her family and friends, Rasha went through the motions of going to the bakery and to her room after dinner, the routine making the situation only worse.

Chapter 29

August 11, 2007
Beirut, Lebanon

Captain Paul Stephens's official title was the American Legation, United States Naval Attaché and Naval Attaché for Air, more simply referred to as ALUSNA. Two months into the job after training at the Defense Intelligence Agency—Paul was an infantry officer but was selected because he spoke French—he was still learning how to write reports and serve around foreign service officers, the FBI legal attaché, a political appointee ambassador, and the army colonel senior defense official, who was his boss. With no prior experience working in a diplomatic environment, he was experiencing a true fire-hose indoctrination.

He and Rachel were married almost three years now—officiated by Pastor Stinson—with one daughter fourteen months old and, unbeknownst to them, another on the way. She had adjusted well to life as an officer's wife, having resigned from the State Department after the hijacking to raise their child and recuperate from the trauma of being shot. Although she wanted to live in Beirut with Paul, his tour there was unaccompanied, mainly for security reasons, even though the environment seemed benign as he traveled around the country meeting other diplomats, military officers, and official contacts.

As he had been told in attaché training, more diplomats die in car accidents abroad than for any other reason; he relied on his driver, Suleiman, to navigate the perpetual gridlock of Lebanon's capital city and his trips north across the Dog River toward Tripoli and south past Tyre, the first throne of Pygmalion's sister Dido before she fled to Carthage to escape his tyranny, on the road to the Israeli border.

Free web-based videoconferencing had been released two years earlier, allowing Paul and Rachel not only to speak but also to see each other almost daily; even in the two months since he left home, he could see her belly growing, getting periodic updates through e-mailed medical exams and ultrasounds and verbal reports from Rachel and their parents. It wasn't as good as being there, but it was the best substitute they could devise. They were otherwise inseparable, but Paul and Rachel answered the call of duty with the attendant challenges, she on the home front and he on the front lines of diplomacy.

The Beqaa is only thirty kilometers east of Beirut, but a world away—a fertile valley with agriculture as its most important industry. Infamous from the early 1980s when Westerners were held hostage by a nascent but evolving Hezbollah in the Sheikh Abdullah military barracks at Baalbek near the village of Majd al Anjar on the border with Syria, successive governments in Beirut agreed with Bashar al Assad's Ba'ath regime in Damascus to allow industry to flourish as it had for millennia. Syrians still manned checkpoints throughout the valley, ensuring they knew who was coming and going, particularly as the village sits directly on the road and is considered the entrance to Damascus.

Paul was well aware of Hezbollah's violent history in the region, with the movement having conducted the U.S. embassy bombing in Beirut in April 1983 and the Marine barracks bombing at Beirut International Airport six months later, among many acts of terrorism, leaving hundreds of dead and injured in their wake. Twenty-one years later, the Iranian Revolutionary Guards would unveil a monument in Tehran celebrating the martyrs responsible for the twin attacks. News reports from Lebanon in the 1980s were replete with hostage-taking, assassinations, bombings, and rocket attacks; and yet life continued in true Lebanese spirit: bars, nightclubs, and restaurants remained open and busy during the Lebanese civil war from 1975 to 1990.

Suleiman slowed the car, a modified Chevy Tahoe with Level 4 bullet resistant windows, armor plating capable of stopping small arms fire, and run-flat tires as they approached Majd al Anjar. Both men were armed and wearing concealed body armor under their jackets, a necessity given the circumstances. They had cleared this checkpoint going into the valley earlier today and recognized many of the same guards still on duty.

As he was trained, Suleiman stopped ten feet behind the truck in front of them, left the car in drive, and reached for the road pass and identification papers they would inevitably be asked for. They continued scanning the surrounding area to identify potential threats, and exchanged information between them calmly and casually; although crossing checkpoints could never be described as routine, in this instance, everything seemed normal.

"The vehicle behind us is really close," Suleiman told Paul, checking out the license plate as it approached, the details he could discern about the driver, and the condition of the car, an old Mercedes sedan that had seen better days.

Before Paul could answer they were hit from behind and pushed forward toward the truck to their front despite Suleiman standing on the brakes. Cars suddenly appeared on either side of the Tahoe, helping push it forward into the narrow chokepoint ahead to prevent escape. The truck reversed into their hood, closing off the last option to evade capture.

Four men exited a Land Cruiser with guns drawn; in typical Lebanese fashion, they were dressed in jeans and polo shirts with collars turned up and wearing Ray-Ban glasses to hide their eyes. They were sporting automatic pistols, and two of them had cigarettes dangling from their lips as they approached the car.

"Please step out of the car now," one of them said casually as though he were instructing visitors at the Space Mountain ride at Disney World. Paul and Suleiman remained seated.

The man issued orders in Arabic to the others, whereupon they attached what appeared to be C-4 plastic explosives under the driver's side of the car. "If you don't want your driver killed, open the door and get out now. You have ten seconds."

Paul looked at Suleiman, shook his head, placed his handgun on the seat, removed his ballistic vest, and exited the car, closing and locking the door behind him. He was immediately frisked, plastic zip cuffs were applied to his wrists, and a hood was placed over his head; the border guards watched dispassionately. The truck pulled away, the C-4 was removed, and Suleiman was ordered back to the embassy.

Forced to sit in the back seat of the Land Cruiser between two of the men, Paul gave up trying to remember the twists and turns of the route to wherever he was being taken. The SERE training—survival, escape, resistance to interrogation, and evasion—he underwent at the Marine Corps Air Station, Cherry Point, North Carolina, taught him to remember details that might be useful.

Their limited conversation alternated from Arabic to French to English and back again but yielded no useful information about intentions or circumstances. Although it was difficult to see through the hood, he was able to glimpse a road sign indicating they were entering Safita, Syria, just above Homs, about halfway between the capital Damascus in the south and Aleppo to the north.

Paul felt fortunate under the circumstances that he was being taken to Safita, site of the former Phoenician city of Sumur, identified as Tell Kazel in the Amarna clay tablets that served as official correspondence between the Egyptian government and its counterparts in the neighboring kingdoms of the region in the fourteenth century BC, the earliest known examples of international diplomacy.

Much of the land in that region was given to the Knights Templar, who built a network of interconnected fortresses of the Templar Order; Chastel Blanc in Safita could maintain direct eye contact with Arwad and Tartus to the northwest, Chastel Rouge in the southwest, and the famous Krak des Chevaliers in the southeast. Safita ultimately fell to Baibars, the fourth sultan of Egypt in the Mamluk Bahri dynasty, who converted the inhabitants to Islam.

Paul believed he was better off in the hands of Sunni captors rather than the radical Hezbollah Shi'a extremists in Southern Lebanon—a belief he would soon come to regret.

Chapter 30

December 3, 2007
Abu Dhabi, United Arab Emirates

Mark noticed her immediately as she walked through the restaurant with three other women and sat a few tables away. The intensity of her eyes captivated him, and she caught him looking at her several times over lunch, embarrassing both of them but also secretly pleasing both.

"How are you going to handle it, Mark?" J-Mac asked. He looked up from his meal at Mark when his question went unanswered. McDaniel followed Mark's stare to the table where she was sitting. He put his hand on Mark's arm. "Are you OK?"

"Yeah, I'm fine." Mark broke his gaze toward the woman and refocused on J-Mac. "What was the question?"

Mark was a newly promoted lieutenant colonel and sixty days into a two-year assignment as the commanding officer of the Marine Security Guard company in Abu Dhabi. Since the late 1940s, Marines have guarded American diplomatic missions abroad, and the program grew to over eleven hundred Marine Security Guards, or MSGs, organized into five companies around the globe. Originally slated to take command of an infantry battalion, poor judgment by and an untimely relief of command of his predecessor in Abu Dhabi resulted in a last-minute change of orders that transferred Mark to the UAE instead. Disappointed in not getting an infantry unit, he once again accepted the fate of his trajectory in life and headed to the Middle East.

The enlisted guards must remain unmarried for the duration of their assignment, available at a moment's notice to protect and defend the embassy and its occupants. J-Mac, now also a lieutenant colonel and assigned to the MSG battalion headquarters at Quantico, Virginia, was on a regional tour and arranged a couple of extra days in Abu Dhabi to spend time with Mark. One of the Marines in Cairo was secretly dating an Egyptian Coptic woman without authorization, and Mark had to decide how to handle the situation.

"Corporal Williams was warned previously, so we curtail him in the program and return him to the Fleet Marine Force. I've already requested a relief. Lance Corporal Cuifen Chen should arrive on station next week." Mark had reviewed the case and knew there were no other options. He also knew J-Mac and the battalion commander agreed; but as the company commander, it was his decision to make. Mark looked up and saw the woman heading to the ladies' room. "Be right back," he said as he rose from the table and moved in her direction.

Mark timed it so they arrived at the restroom door together. "Hi, I'm Mark Masterson," he said, not knowing if the woman even spoke English.

"Mr. Masterson, my name is Rasha. Have we met?" Mark could see her dark eyes shining as they shook hands, and he noticed an almost-invisible small scar above her lip.

"I don't think so. I just arrived in Abu Dhabi a few weeks ago and don't really know anyone yet." They stood awkwardly in front of the restrooms, reluctant to move away from each other but also aware of people staring at them from the adjacent tables. "Would you join me for a cup of coffee in the lounge after lunch?"

"That would be nice," Rasha said with just enough inflection to show she was interested in this man, who was obviously interested in her. As she walked into the ladies' room, she felt a warm sensation in her stomach and a tightness in her throat; she wasn't sure why she was immediately attracted to him, but it was a nice feeling.

She wanted lunch to be finished now but returned to her table, intrigued by the thought of the pending cup of coffee. She was used to men hitting on her, but it was usually Arabs who were interested in only one thing, also reminding her she was divorced. This American man—*He is American, isn't he?*—seemed different, and it pleased her that he was direct but polite, eager but respectful.

Mark returned to his table with a look J-Mac had not seen in several years. "What did she say?"

"She said yes," Mark answered absentmindedly, not even volunteering the question he asked her. Mark had the same warm sensation after meeting Rasha, a feeling to which he was unaccustomed. He had not looked at another woman since Anisa's death six years ago, and he accepted with grace occasional attempts by family and friends to introduce him to prospects to take her place. He glanced at Rasha a few more times while they finished lunch, pleased to see her smile when she saw him looking.

McDaniel wasn't sure what to do. J-Mac stood with his friend over the last several years and had been with him on several occasions when Mark was almost paralyzed with grief. Although careful to not let it affect his job, Mark's personal life was devoid of . . . *life*. He rarely went out, then only with J-Mac or a few other officers, and spent most of his personal time at home reading or watching videos, often not remembering afterward what he read or watched.

J-Mac never saw his friend react this way before; Mark and Anisa were already married when McDaniel met them at the Basic School. He silently willed the woman to tread carefully with his friend; six years was a long time to heal, but the wound was still open. Although he would always stand by his friend, he didn't want her instigating another cycle of depression and recovery.

"What are your plans?" J-Mac asked.

"We're having a cup of coffee in a few minutes, and then I'll be back at the embassy. Why don't you take the car and I'll grab a taxi? I should see you around 1500."

"I think I'll join you for coffee." J-Mac waited for his friend's grimace, replying afterward, "OK, Mark. Please be careful."

"Yes, Mother," Mark chided his friend. "I'll catch up to you shortly."

J-Mac headed out of the restaurant, and Mark went to the lounge to wait for her. He replayed the brief encounter in his mind, trying to understand what this woman had that attracted him so powerfully. He could see the far end of Rasha's table in the mirror behind the bar but could not see her, so he was surprised when she spoke from behind him.

"May I join you, Mr. Masterson?" Rasha asked.

"Of course, and I go by Mark," he answered as he stood to pull out her chair, noticing that she blushed when he did.

The waiter appeared and took their coffee orders, hers a double espresso and his a decaffeinated latte.

"If you drink coffee, why do you have it decaffeinated?" Rasha asked, not quite understanding the logic.

"I like the taste of coffee, but the caffeine gives me a headache," Mark confided in her. "About the only thing I drink with caffeine is Coke because I don't like the taste of the decaf colas. A double espresso like yours would cripple me for a couple of hours."

"You said earlier you arrived a few weeks ago. Are you visiting Abu Dhabi?" Rasha asked the question to encourage him to talk.

"I was transferred to the UAE from the States, and I work at the American embassy." Mark turned the conversation to her. "How long have you been in Abu Dhabi?"

"All my life." Rasha let that hang for a minute. "I was actually born in Syria, but my family moved here when I was a baby."

"Really? What part of Syria are you from?"

"I'm Aleppian." Rasha gave only as much information as he asked and watched his reaction.

Mark smiled. "In the north near the Turkish border. I was there two years ago and stayed at the Baron Hotel."

Rasha was stunned. She had met only a few Americans and none who had ever been to Aleppo. This stranger sitting in front of her had not only been to Syria but to her birthplace. "Why?" Rasha tried to act casual, but the abruptness of her question and the tone of her voice betrayed her.

"I was curious. I took leave and traveled throughout Syria, but Aleppo was by far my favorite place. I stayed in room 202 at the Baron where Lawrence of Arabia stayed shortly after the ceremonial opening of the hotel in 1911 when he was spying on the Germans while they built the Berlin-to-Baghdad railroad. It's no longer the nicest hotel in town, but it has a lot of character and history. I love the bar—one day when I have enough money, I'm going to buy it, take it to the States, and build a house around it."

Rasha's head was swimming. This man was talking about her hometown like he grew up there, something she definitely had not. "I've never been to the Baron Hotel, but I've heard it's very . . . historic." She was so startled she could think of nothing else to say; the Baron was nothing like the five-star hotels in Dubai and Abu Dhabi to which she was accustomed.

"I would walk down to Bab al Nasr every morning for coffee and a croissant sprinkled with *za'atar Halabi* or have lunch flavored with *dakka*. Whenever I return to Aleppo, it's the first place I go. But I've also visited Damascus, the Krak des Chevaliers, and the Roman ruins at Palmyra on the Silk Road—I know you call the city Tadmur."

Before she could reply, her mobile phone rang, and she glanced down, irritated at the interruption. "Please excuse me, it's my father." Rasha answered the phone in Arabic and carried on a brief conversation with Ahmed. "I'm sorry, but I have to go."

Mark responded immediately. "I understand. Sounds like he needs you to deliver something."

For the second time in minutes, Rasha was startled. "You understood my conversation?"

"I did. I'm sorry, I wasn't trying to listen in, but . . ." His voice trailed off as he tried to decipher her reaction.

"You speak Arabic?" she asked incredulously.

"I do."

"Who are you?"

"Nobody. I mean, I'm Mark Masterson. I'm not sure what you mean." Mark was now fumbling for words and trying not to walk into a minefield.

"I have to go. My father needs me at the store." Rasha was suddenly flushed and unsure whether she could keep her balance. As she stood, Mark rose to meet her, extending his hand to help her from her chair.

"May I call you? Would you like to go for dinner sometime? How can I reach you?" They both laughed as he fired questions at her one after the other.

"Why don't you come by the store and we can discuss it when I have a little more time." She handed Mark a business card. He was pleased to see it included her mobile number. He reached into his pocket and handed her his card.

"Great! When would be a good time to stop by?"

"I'm usually in the store until lunch. Any morning except Friday is fine. Our driver was in an accident, so my father needs me to deliver something to a customer urgently."

Mark had the information he needed to reach Rasha and the desire to do so. "Thank you for joining me for coffee, and I hope to see you again soon."

"Thank you for a lovely time, Mark. It was quite interesting and a pleasure to meet you."

"Likewise, Rasha." He walked with her and opened the restaurant door, noticing her blush a second time.

"Good-bye now." Rasha shook his hand and walked to the parking lot. Mark watched her pull out and drive off.

Mark returned to the table and finished his coffee while the receptionist called a taxi. He replayed the conversation several times in his mind and tried to analyze every statement and nonverbal cue.

"On my way back to the embassy, J-Mac," he told McDaniel on the phone.

"How did it go?" J-Mac was curious why Mark was returning to the office so soon.

"Her father called, and she had to go back to work. But I got her number!" Mark said a little too excitedly.

"Steady, Hoss. Who is she? What does she do?"

"Her name is Rasha, and she's Syrian. Her father apparently works at a bakery, and I guess she works for him. She wants me to come by the store one morning to discuss when we can grab a bite somewhere." Mark turned her card over to the Arabic side and then back to the English. "I got her number."

"Yeah, you said that already. OK, I'll see you in the office." J-Mac was cautiously optimistic that his friend might have found someone to go out with and start living a more normal life.

Meanwhile, Rasha was trying to drive, read Mark's card, and remember the chance meeting in detail. *He's a* muqaddam—*lieutenant colonel—in the United States Marine Corps,* she read, *and a commanding officer of something to do with security. He speaks Arabic and has been to Aleppo.* Rasha felt strange as she drove to the bakery, trying to understand why this man affected her so much and dizzy at the prospect of him actually coming to the store to see her. *Will he call before he visits? What will he think about me working in the bakery? Will it matter to him that I'm divorced? Will he like me once he gets to know me?* A hundred questions flashed through her mind. *Will he even show up?*

Mark sat in the back of the taxi heading down Airport Road toward the embassy. He used so much adrenaline during the brief encounter with Rasha that he was suddenly tired. *What is it about her that's affecting me this way? As incredibly beautiful as she is, there must be a line of men ahead of me. I wonder how she got that little scar?*

Mark entered the embassy to the salute of the Marine on post 1. Since he was not in uniform, he could not return the salute but nodded and greeted the Marine. The guard pressed the release for the steel door to the chancery, and Mark headed to his office where J-Mac was waiting.

McDaniel could hardly contain himself. "Tell me everything!" Mark offered him Rasha's card, and J-Mac read it carefully. "Rasha M. Al Shibli. No job title, works at Al Shibli Bakery on Hamdan Street, phone, fax, e-mail, and mobile phone included. I wonder what the *M* stands for?"

"Arab culture requires children to take their father's first name after their given name. If her father's first name is Mohammed, then her name would be Rasha bint Mohammed Al Shibli. *Bint* means 'daughter of.' From the name of the bakery, it looks like her father owns it, probably with a local partner." Mark studied enough in the Foreign Area Officer program to know the customs of the region.

"She's Syrian, Mark. That's one of the criteria countries on some list in Washington that requires special consideration."

"Syria is on the list for state-sponsored terrorism, mostly for its involvement with and in support of Hezbollah in Lebanon over the years. I'll declare it to the battalion headquarters and keep you informed if anything happens." Mark would play by the rules but also didn't want this chance to slip by, assuming she would even go out with him. "She's been here her whole life, so I'm not sure what ties she really has to Syria other than the nationality."

The two officers went about their business as McDaniel prepared to return to Washington that evening. They drove to Mark's apartment for his luggage, grabbed Mexican food for dinner at Hemingway's at the Hilton Hotel on the corniche, and Mark dropped him off at the airport.

"Keep in touch and let me know about her after you meet." J-Mac was secretly glad that Mark showed such interest in a real woman, and if looks were any indication, Rasha was indeed a real woman. J-Mac also knew Mark's radar was on full alert, and he would protect himself from any pain until he was comfortable in the relationship. *Mark is a big boy, a badly bruised big boy, but he can handle it,* J-Mac thought to himself.

The weekend in much of the Arab world is Friday and Saturday; Friday is the holy day in Islam when practicing Muslims pray at the mosque and most businesses are closed. Government departments are closed on both days, but many private sector establishments open for business on Saturday; some are even open on Friday evening. Mark took the chance after attending church on Friday morning to drive downtown to find the bakery.

As he expected, it was closed, but he was able to establish the landmarks he would need to return during working hours. He dressed casually on Saturday morning and went back; the store was open, but he could not see Rasha inside. He sat in the car for a few minutes to see if she showed up. Mark also did not see a man who could be her father; it seemed like mostly young Arab men and an occasional Indian were working the weekend shift. He left and headed to the Marina Mall for lunch and to buy a hands-free kit for his mobile phone.

Midday on Sunday, Ahmed watched a young man enter the store and move toward the counter. Since his customers were mostly local and expatriate Arabs, a Western man in a suit and tie stood out from the normal crowd buying bread, sweets, and chocolates. The man seemed to be searching for something but wasn't looking at the baked goods or freshly squeezed juices. "May I help you?" Ahmed asked.

"Yes, sir. My name is Mark Masterson. Can you please tell me where I might find Rasha al Shibli?" Mark thought he saw the man recoil slightly, but he recovered quickly.

"Rasha is not feeling well and won't be in today. Can I help you?"

"If I'm here tomorrow at the same time, do you think she will be here?" Mark was trying to gauge if this was her father and how he might react to his daughter going out with an American—worse yet, a Marine.

"Assuming she's feeling better, she will be here tomorrow all morning. You might try back then."

"Thank you, sir. I'll do that. Bye now." Mark headed out of the bakery but could see the man studying him intently as he walked past a mirror beside the door; there was no doubt he was Rasha's father.

Rasha heard her mobile phone vibrate and looked to see what text she received.

```
Rasha, I understand you're not feeling well. I hope to see
you tomorrow when I visit the bakery again. Best regards.
BFN - Mark
```

Rasha read the text again. Mark visited the bakery and she wasn't there! *I'll be there tomorrow regardless of how I feel!*

```
Mark, thank you so much for thinking of me and I will be
at the bakery tomorrow. I'm sorry I missed your visit today.
BFN? Rasha
```

```
BFN=Bye for now
```

```
Thanks and BFN! ☺
```

I can't believe he came by the store on the one day I wasn't feeling well. Rasha considered what to wear and what she would say when he arrived. She replayed the conversation from Thursday and thought of questions she wanted to ask tomorrow.

Mark laughed at the emoji smiley face and appreciated that she adopted his shorthand so quickly. He was glad she remembered him; it would've been embarrassing if she asked, Mark who? He pulled out of the parking lot of the bakery and into the midday traffic, heading back to the embassy; one last look toward the shop confirmed her father was still watching him.

Chapter 31

February 9, 2008
Abu Dhabi, United Arab Emirates

Mark and Rasha had been seeing each other almost daily over the last three months when Mark wasn't traveling despite her father's objections; although she didn't want to antagonize Ahmed, she really enjoyed Mark's company, his respect for her, and how he expanded her perspective on many issues.

To ensure there were no problems later, Mark informed his commanding officer that they were dating; with J-Mac's help at the battalion headquarters, approval was granted, allowing them to continue seeing each other. Mark understood he would be subject to a lifestyle polygraph at the end of his assignment to confirm he wasn't passing classified information to her; although unnecessary, he gladly accepted the requirement.

Rasha became a regular at the Marine House, the accommodations for the MSGs on the embassy compound, becoming known as the Tiramisu Lady because of the dessert she brought to accompany her visits when they had house parties.

The young Marines were curious about Arab women and took the opportunity to ask her questions, often beginning with, "I don't want to offend you, but . . ." She appreciated their naiveté, answering anything they asked, helping them understand the cultural similarities and differences, and teaching them a few phrases in Arabic they could use when out shopping or having a meal. The Tiramisu Lady also became a big sister to the corporals and sergeants only five or six years her junior.

They went to the beach and enjoyed dinner most evenings in one of the outdoor restaurants, finding they liked the same cuisines, Prosecco with the appetizers—called *Prosegkar* by the Slovene-speaking population living in Italy in the 1700s—and beef or pasta with Chianti in the requisite straw basket called a "fiasco." The moderate weather of Abu Dhabi in the winter offered ample outdoor settings for dinner and drinks with friends or just the two of them, only venturing inside when it got too chilly or windy. They also enjoyed finding restaurants that offered the chef's table in the kitchen, sometimes having to convince the restaurant manager to allow them to eat with the kitchen staff.

For the second time in a year, Mark's orders were changed on short notice; in this case, the commanding officer of a battalion in Iraq was injured and evacuated to the United States. J-Mac informed him to pack his bags, fly a commercial carrier to Kuwait, and from there catch military air transportation to Baghdad. He would take over Battalion Landing Team 2/6, reporting to Regimental Combat Team commander Colonel Jim Dowdy in his fourth tour in Iraq. Mark finally got his infantry battalion, but it also meant leaving Rasha behind, at least for now.

Chapter 32

February 16, 2008
The White House

Rush lay quiet and unmoving, her husband breathing softly beside her, not wanting to wake him on this frigid Saturday morning. *It'll be another long day*, she thought, *as they all are.* It seemed like all days were complicated, not only for her but for many people in the United States after the tragedy brought on by the attacks in New York and Washington and the crash in rural Pennsylvania even seven years later.

What must they have felt? she asked herself again of the people on those flights who at some point knew what was happening, who knew their lives were ending, who had no control beyond prayer, redemption, and salvation. *Was there really a feeling of peace as they hurtled to the ground, or were they as terrified as I am just laying here thinking about it?* It was one of many questions she wrestled with over the years since the attack.

The world was different before September 11, she thought to herself, and wondered what her predecessor felt when it happened. No president since Franklin Roosevelt had faced attacks on U.S. soil, and the response the former president initiated had been debated every day of his presidency and into hers, in the liberal media, in the liberal think tanks, and in the liberal universities, never in his favor despite him being a very liberal Democrat.

As with any president she wondered if she would've handled responses to the attacks any better, to make the right decision of the few good and many bad options available to her. She knew every decision would be a collaborative effort by thousands of people in hundreds of offices of the federal government across the country and around the world, yet she alone held absolute and complete responsibility for those decisions and their intended or unintended consequences.

She had asked for courses of action to be briefed today, even though it was Saturday, and a decision to be made on the direction this country would take to counter the growing threat of terrorism that to date had taken several thousand American lives before and since September 11. The sleeping giant was awakened, slowly unsheathing its sword, deciding how to wield it in response to the attacks. Given the number of incidents around the world and the increasing number of American and foreign casualties, the options before her were wide and varied.

Barker blew it, she thought of her immediate predecessor. *He didn't have the intestinal fortitude for this sort of thing. Had he acted when the time was right*, Rush told herself, *we likely wouldn't be in this position now. I wouldn't have to be deciding the next steps in this war, to send our young men and women possibly to their deaths to protect our country and defend our way of life. He lobbed a few cruise missiles in their general direction instead of confronting the enemy head on.*

Remember, though, she reminded herself, *the two stupidest people in the world are your predecessor and your successor*, she thought, laughing to herself so she wouldn't wake Steve.

Former President Charles Linden Barker was now on the television news shows telling the world how he would handle the current situation, yet when he had the chance to do so during his administration, he had failed to—and was even criticized by the same journalists, politicians, and professors who now attacked her.

In his effort to show the world that the United States was not a bully, he had instead projected the image of a weak and timid nation, "leading from behind," as he called it, afraid to act even in its own self-defense. Emboldened by repeated lack of responses to acts of terrorism, the attacks grew larger and more destructive, culminating in the first strikes on American soil since 9/11 and the Japanese assault on Pearl Harbor sixty years previously.

I can't leave this for the next president, Rush thought, *as Barker did for me. Even if what I do is unpopular, I have to go for the jugular, or we will never again be safe.*

Barker always talked big. "One way or another, we are determined to deny Iraq the capacity to develop weapons of mass destruction and the missiles to deliver them. That is our bottom line." He delivered those words almost nine years before in another speech to another audience that again believed he would do something. Even when he had the authority to do so, he did nothing, and Iraq continued its concerted efforts to obtain chemical precursors, triggers for nuclear devices, and biological weapons. He didn't after Lockerbie and he didn't after USS *Cole* was hit in Yemen. He just didn't; he left it for the next president to deal with and then told everyone who would listen what he would've done differently given the chance.

Rush felt Steve stir next to her and reached out to him under the covers. He instinctively moved closer to her, making them like two commas pushed together into quotation marks, their bodies side by side—spooning. She credited him with her strength, her conviction, and her many successes. He was always there at her side to nudge her in the right direction or whisper another option or viewpoint in her ear. Or simply stand to the side and support her. *The wind beneath my wings,* she reminded herself. *Don't fool yourself into thinking otherwise.* She smiled at herself in the dark.

JoAnne Alice Rush was elected forty-third president of the United States on November 5, 2004, in the closest election in American history. The Democrats always believed they would elect the first woman president, but here she was, less than a year from finishing her first term, possibly departing the White House if the voters didn't want her to continue.

Barely eight months after the inauguration, just as she was getting comfortable with the Oval Office, Air Force One, the invasion of privacy, and the countless challenges of her office, terrorists attacked again in the American heartland, this time Mexican drug cartels trying to stop construction of a border wall hampering the free flow of their poison—drugs, prostitution, smuggling, and human trafficking—into America. In a few moments of history, she was transformed from a peacetime president wrestling with a lingering recession begun under the forty-second president to one facing the prospect of a protracted war of attrition, fighting one drug terrorist at a time, hunting them down one by one, one tunnel under the border after another, and ending both their individual and collective threats. The human toll was unthinkable. Economic effects of the attacks reverberated throughout the American economy and quickly echoed globally; it would take half a decade at least to reestablish equilibrium, she thought, if not longer.

She slipped out of bed and moved to the family room, with Special Agent Natalie Sizemore close behind. "Jarhead moving to twelve," Sizemore reported, giving the numeric code word for the family room. She knew JoAnne would not engage in small talk right now, she knew the president wasn't being rude or unfriendly, and Sizemore knew she just wanted to be alone for a few minutes as she always did this time of the morning. She watched her enter the family room, notified the remaining Secret Service detail on duty in the White House and in a dozen other locations around the country that Jarhead had arrived, and then withdrew.

The Secret Service learned that *Jarhead* was one Rush picked up during her Marine Corps service. A pejorative name the Marines call themselves, it also used her initials—JAR—to form the nickname her Basic School classmates used since Quantico. The president had heard it so many times since then it no longer registered when the Secret Service agents used it when referring to her.

Rush heard the door close and appreciated Natalie's discretion. Although the Secret Service never wanted her to be alone, even in some parts of the residence in the White House, Natalie realized JoAnne needed private time just like everyone else. The mother of two teenagers, Sizemore also appreciated those quiet moments to herself during a hot bath or curled up on the deck of her Annandale townhouse in northern Virginia, reading a magazine or just being alone doing nothing. She also admired the president's faith and her indefatigable habit of praying every morning, regardless of what was going on around her, regardless of where she was or who she was with.

Lord God, JoAnne began, *let Your holy angel be with me. I am Your servant, in awe of the immense sacrifice You made for me so long ago. Through Your mercy, I come, hopeful that with Your grace we will be able to stand against our enemies with courage and conviction. I look for Your guiding hand, for the strength of character, the wisdom and insight, and Your leadership as we go forward. In Your most holy name I pray. Amen.*

Rush sat on the couch and stared out the window into the District of Columbia, the city surrounding the White House. *They always say the weight of the country is on the president's shoulders*, she thought, *yet I feel uplifted and at peace. The national security meeting this morning is probably the most important and consequential of my presidential life so far, but I know that we'll do what is right and just. I can feel it in my heart.*

When JoAnne finished her morning prayer and reflection, she opened the door and greeted Special Agent Sizemore, appreciating more every day the sacrifices Natalie and thousands of others like her made to protect the president, protect the American way of life, the democracy, the freedoms and liberties, and the government. Regardless of their individual personal political persuasions—she had never thought to ask Sizemore how she voted—she stood there protecting the president of the United States of America against all enemies, foreign and domestic.

"Happy birthday, Natalie. Please go home at a reasonable hour so you can celebrate with your family." Rush knew her PSD (personal security detail) well and knew without being reminded many personal things about their lives.

"Thank you, Madam President. I'll secure by 1700 or so." Natalie would be lucky to get home by 2100, but she argued with the president of the United States only when it involved her personal security.

Within seconds, a member of the kitchen staff arrived with a pot of decaffeinated coffee, a glass of cranberry juice, and a dozen newspapers. Rush started with the weekend edition of the *Wall Street Journal*—she always started with the *Journal*—and then worked her way through the others. Each published its own opinions of what she should do regarding the drug cartels now in open warfare along the southern border, with

Libya, Iraq, and Afghanistan; what measures she should take; and how she should respond. The liberal papers always advocated economic and political sanctions, whereas the right wing media wanted war. It was never a simple, straightforward, binary choice. *I can't send American men and women into harm's way without the best plan, the best equipment, and the best leaders. It doesn't have to be the last option, but it has to be justified.*

Jeffers got it right again, she thought. Greg Jeffers was a young journalist covering the Pentagon for the *Wall Street Journal*, and although he had no military background or service, he came at every article with insightful research and a dogged determination to get the facts. This time he laid out five courses of action the president could take to counter another growing threat from the Middle East, from no reaction to a full response. He stepped through each scenario with a careful analysis of risk and gain, the monetary and human costs, and the political ramifications of each. Rush wondered how much of Jeffer's analysis would be fed back to her by her own staff in today's meeting.

Steve came up behind her, touching her cheek and kissing the top of her head. Husband and wife for thirty-five years, they were secure in their marriage, secure in each other, and acutely aware of each other's wants and needs. Her routine of morning solitude was a habit developed decades ago, and he always gave her this special time to herself.

"When can I expect you this evening?" he asked, knowing it would undoubtedly be another long day. They had a dinner party at 2000 for some members of the U.S. Senate and their spouses who didn't return to their districts for the weekend and he didn't want to do that one alone, even for a while.

"I assume it will be late, but I'll try to make it by 1900. I'm not sure how long the NSC staff meeting will run," referring to the National Security Council personnel whose job it was to keep the president informed of global political and military activities that might affect the United States and her allies.

"You know, whatever decision you make, people will die." Steve stated the obvious, but it was something his wife needed to hear. "And regardless of what you do, someone will always have a better answer."

Rush rolled her eyes and laughed quietly. "Yeah," she started, "I know. I just hope it doesn't devolve into the same food fight we saw consume the country after 9/11."

She moved through her morning routine, showering and dressing for the day's events. Before she was really ready for the meeting, the NSC was assembled in the large conference room, and the discussion began in earnest. The team was augmented this morning by several junior analysts with particular expertise in Iranian, Iraqi, Afghan, and Libyan affairs; global narcotics; weapons of mass destruction; and even an energy analyst. She had asked for the desk officers to be present because she wanted unedited and unfiltered answers.

The National Security Advisor was finishing the analysis of the global threat and summed up his recommendation. "The deliberate attacks on the fleet in Naples in August 2001, Pan Am 103, and the London police murder before that, hit squads going after President Reagan, the Berlin disco bombing, 9/11—all of those events and others fully justify a firm response." He continued for several minutes.

There are too many things we don't understand about them, Rush thought to herself. Unable to comprehend how they could use religion—in this case Islam—to commit these acts, she remembered justification for hundreds of thousands of Europeans moving across the Levant toward Jerusalem eleven hundred years ago when Christianity was used to justify the Crusades. Even though Pope Urban II launched the Crusades in an attempt to unite the church under him and not the kings and queens of Europe, the two events weren't alike but were remarkably similar. *The Crusades had not succeeded*, she observed to herself, *and neither will this wave of Islamic militarism.*

The meeting went on for several hours with intermittent breaks for smaller meetings and meals. Rush called for adjournment at 1800 and asked the senior staff to remain behind. The vice president, chief of staff, secretary of defense, secretary of state, national security advisor, and a few others moved to the Oval Office for a private discussion. Rush was anxious to have a more candid talk and see where all of this was heading.

The secretary of state began almost immediately after the door closed. "Madam President, you must consider suspending Executive Order 12333 prohibiting assassination of foreign leaders and go after these guys. We've got a half dozen leaders, some even claiming to be our allies, helping these groups with weapons, equipment, intelligence, and money."

Chairman of the Joint Chiefs and Marine General Russell "Rusty" Blackman agreed. "If we decapitate this monster, we'll be in a better position to prosecute the war against those who are left. We take out one of them as a message to the others and give them a chance to stop what they're doing. If they don't, well, we might just turn the big dogs loose."

The vice president added, "Congressman Barnes of Georgia reintroduced House Resolution 19 and already has fourteen bipartisan cosponsors. The bill would allow surgical strikes to take out the leadership instead of carpet bombing a city to get one guy. Bob thinks it has a real chance of passing the House."

"General, draw up plans for a surgical strike to take out one of the leaders. Who does it make sense to hit?" Rush asked although she was fairly sure what the answer would be.

Blackman didn't hesitate. "We go after Gaddafi in Libya. His fingerprints are on too many things we've ignored far too long."

The secretary of state agreed. "He's been there the longest, and even though most of the other leaders don't like him, they'll still get the message when he goes down. You know the drug lords along the southern border will also sit up and take notice."

"Madam President, perhaps we should look at President Assad in Syria instead," an analyst in the State Department's Bureau of Intelligence and Research spoke up for the first time and drew some curious looks from the more senior officials in the room.

Rush recognized him from the larger meeting but couldn't recall his name. "Why do you say that?"

"Jonathan Winston, ma'am, INR. Striking Gaddafi will be easy. If we go into Syria, a much more difficult target, we will demonstrate the U.S. military's supremacy on the battlefield, ma'am."

"Mr. Winston, we're the only military force in the world with credibility. We don't have to prove our supremacy to anyone," General Blackman asserted, "and we want a quick in and out, no large buildup of forces, and no footprints to follow." The chairman left no room for discussion on the issue, and Winston dropped it even as he made a note of it in his Moleskine.

"Bring me the plan when you get it done. If Barnes gets the resolution through the House and can get sponsors for it in the Senate, I'll sign it. Make sure the congressional leadership knows that and they get it done. Just in case it doesn't happen, though, ask the attorney general to get the language together for me to rescind 12333 by Executive Order."

Rush stood as she spoke and everyone in the office followed suit. "Let's kill the dragon, or at least one head of it. And don't give me a strategy of tactics: I want a comprehensive plan that solves the problem, not one that just puts a bandage on it. A Title 10 military operation with any support you need to get it done." She walked out of the Oval Office to the residence, definitely not looking forward to dinner.

Jonathan Winston left the White House and walked two blocks to Farragut Square, stopping at one of the few working pay phones still remaining in the District, depositing the required change and dialing (202) 364-5500. A recorded message announced that the Embassy of the State of Israel was closed until 0900 on Monday. Jonathan pushed 721 and got another answering machine that had no message. After the beep, he entered the code 670610 signifying June 10, 1967, the last day of the Six Day War, hung up, crossed the street to the Army and Navy Club, went upstairs to the Daiquiri Bar & Lounge on the first floor—where Rear Admiral Lucius W. Johnson first introduced Americans to the rum and citrus drink created by Jennings Cox in Cuba in 1898—and ordered a cocktail. It was busy on a Saturday night when the area's military retirees came for a nice meal with a 20 percent discount, good wine, and a jazz combo performing in the main dining room, reminiscent of an earlier day and more genteel world.

Twenty minutes later, a man entered the bar, sat next to Jonathan, and gave his drink order to the bartender. Two men meeting for a drink and catching up on a Saturday night—they looked like every other table in the club.

"So, Jonathan, what's up?" the man started in right after his drink arrived and they were alone in the crowd. They spoke for twenty minutes, paid the bill, and left the club, each going different directions into the crisp winter night.

Jonathan didn't notice the young officer who had previously entered the club and now observed him as he departed.

General Blackman organized his thoughts about the day's meetings and called his office on the secure cell phone. "Sergeant Greco, please find Colonel Bob Robichaux in Old Town Alexandria and invite him to my quarters tonight at 1930. His number is in the database on my computer. And let my wife know we're having company. I'm going straight home," he announced to his office staff and driver at the same time. The driver made an immediate left at the next traffic signal toward the general's quarters instead of returning to the Pentagon.

Robichaux took the call from the chairman's office and got his jacket from the hall closet. "Going to the Blackmans'. Do you want to come?" Robichaux asked his wife, Joan.

"Yes, I do. Peggy and I can work on that quilt while you and Rusty talk." Beth Robichaux and Peggy Blackman were friends in high school and college long before they each met and married their respective Marine husbands. The Blackman and Robichaux families vacationed together, one of the few bits of intelligence known only to a few inside the Capital Beltway—originally called the Circumferential Highway when construction was approved in 1955—surrounding Washington DC.

Blackman got out of the car, sent the driver home, and went into the house. He showered and changed quickly and reviewed the material he brought home in his briefcase. By the time Bob and Joan arrived, he was refreshed and ready to talk.

"Bob, the president wants to go after Gaddafi. Surgical. Decapitate these groups that think we won't respond."

"It's about time, Rusty. We've let that maniac get away with too much for too long. We need to shut him down *now*."

"One of the State Department analysts suggested to the president that we go after Assad instead. What do you think about that?"

"After the attack on the ARG in Naples and Pan Am 103, Gaddafi's a no-brainer. Wonder why he would suggest Syria instead of Libya?"

"I'm asking the same question, Bob. And while both of them are dirtbags, the two aren't even close to being equal, at least regarding the U.S. I asked about the analyst—Jonathan Winston is his name and he works in INR at State—and he's never worked Syria before. It doesn't add up."

"What's the plan, Rusty?"

"It's being drawn up now. Got any suggestions?"

"As a matter of fact, I do. When I was a staff platoon commander at the Basic School, I had a Marine who was the best shooter I've ever seen. If she's still in the Marine Corps and can get within fifteen hundred or two thousand meters of Gaddafi, she can take him down."

Rusty looked at him with eyebrows raised. "We send a woman in there and she gets rolled up—how do you think the press and the American people will handle it, particularly if she's tortured and raped in captivity, Bob?"

"I don't know, but she's outstanding at hitting targets at very long range. What's more, she grew up in Libya, Rusty, and she speaks Arabic." Bob knew he got the general's attention.

"What's her name, Bob?"

"Katy Morgan." Robichaux picked up his cell phone and hit a speed-dial number. "Colonel Robichaux for First Sergeant Mersino, please," Bob said into the phone. "John, how are you? How's the family?"

After catching up briefly on each other's lives and careers, Robichaux asked Mersino about the officer. "Do you remember her, John? Her name is Morgan."

"Colonel, she shot better than me and at greater distances. She's even better than Matt Hamel, and he's the best in the Corps. She'd be in a scout-sniper unit, but they don't accept women, and she's left-handed too."

"Thanks, John. We have a mission coming up, and I'll give you a call. How much advance notice do you need to start rolling?"

"Twenty minutes, sir—ten if it's an emergency," Mersino said, and Robichaux laughed but knew he was serious.

While the colonel was on the phone, General Blackman received a call. He listened, thanked the caller, and hung up. "You know that analyst I told you about—Winston from INR? He left the White House right after the meeting, walked to the Army-Navy Club, met with the Israeli defense attaché Brigadier General Uri Shetzer, and both departed after a brief conversation. My guy heard Winston say "Libya" and "Gaddafi" but couldn't make out the rest of the conversation."

Robichaux thought that over for a minute. There was an explanation but whatever it was wasn't obvious. Blackman got another call from Headquarters Marine Corps, asked a few questions, and hung up.

"She's still on active duty, a captain and currently in an intel billet with SEAL Team 3 at Coronado." SEALs—officially the Naval Special Warfare Group—operate globally from the Naval Amphibious Bases at Little Creek, Virginia; on the Atlantic coast and Coronado, California, out west. NSWG 3 trains to deploy assets from submarines and in the use of underwater swimmer delivery vehicles to approach beaches and coastlines clandestinely. Katy was part of the N-2 section with her navy colleagues providing fusion of all-source intelligence and intelligence preparation of the battlefield plans for the SEALs.

"I'll find Morgan and get orders cut bringing her to Quantico," Robichaux replied. "We can create a working group so it doesn't raise questions. The CO of SEAL Team 3 is Commander Mike Mitchell—we were classmates at Marine Corps Command & Staff College and served together before that. I'll give him a call to work things out."

The two officers joined their wives for dinner and tried keeping the conversation light even as their brains were racing with questions and ideas. Both women saw through the façade, and after dinner, they moved to the den to survey the quilt, leaving the men to continue their discussion. Blackman took another call before they resumed.

Chapter 33

February 19, 2008
Coronado, California

Katy Morgan answered her cell phone while negotiating the traffic heading into the Naval Amphibious Base, leaving home later than usual this morning, tired after spending the weekend skiing at Big Bear Mountain with Elyse Anderson, a navy lieutenant commander in the intelligence section where she worked. They took advantage of the Presidents' Day long weekend to make the five-hour drive Friday after work. They skied all Saturday, Sunday, and Monday morning before heading back to San Diego in the afternoon. She glanced at the clock on the dashboard, wondering who would be calling her at 0620.

"Captain Morgan, this is Commander Mitchell."

"Good morning, sir," she said, getting an immediate answer to her question. "How can I help you?" She went through her mental schedule quickly but couldn't remember a meeting this morning with the commanding officer.

"I'm sending you to Quantico today for some temporary duty. Please see me as soon as you get in."

"I'll be there in ten minutes, commander," hoping he would elaborate on the nature of the assignment. He simply hung up.

Traffic seemed to slow to a crawl even though she was driving thirty miles per hour, slowing to fifteen in the school zone. She parked in the first available spot rather than wasting time looking for something closer to the building and ran to her office to check her uniform and get a pen and a notebook. She knocked on Mitchell's door eight minutes after the call.

"Have a seat, Captain. I got a call over the weekend from Colonel Robichaux, who I believe you know."

"Yes, sir, he was my staff platoon commander at the Basic School," she answered matter-of-factly.

"He needs you for a working group they're conducting on Marine integration in SEAL units. You'll report to him at Quantico." Mitchell didn't really know the nature of the assignment beyond what he told Katy but let her assume he did. "The orders are open-ended, so you might be gone for several weeks. Call the colonel after this meeting for travel and uniform requirements, bachelor officer quarters availability, and other details. The duty driver will take you to the airport. Any questions?" He wrote a phone number on a piece of paper and slid it across the table.

"None, sir. I'll call the colonel ASAP and let you know what he says."

"No need. You report directly to him as of now." Mitchell seemed irritated one of his officers was getting pulled on short notice, particularly as Katy was the best tactical intelligence officer in the group. She worked hard, anticipated the SEALs' questions before they asked, and made sure she had the right answers when they needed them. They were preparing for joint exercises with U.S. and foreign special operations units, and he needed her expertise and energy. That said, he knew Robichaux well enough to realize the working group story was bogus; Katy had over a year with the group, but the CO knew many Marine officers far more experienced and knowledgeable for a working group on integration. "You're dismissed."

"Thank you, sir." She exited the office and headed back to her desk and dialed Robichaux's number. He answered on the first ring in Washington, as though he was expecting her call.

"Good morning, Katy. Thanks for calling."

"Good morning, Colonel. How are you, sir?"

"Great. The CO filled you in on the assignment?"

"He didn't say much, sir, except I report to you and I need to be in Quantico by this evening."

"Senior Chief Carl Zemanski from the chairman's office will pick you up at Dulles Airport. He'll have more information for you when you arrive."

"The chairman of what, sir?"

Robichaux smiled before he answered. "Chairman of the Joint Chiefs of Staff, General Blackman. Your flight's at 1145, so you need to get moving. Commander Mitchell will support you on the ground there." He passed the phone to Zemanski, who briefed Katy on the details she needed to prepare for the temporary duty assignment.

After she hung up the phone, her mind went in a hundred directions trying to figure out why she was needed at Quantico, what was so important that CJCS's driver was picking her up from the airport, and how she was going to juggle her schedule to provide the intelligence to the SEALs for the exercise.

Katy's five-hour flight landed at 1945. She went to the baggage carrousel and immediately saw a uniformed senior chief in the navy peacoat waiting by the exit door. Their eyes met when he saw her uniform and moved to meet her as the luggage began arriving.

"Captain Morgan, welcome to DC."

"Good evening, Senior Chief. Its colder here than in San Diego!"

"Yes, ma'am, it is. The car is waiting right outside the door so we won't be in the weather very long."

True to his word, an unmarked Lincoln Town Car was waiting with the engine running and the heat on; the driver had to show his CJCS credentials four times so airport security would allow him to stop directly in front of the building. He opened the rear right door for Katy to get in while Zemanski moved around the car and slid into the backseat next to her.

"Colonel Robichaux will meet you at the Willard Hotel where you'll be staying for the next few days."

"Senior Chief, there's no way my per diem will cover the cost of the Willard, and my CO won't approve any reimbursement claim above that rate. Any other hotels near there more reasonable?"

"Don't worry about it, Captain. I'll take care of the hotel bill. It'll be paid from another account and won't be billed to your command. Just charge all meals and drinks you have at the hotel to your room. General Blackman and Colonel Robichaux thought it best to have you stay close to the Pentagon and the White House."

Katy's turned to face Zemanski. "Why do I need to be close to the White House?" Zemanski hit redial and handed her the cell phone.

"Katy, welcome to DC. I'll see you in twenty minutes and answer all your questions," Robichaux announced as though he was listening to the conversation in the car, something she didn't immediately rule out.

Katy spent the remainder of the drive processing everything she heard and experienced throughout the day. Just as she never had all the details she wanted when fusing all-source information into actionable intelligence for her SEALs, now she didn't have everything she needed for this assignment. She organized her thoughts for the meeting with Colonel Robichaux, preparing a list of essential elements of information or EEIs she needed to do the mission, although she still was unaware of what she was being asked to do. *It must be important,* she told herself, *if it involves the White House, getting me across the country on short notice, and committing resources from CJCS's office for such a junior officer.*

Don't wimp out, Katy admonished herself, and then almost laughed out loud. How many times had she told herself the same thing, and every time she hadn't wimped out and always had succeeded. This time would be no different.

Stop asking why this is happening to me and figure out what it's trying to teach me. Stay inspired, stay passionate, stay motivated, stay grateful, and stay open-minded. I never lose. Either I win or I learn. So what will I learn today? Katy remembered then Captain Robichaux's wisdom during the "Company in the Night Defense" exercise at TBS; now she was asking herself, *What would Robichaux do?*

She saluted the colonel as she stepped out of the car even though he wasn't in uniform, opting instead for an open-collar button-down shirt and sports coat. She turned back toward the car just as Zemanski, reading her mind again, told her the luggage would be delivered to her room as he handed her a key. Katy and Robichaux entered the hotel and headed to the Round Robin Bar; they were directed to a reserved private table where they could speak without fear of being overheard, a rare commodity inside the Washington Beltway. They ordered drinks and sandwiches, and he spoke before the waiter returned.

"Katy, General Blackman selected you for a very special classified mission, which he'll tell you about tomorrow at the Pentagon, and then you'll spend a few months training at Quantico, Hurlburt Field in Florida, 29 Palms, Fort Benning, and other locations. It will test all of your special skills, including marksmanship, Arabic, operational intelligence, and physical fitness. You'll be on your own during the op, with a thousand people supporting you. There's a clear and present danger that you'll be asked to eliminate."

Katy wasn't sure what he meant by "eliminate" but knew better than to ask questions the answers to which were classified, so she asked the one that had been nagging her since the conversation in the car.

"Colonel, Senior Chief Zemanski said I'm staying here to be close to the White House. Why is that, sir?"

"For this operation, you are a Tier 1 asset. You'll get whatever equipment, transportation, and funding you need to complete the mission. You will be the supported unit. Supporting units will come from across the Department of Defense and other agencies and organizations within the government." He let that sink in for a moment. "And the president wants to meet you Thursday morning."

Katy tried to focus on the rest of the evening; dinner came and went, the conversation drifted from duty stations and assignments to family and her TBS class. When she got to her room—Zemanski had arranged a one-bedroom suite larger even than her entire apartment in San Diego—she was confused, exhausted, exhilarated, and tired. Before she could start sorting out the day's events, she heard her cell phone buzz. The text message was from Colonel Robichaux.

```
I'll pick you up tomorrow at 1000. We're meeting with CJCS
so wear your dress uniform. Call hotel laundry and get your
Dress Blue "A" uniform cleaned and pressed for the meeting
on Thursday. OPSEC on all above. Keep it close hold and don't
share it with anyone including NSWG 3, your boyfriend, or
your parents. Get some rest! Goodnight.

Aye aye, colonel. I'll be ready. Goodnight.
```

This morning she was in San Diego after a fantastic weekend skiing with Elyse, enjoying the après ski hot tub at Bear Mountain Ski Resort where they stayed, flirting with supposedly single guys and dancing well into the night at Snow Summit Ski Resort and Slopeside Speakeasy, and finishing with nightcaps at Whiskey Dave's. The weekend that ended twenty-four hours previously already seemed an eternity ago.

Katy snapped out of it, unpacked, and got the hotel iron from its cradle to press her dress uniform for tomorrow's meeting. She checked her pumps, the necktab, and the alignment of the ribbons and badges on her uniform coat. When she was sure her dress uniform was ready, she called the laundry service and asked them to pick up her blues. A man roughly her parents' age, whose nametag indicated he was Abner Dalupang, arrived to take the uniform. After discovering he was Filipino, she started to explain what she needed before he interrupted her.

"Captain, I'm a navy senior chief moonlighting here at the hotel. I've been a steward for several flag officers and have worked around Marines all my career. I'll take good care of your uniform and have it back to you any time after 1500 tomorrow, if that's acceptable. Please also give me your decorations, and I will make sure they are properly displayed."

Filipinos can be recruited for service under the provisions of Article XXVII of the Military Bases Agreement of 1947 between the United States and the Republic of the Philippines, assigned to stewarding duties in the navy; laws and regulations later were amended to allow them to serve in other specialties, both as officers and enlisted personnel. Filipinos who serve honorably for at least three years can apply for citizenship without having to meet some requirements for naturalization.

"Perfect, Senior Chief. Salamat, po!" she thanked him in Tagalog. To which he answered, "Walung anuman, Kapitan!" *Po* is usually included at the end of a sentence recognizing the person being addressed as older or more senior. Katy acknowledged his age, whereas he respected her rank. They laughed at each other and agreed to meet the following day to "inspect" her blues together after the cleaning and pressing.

Before she was fully rested, Katy was awake, in the gym for a quick workout, then back to the room to shower and dress. She went downstairs for breakfast in mufti, saving her dress uniform for the meeting later in the morning. She was surprised to see Zemanski in the lobby and invited him to join her.

"Good morning, Captain," he said as they were seated by the maître d'hôtel. "Did you get some rest?"

"Not really. I'm not sure what's going on or how I fit into the plan, so it was a restless night with lots to think about."

"Well, ma'am, I believe it'll be clear after the meeting with the chairman this morning. He and the colonel will lay out the plan and then let you get on with the training part of the op." Zemanski knew but couldn't share the details with her. "That said, there's only one Marine with the skills, training, and background to do this mission, and it's you, Captain."

Colonel Robichaux arrived as they were finishing breakfast and ordered a cup of coffee. "After the meeting, we'll meet with some of the people who'll support you with intelligence and logistics. Don't be afraid to speak up if you see something you need that they don't offer. We'll get anything you want."

That in no way soothed her nerves.

"Good morning, Captain Morgan. Take a seat." General Blackman was already watching to see if she was easily rattled or intimidated; he saw nothing of the sort.

"Thank you, General. Good morning." Katy did as she was ordered and kept calm, at least on the outside. "Sir, I heard you speak at the Marines' Memorial Club in San Francisco last October on force projection in the Middle East. I used some of your remarks for an assessment I was preparing for SEAL Team 3."

"Good, I hope it was helpful. Colonel Robichaux tells me you're one hell of a shot. Longest range?"

"General, I hit the target center mass nine out of ten times from seventeen hundred meters at Camp Pendleton last September." When she saw a puzzled look on his face, she continued. "On the tenth shot, one of the corporals threw a bucket of ice water on my head just as I pulled the trigger. That time I hit the nine-ring." She said it matter-of-factly and not as an excuse.

"What's the farthest you feel you can hit the target?"

"With the correct rifle and ammunition, General, I feel confident I can hit the target from two thousand meters. I'll need a good spotter and decent weather, sir."

"Do you have anyone in mind for the spotter?"

"Sir, Staff Sergeant Mersino was at TBS when I learned to shoot. He would be the best spotter for me, if he's still in the Marine Corps."

Robichaux spoke for the first time since the meeting started. "First Sergeant Mersino is driving up from Camp Lejeune today. He'll join us for dinner this evening."

Why am I not surprised? Katy asked herself.

"If this is the right time, General, what's the mission?"

"It's the right time, Katy O." She didn't fail to notice reference to her TBS nickname; the general obviously had intel on her too. "We're going to drop you into your old stomping ground, the Libyan desert, to take out Gaddafi. You and First Sergeant Mersino will be inserted from *Pasadena* near Benghazi, work your way inland to his desert compound at al Aziziyah, and when the opportunity presents itself, you'll pull the trigger."

USS *Pasadena*, SSN-752, is the third ship in the U.S. Navy to be named for the city of Pasadena, California, and the forty-first boat in the *Los Angeles* class of nuclear-powered attack submarines to be launched. With twelve officers and ninety-eight seamen, she is a multimission platform; in this case, it would be to insert Morgan and Mersino clandestinely along the Libyan coast before continuing operations throughout the Mediterranean Sea.

Katy realized she was holding her breath as the chairman was speaking; she didn't want him or Robichaux to see her gasping for air, so she forced herself to breathe slowly as she recovered her composure. "When would you like this done, sir?"

"We'll get to that later, Katy," Robichaux said as he and Blackman exchanged amused looks. "Right now we want to get you refresher training, so it's ten of out ten, center mass, every time, ice water or not. You might get only one shot, so it has to count."

The three Marines talked for another fifteen minutes before Zemanski knocked and entered the chairman's office.

"I believe you already met Senior Chief Zemanski, right?" He didn't wait for an answer. "He'll be by your side throughout the next few months as you get ready for this deployment. Whatever you need, tell him. If it's difficult, he'll do it immediately. If it's impossible, give him a little extra time to deliver."

Blackman finished the meeting by saying, "Captain, I think you know how important discretion is for this operation. Other than the four of us, First Sergeant Mersino, and President Rush, you are not to discuss this with anyone else for any reason. If someone asks you about it, even if they appear to know what they're talking about, don't assume they do and report it to the colonel or senior chief immediately."

"Aye aye, General."

With that, Zemanski led them down the hall to Colonel Robichaux's office and closed the door. The conference table was littered with topographical maps, nautical charts, and binders of information about Libya marked Top Secret. For her job with NSWG 3, Katy was already cleared for TS codeword material.

"Katy, the most important resources you need are courage, decisiveness, and physical and mental agility. You need to think on your feet, keep your head on a swivel, adjust to a changing situation, and revise the plan if you need to without hesitation. It'll be a VUCA operation."

"VUCA, sir?" Katy wasn't sure she heard him properly.

"Volatile, uncertain, complex, and ambiguous. Just when you have everything figured out, something will change, and you'll have to adjust. There are no straight lines in this mission, not even the gun target line. At that distance, even your shot will curve with the wind and gravity. The mission will do the same, moving one direction and then make a sharp turn in another. We want to give you everything you need to succeed, so the next few months will take everything you have and then some. Failure is not an option."

"I understand, Colonel." Katy wasn't sure she did but couldn't think of anything else to say at this point.

"You'll depart the hotel at 1830, and we'll meet at the Capital Grille for dinner. First Sergeant Mersino will join us, as will Congressman Steve Bossie and his wife, Tara, and my wife, Beth. It's social for now. The congressman will be read in on the operation later, so we want him to know who you are when that happens. He's a retired Marine colonel, so there'll be plenty to keep the conversation going." Robichaux handed Katy an itinerary for the next few days.

"As you can see, the driver will pick you up tomorrow at 0900 and take you to the White House. We'll meet beforehand and drive through the Lafayette Park entrance. The meeting is at 1030, so there's plenty of time to clear security and get to the right place."

"What am I supposed to tell the president, sir?" Katy still wasn't sure why the meeting was occurring.

"She wants to meet you and First Sergeant Mersino now before you begin training when it will be more difficult to get the two of you here without raising suspicion. She wants to express her appreciation for your service. General Blackman will also be there.

"If you check the itinerary, you'll see there's a visit to see your folks in Charleston. Senior Chief already bought you a ticket to fly down tomorrow afternoon, departing Reagan National Airport at 1530, and back up here on Sunday at 1845. Take the time to be with them and use the working group as the reason you're up here. You can tell them another officer dropped out at the last minute with the flu, so they sent you orders instead. Leave whatever you don't need for the Charleston trip in your room at the Willard. You'll be staying there for the next couple of weeks.

"Training starts Monday at Quantico. The driver will pick you up at 0700 and drive you to the Marine Corps museum. I'll meet you there with First Sergeant Mersino, we'll transfer to a government vehicle, and go on base. The driver will be there to pick you up when we finish each day and take you back to the hotel. Any questions?"

"No, sir. I'm ready to go."

They finished the brief meeting, and Zemanski took her back through the Pentagon maze to the car. After getting to her hotel room, Katy called her parents to let them know she was coming and when to pick her up from the airport. They were, of course, delighted, believing she was still in San Diego. Just as she hung up, the hotel phone rang.

"*Kapitan*, this is Abner from the laundry. May I bring your uniform to the room?"

"You certainly may, Senior Chief!"

As expected, Katy's blues were immaculate and the ribbons and badges accurately displayed with precision. Abner had obviously spent considerable time making sure every detail was perfect, even going so far as to replace two ribbons that were slightly soiled.

"There was a navy officer named Michelle Dalupang in my intel class at NMITC in 2000. She graduated from the Naval Academy and was a superb officer. I'm not sure if she stayed in the navy."

"Thank you, *Kapitan*." Abner beamed with pride. "Michelle is my eldest daughter of four. She's now stationed at the Naval Submarine Base New London in Groton, Connecticut. She's up for lieutenant commander next year."

"Please pass her my regards, Senior Chief. And thank you for taking care of my uniform—it's perfect!" Katy tried tipping him, but Abner wouldn't accept it.

"It's my honor to help. As before, please let me know if you need anything else. I'm on duty 24/7, so all you have to do is call Guest Services and ask for me."

After he departed, Katy dressed for dinner, choosing a long-sleeved A-line dress, a birthday gift from her mother last year, with heels and a matching handbag. She looked professional and feminine in a style befitting a Marine officer. She stepped out of the elevator into the lobby at 1825. The driver was waiting just inside the entrance to the hotel.

Robichaux made the introductions once everyone arrived to the dinner table. Katy learned that Congressman Bossie sat on the House Armed Services Committee after serving thirty years in the Marine Corps, retiring from the infantry as a colonel. His wife, Tara, was the vice president's director of legislative affairs. Beth Robichaux was a docent at the National Museum of the Marine Corps in Triangle, Virginia, just outside the front gate of the sprawling Marine Corps Base Quantico along the Potomac River. Mersino was now the first sergeant of A Company, First Battalion, Eighth Marine Regiment at Camp Lejeune, North Carolina, having just returned from a deployment to the Mediterranean Sea, his fifteenth six-month deployment since enlisting in the Marine Corps seventeen years previously. Zemanski joined them as did Senior Chief Dalupang. Katy was again surprised, learning he also worked in CJCS's office, purposefully inserted into the hotel staff to watch over and protect her, and was read in on the operation.

Katy enjoyed the conversation as it moved from the Corps to public service and life and work inside the Capital Beltway surrounding Washington DC. Bossie was Robichaux's Marine Expeditionary Unit commander when the latter's battalion was attacked in the Naples harbor. As she found out over dinner, Mersino—Robichaux told the story because he knew the first sergeant never would—was a platoon sergeant in the same battalion and was awarded the Navy and Marine Corps Medal, the highest non-combat decoration for heroism. He suffered third-degree burns on his hands and face when he rescued dozens of sailors and Marines from USS *Sumter County*. Mersino boarded the ship singlehandedly not once but seven times before she eventually sank, carrying the last sailor he could reach off the ship on his shoulders, his uniform and hair on fire, his face streaked with dirt, sweat, and blood, clinging to the accommodation ladder being dragged underwater with the ship until the end fixed to the pier broke loose just as he jumped ashore. Mersino received a Christmas card from the sailor every year with notes of gratitude from the man's wife and children.

Their husband and father made it home alive unlike dozens of others who died in their sleep on the ship.

Robichaux also told the group of Zemanski's heroism and quick thinking in destroying two of the motorboats in Naples, saving hundreds of lives in the process. "He acted without hesitation in self-defense to degrade the enemy's full attack on our forces."

Bossie was interested in Katy's work with the SEALs. She described getting orders to Camp Lejeune after completing intelligence training, deploying aboard USS *Nassau* providing intelligence support to the embarked Marines after promotion to captain, before being assigned to NSWG 3 at Coronado.

"Colonel Robichaux told me you grew up in Libya. Was your dad in the air force stationed at Wheelus?"

"No, Colonel, he worked for an oil services company. My parents put me in a Libyan school, so I had class in Arabic eight hours a day." Katy valued Bossie more as a Marine officer than as a politician.

Robichaux added to her story, making it Katy's turn to be embarrassed. "Steve, Katy maxed out the language proficiency tests and is a qualified Foreign Area Officer in Arabic, German, French, and Italian—any others I don't know about?—and is a sniper-quality sharpshooter. She was the cadet regimental commander and valedictorian at The Citadel and the top graduate in her TBS class as well as the intel class at NMITC. And her CO at NSWG 3 told me she's his best analyst."

"The colonel was my staff platoon commander, and the first sergeant was my shooting instructor at TBS, so everything I know about being a Marine I learned from them," Katy said, hoping to shine the spotlight away from her.

"Captain Morgan is the finest shooter in the Marine Corps today, bar none," Mersino volunteered.

Katy was stunned. "You can't be serious, First Sergeant."

"I am, Captain. I taught at the First Marine Division Scout Sniper School at Camp Pendleton after I left Quantico. I know every shooter in the Marine Corps. They're all outstanding snipers, but none of them consistently can hit long-distance targets as well as you do, ma'am."

Mersino spoke so matter-of-factly no one doubted him. "I only wish women were allowed to go through the course—at least one woman I know of." He smiled, briefly, acknowledging her competence.

"Can't you get your congressional buddies to pass a bill letting women go to that school? I'll get the president to sign it into law!" Tara chided her husband, whereupon everyone at the table laughed.

"Here's to women attending that sniper school place!" Beth spoke up as they toasted Katy's success.

Toward the end of the evening Robichaux signaled it was time to depart. Katy thanked everyone for the evening and moved toward the door while Zemanski paid the bill and escorted her to the waiting vehicle. On the way to the hotel, he reviewed the schedule for the next morning and reminded her to have her suitcase packed for the weekend in case the meeting at the White House went later than expected; they could leave it in the car should she not have time to return to the hotel before her flight.

Senior Chief's intuition proved correct; the meeting was delayed until noon, and then again until 1300. He had an alternate booking for Katy departing at 1700 through Detroit that wouldn't get her into Charleston until 2200.

President Rush was genuinely happy to meet Katy Morgan and Dave Mersino, having been briefed on their personal and professional backgrounds. The twenty-minute meeting lasted an hour—the West Wing staff had to reschedule two other meetings, unusual in the Rush administration—with the president asking questions of each Marine and confirming her support for the mission.

"You know, Beth Robichaux and I went to the University of North Carolina together, and I introduced her to the colonel a few years after we graduated. Bob and I served together on a promotion board at Headquarters Marine Corps, and he seemed the perfect match for her. I take full credit!" The president laughed with everyone. "So you see, we're all related to Colonel Robichaux in some way.

As they got up to leave, President Rush asked Katy to remain behind in the Oval Office. Even the Secret Service agent stepped outside.

"Katy, you know how important this operation is. I never faced anything like it when I was in the Corps, so I can't say I know how you're feeling right now. Just know there are a bunch of folks pulling for you, and they don't even know who you are or what you're gonna do. Do it well and come home safely. I'll see you again when you get back. Good luck and Godspeed, Marine."

"Thank you, Madam President. I won't let you down." Katy was sincere as she said it, not quite sure how she was going to deliver such a tall order.

They left the White House and drove straight to Reagan National Airport. Katy made the early 1530 flight and was met on arrival in Charleston by her family. They dined at Slightly North of Broad restaurant on East Bay Street before heading home for the weekend. Halfway through dinner, she noticed people glancing at her, finally realizing she was still wearing her dress blue uniform. Two girls not more than seven years old asked to take a photograph with her; she enthusiastically agreed and had to take two more before Katy admitted to her family she was exhausted and it had been a long couple of days. Her folks felt there was more to the story than she was admitting but knew better than to ask.

Her dad paid the bill, and as they left the restaurant, the other diners stood and applauded, proud of this young Marine officer even as they had no idea what she was being tasked to do.

Chapter 34

March 17, 2008
Tel Aviv, Israel

"What's JoAnne Rush thinking?" Shlomo Klingman had just been appointed prime minister, and one of the first briefings was on the evolving situation regarding their man in Tripoli. "I know Uri Shetzer, and if he says they have a real chance to assassinate Avraham Abelman, then it's true. We can't reveal to them that we know about the operation, so the only option is to stop the sniper from pulling the trigger. They'll believe the Libyans intercepted him."

"When you say stop him from pulling the trigger, do you mean kill the American, Shlomo?" The defense minister wanted to understand the PM's thoughts and intentions.

"Ari, we have no choice. We've been able to keep the region destabilized for two decades using Gaddafi as the foil to focus attention away from us and on the Libyans, the Iraqis, the Yemenis, the Syrians, or the Palestinians. We can't afford to lose the asset. Disable him if possible, kill him if you have to, but don't allow the American to take out Avraham."

Ari continued pressing; he knew if there was blowback from killing the American, it would likely fall on his shoulders. "Can't we accomplish the same thing without Gaddafi?"

"Avraham is on the inside, unchallenged in Libya and respected by many countries opposed to Israel. He can snap his fingers and a

221

thousand fighters will march off to Paris to kill Christmas shoppers if that's what we want. If we can't redirect frustration against us in a different direction, expansion of the settlements and our operations in Gaza will see the light of day; we can't allow that! End of discussion. We also can't let the Americans know all of the their people killed over the last two decades were carried out by our man, not the real Gaddafi.

"You know the Americans will send a SEAL Team to Tripoli, so tell Uri to keep an eye on them through his network of informants at the bases. We want to account for every unit every day, where they are, what they're doing, and who might sneak away to conduct a separate operation. And tell our ambassador to put pressure on the White House to call it off without telling them we know what's going on."

Defense Minister Avi Goldman excused himself and returned to his office, ordering Major David Pearlman, commander of the Sayeret Matkal to visit him immediately. When he arrived, Goldman tasked him with stopping the American team at all costs.

Chapter 35

April 4, 2008
Safita, Syria

Although Paul Stephens was only thirty years old, after eight months in captivity, he looked twice that age: gaunt with drawn eyes, a full graying beard, and injuries suffered from repeated beatings and torture. He shuffled like an old man, hunched over with a slow gait. His captors didn't immediately interrogate him, instead simply hurting him for its own sake and their enjoyment. Immediately after being taken in Majd al Anjar and transported to Safita, his captors began with the usual and expected sensory, food, and water deprivation common to interrogations and intimidation; Paul handled it far better than even he expected. He prepared himself mentally for the interrogation that only began a full month after his capture.

"Good morning, Captain Stephens," the Syrian interrogator said with the slightest accent but in idiomatic English, "my name is Yousef. May I call you Paul? You and I will get to be good friends if you help me, otherwise it will get very difficult for you. I hope you understand that." He nodded his head in agreement, eyebrows raised. Paul said nothing.

"It's all right, Paul. I know your survival training at Cherry Point taught you to remain silent. The harder I work to get answers, though, the more you'll suffer, and I really don't want you to suffer. Neither would Rachel, Victoria, or your unborn daughter. Rachel was on television the other day saying she felt sympathy for me because I didn't know her husband and what he was capable of." He paused for effect. "We'll see. Now, please tell me about the intelligence reports you sent to Washington. What were the subjects of those reports, and who did you report on?"

Paul felt a gut punch when Yousef mentioned Rachel's and Victoria's names and discussed his survival training, more surprised he even knew where he underwent the training. He was unaware of the many details of his life and career being shared on the mainstream media, giving fodder to those holding him and insights into his training and fortitude.

"I'll give you one more chance to discuss the reports."

Paul noticed how gentle Yousef's voice was, as though he were speaking to a child who just didn't understand the rules. When Paul didn't reply, he shrugged and spoke a few words to a colleague. "Mr. Mahmoud, would you please proceed?"

What happened next would haunt Paul for the rest of his life. Mahmoud began rubbing olive oil on the soles of Paul's feet, massaging it well into the pores until they would accept no more. He then lit a small butane blowtorch, the type a chef might use to caramelize sugar on crème brûlée, rendering it golden brown. Yousef looked at Paul again. When he got no reaction, he nodded once at Mahmoud.

Paul couldn't comprehend the popping noise he heard above the sound of his own screams, his brain not accepting that the oil was expanding as it got hot and causing the pores to explode. The soft, tender skin on his soles was sending urgent real-time megadata to his central nervous system: just in case he wasn't aware, his body was transmitting unmistakable signals of pure pain. Within thirty seconds, his feet were ravaged, he was sweating profusely, tears ran from his eyes, and he was hoarse from screaming.

"Let's let that sink in, shall we?" Yousef walked out of the room as Mahmoud and another man dragged Paul back to his cell.

Three days later, they hauled him back to the torture chamber and slapped his soles with a leather riding crop used to encourage horses and camels to run faster. They hung him from the ceiling and took turns driving their fists into his gut, his kidneys, and his groin. They also applied olive oil and the blowtorch to his back, leaving open welts that hurt him whenever he moved or breathed. After a few days, they would repeat the process, stopping only to ask Paul questions, many about things he had no knowledge of.

Every person undergoing torture eventually breaks down and obeys his captors. Although Paul was determined not to do so, he felt his willpower getting weaker with each episode, holding back as long as he was able. Yousef added ten minutes to each session, knowing Paul would eventually break, in the meantime searching for the least amount of pain he could endure before that happened. He understood Paul did not consider Yousef an authority figure, at least not in the beginning, so he had to train the Marine, using innate cruelty, dehumanization, and disinhibition, to the point where the only option short of death was to cooperate. It was nascent evil on full display.

Paul knew better than to lie; it was too easy to make a mistake under duress. On top of that, he was tired, hungry, thirsty, and in pain; and Yousef would've seen through his deception immediately. Instead he decided to relate actual stories from his life experiences. In one instance he told of an incident where a team of special operators attacked an enemy prison and rescued a CIA officer who had been captured; it was the plot from *Spy Game*, a movie he saw a few years before. In another instance, he changed the location from Nigeria to the Middle East of *Tears of the Sun*, a Bruce Willis movie involving SEALs. Because he wasn't creating the deceptions from scratch, he only had to remember a few discrete details to keep the story accurate and consistent.

And so it went month after month, the beatings and torture, the destruction of his soles and soul, and the deprivation of freedom that slowly took its toll. Paul was psychologically crushed, until Ambassador Roger Pugh was thrown into the cell with him, a serving foreign service officer and ambassador to Afghanistan until he too was captured a few weeks previously in Kabul. Paul recognized him from photographs of the Heads of Missions meeting in Muscat, Oman, in January that year. They traded news and kept each other motivated, they practiced stories to tell their captors, and they talked about going home.

This morning was different, though. The guards brought clean clothes—Paul's first in eight months—with a bar of soap, a washcloth, and a bucket of water. He and Roger were told to shave, brush their teeth, bathe as best they could, and change clothes. Although the ambassador had only been a captive for a couple of weeks, his bucket was just as black and filthy as Paul's after the cat bath. But it drove their morale sky high, something they cautioned each other against in case this was just psychological torture to raise hopes and then crush their spirit even further. They weren't sure what was happening, but it sure felt good.

The guards returned and put hoods on the two, loaded them into a four-wheel-drive, and headed south. Paul assumed they were going to be flown somewhere when he heard aircraft engines nearby; they were being taken to the Sharyat Air Base near Homs, where they were loaded onto an Ilyushin Il-76 strategic airlifter. Before they departed, Yousef informed them they were sold to another group, fetching 5 million dollars each. "Somebody must really want you badly, even more than *Daesh*," he said, using the Arabic name for the self-proclaimed caliphate of the Islamic State of Iraq and Syria. He stepped out of the hatch and closed it behind him. They were airborne in two minutes.

The six-hour flight provided a brief respite from the conditions in Safita, permitting Paul and Roger much-needed sleep. The enthusiasm would be short-lived, however, when they realized they were landing at Tripoli International Airport in Libya, dashing any hopes they were being released directly to the U.S. government or an intermediary and on their way home.

They were loaded into an armored personnel carrier and immediately driven off the airfield south out of the city. The vehicle was hot; there was no air-conditioning or, for that matter, *air* in the back where they were being held. Even the two Libyan guards were suffering, taking turns sticking their nose out the small window covered by bars. They did not allow the Americans to do the same.

Paul could tell they were entering a compound of some sort, and they were only twenty minutes outside the city. The back door opened suddenly, flooding the compartment with sunlight and forcing everyone inside to shield their eyes. They were dragged out of the vehicle and thrown to the ground, kicked and hit with the butt of a rifle, and finally taken to a small building off to the side of the gate they had just come through.

"So this is the coward who abducted the patriot Khalid Jalili from his hotel room in Dubai," Colonel Gaddafi said as he approached the two men still on the ground. "Well, Captain Stephens, you did yourself no favors. You will spend the rest of your natural life paying the price for such arrogance, and we'll treat you the same as I'm sure your President Rush is treating Khalid at Gitmo."

Paul thought momentarily of assuring Gaddafi that Jalili was being treated far better than this, but he lacked the strength to muster that many words.

"Don't kill them," Gaddafi said over his shoulder as he left the room, then paused and turned back to his people, adding, "yet."

Unlike the tactics in Safita, interrogations began immediately, but both men were prepared with stories honed over several months' practice. Gone was Yousef's annoyingly friendly voice just before inflicting immeasurable pain on the men, enjoying their suffering, replaced by what can only be described as thugs. Yousef's torture contained a certain amount of finesse, a ball-peen hammer compared to the Libyans' wrecking ball. Paul and Roger were beaten until they could no longer stand; with enough energy, they might've been concerned about the amount of blood in their urine, but in their condition it didn't matter.

Also unlike Safita, the beatings were daily, sometimes more often, with no time to recover from the last one. If they answered immediately, they were beaten; if they hesitated, they were beaten. Sometimes they used clubs, other times a bicycle chain that dug into the flesh of their backs and legs. One of the interrogators enjoyed making multiple cuts in their chests, sometimes leaving a hundred lacerations oozing blood.

Roger estimated they were getting two hundred calories a day in the meager rations they were given but were easily expending five times that

many under torture. The diminishing returns forced the Americans to
think only about survival, pushing everything else out of their minds
and wreaking havoc on their morale and spirits. Day in and day out,
they were slowly dying.

Chapter 36

May 12, 2008
Quantico, Virginia

Katy and the team were only two weeks away from deploying to the Mediterranean Sea for the mission, now named Operation Desert Wind; most of her days were spent reading the latest intelligence reports on Gaddafi and Libyan military operations. Much of the top secret/sensitive compartmented information she reviewed was generated by the Talent photographic reconnaissance aircraft program and the Keyhole satellite communication intercepts—most of it further designated UMBRA as the most sensitive material—to which Katy already had access from her job with SEAL Team 3. Now she also had a need-to-know, the second criteria for gaining access to such information.

First Sergeant Mersino catalogued every shot Katy took over the last ninety days, totaling almost 25,000 rounds at distances from five hundred to two thousand meters, miraculously hitting the X ring, often referred to as the bulls-eye, all but forty-six times. Her rifle and his spotting scope accompanied them everywhere, and Katy also carried a short-barreled shotgun while Mersino preferred the 9mm semiautomatic pistol designated the Beretta M9 with a standard fifteen-round magazine, in addition to the M4 Carbine folding-stock rifle with an infrared night scope and M203 grenade launcher under the main barrel. The two Marines represented formidable firepower at short and long distances.

Together they practiced parachuting with the U.S. Army at Fort Benning, desert training with the Marines at 29 Palms, and other skills they would need during the mission. They took only enough time off to clean and repair weapons, rest and recuperate, and prepare for the next training episode. Every chance they got across bases in the United States, the two Marines practiced shooting at long ranges. After three months of intense mental and physical training, they felt ready for the mission.

Colonel Robichaux and Senior Chief Zemanski arranged the schedule and movements for Morgan and Mersino, letting the pair know where to be for the next training session. Senior Chief Dalupang was also close by, taking care of their uniforms, meals, supplies, and other administrative requirements. Robichaux promised them the equipment they would need for the mission, and the team delivered everything they requested. Katy—codenamed Ariel—and Dalupang supervised packing and loading the equipment onto pallets and into the C-17 aircraft that would take them to Spain. Katie made a quick trip to Charleston to see her parents one more time, hinting that she was deploying overseas and would return in a few weeks. Likewise, Mersino drove home to Camp Lejeune just in time to witness the birth of his third child and second daughter before meeting Katy back at Quantico.

The team landed at Naval Station Rota on the southern coast of Spain, west of Gibraltar, across the Bay of Cádiz near the city of the same name, and immediately moved the palletized gear into an aircraft hangar on one end of the runway, remote enough that there were no casual visitors but close enough to the facilities they needed to prepare for the mission.

The equipment was unpacked and checked for damage, batteries were recharged, and communication uplinks were established with the chairman's office and the National Military Command Center at the Pentagon. For the first time since dinner at the Capital Grille only twelve weeks earlier, the whole team met for a meal and drinks together before heading back to their respective quarters.

D-Day was only two weeks away, with June 3 having been selected because of the new moon, and Katy had a list of things she wanted to do in preparation for the mission so she didn't forget any details that might compromise their presence in Libya or the success of the operation. For now, though, she needed some rest to recharge her own batteries and take time to process the activities of the next three weeks, including the insertion, the operation, and the extraction.

She made last-minute corrections to the checklist created over the last three months and inspected her equipment one more time before retiring for the evening. Sleep came hard, not only because of the jetlag but also because of the adrenaline coursing through her veins. She woke several times after living through parts of the mission in her dreams, only to fall back asleep to experience another episode.

Chapter 37

May 25, 2008
Aboard the USS *Pasadena* in the Mediterranean Sea

My name is Ariel
and I want to be free.

—"Ariel," October Project

"USS *Pasadena*, this is the captain. It's another beautiful day topside! We have some visitors aboard who have important work to do over the next two weeks, but *Pasadena*'s work is equally important. We'll be supporting the operation and providing intelligence and communications throughout, and respond as required to the National Command Authority and Sixth Fleet directives. There will be a lot of moving parts going forward, so stay sharp and be flexible. Set the watch. Under way. Out," Commander Jeb Larson informed and motivated his sailors.

The submarine sailed just after sundown with the team having spent the last two nights on the boat running drills and testing weapons and systems. The immediate gear needed to get ashore was already loaded and dogged down—secured in place—on the Rigid Raiding Craft/ Rigid Hull Inflatable Boat, or RHIB, and covered to protect it from dust and salt water. Individual pieces of equipment were further protected from the weather in waterproof bags, and the radio equipment was the last to be loaded; the communication and cryptologic technicians checked and rechecked every switch, every piece of software, and every frequency Morgan and Mersino intended to use.

The weather had turned decidedly nasty as the submarine approached the Libyan coastline near Derna in the Cyrenaica Province, a place famous in Marine Corps history as the first land battle by American forces on foreign soil. First Lieutenant Presley Neville O'Bannon marched his mercenary army 520 miles through the North African desert from Alexandria on the Mediterranean coast of Egypt to the eastern port city of Derna in 1805 to restore the rightful heir to the Libyan throne. Supported by cannons from an American naval squadron and under heavy fire from a superior force in the city, O'Bannon and his Marines attacked at 1445 on April 27; less than ninety minutes later, the city fell, the governor's palace was overrun, and O'Bannon raised the fifteen-star, fifteen-striped flag over the battery, the first time an American flag flew over fortifications on the other side of the Atlantic Ocean. After several skirmishes over the next six weeks, a treaty was signed on June 10, ending the hostilities and enabling foreign forces to return home.

Katy was not considering any of that history as they neared the launch site for the RHIB. She and Mersino moved topside and made one last check of their equipment and weapons, boarded the RHIB, and prepared for the boat to be lowered into the water. After a calm underwater transit from Rota, the cylindrical submarine was now rocking violently on the surface. The deck sailors did their best to steady the small boat as they craned it slowly to the water's surface, almost impossible with ten- to fifteen-foot waves and an occasional and unpredictable one twice that size, made worse by a driving rain in a thirty-mile-per-hour gale. Although the decision makers considered aborting the mission for that evening, too many individual and well-timed support operations were already in motion that would've been extremely difficult to rearrange at this late hour. It was time.

Prussian chief of the general staff Field Marshal Helmuth von Moltke famously said no plan of operations extends with any certainty beyond first contact with the enemy; on this night the enemy was

Mother Nature, hell-bent on causing as much disruption to Operation Desert Wind as she could. Two sailors were washed overboard with search-and-rescue teams quickly retrieving them. One sentry lost his footing and dropped his M16 rifle into the unforgiving sea. None of the crew admitted they felt seasick, staying at their assigned stations but with a trash can nearby just in case. Some even felt sorry for Morgan and Mersino having to make the fifteen-mile transit to the beach in the small inflatable boat.

No one could have predicted the wave that hit the RHIB just as it settled on the surface of the water, ejecting Mersino and slamming him against the hull of the submarine, breaking his right leg in four places. Katy managed to steer clear of the vessel, holding the RHIB fifty feet away watching the deck crew pull Mersino out of the water. When it was obvious he would not be joining her, Katy gave the crew a thumbs-up and turned the bow toward the Libyan coastline, checked the compass bearing, and opened the throttle.

Colonel Robichaux called General Blackman on the super-high-frequency radio, relayed through orbiting satellites supporting the operation, to update him on the events of the last twenty minutes. After a quick analysis, they decided to continue the mission, knowing there were a half dozen phase lines over the next week when they could recall Katy and cancel or reschedule the operation if needed.

The radio operator signaled the National Military Command Center a simple message: "Ariel is away, one soul on board." The message was transmitted to the White House Situation Room and to President Rush, prompting her to ask why Katy was alone in the boat. The feeling she had after speaking with Blackman on the secure phone was not encouraging, secretly asking herself if she would feel the same if she hadn't met and didn't know Katy.

Katy made it ashore, soaked to the bone, cold despite the late spring weather, and exhausted after depleting all her adrenaline and dipping into her body's store of ketones. Her first priority was to get the RHIB off the beach and concealed. Although she was a few miles southwest of Derna halfway to Susah, the ancient Greek city of Apollonia, with no visible settlements nearby, she could not allow the boat to be discovered and compromise the mission. Even if someone was up at that hour, the rain and wind would discourage them from venturing too far out into the night. She used the boat's winch to drag it into a small cave a hundred meters from the beach, arranged rocks and boulders around the mouth of the enclosure, and checked to see if she lost any equipment during the run ashore. Fortunately, she had not.

She made a small fire in the cave and heated some water for coffee. While she waited for the water to boil, she dried off and changed clothes. Once dressed and the coffee was ready, she turned on the radio, tuned it to the correct frequency, enabled the crypto, and called *Pasadena*.

"Rose Bowl, this is Ariel. Whiskey Bravo November, over." WBN was a code letting the crew know she hadn't been captured and wasn't under duress.

She smiled when the radio operator answered immediately; they must've been anxiously awaiting her call. "Ariel, this is Rose Bowl, Victor Uniform Golf. Sitrep, over." VUG confirmed to her it really was the submarine at the other end of the radio signal.

"Rose Bowl, Ariel. Position Delta Two secure at A6GB7N. Mission capable. Over." Katy gave them a position location with an alphanumeric code they had developed over the last couple of days. No one outside the submarine knew what it meant or could use it to figure out where she was hiding. She knew they were also watching her from the satellites overhead but wanted to reconfirm she was all right. And she knew better than to ask about Mersino, as much as she wanted to.

"Ariel, Rose Bowl. Roger. Out." And that was it. In less than ten seconds, they knew she not only was alive and in a secure location but also ready to continue the mission.

Katy sat back and sipped her coffee, knowing she had to wait sixteen hours for the next phase of the operation. With boulders, brush, and a hastily made sand dune in front of the cave, she was all but invisible to the outside world, offering her a chance to recuperate from the exciting start to the mission. She unpacked, cleaned and loaded her shotgun and Mersino's 9mm pistol, now hers to use. She rehydrated and heated breakfast and ate quickly, not realizing how hungry she was until she smelled the food.

Before the sun rose, she ventured outside quickly to set up discreet motion sensors that would alert her if anything approached the cave. She rechecked the camouflage and looked for signs of her presence or that of the boat, and again retreated to the temporary safety of the enclosure. She organized the weapons and ammunition and drank the last of her coffee. Once she was sure everything was in order, she crawled into the RHIB, pulled a poncho liner over her, set the alarm on her watch for 1600 and went to sleep.

Katy reached for the shotgun when one of the sensors woke her, realizing after a few tense seconds it was the alarm clock and not an intruder alert. The first thing she did was brew another cup of coffee to clear the fog from her heavy head. She had slept ten full hours without waking, and now it would take time to shake off its effects. She moved slowly, knowing it would be another long day, made more taxing without Mersino's help.

I can do this, she told herself, realizing afterward that she was actually speaking out loud, then laughing as she added boiling water to a package of oatmeal, mixing it with powdered coconut milk to take advantage of the cognitive and physical enhancements the fibrous dry drupe's extra ketones offered her. Thirty minutes later, she felt awake and alive, ready for today's activities and more confident she could accomplish the objectives of the mission despite being one man down.

"Rose Bowl, Rose Bowl, this is Ariel. Tango Bravo Mike." She made the call precisely at 1738 per the agreed schedule. The unusual time was further confirmation Katy was not under duress; any other time would've been a signal to send the cavalry.

"Ariel, this is Rose Bowl. Roger Mike Mike. State status. Over." USS *Pasadena* was dedicated to this mission until its completion and would be her immediate contact with Colonel Robichaux on board.

"Rose Bowl, Ariel. Alpha Sierra Mike Charlie at Delta Two." Katy used the brevity code for all secure, mission capable, and reconfirming she was at Delta Two, the codename for the beach they had chosen as the landing site near Derna.

"Ariel, Rose Bowl, roger. Mark twenty-two thirty. Dash Two recovering. Out." The radio operator signaled that the next activity would begin at 2230 that evening, the next major event of the mission. Katy would feel much better once that was done.

"Rose Bowl, Ariel. Confirm 2230. Thanks. Out." Dash Two referred to Mersino; at least she knew he was safe and his injuries weren't life threatening.

Katy set about organizing her equipment, occasionally surveilling around the cave for any activity indicating humans were out and about. A pair of Ouaddan gazelles native to Libya tripped the sensors a couple of hours later, but otherwise there was little movement in the immediate area. She remembered from her childhood that the family stayed at the Ouaddan Hotel in Tripoli when they first arrived in the capital twenty years before, at the time the best hotel in the country. Popular with visiting Western oilmen, the hotel even featured an Italian dance troupe and floor show with the mediocre dinner menu, ameliorated only by the topless dancers and pop music of the time.

By 2200, Katy had eaten, surreptitiously bathed in the Mediterranean—probably the last chance to do so for several days—and was ready for the night's activities. She moved by foot about seven hundred meters south of the cave, using her night-vision goggles to navigate through the unfamiliar terrain, recognizing the flat open area identified by satellite imagery she had viewed with the team what seemed a million years ago. She found a good position to view the area and protect herself from someone coming up behind her. At 2220, Katy flipped the switch on a small handheld device and watched as the soft red glow gave way to a green light indicating it was on and working properly. And then she waited.

Ten minutes later, the device beeped once. Katy scanned the night sky, but it was really too dark to see much; the waning moon would not rise for another hour. There were more stars visible than she had seen since her trips to the oilfields deep in the desert with her father and sister two decades ago, but they offered little help in spotting the aerial delivery she was expecting.

The device began a slow beeping sound, letting her know it was getting closer. As the speed increased, she looked skyward again hoping to glimpse the package. The tone changed, indicating it was below two hundred feet above ground level. Katy knew it was nearby—the light indicated it was right on top of her—but she heard it before she saw it. At the last second, she heard the silk parachutes ripple in the breeze, causing her to look directly above her position, and dove out of the way just as the payload hit the ground where she had been standing. Two seconds' hesitation would've resulted in a disaster from which Katy likely would not have recovered, being crushed and buried under the gear, suffocating if she could not extricate herself from underneath the pallet.

After collapsing and gathering the parachute and releasing the straps tethering it to the vehicle, Katy unloaded the cargo. The vehicle was preloaded with everything she needed for the mission except fuel, but she saw a second parachute land fifty meters away attached to a fuel bladder for that purpose. She rolled the bladder to the vehicle, filled it quickly, stowed the equipment, dismantled and folded the custom-made insulated pallet that she attached to one side of the ALSV—she would need it later—and returned to the cave.

Chenowth Racing Products in San Diego built the advanced light strike vehicle, or ALSV, as a third-generation high-performance surveillance, light strike, and reconnaissance vehicle for the Marines and SEALs. Katy and Mersino spent hours training with the ALSV, learning its field maintenance, changing tires and other parts, and putting it through its paces to understand the vehicle's capabilities and limitations. The ultimate all-terrain four-wheel-drive vehicle powered by a 160-horsepower Porsche diesel engine, the pair enjoyed that part of their training package at 29 Palms as much as anything, splitting driving and repair time equally to ensure both could do everything well. Two vehicles had been stored in the hangar in Rota with a parts package and maintenance crew supporting the mission; Katy was driving the one with a camouflaged "Go Bulldogs" bumper sticker inside the cockpit in reference to her alma mater.

Katy loaded the remaining gear from the cave onto the ALSV, put the parachutes and other unneeded equipment in the RHIB, let Rose Bowl know she was moving, and set off on a preselected course of waypoints programmed into the global positioning system, privately thanking her great-aunt Gladys who developed the satellite geodesy models that made the locating system work; Dr. West was among the hidden figures of the early space program specializing in geodesy. Katy had to reset the GPS twice until it was functioning properly, knowing she didn't have a backup other than map and compass; Robichaux had required his platoon at TBS always to check the technology manually, so she was confident she could navigate without the GPS if required.

She drove south from the coastline into the Libyan desert, away from settlements and trade and smuggling routes, toward an uncertain week of activities worthy of a Tom Clancy novel. She missed Mersino's company but assured herself she could accomplish the mission without him; unless they postponed the operation or sent a replacement, at this point, she had no choice but to proceed alone, allowing more time to do things he would've helped her accomplish.

Armed with a stabilized .50 caliber M2 Browning machine gun she could operate remotely from the driver's station, the ALSV could average sixty miles per hour across the desert floor, sprint to a hundred if needed, although Katy was forced to slow occasionally to avoid rock outcroppings among the prehistoric *wadi*s, or dried riverbeds, in the Sahara, especially at night despite a waxing gibbous moon.

Weighing almost two tons empty with another twenty-five hundred pounds of equipment and personnel—two hundred pounds lighter without Mersino on board—the vehicle could navigate seventy percent gradients and fifty percent side slopes, something Katy would do only if forced by circumstances. Some creative engineering also muffled the engine noise; even at full speed, it was difficult to hear the ALSV from more than seventy-five feet.

Katy made good time to her first stop, a series of low caves near the mountainous Gilf Kebir plateau near the Egyptian border, where she could hide until the next night. She saw the Cave of Swimmers, popular with intrepid tourists who came to view the ancient rock art of the Neolithic period discovered in 1933 by Hungarian explorer László Almásy. About ten thousand years old, the pictographs appeared to represent people swimming and included giraffes and hippopotamuses, indications of a wetter and greener Sahara before a previous climate shift from temperate to xeric desert caused by changes in solar insolation.

Other researchers in the early 1950s found ancient underground megalakes from the same period almost 125 miles south of the caves. With no natural potable water sources closer to the main cities in Libya, self-promoted Colonel Mu'ammar Gaddafi embarked on the largest underground network of pipes and aqueducts in the world, transporting fresh water from the Nubian Sandstone Aquifer System to the coastal areas inhabited by 98 percent of Libya's population. Gaddafi even described the Great Man-Made River as the Eighth Wonder of the World.

Katy quickly ventured into the Cave of Swimmers and took photographs; although not on the official operations plan, it seemed likely she would never be this way again and wanted to explore where few had been before. Robichaux watched the live feed from the orbiting satellites as she entered the cave and made a note for her to share the photos when she returned.

She deserves a minute to sightsee. He smiled to himself, confident that no accidental tourist would stumble on her at 0300 in this remote corner of the world. He admired her nonchalant demeanor given the magnitude of the operation she was conducting singlehandedly. And he knew Big Brother was watching every move from above and could alert her to any perceived threats. Such were the benefits of Katy being a Tier 1 asset, something she only recently came to appreciate fully.

Katy drove the ALSV to another fuel bladder dropped near the cave complex and refueled before finding shelter. She chose a cave several hundred meters south where imagery confirmed no one had visited in the previous three months, backing the Chenowth into the enclosure and camouflaging the exterior. As was becoming routine, she heated water, ate, and settled in after contacting *Pasadena*.

Just before sunrise, she observed vehicles approaching the area, as expected. Five four-wheel-drive Land Cruisers loaded with what appeared to be Europeans went directly to the Cave of Swimmers and took turns viewing the pictographs and surveying the surrounding area from the high ground. Katy watched them through binoculars, confirmed they presented no obvious threat, and saw the vehicles retreat along the same track north toward the coast a couple of hours later. Knowing the next set of tourists would likely come just before sundown—it was too hot to make the trip during the day—she stretched out to rest until the afternoon.

After another sound sleep without interruption, Katy awakened with the gnawing feeling about what she saw that morning. Did five vehicles arrive but only four depart? In her fatigue, she was unsure, and although she *heard* nothing outside the cave, she *felt* something instead. She slung the shotgun over her shoulder, holstered Mersino's 9mm, and also retrieved and loaded the M4 Carbine rifle with its attached M203 grenade launcher. She felt like Rambo with a legendary Marine Corps Mark 2 Ka-bar combat knife strapped to her calf as she eased toward the opening of her cave, each weapon serving a different purpose depending on the distance to the threat.

She saw something move in the twilight and flipped down her night-vision goggles. She waited quietly for what seemed an hour, moving only her head and eyes to scan the area. Something rustled to her left, but she detected movement again to her right. She flipped up the NVGs and watched with the unaided eyes. Nothing moved. And then there it was, neither tourist nor assassin but, instead, a leopard. Believed to be extirpated in North Africa, the wildcat moved noiselessly from Katy's right to left, stopping periodically to sniff the air for threats or opportunities. He seemed not to know of or not to care about Katy's presence only thirty yards away, and she let him pass undisturbed. But she still felt uneasy.

"Rose Bowl, this is Ariel. Alpha Mike Charlie. Do you see activity near my position? Over."

"Ariel, Rose Bowl. Hotel Victor Zebra. That's negative. Over."

"Rose Bowl, Ariel. I counted five inbound to my position this morning but only four outbound."

"Wait, over." The analysts were obviously checking this morning's satellite imagery.

"Ariel, Rose Bowl. Concur. Five in, four out, over."

"Roger, Rose Bowl. Interrogative—proceed? Over." She waited ten seconds for a response.

"Delta Whiskey 6 confirms proceed. Depart present location thirty mikes after Echo Echo November Tango. Out."

The commander of Desert Wind, Colonel Robichaux, designated Delta Whiskey 6, instructed Katy to leave the cave and continue traveling west-northwest thirty minutes after end of evening nautical twilight, or EENT, the period between sunset and dusk. In so doing, he wanted her to begin the next leg of her trip just before full darkness set in; if someone were indeed following her they would expect her to leave two hours after dusk to take full advantage of the dark night. Robichaux also knew the satellite angle was at its best to observe her intended route and anyone following her to the next stop.

Katy saw immediate activity at the Cave of Swimmers as soon as she got underway, accelerated to over eighty miles per hour to egress the area, and trusted the *Pasadena* team to deal with the threat. A thousand questions crossed her mind, the most obvious being who was following her, and how did they know she was there, given the strict operational security of the mission.

She saw her pursuers one more time the following evening, confirming they were indeed following her. Rose Bowl assured her plans were being drawn up to counter what they could only assume was a threat to her safety and security, and for her instead to focus on the mission. She did as instructed but kept one eye open for any surprises.

And so her days went as she traveled roughly 800 miles through the interior of Libya northwest toward Tripoli, arriving at Gaddafi's desert camp at al Aziziyah only 20 miles south of the capital at 0100 on May 30. The team planned her route to avoid detection, particularly by human traffickers and drug smugglers on the Sahel superhighway crossing Africa east to west. Although she stayed north of the Sahel—the area bounded by the Sahara in the north and the Sudanian savanna to the south—groups would travel outside the transition area to buy the smugglers' commodities and sell them food, guns and ammunition, and other supplies. Katy would command a good price if she were caught, assuming they did not surrender her for the bounty to one of the governments along the way if they discovered her true identity and purpose.

Katy unfolded, assembled, and locked the pallet open, placing it on top of two dunes to provide an insulated carport for the ALSV with the opening facing away from the target. She added an eighteen-by-thirty-two-foot camouflage net on top and placed a periscope embedded in scrub brush through a small opening, offering her unimpeded surveillance for at least two hundred meters in every direction. Moving away from the prepared position, Katy constructed an unobtrusive sand mogul chicane to retard other vehicles' approach and unconsciously force them into a kill zone, placed the sensors in strategic positions to cover avenues of approach, and implanted command-detonated Claymore antipersonnel mines with the wires buried under the loose sand. She also arranged solar-powered radars able to see out to a thousand meters, the final capability in her defense-in-depth for advance warning of anyone approaching the camp.

While Katy worked, her meal was heating on the ALSV's cylinder head; this close to the target, she could not afford to light a fire, particularly at night. She was far enough from the desert camp that discovery was unlikely, but close enough that if she wasn't careful, she could inadvertently alert security forces and give away her position. Two fuel bladders—she loaded one of them onto the ALSV for later use—had even been dropped thirty miles south of al Aziziyah; any closer would've been an unnecessary risk. A full hour before sunrise at 0600, she was in the hideout, organizing herself for the day.

"Rose Bowl, Ariel. Touchdown, over." Katy tied the *Pasadena* team into a live video feed at her location, with six cameras and the radars placed around the redoubt to give her, and them, a 360-degree view from her position. Feeling much like an astronaut in a small capsule broadcasting from space, Katy sat in the ALSV, briefed Colonel Robichaux on her preparations, reviewed the checklist, and voiced her concerns.

"Sir, do we know yet who's following me?" She addressed the eight-hundred-pound gorilla sitting directly beside her.

"Not yet, but the Twenty-Fourth Marine Expeditionary Unit in the Mediterranean has a QRF standing by to intercept them. Satellite surveillance shows one vehicle with four armed men currently stopped seventy-five miles south of your location. Although we intercepted encrypted radio traffic between them and the camp, we're not yet sure who they're talking to, but we'll keep at it." Deployed Marines always have a quick reaction force composed of Marines and navy SEALs available for extremis situations.

"Any special considerations I should focus on, Colonel?"

"Don't get caught," Robichaux implored as both of them laughed.

"I'll try my best, sir."

"OK, get some rest and let's talk again tonight. Reaper on station at 0800 local. Be safe."

"Thanks, Colonel. Out here."

Katy sat back reviewing the conversation. If the men following her were in contact with someone at the camp, and they correctly surmised where she was, her safety and security were tenuous at best. Perhaps they were unaware of her purpose and mission, maybe they wanted to catch her in the act, or they were waiting for an opportune time to strike. She suppressed her imagination, knowing the Twenty-Fourth MEU had her back; she even knew the intelligence officer in the embarked Battalion Landing Team who graduated with her from NMITC.

Between bites of spaghetti and meatballs, Katy opened two sealed packages and dumped them into a small pan made for that purpose.

The toxic chemicals—ammonium thiocyanate and barium hydroxide octahydrate—created an endothermic reaction that absorbs heat from the surrounding air and turns cold, even to the point of freezing water. Attaching alligator clips on the electrical leads from the container to a six-inch-by-six-inch solar panel powering a small fan, she placed the contraption outside the carport with a small duct hose to vector cool air into her shelter. The insulated pallet overhead provided some relief from the heat; cool air created by the chemical concoction made it downright comfortable. It wasn't the Ritz-Carlton, but considering the temperature would exceed a hundred degrees Fahrenheit by midday, and the fact that she needed two days of good rest before the operation, it would do nicely.

Katy moved out of the enclosure at 0800 with the comfort of knowing an MQ-9 Reaper was overhead as an additional eye in the sky. Barely one year into its service with the U.S. Air Force, this hunter-killer drone provided not only optical infrared surveillance from an operational altitude of 25,000 feet but was also armed with four air-to-ground Hellfire missiles, providing Katy immediate close air support. First Lieutenant Bill Bartels, pilot of the unmanned aerial vehicle, was sitting in the Nevada desert in direct secure communications contact with both *Pasadena* and Katy; even a few seconds' delay relaying firing instructions could mean the difference between life and death, and he wanted to be able to respond to Katy immediately if she called. Bartels would keep his Reaper overhead for ten hours before landing it back at Naval Air Station Sigonella in Sicily when First Lieutenant Maria Rodriguez would relieve him flying another Reaper.

Katy steered a small noiseless four-wheel electric-powered scooter with balloon tires toward the desert camp; she would conduct reconnaissance and surveillance for a few hours to review the layout of the camp in daylight, observe the scheduling and movement of the guards, and confirm the best vantage points from which to shoot.

The team had already plotted proposed shooting points 750 to 2,000 meters from the target, but she checked and rechecked every detail: wind speed and direction, cover and concealment, and altitude of the target relative to the line of fire, among others. She saw the tent where Gaddafi relaxed on pleasant evenings, often having dinner with his family and close friends and finishing the night by adding a half teaspoon of orange blossom water to his coffee in true Libyan style. She also located the lounge in the southernmost building he used as an office and *majlis*, the parlor where visitors and guests are received and entertained.

Although the early-morning coolness would soon recede, right now the windows of the *majlis* were open and a slight breeze was blowing the curtains. Katy watched for a few minutes, and when she was certain no one was in the room, she aimed her sniper rifle toward the far wall and fired a small projectile. Even at a distance of 800 meters, Katy hit the intended spot in the soft wood fascia near the ceiling, embedding a small microphone capable of picking up sounds in the room.

Twenty minutes later, one of the orderlies came to close the windows; she used that activity to check the audio feed, made some adjustments, enabled a relay that would allow her to activate and deactivate the system and listen from her camp, and shut off the microphone remotely to save the battery.

Katy began packing up to return to her hideaway when a door opened on another building and guards dragged two men, one about forty years old and the other appearing to be in his sixties, to a small warehouse at the center of the camp. Although they were blindfolded, she could tell one was Caucasian, the other black; from their clothing, they both appeared Western, but their unshaven faces masked other identifying features. Katy used the scope on her rifle to get a better view before they were pushed into an open door, so quickly she didn't see much more.

I wonder who they have out here? she asked herself, hoping the Reaper crew saw what she did and recorded it to review in detail.

With another full night of exhausting work behind her, Katy crawled into the makeshift cot, pulled the poncho liner over her, and was asleep within minutes.

The next two days and nights were rehearsals for the main event on June 3 when the new moon would mask her presence and conceal her egress after the shot. Another night of rain provided additional protection from roving patrols and observation; and although there was wind, it was light, and Katy felt it wouldn't hamper the accuracy of her shots.

She took advantage of an early thunderstorm to move the ALSV forward to a defiladed spot thirty meters behind the shooting position. She estimated it would take two hours to deploy the necessary equipment for the mission; had Mersino been there, it would've taken half that much time. But he wasn't, and they had rehearsed operating alone so she was prepared.

Once everything was set up, Katy drove the electric scooter back to the hideout to change clothes, eat, and call Rose Bowl. She briefed the colonel on her preparations, reviewed the checklist with him one more time, and buried items she would not take with her when she departed the area. She set explosives around the redoubt; should the Libyans find it, tripwires would set off several pounds of C-4 plastic explosives to eradicate what was left behind. The Reaper was also prepared to finish the job with Hellfire missiles if any significant evidence remained.

Robichaux signed off by saying, "Godspeed, Marine. There are a thousand of us here if you need us, including the lady in the White House. She called about an hour ago and asked me to pass on her well-wishes. Weapons free. You're cleared to execute the operation. Do us all proud, Katy O."

"Thanks, Colonel. I'll check in after the op, and I'll definitely call if I get in trouble." She set the alarm clock to wake her in one hour.

Katy bolted from her sleep, startled by nearby gunfire. Despite sound suppressors—civilians referred to them as silencers as did Hiram Percy Maxim, the original patentholder of the device—the guns sounded loud even in the rain—at least until she realized it was coming from immediately outside her shelter.

The QRF had been inserted when it became obvious the men following her were moving toward the encampment. She pulled on a ballcap—she allowed herself the luxury of carrying a dark-blue Citadel hat on the operation—to keep the rain out of her eyes and pumped the shotgun as she stepped outside. The QRF leader, a Marine captain, handed her a cherry lollipop and greeted her, "Good afternoon, Marine. Captain America at your service! All secure."

Still dazed from being awakened so abruptly—it had been only fifteen minutes since she lay down—she laughed and replied, "Thanks for covering my six. Any idea who they are?"

"We'll send photos and fingerprints back to the ship. They'll run them through Interpol and the FBI, but I doubt they'll find anything. The weapons are clean, and there's no identification on the bodies or the vehicle. It looks like a special operations direct action unit that just wasn't expecting us to be here when they arrived."

"I'm glad you were. What's next?"

"We'll take the bodies and the vehicle and get out of your way. Need anything?"

"I'm good. See you back at the barn." She snatched two more lollipops from his breast pocket before he departed.

"I've shot people for less than that!" he declared, laughing as he reached in a cargo pocket and threw a bag of twenty at her.

"Carry on, Marine!"

"Aye aye, Ariel," he said, saluting, and just as quickly as they arrived, Captain America—she saw his name tape said LeBlanc—and the QRF were gone, no one in al Aziziyah save Katy any wiser.

Sunset came at 2012; Katy was in position forty-five minutes later, sipping on another coconut milk solution to boost her ketones. The rain precluded most outdoor activity, and she saw some of the guards huddling under overhangs rather than standing at their assigned posts. The Libyan flag in the compound wasn't waving, made heavy by the water and no wind to move it. By 2200, the landscape in every direction was dark except for the lights of the compound. With proper cover and concealment, she was invisible among the dunes surrounding the camp. The rain even allowed her to move closer to the target, shooting from eight hundred meters instead of fifteen hundred meters or more.

Arabs are a nocturnal culture, coming out late at night and socializing until early morning; the Libyans were no different. Today was Friday, though, the holy day in Islam, which tempered some of the revelry found on other days of the week. The garrison's mosque called them for the Maghrib sunset prayer, after which they ate dinner and drifted off to their respective accommodations. Ramadan had ended two weeks before, most of the guards were broke from the festive holidays after a month of fasting, and summer was approaching. Many found it nice to take a break, play cards or backgammon with colleagues, and get some rest.

At midnight, a new shift of guards took their posts as expected. Katy was concerned they might be on higher alert, but there was no discernable difference in their demeanor, weapons, or behavior. As she scanned the compound, she saw familiar faces: Geppetto and Pinocchio guarded the road approaching the compound from Tripoli and were armed with Russian-made AKS-47 folding stock assault rifles; Dumbo manned the watchtower equipped with a Bulgarian-made 12.7mm caliber heavy machine gun capable of firing seven hundred rounds per minute out to two thousand meters; and the Three Stooges Moe, Larry, and Curly patrolled around the *majlis* and surrounding buildings, armed with fixed-stock AK-47s. There was no deviation from the schedule or personnel from previous evenings; everything was as it should be.

Katy watched for activity in the *majlis*, her senses moving to full alert when Gaddafi entered and sat on a couch facing the open window through which she previously fired the microphone. She switched on the audio and started the recording. And then she froze.

Gaddafi and the two men with him were conversing in *Hebrew*.

There was nothing in the intel pack that indicated Gaddafi spoke Hebrew, and although his mother was Jewish, it made no sense for him to do so now. She picked up a word or two common to Arabic but for the most part she didn't understand their conversation. Trying to put the puzzle together, Katy watched as the three men quickly switched to Arabic when others entered the room but reverted to Hebrew again as soon as they departed.

Although they were in a communications blackout, reserving radio calls only for true emergencies, she wanted to inform the team on *Pasadena*. She transmitted a quick data burst of the conversation to the submarine and then continued the stakeout. This was certainly abnormal—bizarre seemed a better description—but it posed no additional threat to Katy or the mission that she could discern. In the distance, she heard the approach of another thunderstorm, made final adjustments to her weapons and equipment, and waited for its arrival.

Then it dawned on her. The direct action team must've been Israeli, maybe from the fabled Unit 269 she had read about. Gaddafi was speaking Hebrew, so were they protecting him? If so, why? Colonel Robichaux said they were in touch with someone at the compound; were they speaking with Gaddafi and the two men sitting with him?

She had been questioning how the four men got so close to her camp without setting off sensors in the radars. The QRF all carried Identify Friend or Foe (IFF) devices synchronized with the sensors that confirmed they were friendly forces, but the Israeli team didn't—at least until Katy remembered the radars were manufactured in Israel; the company must've provided the frequency to Unit 269, giving them the same tactical advantage. That fact probably wouldn't go over well at the Pentagon, but there were too many questions right now that served only to take her focus away from the mission.

Katy organized her shots sequentially according to the threats they posed. After Gaddafi, she would next focus on Dumbo since his machine gun could interdict her egress from the area. If any of the others moved out of the compound toward her, they would be next. But her primary objective was to take out Colonel Gaddafi and his advisors quietly and efficiently. With any luck, it might be several minutes before anyone realized they were dead.

The gun-target line to the three men was unimpeded, the overhead thunder and the noise of the rain would further dampen the sound signature of her silenced CFSR, and the window was open, so there was no chance of someone reacting to the sound of breaking glass. Worst case, she would have to take out Dumbo, Moe, Larry, Curly, Geppetto, and Pinocchio in that order so they couldn't raise the alarm to others in the compound. Nine shots, nine kills, and she had the tactical advantages of surprise, weather, and darkness.

She also had to consider Gaddafi's personal security detail led by Captain Aisha. Would they respond and chase her if they knew he was being shot at? She had not seen the amazons in her daylight and nighttime recons of the camp, so perhaps they weren't at the desert compound this evening. She hoped that was true, but hope is not a strategy; she would plan for them to protect Gaddafi and be pleasantly surprised if they didn't.

By 0030, things had settled down to the point that Katy was ready to take the shot. With the arrival of the thunderstorm, she focused again on the three men in the *majlis*, aligned her sights on the primary target, looked down the barrel for a perfect sight picture, and squeezed the trigger.

Gaddafi's head first snapped backward with the impact of the round, and then his upper body slumped forward. He was dead immediately. Katy instinctively aimed at the man sitting next to the Leader and fired, hitting him squarely in the forehead. The third man inexplicably ran to look out the window into the dark night, presenting Katy with a perfectly silhouetted target against the light of the *majlis*; he was propelled backward over the sofa when the round hit him in the chest. She took a breath, saw that none of them were moving, and heard no signs of life in the room. She knew the audio and video feeds would confirm the kills.

Once she was confident the primary mission was completed, she turned her sniper rifle on Dumbo, hitting him where he sat, his head dropping into his chest without a sound. Katy waited to see if anyone was alerted by the gunfire, but the remaining guards continued chatting and smoking as if nothing was wrong. Forget the new moon;

she wondered how different things would've been had the storm not arrived when it did.

After a full thirty seconds, the same door opened again, and the guards dragged the two prisoners—she called them Butch Cassidy and Sundance—outside and tied them to posts in the courtyard. Katy watched as they bound the prisoners' hands and feet, preparing for what looked like an execution.

She took in a full breath and then exhaled. Swinging her rifle to the left, she shot the Three Stooges in rapid succession. With her OODA loop—a decision-making tool including observe-orient-decide-act—in full cyclical mode, she quickly shot the four guards with the prisoners as well as Geppetto and Pinocchio at the gate. No one reacted to the scene with thirteen bodies strewn about the compound. She had to take advantage of that fact before she missed the opportunity.

"This is a bad idea," she said out loud to everyone and no one in particular.

Jumping into the driver's seat of the ALSV, Katy headed directly toward the gate where Geppetto and Pinocchio had collapsed and drove into the compound. Acting on impulse, she jumped off the vehicle and approached Butch Cassidy and Sundance, announcing herself as she did, "I'm Captain Morgan, United States Marine Corps, and I'm here to rescue you."

The younger man, obviously injured from what she could only imagine was prolonged torture, quite incredulously asked, "Katy O, are you still mad about that flare I shot at you at OCS?"

"Paul," she said, not believing what was happening. "This is impossible!" She was cutting away his bindings as they spoke. The beard, the bruises, and the swelling made him almost unrecognizable.

"What are you doing on the shores of Tripoli?" Paul laughed at his own joke despite several broken ribs sustained months ago that had not been allowed to heal.

Katy helped get him to the ALSV and strapped into the passenger seat. She returned and cut the other man off the post. She quickly fashioned a makeshift seat behind Paul and lifted the man starved to less than ninety pounds into the vehicle. Just as she got him secured, a bullet hit her in the left arm through and through the meat without shattering the bone or severing any arteries. It stung, but it wasn't fatal.

"Katy, this is Ambassador Roger Pugh," Paul informed her, just as gunfire started to hit around them. She handed Paul the 9mm pistol while she moved to a firing position overlooking the guards' avenue of approach, hitting five of them with the M4 before they even fired a shot. What appeared to be a noncommissioned officer barked some commands; the squad dispersed and set about trying to flank her. Lights came on elsewhere in the compound, and people started coming out in small groups with rifles and handguns.

"Use the joystick for the Browning," Katy yelled to Paul. He swung the machine gun toward the enemy's point of main effort and fired, sending 1,200 rounds per minute in their direction and forming a lead curtain around the trio. Katy was hit again, this time on the right side of her abdomen; unbeknownst to her it made a small laceration on her appendix that also hurt but was not life-threatening. Treating it would have to wait.

Katy saw a tall, lithe figure coming out of the shadows to her right, sprinting directly toward her, arriving at her position before Katy could shoot. She sidestepped the woman—she recognized Captain Aisha from the intelligence files on Gaddafi's all-female guard force—but watched her stop, turn quickly, and launch another assault, landing a blow to Katy's chest and knocking the wind out of her. Before she could recover, Aisha was kicking her in the back and ribs. If allowed to continue, or if Aisha kicked the abdomen wound, Katy would soon be incapacitated and taken prisoner, if not killed.

She rolled just in time to catch Aisha's foot, twisting it and breaking the ankle, and pushing her to the ground. Paul fired his pistol before Aisha could shoot Katy, hitting her in the left shoulder, severing the brachial artery and dorsal scapular nerve, thereby disabling her left arm. Displaying nothing approaching the pain she must've been feeling, Aisha attempted to rise using her good arm but was shot again by Paul, this time permanently ending her service to Colonel Gaddafi even if he were still alive.

Shooting out the main floodlights facing south toward her encampment, Katy vaulted through the open window of the *majlis* to collect DNA samples of Gaddafi and his advisors and anything of intelligence value she could find, managing to grab two laptops, some maps, and a folder of papers. She returned to Paul, got in the driver's seat, fired up the ALSV, and headed out of the compound, sending commands to the Browning mounted on the vehicle and to three other machine guns emplaced near the firing point from which she shot Gaddafi and the others.

The guns were programmed remotely to shoot on either side of the vehicle, recognizing its moving location by means of a radio-frequency identification beacon she activated. The three guns acted in unison, augmented by the Browning, setting up a wall of lead through which Katy could navigate the ALSV; they shot everywhere the RFID wasn't. Katy took a third round in her right shoulder, breaking the clavicle and lodging itself on top of the sternum. She ignored the pain as much as possible and relied more on her dominant left arm and hand.

The storm had abated somewhat, although she was hoping it would continue a while longer. They could hear the three machine guns covering their egress, alternating back and forth as movement drew their fire in different directions. Nonetheless, three BRDM-2 armored patrol cars were able to make their way out of the compound and follow the route taken by the Americans. Katy was already on the radio with *Pasadena*, but before she could ask for air support, the sky was lit up behind them as Hellfire missiles destroyed the Russian-made vehicles.

The Fulton surface-to-air recovery system, or STARS, named after inventor Robert Edison Fulton, Jr., uses a self-inflating balloon with an attached lift line to recover persons on the ground using fixed wing airplanes such as the MC-130E and Boeing B-17. The airplane snags the line with a V-shaped yoke, whereupon the person is reeled aboard the plane.

After surveying their wounds, Katy decided against sending Paul on the STARS; the broken ribs might puncture the lungs or damage his spine. Instead she buckled Ambassador Pugh into the harness, activated a strobe on top of the balloon and lights on the lift line for the pilots to see in a nighttime recovery, and allowed the balloon to ascend five hundred feet with its braided nylon line attached. Within sixty seconds the roar of four Allison T56-A-15 turboprop engines could be heard approaching; and in another twenty seconds, the ambassador was there one minute, gone the next, pulled into the night sky by the MC-130E and away from his captors.

The STARS system was supposed to be her ticket out of the area but given the changing situation—Robichaux characterized it as VUCA—she and Paul had to move immediately to avoid being captured or killed. He was in rough shape, far worse than she was, so she threw a poncho over him to keep out the rain, set the charges on the camp, and secured the last pieces of equipment they would need for the journey.

Katy floored the accelerator heading southeast away from al Aziziyah, retracing her steps of just a few days ago. Explosions in the direction of the three machine guns meant the Libyans had reached them; the mines were set to explode if proximity sensors were tripped within ten feet of the emplacements. A much larger explosion a few minutes later indicated the carport was destroyed, also tripped by someone approaching it, hopefully erasing any evidence the Libyans could use to identify its previous occupant.

Katy drove almost two hundred miles deep into the desert before stopping in the Jebel Sawda; the sun would be up in ninety minutes, and she needed to prepare and secure their encampment and accommodations. After offloading Paul near the site she selected, Katy used the plow shovel at the front of the ALSV to create a three-sided hastily constructed sand fortification, leaving an egress point for the vehicle on the south side facing away from the direction any pursuers would likely come. She anchored another net on top of the dunes, added some local camouflage in the form of scrub brush to the site, and finally moved Paul and the vehicle inside the hideout.

He was injured far worse than she first believed. Once she was able to triage and treat his wounds, it was obvious he was in a great deal of pain, not only from his broken ribs but from several other injuries as well. As he faded in and out of consciousness, she worked quickly to clean and dress the deepest cuts. Although he passed out, he moaned when she moved his left arm; only then did she realize both the radius and ulna were broken. She fashioned a splint and bound it with a stretch gauze wrap, hoping she did no further damage.

She duct-taped three fingers together on his right hand that were at odd angles with the remaining two fingers, making a large mitt with the tape to immobilize the entire hand; for the rest of the journey and any time he spoke about it in the future, he delivered what he called a Silver Salute, palm facing forward, whenever Katy instructed him to do something.

Katy cut off what remained of Paul's clothes and gave him a sponge bath, as much to remove the dirt and grime and the smell of sweat, urine, and feces as it was to see what other injuries he sustained. There were dozens of bruises and contusions, some obviously months old, his face swollen from the beatings. But it was not until she removed the rags from his feet that she found what smelled so bad; his soles looked like putrid ground meat, and she wondered how he could even walk. Before he woke, she cleaned them and poured hydrogen peroxide on the wounds, wrapping and binding them, and slipping Mersino's spare socks and boots—fortunately two sizes larger than Paul's—onto his feet to protect them from more damage and to keep them clean. Once she was done, she dressed him in Mersino's spare uniform and dragged him to the passenger's seat of the ALSV, knowing they might be forced to leave on short notice. Katy sat back, exhausted.

Once she regained some energy, she heated more water, enjoyed a cup of coffee, and then tended to her own wounds. She found two more bullets had struck her, one that grazed her calf, the other hitting a rib on the right side. A sixth round had hit her left hand, saved only because it was deflected by her Citadel class ring; it was so disfigured and cutting off the circulation to her finger that she removed it and placed it on the chain with her dog tags, something else to worry about later.

Even though she had been hit six times in less than two minutes in close combat with multiple enemy combatants, she felt blessed there was not more damage, and none of the injuries were too serious for her to handle in the expeditionary state of the mission. She bandaged the minor wounds, dressed in a clean uniform, and then used half a roll of duct tape to bind and stabilize her clavicle, deciding to leave the bullet lodged in her breastbone for now; as informed by her father when she was growing up, "If you can't fix it with duct tape, you're not using enough of it." She felt like she was wearing football shoulder pads, but only on one shoulder.

Fifteen minutes later, she heard a plane overhead; looking out of the netting, she saw a Reaper approaching less than two hundred feet above the ground, rocking its wings back and forth to let her know it was there. She found great comfort in that gesture; even though she knew Big Brother was watching, it was nice to see a friendly face, or in this case, a friendly aircraft. On the drone's next pass, she gave the camera a thumbs-up and signaled she would call them soon. Drone pilot Lieutenant Rodriguez acknowledged by again rocking the wings and dropping a fuel bladder close to Katy's position.

Katy fell asleep when she sat down to change her socks, waking two hours later with a sore back and stiff neck, aggravated that she dozed off but also keenly aware how exhausted she was. Paul had not moved. She immediately flipped on the radio and called *Pasadena*.

"Rose Bowl, Rose Bowl, Ariel. Mike Alpha Charlie. Over."

"Ariel, this is Rose Bowl. Sierra Tango Hotel. You have two vehicles twenty klicks out approaching from the northwest. Intent unconfirmed. Is your position secure? Over."

"Rose Bowl, Ariel. Position is secure with good fields of view. Over."

"Ariel, Rose Bowl. Understood. Request medical status of you and Papa Sierra. Over." They knew Paul Stephens—Papa Sierra—was with her after interviewing Ambassador Pugh.

"Rose Bowl, Ariel. Serious but nothing life-threatening, and we have enough medical supplies and ammunition to last; on second thought, I could use more .50 cal ball ammo for the Browning. Papa Sierra unable to evacuate by STARS. We'll work our way back to Delta Two and

RTB from there unless you have something better. Over." RTB meant return-to-base.

"Ariel, Rose Bowl. Expect two days of intense thunderstorms with the seasonal *ghibli*, fifty-mile-an-hour sustained winds, gusts to eighty. Move to Delta Two, stay in touch, and be safe. Rose Bowl out."

Libya is famous for the hot, dusty *ghibli* winds descending from the highlands toward the Mediterranean Sea. At that speed, the winds would drive the rain perpendicular to the ground and move sand dunes hundreds of feet from their original location. The *wadi*s, or dried riverbeds, would fill quickly and create flashfloods in their path. Katy understood the risk but also realized evacuation by air was unlikely and unsafe. As she had already demonstrated, Mother Nature was affecting the mission—sometimes in a good way, other times not.

She watched the vehicles pass her location without slowing; it appeared to be a family heading toward Egypt or Sudan to the east or Chad to the south. Paul stirred after they passed and asked for water to which Katy added some ketone-rich coconut milk and liquid antibiotics. He grimaced at the cocktail but was so thirsty he drank it anyway. She filled the canteen cup with more water, which he drank in three gulps, finally noticing his right hand was wrapped tightly in gauze and duct tape. He also noticed boots on his feet, something he hadn't felt in several months.

"Thanks for coming to get me, Katy. How did you know I was there?"

Katy decided to level with him. "You weren't my mission, Paul, Gaddafi was. No one on our side knew you were there. During my reconnaissance, I saw them take the two of you from the building to the warehouse, so after I took the shot, I came to get you, not even realizing who you were. We just got lucky."

She continued, "I didn't want to give you painkillers without asking, but I believe you're gonna be in a world of hurt soon. Want some?

"Sure, give me what you have. Do I have to stay in the vehicle?" he asked, both of them laughing as Katy helped him to his feet.

"No, you can get out. If we were attacked, I just wasn't sure I could shoot and lift you into the seat at the same time, and I really didn't want to leave you behind." She winked as she said that. "I just spoke with Colonel Robichaux, so Rachel knows you're safe. I also told him we might shove off from here after we get two or three hours of sleep if you're up to it."

"I'm good. Robichaux is part of this?" Paul thought about that for a minute. "And just in case you didn't hear me, thanks for coming to get me, Captain, whether or not I was your primary mission." He ended his remarks with a Silver Salute.

She smiled. "You're most welcome, Captain. Glad I could be of assistance." The TBS classmates laughed together and got some rest after a hot meal and catching up on the latest scuttlebutt.

Katy heard metal-on-metal and instinctively reached for the shotgun and M4, both already loaded with a round in the chamber, as was the .50 cal. She placed her hand over Paul's mouth, woke him gently, and whispered for him to get armed and ready to fight. She checked the periscope and saw at least eight armed uniformed men moving up the slope toward their position, weapons drawn and in tactical formation. The rain had stopped temporarily, and the sun breaking through the clouds was directly in their eyes, giving Katy and Paul one small advantage.

She keyed the radio handset and called Colonel Robichaux. "Rose Bowl, Ariel. Xray Bravo Lima."

"Go, Ariel." She recognized the radio operator's voice so was unconcerned he hadn't replied to her challenge; the call was unplanned, so he rightfully assumed it was urgent.

"Rose Bowl, Ariel. We have eight hostiles at six hundred meters out approaching our pos. Small arms and uniforms. Interrogative—weapons free? Over."

"Ariel, Rose Bowl. Sorry we didn't see that coming—we had to pull Reaper because of a stabilizer problem and have another one inbound. It'll be on station in five mikes. Wait, over." He returned ten seconds later. "Ariel, weapons free. We'll monitor radio traffic to see if they're talking to anyone. Out."

Katy quietly removed the CFSR from its case and flipped open the daytime sights. "I'll keep them together but if one tries to outflank us, he's yours, OK?"

"Hand me the M4 and some grenades for the M203," Paul asked as Katy passed him the weapon and ammunition.

"As soon as they're down, I'm going to see if anyone else is out there. Please stay near the radio in case Rose Bowl calls. And, Paul, please don't get hit again. I already plugged too many holes in you." Katy grinned with him as she moved to a firing position.

In the distance, she heard but couldn't see a helicopter approaching; that probably meant reinforcements were on the way. After a moment, the Mi8 gunship burst out of a cloud heading directly toward her position. Using the laser rangefinder, Katy determined the helicopter would be in firing range in no more than ten seconds. She quickly loaded a magazine of armor piercing rounds and checked her sight picture.

Katy's shot hit the pilot directly in the helmet's visor, bouncing him off the seat and forward toward the windshield, pushing the stick forward and the nose of the aircraft down. As the copilot reacted and tried to regain command of the helicopter, Katy fired several times directly at the rotor assembly that joins the blades to the shaft, cyclic and collective mechanisms; the exploding rounds sheared the vertical mast connected to the rotating blades, thereby creating an unrecoverable situation.

The helicopter raced uncontrollably to the ground at over 120 knots, auguring into the side of the mountain and scattering bodies and equipment over a one-hundred-meter area. With the advancing soldiers fixated on the crash, Katy began picking them off one by one. Eight shots, eight kills. After everything went quiet, Paul offered sarcastically, "Let me know if you need help, OK?"

"Will do," she laughed and exited the position, sprinting down the hill past the dead soldiers and finding two vehicles five hundred meters below their location; there was no one inside either Land Cruiser. She punctured the tires on one car with her Ka-Bar and shot holes in its radiator. She quickly grabbed a pack from the front seat and filled it with maps, a laptop, radios, and papers she would review later. Katy jumped in the remaining vehicle and drove it up the hill, waving at Paul as she approached his position so he didn't shoot at her. The helicopter was burning to her right, and bodies lay strewn on the mountaintop to her left. She pushed the thought out of her mind that she was responsible for both events.

"We have to move now, Paul," she said, a command rather than a request, getting a Silver Salute in reply. She loaded the equipment into the ALSV, got in the driver's seat, and pulled twenty meters away from the hideout. Katy drove the Land Cruiser directly over their hideout and set it on fire; the clouds had returned, it was drizzling again, and it would be dark soon anyway, so the residual smoke wouldn't be noticed. Once she was confident everything of value was destroyed, Katy returned to the vehicle and started down the mountain heading southwest.

"I want to make it to the Waw an Namus volcano before sunrise. It's about 250 miles from here across flat desert most of the way. The moonless night will mask our movement, and the rain will cover our tracks. Even though its only fifteen hundred feet elevation, it'll give us a good vantage point to observe the avenues of approach." The volcano is located in the eastern Fezzan region and dates back to the Pleistocene era some two hundred thousand years ago.

Katy realized she was talking to herself; Paul had slipped into a deep sleep out of sheer exhaustion, and although he was doing better, each activity quickly depleted his energy reserves. She let him sleep and tried to keep the ride as smooth as possible. As the sky got darker, she slowed the vehicle and turned on her night-vision goggles to navigate. Eight hours later at 0330, they arrived on top of the volcano, scouted locations, and set up camp away from the natural lakes created in the caldera. Paul suggested they camp next to a lake so he could wash the remaining remnants of the last several months off his haggard body.

"*Waw an Namus* means 'oasis of mosquitoes' in Arabic. If we stay near the lakes, we'll be eaten alive, although the rain might keep them away for now. I thought this was a better location, plus I saw a palm grove just below us where we might get some fresh dates. Need anything?"

Paul shook his head, obviously feeling more pain after the trek across the desert. He stretched and unthinkingly arched his back, dropping to his knees with tears in his eyes when he strained the broken ribs. Katy watched and stayed close but decided to help only if asked. Both officers hobbled around the encampment, nursing wounds and trying not to make them worse.

They ate quickly and settled in for the day. Colonel Robichaux assured Katy the team aboard *Pasadena* would focus on surveillance and reconnaissance while she and Paul rested, and would alert her to any potential threats. Both slept until midday, although Katy woke periodically to check the flat terrain leading to the volcano's base for evidence of visitors. Another fuel bladder and fifteen thousand rounds for the Browning were waiting near their camp when they woke up.

They were on the move again after a good meal and two cups of Katy's coffee. They reviewed the map, conferred with *Pasadena*, and decided the next stop would be at the Ribiana Sand Sea near Kufra in the southeast corner of the country. Analysis of the Libyan military's reconnaissance flights indicated little interest in surveilling that sector of the Sahara as long as the government got its share of money from the slave and drug trade through the area. Robichaux updated Katy on the weather, now dry but with temperatures approaching 115 degrees in the noon sun. Summer was definitely coming to this part of the Mediterranean.

With another 250-mile drive ahead of them and Paul now feeling somewhat better, they donned tactical noise-canceling headsets and talked about TBS, family, and losing friends in Afghanistan and Iraq during the drive. Paul opened the subject of his capture and incarceration, and even confided details of why his feet were so mangled. They talked about their careers in the Marine Corps and what plans they had for the future. The discussion was upbeat and energizing; they both felt better when they arrived in Ribiana.

Forty million years ago, shifts in the tectonic plates began pushing the African continent against Europe, closing the Tethys Sea that extended from the Mediterranean to what would become the Indian Ocean, an oceanic trench covering 80 million square miles and depositing marine sediments from northern Turkey through the Caucasus, Northern Iran and Afghanistan to China, the Kunlun Mountains of Tibet, and Indochina.

As recently as eight hundred thousand years ago, the Sahara experienced a period of heavy rains that lasted a hundred thousand years, covering the landscape with swamps and dense vegetation, teaming with hippopotami, rhinoceroses, crocodiles, and elephants. Three giant megalakes provided fresh water for the area, one in Tunisia that today is the tiny Chott el Djerid; the existing Chad megalake; and the Fezzan lake in Libya, the only one of the three that provides a long-term record of climate change in the central Sahara.

An abrupt change in the earth's axis from 24.14 degrees to its current 23.45 degrees seven thousand years ago left Libya closer to the sun and transformed it from lush and wet to a xeric landscape. Bedouins and other nomadic travelers identified tracks on which to travel through the sand sea, earlier by camel and now in four-wheel drive vehicles. In another fifteen thousand years, though, the cycle will again soak the Libyan desert and restore its indigenous flora and fauna.

None of that was on their minds as Katy and Paul drove southeast toward Ribiana in the eastern Cyrenaica province. At times they retreated into their own thoughts, other times they discussed the operation and next steps. Sometimes Katy would look over and find Paul dozing while she drove on through the night, taking advantage of the flat areas to speed up and slowing through the rougher terrain. They arrived for the next stop at 0400, fifteen miles west of Kufra and south of the village of Buseima, hopefully far enough away from curious eyes. They could see the village from the high ground, observing a few lights starting to come on as night ended and people awoke.

Eighty-eight years before they arrived to this location, Ahmed Hassanein met the Faqrun family, there as an emissary of King Fuad of Egypt. Oxford educated, he rose to be chief of the Diwan and chamberlain to King Farouk twenty years later. He would shortly also be designated *pasha* under the Ottoman system, but for now he was addressed as *effendi*. Ahmed was a diplomat, Olympic athlete in fencing, and geographic explorer sent on a diplomatic mission to cross the region around the Kufra oasis defended by the fierce and puritanical Senussi tribe. He met the emir and later king of Cyrenaica, Idris al Sanussi, about whom Ahmed chronicled the tribe's history and traditions. Idris would soon become king of the unified country before being ousted while in Turkey for medical treatment by Gaddafi in 1969. On this occasion, though, the men agreed to peace between the two kingdoms and signed a treaty to support each other if attacked.

Katy and Paul would've been in the photograph memorializing the event had they arrived at that location eighty-eight years earlier, setting up their camp among the dunes exactly where the agreement was signed in 1920.

Although they discussed the idea, *Pasadena* ruled out a helicopter-borne tactical recovery, assessing the danger of flying that far into Libyan airspace wasn't worth the risk unless Paul and Katy's situation turned extremis. So far it hadn't. Every objective of the mission had been accomplished without friendly casualties, so there was no need to lose an aircraft or personnel in an unnecessary operation. The pair could always be discovered, but the team's prudent use of satellite imagery and armed drones, the QRT primed and ready to go, and close air support from Sigonella and the carrier battle group in the Mediterranean meant there would be an instant reaction to any hostile threat. For now, though, the pair would continue on their desert egress until it was safe to extract them.

Just after sundown, they headed north toward the Great Sand Sea along the border with Egypt, threading the needle between Kufra to the east and Tazerbo to the west, driving through the esparto grass plains along the way. Through their NVGs, they spotted Toubou nomads with their goat herds, although nothing in their demeanor suggested they were remotely curious about a vehicle traveling without lights in the dark at fifty miles per hour, probably assuming Katy and Paul were smugglers making a run to drop off their goods. Katy had to avoid a herd of goats that walked out from behind a dune just as they reached it, but that was the biggest excitement of the evening.

As before, Katy used the plow to create a box canyon in the dunes almost eight feet high where they could park and camouflage the ALSV, augmenting the site with the camouflage net and local bushes. Paul was preparing their meal and heating water for coffee, anxious to get some rest for the final run to the coast planned for the following evening. Paul asked how much longer she needed before she was ready to eat. As she turned to answer him, she froze.

Standing thirty feet to the east was a man faintly outlined by the sun still forty-five minutes from rising. Had she thought about it, she would've described it as the beginning of morning nautical twilight when the sunrise was still just a faint glow, but that wasn't what was going through her mind at that point.

Paul heard Katy speak, surprised at the strength of her voice. *"Assalamu allekum,"* she addressed the man.

"Wa allekum asalaam," he answered.

"Tashrab gahwa?"

"Na'am," he replied.

"Please tell me the coffee's ready, Paul," Katy implored, not removing her eyes from the man.

"Three cups of joe coming up," Paul answered after seeing him.

"Tafadul, istareeh." Katy asked him to have a seat, after which she and Paul sat opposite him. The man took both sugar and powdered milk when offered, and they sat quietly enjoying the hot coffee in the early-morning chill, each watching the other and trying to guess intentions.

Although the man had a breech-loading Martini-Henry single-shot lever-actuated rifle, he made no move to take if off his shoulder; Katy guessed it was a hundred fifty years old, in reality older than her estimate

by only a decade. He appeared otherwise unarmed, but she assumed he
had a knife of some sort, less a weapon and more a tool. As the sunrise
progressed, she could now discern a blue tint to his headdress.

"Min Tuareg?" she asked.

"Na'am."

"Min ay qubila?"

"Min Kel Ferwan."

"Hal taearafuh Mohammed abu Omar min Kel Ferwan?"

The man hesitated and answered slowly, "Ana Omar ibn Mohammed
min Kel Ferwan."

"Jawzak Hinan?"

He hesitated again. "Na'am, jawzi Hinan."

"Omar, ana Amira!" Katy said with enthusiasm and emotion.

For the second time in just a few days, Katy was dumbfounded. Here
was the son of the old man Mohammed she'd met in the desert twenty
years before. Mohammed's son Omar had indeed married Hinan after
recovering from the accident at the oil rig and was now sitting in front
of Katy. Over the next thirty minutes, she related the story to Omar
of meeting him at the hospital when she and her family lived in Libya
two decades ago. She learned Omar's father and mother had died—she
immediately offered condolences—he and Hinan had six children, and
they were still living the nomadic lifestyle of their forefathers in the
Kel Ferwan tribe. Paul sat listening quietly to the language he didn't
understand, content to laugh when they laughed and nod in agreement
when they did.

After two more cups of coffee—Omar found it strange that the
man had a hand wrapped in silver and was brewing the coffee—he
finally got around to asking Katy why they were camped in the desert
wearing uniforms and carrying weapons. In reply, she asked him what
he thought of Gaddafi, assuming he was less than enamored with the
mercurial man who drove the Tuareg deeper into the desert if they
didn't obey his dictatorial edicts.

Omar pondered the question for a minute, finally replying in
Arabic, "So you're the soldiers the army is looking for. But where are

the others?" The back-and-forth discussion was interrupted only long enough for Katy to translate for Paul what she learned.

"He said the government offered a cash reward for our capture. Omar overheard the soldiers who searched his camp say they've been told we're going east across the border into Egypt. And he said they were broadcasting to the public that a force of two hundred trained mercenaries conducted the operation!" She laughed as she said it. When she saw the look in Paul's eyes, she assured him Omar would not turn them in regardless of the bounty, informing him of the Tuareg's visceral dislike of governments in general and this one in particular. And if nothing else, she and her family helped his father twenty years ago. Omar would never dishonor Mohammed over something as insignificant as money.

Katy told Omar they needed to rest; he understood and told her he would stay nearby in case they needed his help, assuring her he would sound the alarm if anyone approached. The three of them ate and settled in for another day sleeping in the desert; Katy mixed the chemicals again to counter the rising heat, finished her coffee, and lay down. *Pasadena* and the drone were also keeping watch while they slept.

Katy was packing up for the final 250-mile trip to Derna when Paul awoke. Omar stood by to help; she told him good-bye when they were ready, gave him some extra equipment, and all the food and water he could carry, and pressed five hundred dollars in his hand. When he glanced at her Ka-bar, she unhooked the sheath and knife from her calf and handed it to him.

"Ma'asalama, Amira. Allah ya'teeki al afiya!" He said good-bye, wished them strength, then turned and headed off toward the east. They watched him crest one dune and in a few minutes a second one, and then he disappeared into the vast desert the same way his father had twenty years previously.

Paul prepared some snacks for the trip, not knowing if or when they would have time to stop. They both drank a coconut milkshake;

Paul had figured out how to use the cooling device to make an icy slush they both enjoyed in the late afternoon heat. They cleaned and loaded the guns and checked the magazines, organized their personal gear, and spent a few minutes gathering their thoughts. Katy reviewed the checklist, radioed *Pasadena*, changed the dressings covering their wounds, and when the time was right, they set off north toward the coast.

Ninety minutes later, they stopped for Katy to change a flat tire while Paul made another check of the equipment and dogged down some loose gear. They decided to fill the tank with diesel from the last remaining fuel bladder and then buried it in the sand. They jettisoned other commercially available equipment that could not be traced back to the U.S. government, added oil to the crankcase, changed the batteries on their NVGs, refilled their coffee cups, and got under way again twenty minutes later.

The officers knew they were now committed to leave the Libyan mainland before sunrise; there would be no secure location to hide once they made the coast. The army garrisons at Benghazi, Derna, al Bayda, and Tobruk and smaller camps at Cyrene and al Jabal al Akhdar surrounded the Bay of al Bumbah where Katy had entered the country a week ago and where they were now heading. They could either spend another long day south of Derna in the desert, knowing the army was searching for them, or proceed with the egress. They agreed on the latter choice with *Pasadena*.

Katy and Paul approached Susah carefully; although there was no one on the streets at 0200, if anyone saw the pair driving such a vehicle they might contact the authorities to investigate. They skirted the town and headed directly for the site where Katy had stashed the RHIB.

"Ariel, this Rose Bowl. Tango Zebra Oscar. Over."

"Rose Bowl, Ariel. Delta Foxtrot Yankee. Over."

"Ariel, the air traffic controller at al Abraq Airport reporting seeing a military-type vehicle with two souls on board heading north toward

Susah. Six tactical vehicles departed al Bayda, arriving at your location in thirty mikes. Additional eight vehicles departed Derna arriving fifteen mikes later. We put up a second Reaper watching both parties. Libyan navy and coast guard have also been notified. Their Corvette is getting under way from Benghazi. Over."

"Rose Bowl, this is Ariel. We're ten mikes from the RHIB. Should be able to launch within ten mikes after that. Over."

"Roger, Ariel. Come on home. Out."

At that moment, Katy swerved to avoid hitting a camel crossing in front of them, driving the ALSV over a small dune directly into a *wadi* still full from the recent rains. Reluctant to stop for fear of stalling the engine—water already was up to the bottom of the steering wheel—Katy instead drove directly toward the closest bank, willing the ALSV forward. She questioned that decision when the water reached chest deep, but the diesel engine kept running and propelled the vehicle forward up a 70 percent gradient as the marketing material for the vehicle advertised. They came out the other side of the *wadi* drenched but relieved.

Paul simply shook his head and said matter-of-factly, "Only you, Katy O., only you. Or should I call you Amira?"

Katy scrunched her nose as they laughed together.

The cave where she hid the RHIB was undisturbed. Although Katy originally was to be extracted via the STARS system, she planned nevertheless to use the boat again if the need arose, otherwise it would've been surreptitiously recovered by a SEAL team in a few days. She used the ALSV to drag the boat to the water and transferred the required equipment from the vehicle into the RHIB; she also placed the two backpacks of intelligence information gained during the operation in a secure space on the boat.

Katy started the twin 150-horsepower outboard engines and let them idle while she backed the ALSV into a defensive position on the beach to cover their exit. She was stepping out of the vehicle twenty meters from the boat when shots rang out from the southwest. One round hit her in the right calf, nicking the bone.

Rather than try to run through the gunfire on an injured leg, Katy decided to back the ALSV into the water where Paul was in a better position to help her. She fired the remote-controlled .50 caliber machine gun at the approaching vehicles, destroying two of them and disabling a third. The soldiers were now dismounted and running toward her, two of them actually in the water attempting to cut her off from escape.

Meanwhile, Paul was in the RHIB and on the radio with *Pasadena*. He loaded the M203 grenade launcher and shot several rounds in the direction of the troops, hoping to slow them enough to give Katy more time to reach him, not yet realizing she was wounded.

"Give me a hand, Paul. I'm hit," she said, just as he saw the spreading stain of blood on her uniform. He jumped out of the boat, pulled her out of the ALSV now in four feet of water, and floated her to the RHIB. Katy still had the remote control for the Browning and was directing fire toward the men when they moved. Of the thirty soldiers dispatched to capture them, she and Paul had already killed seventeen, including the platoon leader, but the remaining baker's dozen seemed unstoppable.

Katy threw herself with Paul's help into the driver's seat and gunned the engines, almost throwing him overboard. Rounds were hitting the water around them, slowed only because the .50 cal was now on auto mode and shooting at anything that moved. When the gunfire stopped Katy knew it was out of ammunition, having fired over twenty thousand rounds in ten minutes, thankful for the recent resupply of ammunition. The soldiers approached the ALSV just as a Hellfire missile destroyed it and killed all but two of them; one lay facedown in the water and drowned a few minutes later while the one surviving soldier succumbed to his injuries a week later.

Lieutenant Commander Haitham bin Musa Al Mijabri, commander of the Nanuchka-class corvette *Tariq ibn Ziyad*, was determined to capture the people who had assassinated the Leader, less because he cared for Gaddafi—he didn't—and more for the adulation and benefits he would enjoy as a hero of the Socialist People's Libyan Arab Jamahariya. Radio reports indicated a boat was launched near Susah and was heading northwest in the direction of Malta; he adjusted course to intercept the boat while it was still in Libyan territorial waters. The government in Tripoli was warning all vessels to avoid that area informing them the navy and air force were trying to apprehend the terrorists who had killed Colonel Gaddafi a few days ago.

Katy adjusted the boat's transponder to squawk 4787—the last four digits of her social security number—for allied aircraft and vessels to know where they were. Oliver Hazard Perry–class guided missile frigate USS *Reuben James* (FFG-57) launched both SH-60B LAMPS Mk III helicopters, the light airborne multipurpose system designed for maritime warfare and, if needed tonight, search and rescue. The commanding officer of *Reuben James*, Dave Giles ordered the vessel on an intercept course with *Tariq ibn Ziyad*, in position to block the Libyan vessel's approach to Katy and Paul. When *Tariq ibn Ziyad*'s commanding officer refused to yield, Giles order the Corvette's engines disabled with gunfire from the frigate's OTO Melara 76-millimeter gun; twelve rounds later Lieutenant Commander Haitham's boat and career ambitions were both dead in the water.

Newly promoted Lieutenant Colonel John "Striker" James checked the transponder receiver on the CH-53E Sea Stallion Super Heavy-Lift Transport Helicopter and found Katy's location, piloting the massive helicopter fifty feet above the water at the recommended cruise speed of a hundred twenty knots.

"Any bad guys in the area?" he asked co-pilot Captain Terry "Caruso" Orbison, a nephew of the late American singer and songwriter Roy Orbison, affectionately known as the Caruso of Rock.

"Radar's clear," Terry answered. "Hawkeye is on-station and coordinating close air patrol, so we can just focus on the pickup."

The E-2 Hawkeye is an all-weather, tactical airborne early warning twin-turboprop aircraft capable of landing on and taking off from aircraft carriers. The model flying this evening was the E-2D which first flew the previous year, the fourth major revision of the airplane and the first specifically designed for its role of command and control, early warning, and electronic warfare. James and Orbison knew the Hawkeye's crew would keep the skies over the Mediterranean open so the Super Stallion could do its job.

"Going active," Caruso informed Striker, switching on a radio beacon Katy and Paul could follow, a homing device of sorts. The active signal also lit up on Libyan air defense radars, identifying the location, speed, and direction of the helicopter. If the plan succeeded, the CH-53E and the RHIB would end up at the same place at the same time, drawing the mission to an end.

"Victor Bravo, this is Delta Sierra, over." The Hawkeye was calling Striker.

"Delta Sierra, Victor Bravo, go."

"Five Osa-class fast attack boats approaching, twenty miles southwest of your position at thirty-five knots, over." The Libyans purchased twelve of the Russian-made missile boats to serve as coastal patrol vessels and protect offshore oil and gas platforms.

"Roger, Delta Sierra. They have an appointment with *Reuben James* if they get too close. Over."

"Roger, Victor Bravo. Let the good times roll! Out." Striker knew the pilot of the E-2D was from New Orleans, echoing the city's motto *Laissez les bon temps rouler.*

Katy and Paul saw activity in the skies above their location, hoping most if not all of it was allied aircraft. They followed the homing signal toward the predesignated pickup point and saw Striker's helicopter hovering just above the surface with seawater halfway up the open ramp.

One of the fast attack boats fired two of its SS-N-2 Styx antiship missiles at the RHIB; although still thirteen miles away, the crew of *Osorkon the Elder* was aiming at the radar signature of Katy's boat. The Mk 15 Phalanx Close-In Weapons System—abbreviated CWIS and pronounced "sea whiz"—on *Reuben James* automatically recognized the threat and shot down the missiles as they passed the frigate. Commander Giles ordered the offending boat sunk, which happened twenty seconds later.

Katy lined up the RHIB directly behind the helicopter, running it up the ramp, killing the power and pushing a switch as she did. The outboard engines rotated up, allowing the boat to slide into the Sea Stallion, coming to a full stop halfway through the fuselage where an arresting net had been installed. Striker and Caruso adjusted the collective to create lift while pushing the cyclic forward to move the helicopter into flight mode. Despite the additional weight—the Super Stallion could haul thirty thousand pounds inside its fuselage—the helicopter rose majestically into the early-morning sky, veered north-northwest, and signaled the Tarawa-class amphibious assault ship USS *Nassau* they were inbound.

Katy remembered being lifted out of the ALSV and placed on a gurney before passing out from exhaustion and blood loss from her latest wounds. She woke up twelve hours later, drank three glasses of water in rapid succession, and asked about Paul. The corpsman told Katy he was doing much better and was being treated for all his wounds and injuries suffered through torture and during the operation. Katy closed her eyes again, sleeping the sleep of the just, knowing the mission was accomplished. She never noticed Colonel Robichaux standing off to the side.

Chapter 38

The President of the United States of America, in the name of Congress, takes pleasure in presenting the Medal of Honor to Captain Kathryn Emily Morgan, United States Marine Corps, for conspicuous gallantry and intrepidity at the risk of her life above and beyond the call of duty while conducting a direct action hostage rescue mission against an armed enemy at Al Aziziyah, Libya, on 3 June, 2008. On that day and for several days thereafter, Captain Morgan proceeded alone after her teammate suffered a debilitating injury. Killing twelve enemy soldiers guarding the hostages, without hesitation and with complete disregard for her own safety, she personally engaged with the enemy with gunfire, grenades, and hand-to-hand combat. As the fight developed and after suffering six separate gunshot wounds, Captain Morgan released the two hostages from captivity, secured them in the evacuation vehicle, and successfully withdrew from the area, continuing shooting the enemy soldiers with a .50 caliber machine gun mounted on the vehicle, an M4 service rifle, and an M203 grenade launcher. Her courageous actions helped defeat repeated enemy attacks resulting in at least fifty enemy soldiers and combatants killed and one aircraft downed, while allowing the safe return of the hostages. By her undaunted courage, bold fighting spirit, and unwavering devotion to duty in the face of almost certain death, Captain Morgan's extraordinary heroism and uncommon valor are in keeping with the highest traditions of the military service and reflect great credit upon herself, the Marine Corps, and the United States Naval Service.

Katy arrived at the White House that morning for what she believed was a post-mission meeting with President Rush, the Chairman General Blackman, and others in her chain of command, a few months after the operation so she and Paul Stephens could recuperate from their wounds. What she didn't know was the Marine Corps leadership expedited a Medal of Honor inquiry supported by Congressman and retired Marine colonel Steve Bossie, interviewing Colonel Robichaux, Captain Stephens, Ambassador Pugh, and others involved in Operation Desert Wind, as well as reviewing the classified video feeds from the satellites and drones and the radio conversations over the eleven days Katy was ashore in Libya. She also didn't know her mother, father, and sister were waiting in the East Room by invitation of President Rush.

The initial uproar from the international community over Gaddafi's death was ameliorated by news of the hostage rescue; both Captain Stephens and Ambassador Pugh were guests on the Sunday morning talk shows, revealing general details about their incarceration, not only sanctioned by Gaddafi and but also at his direction. When Paul recognized the name of one of the panelists interviewing him, he paused before answering Martin Ensore's question.

"I wear the uniform of a United States Marine to protect all of the freedoms we as Americans enjoy, guaranteed by the Constitution and our system of laws. Included in Article 1 of the Bill of Rights is freedom of the press. What you did by publicizing personal information about me and my family and sensitive information about training and operations I've participated in, Mr. Ensore, was abetting our enemies and giving them tools to use while torturing me. I will die fighting for those freedoms enjoyed by you and others in the media. I realize you might win a Pulitzer Prize for your reporting, but just know that you, sir, directly contributed to the scars and broken bones I suffered. God forgive you because I never will." The outrage at Ensore resulted in only two thousand copies of the book being sold, and although he was awarded the Pulitzer, it was presented in a private ceremony without publicity.

Paul and Katy were also interviewed at Walter Reed National Military Medical Center three weeks after their return. America and her allies applauded the young woman who exhibited grit and perseverance to rescue her Marine colleague and a member of the U.S. Foreign Service. Paul did not describe the brutality he suffered in Syria and Libya, only that he was tortured, and felt shame when he started crying during the interview. But it galvanized American public opinion in favor of the rescue and silenced critics at the United Nations and in governments around the world, save China, Syria, Cuba, and North Korea. Even the Russians were sympathetic.

"We owe a debt of gratitude to Ambassador Pugh and Captain Stephens for their selfless duty that put them in harm's way. I can only say we triumphed, we got them home safely, and we removed a callous dictator from power—permanently.

"And we offer our deepest sympathies to Captain Stephens on the loss of his wife Rachel. Her courage in the hijacking of Emirates flight 001 from Dubai to London Heathrow in December 2003 was exemplary. On behalf of a grateful nation, please know that we share your grief and will keep you and your family in our prayers."

Katy, Paul, and Roger were initially evacuated to Landstuhl Regional Medical Center near Ramstein Air Base in Germany to treat their most serious wounds—among them a laparoscopic appendectomy for Katy—before repatriating them to Walter Reed. Members of their immediate families were flown to Germany to be by their side, including Rachel and their daughter Victoria.

Rachel collapsed after seeing Paul. Damaged in the shooting five years earlier, one of the blood vessels in her brain had never healed properly, the thin endothelium membrane giving way under pressure. The cabin pressure on the flight from the U.S. coupled with the stress of pregnancy and the shock of seeing Paul's broken body increased her blood pressure, exerting too much force on the carotid artery supplying blood to the anterior portion of the cerebrum.

When the blood vessel ruptured, the sudden decrease in blood flow resulted in numbness and paralysis on the left side of her body, a stroke in an otherwise healthy young woman. She was dead before she hit the floor, although the neonatal intensive care unit was able to save the baby. With Rachel's parents' permission, Paul named her Rachel Ariel Stephens, in honor of his wife and their friend, standing beside the president of the United States, who brought him home to his family.

"Those of us who know Captain Morgan—Katy, if I may—are not at all surprised by her actions last June. She faced the enemy head-on and prevailed. She embraced the mission with confidence and competence, using her unique skills and capabilities to do what most of us couldn't, even if we wanted to." President Rush paused for a moment. "Fleet Admiral Chester W. Nimitz, Jr., in describing the Marines who fought on Iwo Jima said, 'Uncommon valor was a common virtue.' So too must we include Captain Morgan among the greats of the Corps who exhibited uncommon valor.

"What you might not know is that Katy is only the second woman to be awarded the Medal of Honor, the first being Dr. Mary Walker, who was a civilian doctor treating wounded soldiers during the Civil War, and even enduring several months as a prisoner.

"Some in the media have also asked how the inquiry to support the award was conducted so quickly. This operation took place under the watchful cameras of satellites and drones, and everyone involved was alive and immediately available for personal interviews. The Marine Corps was able to review and confirm every detail quickly, certifying that Katy's actions merited the Medal of Honor, something the Members of Congress and I support unanimously, enthusiastically, and wholeheartedly.

"This was the second of its kind in another way. The medal was awarded posthumously to Technical Sergeant John A. Chapman, United States Air Force, for his actions in the battle of Takur Ghar during the war in Afghanistan on March 4, 2002. Tech Sergeant Chapman organized and directed the evacuation of the crew of a disabled helicopter and the embarked SEALs, and then stayed behind to rescue another teammate, giving his life in the process. Videos from overhead drones provided the final proof of Tech Sergeant Chapman's selfless valor, the first time an act of heroism warranting the Medal of Honor was validated that way.

"Most of us cannot comprehend Katy's heroism and we certainly don't have a true appreciation for the courage it must take to conduct such an operation. It's why every member of the military, regardless of how senior they are, is required to initiate a salute to any servicemember authorized to wear the Medal of Honor, regardless of how junior they are. Thank you, Katy, for your courage, for your devotion to duty, and for your love for America. I am proud to know you and proud to be president of the United States on such an occasion.

"I have one more thing to give Captain Morgan. The sixth time she was shot was in her dominant left hand that would've been destroyed were it not for her class ring that deflected the bullet and was mangled in the process. I was able to convince the president of The Citadel—not an easy task even for the president of the United States—to have a new ring fabricated from the gold of her original ring, and to entrust it to me for safekeeping until this ceremony. Today I return it to you, Katy, hoping you will continue to wear it proudly."

Paraphrasing a recruiting poster from the earliest days of Corps, Rush finished her remarks, "Long live the United States and success to the Marines!" To which all assembled Marines responded, "Oorah!" shocking some in the audience unfamiliar with the rites and traditions of the Corps.

The applause was deafening and unending, and Katy was supremely uncomfortable being the center of attention. In addition to the president, the chairman, and Colonel Robichaux, she recognized Congressman and Mrs. Bossie from the dinner at the Capital Grille, Ambassador

Roger Pugh, the secretary of defense, the vice president, and several other people whose names she couldn't remember at that moment. First Sergeant Mersino and Senior Chiefs Carl Zemanski and Abner Dalupang were there; Katy hugged Abner's daughter Michelle, who was his "date" for the event. Commander Mike Mitchell, commanding officer of SEAL Team 3 was there, as was Elyse Anderson. It seemed like a lifetime since their skiing trip just six months ago.

After the formal ceremony and reception, President Rush asked the team to meet her in the Oval Office. As soon as they were assembled, she got down to business.

"I'm sorry we haven't had a chance to meet since you returned, but we had a lot going on behind the scenes that we wanted to do today, and I also wanted to give you and Captain Stephens a chance to recover from your wounds. I hope you understand. Before we get into the next phase, I have one question for you, Katy. With the enormity of the operation and its consequences for the war against terrorism, what did you feel when you pulled the trigger?"

"Madam President, I felt a slight recoil," Katy replied, immediately embarrassed when everyone in the room laughed, belatedly realizing the president was asking about her emotional reaction, not the physical manifestation of taking the shot.

"Well, I'm just glad I didn't ask that question when the cameras were rolling! Recoil or not, the success of this operation was better than I could've expected, with a fortuitous decision by Captain Morgan to turn it into a hostage rescue mission on the fly. That certainly made the pill easier for a lot of people to swallow, although I was fully prepared to take the heat for targeting Colonel Gaddafi in the first place.

"A month after your safe return, I asked General Blackman and Colonel Robichaux to establish a permanent hostage rescue team, reporting directly to me, based on the success of Operation Desert Wind. In short, the colonel is the commanding officer, he invited Lieutenant Colonel Mark Masterson to be his chief of staff when his tour in Iraq is complete, and Sergeant Major Roger Pippins is the staff noncommissioned officer-in-charge of the unit. Captain Morgan with First Sergeant Mersino and Captain Stephens with Senior Chief Zemanski will lead the direct action teams, aptly named Scarlet and Gold"—Rush was referring to the official colors of the Corps—"and the leadership will fill in the remaining billets for intelligence, logistics, air operations, and so on. You'll have SEALs, Force Recon, Delta Force, Rangers, the 160th Special Operations Aviation Regiment, the entire intelligence community, and other assets available as needed. I want to keep it small and elite. No more involved than absolutely required by the mission.

"A month ago, two American women were taken off the streets in Naples, Italy, and forced into a global prostitution ring based in Kiev. One of the girls was spotted a few days ago in Rome by an embassy officer, but she wasn't able to communicate with or approach her. I want you to find them and bring them home, and do it within sixty days, sooner if possible. Any questions?"

"Madam President, wouldn't that be a law enforcement issue?" Colonel Robichaux asked the same question everyone in the Oval Office was thinking.

"Under normal circumstances, I would agree, but one of the women is an investigator at NCIS, the other a cryptologist on the aircraft carrier. It doesn't appear the people who abducted them know that, but they could sell the information to interested parties if they find out.

"To make matters worse, the cryptologist is the daughter of Major General Frank Duggan, director of the National Military Command Center. That word is also not on the street. So this is our problem to clean up. Any other questions?"

There were none.

"Very well. Carry on!"

Chapter 39

November 3, 2008
U.S. State Department

Jonathan Winston got off the Silver Line metro at the Foggy Bottom station and made the twelve-minute walk to the U.S. State Department building at 2201 C Street in northwest Washington. Traffic was normal—busy—for a Monday morning, since many employees in the District live in the bedroom communities surrounding the Nation's Capital, drive in on Monday to a pied-à-terre and return home to their families on Friday.

Four men were waiting at the entrance to the State Department when he entered the building; they approached him, informed him he was under arrest, and one recited the Miranda warning customarily given by law enforcement officers to criminal suspects:

> You have the right to remain silent. Anything you say can be used against you in court. You have the right to talk to a lawyer for advice before we ask you any questions. You have the right to have a lawyer with you during questioning. If you cannot afford a lawyer, one will be appointed for you before any questioning if you wish. If you decide to answer questions now without a lawyer present, you have the right to stop answering at any time.

Jonathan heard only the word "treason" even as he acknowledged understanding his rights.

Similar arrests were happening in three others locations across Washington and another at the United Nations in New York City; an investigation conducted by the FBI found a conspiracy to commit treason by informing the Israeli government of classified military operational plans.

One additional person listed in the indictment as interfering in the government response to a previous hijacking, Ned Walker, who claimed he worked at the Federal Aviation Administration, was not found.

The secretary of state summoned the Israeli ambassador to the State Department and informed him that defense attaché Colonel Uri Shetzer was persona non grata and had twenty-four hours to leave the country. The ambassador objected, citing the special relationship between the two countries and Israeli support for the Rush administration, but Secretary Carter made it clear the decision was final. She also said the U.S. government had DNA evidence from the man posing as Colonel Gaddafi and from the team that tried to stop the Libya operation. She had no desire to release the information but would if the ambassador didn't prevail on Shetzer to leave the country; he was on the El Al flight out of Washington Dulles that evening. Immigration and Customs Enforcement confiscated Shetzer's American passport—he naturalized twenty-five years ago as a student at George Washington University—forcing him to travel home on his Israeli passport. The secretary sent official notification that Shetzer's citizenship was revoked.

The secretary of defense informed the Embassy of the State of Israel that its license to sell equipment to the U.S. military was rescinded, and equipment already received was being returned to the manufacturers. Full refunds were expected immediately with ground radars first on the list.

Chapter 40

November 10, 2008
Abu Dhabi, United Arab Emirates

The Marine Corps celebrates its birthday every year on November tenth, the day Congress in 1775 authorized the formation of two battalions of Marines and recruiting immediately began at Tun Tavern in Philadelphia. Wherever two or more Marines meet on that date the anniversary is celebrated, as it was this year in Abu Dhabi hosted by the Marine Security Guards in the ballroom at Emirates Palace, by far the most luxurious hotel in the city.

Mark applied for leave to attend the ball in Abu Dhabi; his tour in the United Arab Emirates was curtailed and he was transferred to Baghdad to assume command of BLT 2/6 when the previous CO was injured in a roadside bomb and required medical evacuation to the U.S. Since most Marines headed home to the States for their leave, Mark explained several times that his girlfriend lived in the UAE and he wanted to see her rather than travel to Tennessee. He had already spoken with his parents, and they supported his travel plans.

Mark placed a call to the embassy in Abu Dhabi. "Lieutenant Colonel McDaniel, how can I help you, sir?"

"J-Mac, this is Mark. How are you?" McDaniel had replaced Mark as the MSG company commander in Abu Dhabi.

"Colonel Masterson, how are you my friend?"

"I'm doing great. How's the company doing?"

"Well, my predecessor left me with more problems than I should have to deal with, but other than that, things are good. What about you?" J-Mac knew what was coming next but waited for Mark to tell him.

"Very funny. J-Mac, I got the CO's approval for leave to attend the ball in Abu Dhabi. Would you invite Rasha and I'll surprise her?"

"You got it. I'll tell Janet, but no one else."

"Who's Janet?" Mark knew McDaniel would have a date, but J-Mac had never spoken of her in their previous conversations.

"She's a foreign service officer in the consulate. She arrived about six weeks ago."

"OK. Can you work out the logistics to get Rasha to Emirates Palace and I'll come in during the reception before the ball?"

"No problem, Mark. I'll take care of it. And you owe me big time." The two officers talked about Marine Corps matters for a few minutes and then signed off.

Mark found the next week interminable as he waited for the flight from Baghdad International Airport to Dubai, where most of the defense contractors had offices and where the charter flights to Iraq originated. He briefed his battalion executive officer, who would assume command while he was out of country and finalized arrangements, spoke with the regimental commander before leaving for the airport, and checked out with the adjutant.

The run to the airport was always an adventure, or as the Marines described it, a "training highlight." Today proved no different when Mark's convoy was caught in the crossfire between two militias. Even traveling in civilian clothing as he was, all occupants in the vehicle wore flak jackets and helmets, and Mark was glad for the extra protection. When he exited the vehicle to assist another car in the convoy, he was hit on the helmet by a stray bullet, knocking him off his feet and putting a three-inch divot in the ballistic helmet. Mark shook himself off and returned to his vehicle with a headache and sore neck but was otherwise unscathed.

The remainder of the trip to the airport was uneventful, as was the four-hour flight to Dubai. J-Mac arranged a driver who took Mark the eighty miles to McDaniel's apartment in Abu Dhabi, where he stored his dress uniforms when he departed Abu Dhabi eight months previously. After traveling all day, Mark finally arrived at 1700.

"I heard you singlehandedly stopped a 5.56 round this morning."

"Bad news travels fast. Got a sore neck, but otherwise I'm fine. Do you have some aspirin?" Mark felt fine, but the dull throbbing headache reminded him of the events earlier in the day, and he didn't want it to spoil the evening. The two officers dressed for the ball, and J-Mac went to pick up Rasha and Janet. Mark's limousine was waiting in the parking lot, and he headed to the hotel, arriving during the reception before the ceremony and dinner.

He spotted Rasha immediately. She was wearing a floor-length gown the same scarlet color as his cummerbund, with only a pair of earrings, the simplicity of her attire making her all the more beautiful. He stood across the room from her as the crowd moved toward and away from the bar. A photographer was taking portraits in one corner of the room with the American and Marine Corps flags as the backdrop. Mark stood still and waited for Rasha to see him.

Rasha appreciated J-Mac inviting her to the ball, although she really wished Mark was her date. She recognized a few people from the embassy and repeated the answer to the question everyone was asking: how was Mark doing in Iraq?

"I thought I saw Mark over by the bar," one of the diplomats offered.

"David, he's in Baghdad with his battalion," Rasha responded. She glanced toward the bar anyway, knowing she would be disappointed. As people moved around the reception area, she caught sight of a Marine officer in evening dress uniform, although there were dozens of them present. Without excusing herself, she started walking slowly toward the bar, looking for the officer but never quite seeing him. J-Mac appeared behind her and told her it was time to be seated for the ceremony and dinner. As she turned toward the ballroom, Mark was standing by the door waiting for her.

"Sweetheart, you're here!" Rasha raced toward him and threw her arms around his neck.

"I am indeed!" Mark embraced her gently and kissed her passionately. "I hope you're glad to see me."

"Glad to see you? I'm delighted!" Rasha put her small hand in his and walked with him into the ballroom to the table J-Mac had arranged. Several people greeted Mark and Rasha as they were seated for the ceremony.

As soon as the ceremony finished and the music started, Mark asked Rasha to dance. J-Mac looked startled.

"Mark, I've never seen you dance. Are you sure you weren't seriously injured this morning coming out of Baghdad?"

"You were hurt in Baghdad?" Rasha asked, looking concerned.

"It was nothing serious"—Mark said looking mildly annoyed at J-Mac—"and a lesser man couldn't stand the pain. Let's dance before I lose my nerve!"

Doing his best imitation of dancing to Aaron Neville singing "Don't Take Away My Heaven"—Mark had arranged with the DJ for it to be the first song of the evening—he waited until the music stopped and got down on one knee.

"Rasha, you have no idea what it's like to be me looking at you," he started, "and how proud I am to be with you. If I promise to always treat you with dignity and respect, will you marry me?"